Pride Publishing books by Angel Martinez and Bellora Quinn:

AURA
Quinn's Gambit
Flax's Pursuit

I0691654

AURA

FLAX'S PURSUIT

ANGEL MARTINEZ
and BELLORA QUINN

Flax's Pursuit
ISBN # 978-1-78430-670-0
©Copyright Angel Martinez and Bellora Quinn 2015
Cover Art by Posh Gosh ©Copyright June 2015
Interior text design by Claire Siemaszkiewicz
Pride Publishing

Published in 2015 by Pride Publishing, Newland House, The Point, Weaver Road, Lincoln, LN6 3QN, United Kingdom.

Pride Publishing is a subsidiary of Totally Entwined Group Limited.

FLAX'S PURSUIT

Dedication

To anyone who purposefully stood in fairy circles as a child, hoping the fair folk would abduct them. — Angel

To Kyrja, who always makes time for me. Thank you for your encouragement, your insight and all the twisty trails our conversations have taken. You rock!
— Bellora

Prologue

From *Gerald Silverstein's* Magic in the Modern World, (12) New York: Hecate Publishing

Some individuals, in hindsight, claimed they'd known it was inevitable once the mixing of tech and magic began. For those who lived through it though, we know the disaster caught the world completely by surprise.

The accident at Berkeley blew out several rooms at Stanley Hall and left nothing of the spellcasters besides bits of char. Consequently, nothing remained of their notes, their laptops, their original intentions or precisely what steps they had taken. All that remained was the RARE – the Random Anomalous Reality Events.

The connection between the explosion at the college and the appearance of a Minotaur in the middle of Times Square took some weeks to sink in. As more inexplicable beings fell out of thin air at random points on the globe, researchers put the pieces together.

Those first few manifestations ended in panic, disaster and tragedy. The Minotaur ate three tourists before the

NYPD took him down in a hail of gunfire. The mermaid who fell six feet to the ground outside Tempe gazed out at the Sonora Desert and killed herself in despair.

Eventually, magic users of all traditions began to come forward to help with these unpredictable manifestations. With good sense, calm words and, occasionally, magic traps, they were able to contain the new arrivals. Some still chose suicide, but many, frightened and disoriented, were taken under the protection of these brave pioneers.

Five years after the accident, the little band had grown into an organized collective, then a government-funded organization. Thus AURA was born, the Agency of Unnatural Resettlement and Assimilation.

A frequent message appeared on many desk plaques and cubical hangings in the AURA building. "It's a weird job, but somebody's got to do it."

Chapter One

"Here kitty kitty. Here kitty kitty."

The old woman called softly, gently coaxing the tomcat with the matted coat. It had rained earlier and the puddles in the alley glistened from the streetlights, sheened with oil rainbows the old woman thought were pretty, despite their source and toxicity. Many things in this city were covered in grime and graffiti and considered by most to be just another sign of squalor and decay, but she had lived within this concrete and asphalt sprawl her entire life. She found beauty where she could.

The tomcat crept slowly from the deeper shadows cast by the dumpster and heaped up piles of cardboard and other debris, lured less by the coaxing call than by the smell of food.

"That's it. There's a good boy," the woman cooed, setting down the can of cat food and backing off a couple of steps. Feeling the back of her neck prickle, she glanced around quickly. Living on these streets did not grant immunity from attack, no matter how well honed her sense of preservation. It was even less safe since the world had started randomly spawning creatures and beasts that should be found by rights only in fairy tales and fantasy books.

Even so, she was less afraid of muggers or goblins than she was of angry landlords and restaurant owners who would chase her away. Or worse, animal control officers who would get her in trouble. If it came down to a choice, she would rather meet up with a goblin in a dark alley than an animal control officer. A goblin might make sport of her, bully and try to intimidate, but a goblin would have no interest in taking away her babies.

She looked around once more, but all was still and quiet beyond the low rumble of traffic on the street. She looked down and the orange tom she had been hoping to tame enough for her to pet tonight was almost finished gobbling the can of food.

Slowly and carefully, she crouched down, trying to keep her long skirt from getting too wet. Nights were growing colder. It was nearly Halloween. Keeping dry and warm were never far from her mind. Hesitantly she reached out a hand to pet the slat-sided feline, noting as she did that he was scarred and his left ear was nearly split in two.

"Oh, that looks like it hurt! Tch tch, who have you been scrapping with, hmm? You shouldn't fight with others, deary. Forgive and forget, I always say. Well, all except Officer Perell. Him? Doesn't deserve forgiveness, not ever." She sniffed. "Not any of them that took my babies away, but especially not him. You could scratch and bite him all you wanted, but you be nice to Momma Cats, hear? She bring you some nice food and is gonna give you a nice warm place to stay just as soon as we can find somewhere."

Her fingers brushed fur and for just a moment, the cat looked like he might accept this and possibly seal his fate, but then he bristled, his tail fluffing like a bottle brush and a low growl in his throat.

"Oh, now, what's all this? Be nice!" Momma Cats scolded. "Be a nice kitty." But the orange tabby was not growling at her, was not even looking at her, but behind her. She tried to turn quickly, but she was crouched down and her reflexes were not what they once were.

She never saw who or what the notched-eared tom growled at. She only felt the touch on her shoulder and the pain that spread down her arm. She gasped and cried out, the pain rapidly moving to her chest and up her neck and the side of her face.

"Help! Help me... Oh, kitty, run!"

Those were her last words, but they were spoken to an empty alley. The notched-eared tom had much faster reflexes than Momma Cats and had already disappeared into his kingdom of trash, leaving the old woman to die a horrible—if mercifully swift—death alone.

Chapter Two

The weird stuff always happens when you're picking up extra shifts. Officer Flax Wolfheart hurried down the street, following the high-pitched brownie laughter. Five of them had broken into a bakery after hours. The bakery assistant said they'd stolen the final bank deposit and everything from the day-old rack.

"I have visual. Pursuing on foot." Flax spoke into his radio as he broke into a sprint. The suspects had ducked into an alley, probably hoping to vanish.

The radio crackled, dispatch answering, "Officer Wolfheart, backup's on the way. Maintain open channel. Location updates."

"As you wish," Flax muttered, not exactly by the book, but fuck it. He skidded around the corner just in time. The last little brownie culprit was phasing through the bricks of the building to the left, pointed ears swiveling—large, dark eyes already dilated from the sugar high.

That was the problem human police officers had tracking brownies. The little shits could walk through walls, which was how they broke into establishments in the first place. Flax bared his teeth in a feral grin. Good thing he wasn't a human police officer. He could still sense their magic trail through the building, and while he couldn't go through the wall, he could still follow.

"Going on the roof. Same street, dispatch. Looks like we're going building to building."

"Damn it, Wolfheart. Your backup can't follow you that way."

The exasperated tone made him grin. "There are reasons why I work alone, you know."

Flax leaped and caught hold, jamming fingers and boot toes in the joinings between bricks so he could scale up to the roof. The little creeps' trails rambled through the building under his feet until they emerged out of the other side. Giggling and tripping over each other, the sugar high as bad as meth for humans, the brownies raced across the next alley. Rail thin, the pack of them, none more than a few inches taller than the trash cans they used as cover, Flax felt a momentary twinge.

Kids. They're damn brownie kids and if they're not homeless, I'll eat my badge.

He waited until they had phased through the wall before he took two running steps and vaulted to the building they had entered. An old, rebellious part of him wanted to let them go. They were just kids. But he had his duty as an AURA officer and part of that duty was getting delinquent brownie kids off the street, hopefully to the help they needed.

His new life wasn't so different from his old in many ways. Duty. Tenacity. The hunt. The solitude. AURA made exceptions for certain talents. Really, AURA was one big mess of exceptions, so they let Flax hunt alone. It was what he did best and how it had always been.

The elven hunter on the edge of civilization, he accepted that—most of the time.

The brownies were meandering through the building below his feet, so he cast about the rooftop for anything he could use. One brownie kid he could corner and slap iron cuffs on to prevent more phasing. Five? Even he had his limits.

People left the damndest things out on city roofs. Rows of tomatoes and beans confronted him on this one, a rooftop garden with plant stakes pointing accusing fingers at the evening sky as if to say, *where are the stars?* Light pollution still pulled him up short sometimes.

There. A roll of wire mesh that humans used to keep animals out and sometimes in. Chicken wire. That could be useful. He undid the twist ties holding the roll together and shook it out as he crept to the edge of the building. The kids were right beneath him now, up against the outer wall, probably on their way back out. The alley ended in a chewed-up wooden fence here, a few bicycles and a dumpster the only obstacles.

He turned off his radio and gathered magical energy to his fingers as the brownie kids started to squeeze out through the wall below him.

"Hear them?" one whispered as they huddled at the end of the alley.

"No. No badges." The tallest shook his head.

"Human badges." The one with a pink scarf snickered, stomping around in a clumsy, lead-footed circle. "Slow. Stupid."

They collapsed against each other in a fit of giggles.

Flax chose that moment to announce himself. "AURA enforcement! Stand where you are!"

The kids took two seconds in their sugar-addled states to register that the voice came from above them.

A couple of them spouted some nasty brownie curses when they spotted him, then they did exactly what Flax had known they would. They ran for the next wall.

A wall of wind slammed out from Flax's hands, hurling the brownie kids off their feet and tumbling them down the alley until they hit up against the wood slats in a tangled heap of limbs and wild cussing. With another blast of magically directed wind, Flax flung the rectangle of chicken wire through the air and slapped it over the heap of brownies. He had his knives out almost before the chicken wire landed. He snapped them down in precision throws, each of his wickedly curved hunting blades thunking hard through a corner of the wire mesh and into the wooden slats, trapping the brownies in an iron net that negated their ability to phase.

"You have the right to remain silent..." Flax gave the Miranda spiel in fits and starts as he clambered down the building to them. His backup was finally here, sirens wailing down the street.

Several officers swarmed down the alley to take the kids into custody. There would be human courts to deal with, but if the judge ruled that they were juveniles, they'd end up at AURA with the counseling and support staff. Maybe something would help this time. Some brownies managed to assimilate all right. They weren't all petty criminals. Flax even knew one with an interior design business.

"Think you're Batman now, lurking on the rooftops?" Lisa McAndrews passed him with a slap on his shoulder.

"I'm an officer of the law, ma'am," Flax growled in mock offense and ruined it with a grin. "And I'm cooler than Batman."

She laughed and walked off to help load the kids into the van. Flax sheathed his knives, waiting patiently for someone to claim him for the ride back to headquarters since he'd been on foot. Batman. Yeah. Though not as dark. They did both work alone, both outcasts in their own way. It was better to be alone, anyway. One-nighters who didn't sleep over, that was best. Who wanted all that tangly, complicated relationship mess?

Flax shuddered and made his way over to Lisa's squad car when she waved for him. Maybe he'd troll the bars and even have time for one of those quickies before he had to turn around and head right back in for the day shift.

A cold shiver ran across his shoulders and he twitched around in alarm. Was there... No, there wasn't anything in the alley now. He shook his head, laughing at himself, and vowed to stop volunteering for so many extra shifts.

* * * *

A single shaft of bright morning sunlight edged around the curtain and settled in a golden stripe across Quinn's face. It worked its way into his dream, insisting that the park that he and Val were in was pleasantly warm and bright. It certainly made being naked more comfortable, if not more explicable. It just seemed like a good idea to be walking hand in hand through Central Park without a stitch of clothing.

Even though he knew the leaves had already turned and dropped and the days were now chilly and often rainy, for some reason this little pocket of park was still at the height of summer with flowers blooming and the grass a lovely green and softly inviting. He couldn't resist settling down on that soft surface and pulling Val down beside him.

"Are you sure you want to do this?" Quinn asked, keeping Val's hand in his own.

"It's a good opportunity, Quinn. More than that, it's something I feel I need to do," Val answered, slipping one arm around him.

"Yeah, but, it's so much more work and responsibility."

"It is, but not so much that I won't be able to do the job."

Quinn waved a dismissive hand. "I know you can do that job. It's not that. It's just..." He trailed off, feeling too embarrassed to finish the thought.

"What is it?" Val asked him gently, placing a soft kiss on his temple.

"I don't want to lose you."

Val leaned closer, kissing a soft line down from Quinn's temple to his ear, nibbling on the lobe and placing a little nip just behind that sent tingles of pleasure down Quinn's back and stiffened his cock.

"You won't lose me."

Val whispered along his skin and Quinn moaned at the way the brush of his lips ignited waves of heat. Quinn guided Val's hand down, curling his fingers to make Val's fingers close around his shaft.

Words went away and for a long time there was nothing but the feel of Val's lips kissing him and his hand stroking him while they sat in the warm sunshine, exposed to the world and anyone who happened by. The pressure building behind his groin was almost unbearable and Quinn rolled and bucked his hips, trying to get more friction on his sensitive cock and desperately needing to come.

"Uhh, God! Fuck me!" Quinn begged breathlessly. Without seeming to have moved at all, he was suddenly on his hands and knees, Val's heavier body draped over him and elven hands gliding up and down his chest and over his straining cock. Quinn could feel the thick nudge between his cheeks and squirmed eagerly. He felt so hot, like he was burning up, and everything was so bright and then...

Then he was blinking his eyes open in the bed he shared with Val, in the apartment he'd moved into a few months ago, and the lush smells of green grass and damp earth and hot horny bodies melted away with the dream.

"Mmph!" He groaned, rubbing his eyes sleepily with one hand and his persistent hard on with the other. "Fuck." He groaned again as he rolled over and remembered that his lover wasn't home, had probably been gone for at least a couple of hours.

Quinn had gotten rather used to a nice leisurely blow job first thing in the morning—which sometimes led to more—in the first few weeks after he'd moved in with Valerian. Those pleasant mornings had tapered off since Val had accepted the Captaincy. After such a hot dream, he was more than a little disappointed to wake up alone. The temptation to jerk off was overwhelming. He had been close to a wet dream as it was, but after a few moments stretching and yawning, he resisted the urge. If he waited, if he denied himself until he could be with Val, it would be that much more intense. With a sigh, he rolled out of bed and let his bobbing boner lead the way to the bathroom.

After he showered and dressed, Quinn made coffee. He was just thinking about his plans for the day when there was a small 'pop' in the air about a foot from his face and a tiny pink fairy appeared, wings a blur.

"Brianna, what did I tell you about just popping in without knocking? It's rude," Quinn said.

She looked at him without any concern and shrugged her shoulders, which was not easy while she was flying.

"If you keep doing it, I'm seriously getting a cat. What does Kai want now? You would think the big techno geek mage would just pick up the phone, you know?"

Brianna clapped her hands together twice and four more fairies popped into the room, each holding the edge of an envelope. They dropped it on the counter and after a swift, curious buzz around the room, they all popped out again.

"Damn it, I'm gonna put a jinx on the apartment to keep them out. I swear I am," he grumbled as he picked up the envelope and opened it. A sheet of paper was inside and Quinn shook it open to see a single line of text,

I wouldn't have to send them if you would turn on your phone and check your messages.
Kai

Quinn snorted and threw the paper down on the counter then flipped it off for good measure before taking a sip of coffee. He hated the cell phone the department had given him. It made him feel tethered. He had told Kai he didn't like it and the drow had just rolled his eyes and asked how he expected to be contacted, telegram? Quinn had reluctantly accepted the phone just as he'd reluctantly accepted the job. Actually, he hadn't accepted the job Kai had offered him, joining AURA's research department full time. Instead, he had agreed to work for them on a freelance basis. It wasn't how AURA usually worked and Kai had pulled some serious strings to get them to allow it.

Quinn was grateful for the job. It was legitimate work and paid well. He'd already taken on three cases. Two involved scrying for crossovers after Events when officers had been unable to locate who or what had dropped into the world. Another case had been helping an AURA team trap a pit demon that had resisted all previous efforts to bring him in. He'd succeeded all three times he'd been called in for help and although he wouldn't admit it to anyone, it had been quite a boost to his self-esteem to know he could do the job.

He drank half his mug of coffee before digging out his phone from under a pile of papers on the end table in the living room and switching it on to check his messages. Kai's crisp, bossy voice informed him that they had found an instructor willing to work with him and had set up a meeting in one of the conference rooms at headquarters.

Part of the provision of his employment was that he began training with a mage who was also an AURA officer. Kai's message told him the meeting was scheduled for ten a.m. that morning. Quinn looked at the clock and cursed softly. He had just barely enough time to get down to AURA headquarters if he was lucky. So much for a nice, leisurely morning.

* * * *

"I can't work with that human!"

Captain Valerian Hartgrove fought the urge to bury his face in his hands as Aello the siren shrieked at him about her new partner. "What, precisely, did Matt say that has upset you so terribly?"

"He called me a screaming Mimi!"

Not sure at all that he could suppress the urge to laugh, Val pulled in a slow breath, placing both palms flat on his desk. He understood that accepting command came with the need to mediate petty squabbles and that such a diverse force of both humans and magical creatures could well be a veritable minefield of prickly offense. Sometimes he fought his own temper when the disagreements were petty or mean-spirited, but the issue before him had little to do with what Matt had said.

"Officer Kensington has an odd sense of humor. It's something one has to become accustomed to," Val said in his gentlest voice of command.

"I don't want to *become accustomed*. He's vile."

"Careful, Aello. I think highly of Matt. He's an excellent officer and a good man. Give it time. I know this hasn't been easy for you."

Aello's beautiful face crumpled, her wings drooped. "I miss Michael. I want him back."

He reached across the desk and took her hand. "There are many things I can do. I can't do that. I'm so sorry. We all miss him, though I know no one can miss him as you do. Try for me a little longer. Matt's a good partner. He saved me several times and he was there for me whenever I needed him. I think you two will work well together if you give it a chance."

She nodded miserably, gaze locked on her feet.

"I'll speak to him, all right? Let him know that what he said was not appropriate or professional." Val sat back, his voice raising just a hair. "Was there anything else, Officer Aello?"

"No...no." Aello's head snapped up as if his tone had startled her, but she understood the dismissal and scrambled to her feet. "Thank you, Captain—for listening."

Val sighed as she shut his office door. Though he was new to the position, he already had days when he just wanted to be an officer again. The need to separate himself from his staff was painful. The easy camaraderie he had with them gone.

But someone had to do it. Someone had to step into Captain Lyons' place when she died. I can't replace her but I can try to carry on and do things as she would have done.

Chirping interrupted his thoughts and it took him a moment to remember that Kai had replaced the harsh ring of his office phone with birdsong.

"Hartgrove here."

"Captain, this is Lou Dominguez over at Twelve. Do you have a minute?"

"Of course. What can I do for Homicide today?" It wasn't often that they heard from human police divisions and Val's heart lurched. Homicide only called AURA when a magical being had been murdered.

"We have something unusual. We're not sure what we're looking at."

"You have a body you can't identify species for?"

"No, we're pretty sure the victim's human." Inspector Dominguez stopped and Val heard a hard swallow. "I think someone from your division needs to come have a look, though."

"I'm afraid I need something more specific, Lou."

"Restaurant owner came out this morning with the trash and found an old lady in the alley."

"Was she killed by magical means?"

"I'm not even sure... Captain, it looks like she was turned to stone."

Val sucked in a hard breath. "Give me your location, please. I'll send someone right down."

There were stories, of course, of beings that could turn flesh to stone with a look or a touch. As far as he knew, there were no gorgons or basilisks in this world yet, and if there were, how had they come through without the Event alarms going off?

A soft knock sounded on Val's door just as he got off the phone with dispatch.

"Come in," Val said, as he typed in details of a report he was working on.

Quinn opened the door and poked his head in to smile at him. "Hey, babe. I have a meeting in a couple minutes but wanted to say hi first."

"Good morning, love." Val managed a smile as he rubbed at the back of his neck. "Whoever you're meeting with, could you reschedule? I have something for which I'll most likely require Research's input. Your particular sensitivities could be helpful."

Quinn slipped inside the crack he'd opened and came over to lean against the side of Val's desk. "I could probably reschedule. Or Kai could reschedule, I should say. I don't know who he's got me meeting. He just told me to show up at ten in room six-B. Something about finding someone willing to teach me." He rolled his eyes, then smiled at Val.

"Ah..." Val hesitated, knowing how long Kai had been trying to set up this particular meeting, and how long Quinn had been trying to avoid it. "Perhaps you should keep the appointment then. I don't want you to make a bad impression with someone you may have to work with for some time."

Quinn's mouth turned down mulishly and he heaved a sigh. "I don't see why I have to do this anyway. I've managed just fine on my own so far."

"And you've managed astoundingly well. That doesn't mean your skills can't be honed. I've studied with several human sword masters since I arrived in this world."

Quinn didn't argue the point, but he looked more resigned than happy about it. "I guess. So, what did you need me for? I mean, if it's important, I'm sure I can postpone the meeting, Val."

Val weighed his desire to have Quinn go with him, and Quinn's obvious wanting to postpone yet another meeting, versus Kai's almost certain temper tantrum and the possible alienation of Quinn's future teacher.

"A compromise, perhaps? Go and meet the teacher Kai has selected for you and explain that I need you. That way it won't appear that you are simply 'blowing him off'." He said the last part slowly, uncertain of the phrase, and was rewarded with one of Quinn's grins.

"Sounds like a plan. I'll be back in ten minutes. You can fill me in on the way." Quinn leaned in to kiss Val quickly before springing for the door and forgetting to close it in his rush.

* * * *

Boots kicked up on the conference table, Flax heaved an exaggerated sigh. Damn Kai for railroading him into this. Give a drow a management position, and it went to his cobweb-filled head. So the kid could do some magic, so what? He was still human. Not that there was anything wrong with that. Some of Flax's best friends were humans. But they weren't magical creatures at their cores and had to struggle with things that came naturally to an elf.

"C'mon. I have work to do." He spun in his chair, checked the clock and finally started to amuse himself making little fire horses run over his fingers.

The snick of the door handle turning distracted him and the flames lost definition then trailed off as he let his focus drop. A little puff of smoke rose and dissipated as the door opened and a young man in a T-shirt, faded jeans and sneakers came rushing in, looked right and left as if he expected to find others in the room, and finally looked at Flax.

"Uh, hi. I'm Quinn. Kai said I was supposed to meet someone here. Are you him?"

Great. A kid. Thanks, Kai. "Kai the Great and Powerful didn't give you a name?" Flax let his feet thump down as he rose with his brightest smile. No need to be rude. "I'm Officer Flax Wolfheart. Apparently I'm supposed to teach you."

The blond kid looked uncertain now, which Flax hadn't intended but was still okay. He had agreed to this only because Kai forced him into it, but he hadn't promised anything beyond meeting him and attempting to teach him. If it didn't work out, that was that. There was no way he was going to take on an actual apprentice just because Kai wanted him to.

"Yeah…Kai did say something about you being a teacher," Quinn said, finally taking the couple of steps away from the door that brought him to the other side of the table. "I didn't expect you to be an elf."

Flax's smile didn't waver, but his tone cooled considerably. "Is that a problem for you?"

Quinn grinned. "Not at all."

What is that supposed to mean? "Well…good." He hitched a hip on the conference table. "So what are you? Listener? Firestarter? Empath?"

Big blue eyes blinked slowly at him and the grin faltered. "Er, no. I mean, I can do some stuff, but I never studied any particular specialty."

"Pfft." Flax waved a dismissive hand. "I don't give two rat's tails about human schools of magic. I need to know what you're good at. Kai must've picked me for a reason besides my dashing good looks and charm." He frowned, staring at his boots a moment before he decided on a different tactic. "I was a finder in my first life. A hunter — you understand?"

Quinn licked his lips and Flax found his eyes fastening there for a moment before he forced them back up, lifting an eyebrow expectantly.

"I'm good at casting a circle. And setting wards," Quinn said haltingly.

"Uh-huh. And I doubt Kai needs you to do either of those for him, the little snob. He said you were contracting. Doing what?"

"Finding crossovers when they disappear before AURA gets on the scene. And Kai has used me for casting circles. Once to hold a lich and a couple weeks ago to trap a pit demon." Quinn sounded suddenly defensive.

Lich? Really? This is that kid? This skinny, raggedy... Flax's jaw tightened. He couldn't help it. Sure, he'd still been at the academy when the whole lich thing happened, but they had known he was there. They could've come to him instead of using some untrained human runt.

Two choices. He could refuse to teach the human and look like he wasn't capable while retaining his internal pride, or he could agree to it and maybe make himself a little nuts.

But not today. He had to get his head in the right place first.

"Great. Finding stuff is good." Flax settled his knives more comfortably at his hips as he rose. "That's where we'll start. Right now, though, I've got casework to catch up on. Call me later this evening. We'll set up a time."

"Call you?" Quinn blinked at him, obviously perplexed. "Kai has a number for you?"

"No, silly." Flax waggled his fingers at Quinn's pocket. "I just put it on your phone." With a wink, he swaggered out, trying to quiet the seething prickles under his skin.

Quinn stared at the open door for a full thirty seconds before he finally dug the phone out of his pocket and pushed buttons, swiped the screen and cursed under his breath at the thing before it brought up the short list of contacts. Sure enough, Flax's name was now listed, alongside a phone number. Quinn narrowed his eyes, unsure if the elf had really just done that or if Kai had programmed it in remotely and the elf was fucking with him.

He could not remember the last time he'd ever felt so rattled meeting someone. This whole encounter had gone nothing like what he'd envisioned. He had figured he would waltz in, shake hands, tell whoever it was that he was happy to meet them but had important things to do and probably piss them off enough to go running to Kai complaining about him straight off the bat.

That hadn't happened. Quinn was still trying to process what exactly *had* happened. He didn't know why he'd expected a human teacher, but he'd had some vague idea of finding an old hack like Jerry sitting at a desk, only too happy to bore him to death with rote drills and theory of magic bullshit.

He had not expected his new instructor to be an elf, and he certainly hadn't expected him to be fucking gorgeous. He immediately felt disloyal thinking it, but he'd be lying to himself—or dead—if he hadn't noticed. Flax was tall, fit, blond and had a face that if he ever decided to give up being a cop would probably do well as a model. Also, he was kind of an asshole.

He hadn't said anything rude exactly, but Quinn could not shake the feeling that the entire time Flax had been looking down his nose at him. He had no illusions that he was some great mage or had a vast store of untapped potential power like Kai seemed to think he did, but he'd never felt lacking before. He wasn't exactly the swaggering type, but he did have a certain amount of pride. It was stinging like hell to have his abilities all but sneered at.

With a start, he realized he was just standing there holding his phone looking stupid while Val was probably pacing. He shoved it back in his pocket and raced for the stairs, figuring that would be quicker than taking the elevator.

He was only slightly out of breath as he exited the stairwell on the second floor and wove his way back through the cubicle farm toward the offices.

"Hey, Quinn!" A cheerful voice called to him and Quinn stopped.

"Matt, how's it going?" Quinn asked with a genuinely warm smile. Matt was no longer Val's partner, but he still looked out for Val, and Quinn understood why Val often turned to him for advice when he had trouble with a case, or when he needed to understand human peculiarities. He was a good man, and he was a nice guy, for a cop.

Matt wrinkled his nose. "Oh, I've had better days. Kinda hoping this is the last time I have to break in a new partner. Val was bad enough..."

"Tough working with a siren?"

"It's not the siren part. She's professional and by the book. But she really doesn't *like* me. Picks on everything I do." Matt let out an embarrassed chuckle.

"Sorry. I sound like a kid in high school or something."

Quinn gave him an appraising look. "You're a likable guy, Matt. I can't imagine she doesn't like you, unless you've given her a reason not to like you, maybe? You're not giving her any of that 'I'm the veteran and you're the rookie' shit, are you?"

"No. Not on purpose, anyway. She's a seasoned cop, you know. Was poor Mike Kennedy's partner for—" Matt cut off abruptly. "Oh. Yeah. There is that."

"What?"

Matt's expression fell as shadows gathered in his eyes. "I'm not Mike."

Quinn put his hand on Matt's shoulder sympathetically and gave him a slightly awkward pat. "No, you're not. But that's not your fault. You're a good person, Matt. She'll either come around or she won't, but if you're treating her decent and she still doesn't like you, then there's nothing much you can do."

"How'd you get so smart so young?" Matt managed a crooked grin. "Gotta run, kiddo. Due on patrol. The big guy looks like he's getting ready to go out somewhere, too. Don't let him do anything stupid."

With a pat to Quinn's shoulder, Matt took off for the staircase, alone. Maybe he and Aello would meet at the car, but there was something sad about partners who didn't really speak to each other, doubly sad since both Matt and Aello had suffered so much during the lich incident. Quinn shook his head and hurried to the captain's office where Val was just shrugging into his trench coat.

He smiled as he watched the way the tailored coat settled on his broad shoulders and allowed himself a wistful moment to let his eyes roam up and down Val's frame. He closed the door behind him and leaned against it, his face full of mischief. "Are you sure we have to run right out?"

Val gave him a smile, though it was a distracted one. "Call from homicide, love. I'm afraid so."

"Aww." Quinn pretended to pout for a second but he moved to the side and reopened the door. "So, what happened? Someone piss off the wrong crossover? Or did some trigger-happy asshole shoot someone?"

"Neither." Val shook his head as they headed for the stairs. "Someone turned an old woman to stone, NYPD claims."

Quinn frowned as he processed that information. "Yeah? That's...unusual. I take it they don't know who or what did it if they're calling AURA in. What can turn people into stone?"

Val frowned, clearly disturbed. "Several things in my world, but none of those have been recorded as coming through here. Basilisks. Gorgons. Cockatrices."

Quinn snickered then stifled it. It wasn't exactly something to laugh about. He cleared his throat. "Could there have been an Event that was missed? Maybe the precogs didn't pick up one?" he asked as they exited the office.

"Oh, yes, it's possible. Or something could have come through in the early days and remained hidden. That's why I need someone with me who can...scent certain things."

Quinn gave him a crooked grin, "I don't exactly smell them. Well, not unless they're particularly stinky." Valerian knew that of course, in fact his nose was far better than Quinn's. "So, are we going right to the crime scene then?"

"Yes, directly there." Val fished the keys from his pocket as they approached the garage. "How was your meeting?"

Quinn hesitated, frowning slightly as he thought about how to answer that. "Not what I expected. He doesn't seem very interested in teaching me. I kinda got the impression that Kai forced him into it."

"That rather sounds like Kai." Val chuckled. "Who was this not interested person?"

"Flax Wolfheart. He's an elf," Quinn added rather unnecessarily with a name like that.

Val leaned in to kiss the top of Quinn's head. "Ah. That one. He's young. Bit of a hothead. Give him a chance. He has skills that mirror yours and could teach you."

Quinn didn't think it was a matter of giving *him* a chance since the meeting had felt more like an interview and not even a mutual one. More like Flax was the one giving Quinn a chance, and would drop him like a hot rock if he felt he was wasting his time. He kept his mouth shut though, not wanting to sound like he was complaining already.

"I guess." He tried not to sound too sullen. "I'm supposed to call him tonight and set up another meeting."

They reached the car and got in. Just as Val pulled onto the street, an annoying jangle went off in Quinn's pocket made him jump. He still wasn't used to the cell phone. Kai thought it was more than a little odd how much he resisted the technology given that every other person Quinn's age was so excessively attached to the devices. Speaking of the devil, or in this case, the drow…

"Hello, Kai," Quinn answered.

"Good. You have it on. I won't have to send Brianna after you again. How did the meeting go?"

"Nice of you to call. I'm doing great. Thanks for asking," Quinn said sarcastically. "It went fine. Why do you ask?" He decided he wasn't going to give Kai the satisfaction of knowing how badly it had gone.

Kai grunted softly on the other end of the connection. "I was certain you would storm up to my office to tell me all about it afterwards."

"I didn't have time. I'm with Val. He might need my help with a case."

"Ah." Rustling on the other end probably meant Kai was tucking the phone between chin and shoulder while he multitasked. "I will save you the trouble of coming to shout at me in person, then, though you seem to enjoy it. I picked Flax because he is much like you, in many ways. And because I have leverage. If he refuses to teach you or if he does less than you feel he should, simply let me know. Easily fixed."

Quinn narrowed his eyes suspiciously, although Kai couldn't see his expression. Obviously Kai was already expecting trouble. The question was why? And what type of 'leverage' was he talking about? And why exactly did he think he and Flax were alike? As far as Quinn could see they were nothing alike, and the elf obviously didn't like him already, for some reason. He didn't ask any of his questions—not yet, anyway.

"Don't worry about it. It'll be fine." That should throw him off until Quinn could figure out what the drow was up to.

"Good." Kai heaved a sigh, most likely at whatever was taking up the other half of his attention. "Tell Val to call me about whatever this thing is that takes the captain out of his department."

"No need," Val said on a chuckle after Kai hung up. "I heard him. How could I forget after his harangue about 'keeping Research in the loop'."

"Well, technically, I'm part of Research, so you did keep us in the loop," Quinn said. "Not that it'll make Kai any less bitchy."

"He is what he is, love. If he were not so prickly, he would never get half the things done that he does."

Quinn chuckled softly. "You know I only pick on him because he likes it, right? If he wasn't playing the part of the put-upon-drama-queen, he wouldn't know what to do with himself."

"Part of it is playing a part, certainly." Val turned a corner and started looking for a place to park. "Part of it is how his nerves are strung. Someday, he will push himself too far—ask too much of himself, because he truly is strung so tightly and wishes for everything to be perfect. If he were human, they would most likely call him OCD and medicate him."

"He could probably do with some medicating anyway," Quinn muttered, only half joking. "Look..." He pointed to where a police cruiser was parked on the street in front of an alley cordoned off with yellow tape. "That must be the place."

"Yes." Val's teasing vanished when he parked the car and exited, all business as he approached the uniforms with his badge in hand. "Captain Hartgrove from AURA. Homicide called me in."

One of the officers leaned into the alley and called out, "Hey, Lou! The elf cop's here!"

Val took a step forward but the uniformed officer held up a hand. "Sorry, Captain, no civies allowed." He gestured at Quinn.

"He is a consultant for the department," Val explained, waving Quinn forward and not stopping.

Quinn kept a serious expression on his face as he moved up by Val's side, but it was hard not to flash a smile. He liked how Val could do that when he wanted. Even though what he said was completely true, the cop could have still insisted, but the way Val said it and the way he kept moving made it seem like he didn't need any approval from anyone to do whatever the hell he wanted. He had never figured that he would fall for a dominant type of guy, but in his heart of hearts, he had to admit that it got him hot when other people automatically deferred to Val without him even having to act menacing or throw his weight around. It was just something people seemed to sense.

Quinn walked at Val's side as they made their way to the mouth of the alley and no one else stopped them. Once they got a view of the crime scene, they both slowed down, taking everything in.

Quinn's eyes went right to the statue near the dumpster. Only he knew it wasn't really a statue. This had been a person, apparently. He could believe it too. No artist would make a statue like this, an old woman dressed kind of frumpy and with a look of pain and terror on her face. Even cast in stone, that expression was hard to look at. She hadn't died quickly or without pain, that was for sure.

"Lou, good to see you," Val's voice was muted, distracted as he greeted the detective. "Anyone able to ID the victim?"

"Not a complete one." Lou shoved his hands back in his pockets. "All the shop owners around here can tell me is her name was Gertie. They just knew she was a crazy cat lady."

Quinn suddenly drew in a quick breath. "Momma Cats."

The detective looked at Quinn, his brows pulled down over his eyes. "You knew her?"

"Sort of, yeah," Quinn said. "She's homeless. *Was* homeless. She's been around forever though. A lot of people know her — knew her."

Lou blew out a sharp breath. "Why would someone wanna hurt a cat lady?"

"It may not have been planned." Val crouched down to get on eye level with the victim. "She may have surprised a being who thought they were hidden or came across something being done that she was not meant to see."

Quinn had shoved his hands in his pockets and looked away when he'd realized who it was but now he forced himself to look back to where Val was examining the…the statue. He didn't want to think of it as a body. He should be trying to pick up any trace of magical residue but figuring out 'what' it was that did this wasn't really his forte. If Val or someone else could tell him the 'what', then Quinn could come up with the 'where'. It didn't seem like his partner was having any luck figuring out who or what had done this to her though.

"Do you think we could take the remains back to AURA?" Val asked after a quick glance at Quinn. "Let our staff see if they can glean anything from the stone?"

Lou shrugged. "Don't think the ME can do much here. I'll get clearance."

Chapter Three

Val dropped Quinn off at the apartment before heading back to work. The cops figured it would take a while to get what had once been Momma Cats transported to AURA headquarters and all the requisite paper work filled out. They had seemed vaguely disappointed that Val hadn't walked up and pulled a suspect out from behind the garbage cans or something—or at least been able to tell them definitively what had done it.

In the meantime, Quinn put the situation to the back of his mind until he could spend some time alone with the statue. It was far more difficult to find someone or something when he didn't know what he was looking for, but he would give it a shot, even if they still hadn't discovered what had turned her to stone.

He extracted a promise from Val that he wouldn't work *too* late then went back out to pick a few items up from the market.

When he'd lived on his own, Quinn had never been much of a cook. He had been too busy with day-to-day survival to be overly picky about what filled his belly. The lack of time and money had meant the majority of his meals were of the microwave variety or from food trucks and vendor carts if he wanted to treat himself.

Now that he didn't have to constantly worry about keeping a roof over his head or where his next meal was coming from, he could apply some of his time to learning to cook and to his surprise, he'd found he enjoyed the process so much it had developed into something of a hobby. He discovered that he liked the challenge of coming up with tasty vegetarian meals. He still ate meat himself, but Val couldn't stomach it and so it was easier to cook mostly vegetarian than to cook two separate meals.

Tonight he wanted to try a recipe for an Indian dish he'd gotten from a friend, and he was going to have to get a move on if it was going to be done before Val got home. He had most of what he needed but they were out of cream and he also needed fresh ginger, bell peppers and cashews to make the *korma*.

When he got back to the apartment for the second time that afternoon, he turned on the stereo and opened a beer before getting to work. Soon the whole place smelled of ginger and garlic and peppers and curry. It was a good, spicy, homey-type smell.

After leaving everything to simmer slowly, Quinn decided to set the mood with some nice candles on the dinette table and put out plates and silverware, making it look nice and cozy. He was thinking back to his dream and was hoping dinner wouldn't actually take too long because he was much more looking forward to dessert.

He still had a few hours to kill before Val got home though and he spent them on some mundane tasks he'd been putting off, like taking care of the laundry and vacuuming the living room. Val was always telling him not to trouble himself, but Quinn didn't work nearly as many hours, so he figured it was only fair to at least pick up around the place.

* * * *

"Flax!" Val leaned out of his office to shout across the squad room. He didn't quite bellow as Captain Lyons had always done, but his voice carried.

The officer in question looked up from his computer with a start and got up to head toward Val's office, his smile not quite hiding his concern. "Captain?"

"Come have a seat. Shut the door, please." Val waited until Flax had settled, straight-backed and alert. "Care to tell me what happened with the medical staff today?"

"Sir? I don't—"

"Don't play me for a fool, pup. There aren't too many things that won't reach my desk eventually." Val tapped a pen on his desk, waiting, watching patiently as some of the bravado leaked out of his newest officer.

"That incubus is an arrogant ass, Captain."

"He can be. Granted. It's part of his nature. But you, youngling, are now an officer of the law. Conjuring spider silk so his feet are ensnared and he falls on his face is not an acceptable reaction to a perceived insult. What if he'd been needed on an emergency call in that instant?"

"Yes, sir." The response was sharp and bitten off, barely shy of sullen.

Val reached across the desk and cuffed Flax lightly on the side of his head. "You're talented and have skills we desperately need. It would be a shame to put you on suspension. Consider yourself reprimanded."

"Yes, sir." Flax sat up a bit straighter, one corner of his mouth twitching, his tone more professional. "Thank you, sir."

"Now. One more thing. I hear you have a teaching assignment."

"Oh, that. Yeah. Some human kid who works with Research. Shouldn't take much of my time."

Val cleared his throat, eyebrows creeping up. "That human kid is my lover. Perhaps you didn't realize. And he's not a child."

"Fu — Oh. Sorry, sir. I didn't...didn't know." Flax's lilac eyes were huge. Chagrin, fear, shock, all of those things could be read in his expression.

"Yes. Well. Just keep it in mind. Be respectful. Teach him well. He's unusually talented." Val ran a hand over the side of his face. "Please try to be more respectful in all your interactions. We have so many different people we have to work with peacefully in order for this department to work. I'm counting on you."

"Yes, sir." Flax nearly raised his hand to his chest in an elvish salute before he caught himself with a crooked grin. "I'll do my best."

"Go on. Go home — or wherever you go after shift." Val shook his head, chuckling as Flax swaggered out. Young elves. Was there anyone more arrogant and sure of themselves on any plane of existence?

Coat, keys, phone… Some days Val felt inexplicably old leaving the office. Part of that was the pressure of a new job, made even more stressful by the challenges of finding new officers and staff. After the deaths and the horror of the lich queen's bid to take over the city, putting the department back together hadn't been an easy task.

His heart began to lighten as he neared his building, though. Quinn would be there. That smile alone, that laugh, those beautiful hands—those would erase the pressures of the day in no time. Not to mention that wonderful, tight... Oh, something smelled amazing. He opened the door, calling out, "Quinn? I'm home!"

Quinn came wandering out from the back of the apartment, shirtless, barefoot and only wearing a pair of loose jogging pants, his hair still damp from the shower. He smiled as soon as he saw Val. "Hey, babe, I was half expecting something would keep you late. Glad you got out of there on time. Dinner's ready."

Unable to help himself in the face of such a beautiful, welcome sight, Val seized Quinn around the waist, dragged him close and claimed his lips in a hungry, growling kiss.

Quinn wrapped his arms around Val's neck, melting easily against him and returning the kiss with his own fevered heat. In the days and weeks following the destruction of the lich queen, there had been a period of learning and discovery. Quinn had not overcome his past all at once, but certainly he'd come a long way, a fact that lightened Val's heart. These days Quinn rarely had nightmares that woke him in the middle of the night in fear, and he no longer tensed when Val pulled him close unexpectedly.

Quinn pushed his fingers into Val's hair and kneaded the base of his skull while their lips pressed and their tongues tasted until they broke off, both breathing deeper.

"Are you hungry? Eat first, or...?" Quinn asked him with a little smile that was somehow both shy and suggestive.

Val's laugh was more of a shaky exhalation. "I think I'd better eat first—food—before I devour you." He let his cheek rest against Quinn's shoulder a moment. "Bit of a headache still."

Quinn's fingers moved down, kneading the stiff muscles of his neck and finding all the right spots. He kissed just below his ear, sending a warm breath of air across the ridges and dips in a promise that almost made Val change his mind about eating first, but then Quinn took a step back.

"I made something new. Cheryl gave me a recipe she got from a guy she says works at an Indian restaurant. It turned out a little spicier than I was expecting, but I think it's good."

"It smells wonderful." Val took a deep breath as he tucked Quinn under his arm and steered them toward the table. He shed his coat and stopped for another tender kiss, but the tantalizing scents were almost as intoxicating as Quinn.

"Go on and sit, I'll bring it out," Quinn told him, disappearing into the kitchen.

Val noted the fresh candles in the holders on the table and lit them. A moment later Quinn was back, balancing two large covered bowls, one with rice and the other with what looked like a rich curry stew.

"You spoil me." Val had to clear his throat to get rid of the growl. When Quinn dished out rice and curry onto both their plates, he had to concentrate on eating like a civilized person. Where was this animalistic need coming from?

Quinn sat next to him and dug in, obviously hungry too.

"Did you eat today?" Val asked him.

"Yeah. Some." Quinn swallowed another forkful.

Val eyed him knowingly. "Did you eat anything other than what you tasted while cooking?"

Quinn had to think about it. "Coffee...um."

"Quinn—"

Quinn held up a hand, "I know. I know. Sorry. I'll eat more. I just get busy and forget."

"It was an odd day, I know." Val caught the gesticulating hand and kissed Quinn's fingers. "Have I told you how peaceful it is to come home to you?"

One corner of Quinn's mouth lifted in a half grin. "You may have mentioned it once or twice." He shifted on his seat and his smile turned more mischievous. "I had a dream this morning. Something about being naked in the park with you."

"Oh? And was there sex involved with the naked?" Val asked, trying to hide his smile.

Quinn took another bite of his dinner and licked the fork clean as he watched Val. "Might have been a little sex involved. Might have been a lot actually."

"We'll have to see if we can't make some of that reality, then. Though I'd rather not the park, if it's all the same to you."

Quinn chuckled. "Wouldn't do to get the Captain of AURA arrested for indecent exposure. It was a good dream...hot. I woke up before the finish though," he said with a little pout.

"We'll have to fix that then, won't we?" Val said softly. He licked a bit of sauce from the corner of his mouth, imagining other uses for his tongue.

Quinn paused, just holding his fork above the food as if he'd forgotten how to eat, then laughed. "If I keep this up, we'll never finish eating. How do you like it?"

"It's marvelous." Val closed his eyes on another forkful. "I'm in paradise."

Quinn ducked his head but sat a little straighter in his chair in a way that Val had become familiar with as they got to know more about each other. He had been confused at first by the response he got from Quinn every time he paid him a compliment. It looked to him as if Quinn were withdrawing, his body language saying that he was uncomfortable. It was one of those things he'd been hesitant to ask Quinn about. He'd sought Matt's advice before broaching the subject with Quinn and possibly making a botch of it. Matt had told him that Quinn probably hadn't had many people in his life give him a pat on the back or much in the way of praise and so he guessed Quinn didn't really know how to respond to a well meaning compliment.

After that, Val had watched Quinn's reactions more closely when he gave him a compliment, and saw there was warmth to Quinn's expression in spite of the shy withdrawal, and a little glow of pride hiding in his eyes behind the tension that looked like discomfort. Val figured Matt was probably correct and it was simply unfamiliarity with praise.

"Good. I'm glad you like it," Quinn said after a moment.

Val reached over, squeezed Quinn's hand and left it at that. He was learning when to step back.

※ ※ ※ ※

They actually did manage to finish eating without tearing each other's clothes off in the middle of dinner, mainly because the food was good and they were both really hungry. Once they'd eaten their fill, Val headed off to the shower while Quinn put the leftovers away. He left the dishes in the sink for later though, wanting to see if he could sneak in and join Val before he finished his shower.

When he slipped into the bathroom, his half-formed plans of seduction got a little muddled because Val was standing under the spray, head bowed and shoulder leaning on the tiles like he was too tired to stand upright on his own. That kiss when he'd gotten home had primed Quinn up for some fun time but looking at his lover now, he figured he wasn't going to push the issue.

"Hey, babe…I was wondering if you wanted someone to soap up your back for you?"

Val shifted and raised his head almost guiltily, as if embarrassed at being caught in a weak moment. "That would be wonderful. Yes."

Quinn hesitated, not sure if he really meant it, but only for a moment, then he slipped his pants off. They had been through that conversation already—the one where they weren't supposed to second-guess each other. Quinn was worse at it than Val, who said what was on his mind without much in the way of hedging. The plain honesty was still sometimes disconcerting to Quinn. Refreshing too, though, once he'd had some time to get used to it.

He stepped in behind Val, the spray of water only misting over him as it was mostly blocked by Val's body. He palmed some shower gel and spread his hands over Val's back. It was a lot of back to wash, not that Quinn minded. He could run his hands over those wide shoulders and sleek muscles all day and night and never get tired of it.

A low rumble vibrated against Quinn's hands, almost a purr as Val spread his feet and let his head drop forward again. His muscles were always hard, but they felt like rocks under Quinn's hands right now, his tension all too obvious. Val reached his arms forward to brace himself against the shower wall, which resulted in him unconsciously pushing his beautiful, rounded ass out toward Quinn.

The posture might not have been intentional but it still had an effect. Quinn had been waiting to get Val alone all day and it didn't take more than running his hands down Val's back and gorgeous ass to get him hard. He ran his hands back upward, pressing his thumbs in and kneading gently, then more firmly when Val groaned. After he'd spent a minute or two on the impromptu massage, he moved in a little closer, pressing his lower body along the curve of Val's and sliding his cock back and forth in the slippery crease of his ass.

He circled his arms around Val and let his hands glide over his chest. Their height difference made maneuvers like this slightly more challenging, but with Val's legs spread out a bit it wasn't impossible.

"My lovely Quinn." Val's deep voice was husky, suddenly liquid sex where he had sounded only exhausted the moment before. "Are you planning on having your way with me?"

"Maybe..." Quinn murmured back. He licked the wet skin of Val's neck and nipped teasingly at the muscle that ran down to his shoulder. Sliding one hand down Val's front, he found him more than a little hard already and he gave his own little purring growl. Rolling his hips, he pushed more insistently in the valley of his cheeks, the shower gel letting him slide back and forth along his skin in a pleasant way. He wrapped his fingers around the shaft of Val's cock and gave a few gentle strokes. "Do you want me to have my way with you?"

A desperate gasp was all he got for a moment, as Val's hips rolled, pushing his cock into the curl of Quinn's hand and pressing his ass back against Quinn's cock. "Yes. Oh, yes, love. Take me. Please."

This was new, this willingness to let go. There was no doubt that Val was a natural born leader, someone who took charge in an instinctive and automatic way. While he was never violent in the bedroom, his dominant side roared to life usually before either of them could think about it. His surrender was surprising and ridiculously hot.

A surge of lust went straight to Quinn's groin. He kissed and licked the nape of Val's neck while he reached into the niche where the soap, shampoo, and stuff were, thumbing open a bottle of conditioner. He kept meaning to put a bottle of lube in there and kept forgetting, but he knew personally that the conditioner was slick enough to be useful, and didn't burn like the shower gel. He leaned back enough to squirt a good blob right where the top of Val's crack started, his cock standing up eagerly there, ready to take advantage of all the slick stuff. He wondered for a second if he should take more time but Val squeezed his glutes and pushed back against him, and lust won out over caution. Besides, he trusted Val to tell him if he needed him to slow down.

All Quinn had to do was draw back his hips a little farther than he had been doing and his cock slipped down. He set his thumb on the top of his shaft and pushed it down a little more, and he was right there, all lined up. He did slow down then, easing just the head into that tight, inviting pucker.

Panting, legs spread as wide as the space allowed, his Prussian blue hair hanging in a curtain around his face as he dropped his head between his arms, Val pushed back with a long, guttural moan. Apparently, he didn't want slow.

Quinn swallowed convulsively as that tight, tight heat engulfed his cockhead and he couldn't resist sinking right in. He still had one hand wrapped around Val's dick and he circled his other arm back around, caressing Val's chest and pinching his nipple while he curled over him. He pressed lips and teeth into his skin and drew back, thrusting forward again harder. Those sexy little growls and moans Val made were turning him on like crazy.

"Uhh, God, Val…that feels so amazing." He breathed the words into the back of his lover's wet hair.

Val bent forward more, thrust his hips back and gasped an elvish curse as he slapped the tiles with his palm. *Bullseye*. That was obviously the right spot.

Another hot surge went through Quinn and he quickened his pace, finding a rhythm between his rocking hips and the stroke of his hand. He pinched Val's nipple harder, pulling it away from his body, sinking his teeth deeper too and it felt like he was suddenly riding a tempest, the way Val bucked and moaned under him. It was a total head rush to know he was doing that to Val, getting him so hot, so turned on. All the anticipation and longing of the day was catching up to him and Val's passionate response was edging him right up.

"Mmm…fuck, babe, that is almost too good." Quinn's voice was husky and shaky but his hips didn't stutter at all, slapping his groin and his thighs against Val's backside in a bid to see just how hard and fast he could do him before he exploded.

Val's breaths were coming fast and uneven, the muscles of his thighs standing out in hard relief as he slammed his hips back in counterpoint to Quinn's

Angel Martinez and Bellora Quinn

thrusts. His body contracted hard around Quinn as he flung back his head and bellowed, jets of white shooting from him to decorate the blue shower tiles.

Quinn stroked his thick, lurching cock in time with every spurt, keeping up with him until he'd pulled every shudder from his tall muscular body and only then did he tip over the edge himself. He let go of Val's cock and gripped his chest with both hands, pulling him back into the arc of his body and yelping softly, his face pressed between his shoulder blades, until he saw stars behind his closed lids.

"Val…oh, Val… Uhh…that is so… God!" He exhaled that last word with a shaky sigh.

With a little chuckle, Val squeezed the hands on his chest and stood carefully, letting Quinn slip from his body before he turned and took him in a gentle embrace. "I haven't felt so cared for in years," he murmured against Quinn's hair. "TV or bed?"

"TV, then bed?" Quinn suggested, a silly, happy, satisfied little grin on his face.

Val laughed again, a deep-chested happy sound, and though he still looked tired, all the tension had dissolved from his features. "I love you. You know that? You've made me a very happy elf."

"Of course you do." Quinn snorted. "I mean, what's not to love?" He teased, but he also wrapped his arms around Val's neck and gave him the most tender, sweetest kiss he was capable of giving and when Val returned it with every bit as much tenderness, he dropped the teasing and whispered, "I love you too."

* * * *

Kai Hiltas paced around the statue-victim in frustration. Puzzles were his life's blood and his addiction, taking a strand and following it to its source, no matter how twisting the path. But this? He had no strand. Nowhere to start.

"Basilisk?"

The young humans who worked for him weren't helping. "No, Jordie. If you would do your research first instead of engaging in blind guessing, you would know that basilisk victims are sandstone. Does this look like sandstone?"

Jordie averted his gaze, muttering something under his breath. Hurt feelings? Most likely. But he didn't have time for sloppiness or incompetence. These pups needed to learn that quickly or find another job.

"I've read that basilisk statues aren't...such good quality?" Vicki said hesitantly.

That one showed real promise, but her male colleagues often discounted her. No confidence, so often her statements came out as questions.

"Very good, Victoria. Yes." Kai nodded toward her, irritated that she blushed at the praise. "Basilisk victims lack definition and fine detail. What else do we know this is not?"

Rudy looked up from his tablet, his thin face pinched under his wire-rimmed glasses. "It's not a gorgon. Those should look smoother. Lifelike."

"Yes. And you would feel the spell residue with a gorgon. Have any of you actually *touched* the victim? Tried to determine if you can detect a spell matrix?"

The three young men in the room cast their eyes at anything but the statue. Vicki raised a hesitant hand.

It was all Kai could do not to shake her until her teeth rattled. With every remaining ounce of his will, he kept his voice soft and calm. "And what did you find?"

"Nothing, Mr. Hiltas," she whispered. "I'm sorry."

Kai turned away and resumed his pacing. "You found nothing because there is nothing to *find*, not because of any personal shortcoming. Actual spells, as opposed to magical manipulations that are part of a beast's nature, leave a signature. One that can be identified and traced."

"So there's no spell, boss?" Terrence, who Kai thought of as *the big one*, asked. Not the brightest, but steady, determined and with a strong native talent.

"There is no *detectable* spell. I don't discount the possibility of one, but this is no drow or elvish spell. That we would feel. Something new? Some human spell we haven't encountered? Some new beast? Some bespelled object? Any of these things are possible."

He resumed his pacing, running his hands an inch above the statue. Something…something… Of course, at the moment he thought he felt something, his phone rang. If it had been any ring other than *Let It Snow*, he would have ignored it.

"Tenzi." He turned away from the youngsters and stalked out into the hall. "I'm working."

"It's past ten, Kai." His yeti lover's voice was soft and aggrieved. "You said you'd be home for dinner today."

"Something important came up."

"Yes. It always seems to these days."

Kai pressed the bridge of his nose between thumb and forefinger. "Dearest, I can't have this conversation right now."

"No. Of course not." Tenzin never raised his voice, but there was an edge there. "You could call. Let me know so I don't worry. Or are you too important for that now?"

"Don't. Don't you dare. I'm working myself to the bone here. If I forget to call —"

Tenzin's soft sigh cut him off. "I'll be here. Waiting...for the third night in a row."

"There's no need—" But the phone had that terrible silence to it. Tenzin, sweet, patient, ever-forgiving Tenzin, had hung up on him.

Exhausted in every fiber of his being, Kai turned back to the holding room where four sets of young eyes watched his every move. "Go home. It's late. We're not solving this tonight."

He waited until they filed out before he closed and locked the door. A large part of him simply wanted to go sleep in his office and avoid the suddenly clingy and passive-aggressive behavior that awaited him at home, but he supposed that would be cowardly. There were times when he wondered if he would have been better off still alone.

* * * *

The dressing down from the captain hadn't been harsh, but it had still managed to cut Flax deep. There were few people he respected in the same way he respected Tesined... No, Captain Hartgrove. He had to keep reminding himself not to think of him as Tesined. He embodied the word though. Battle Prince—a leader and protector of his people. In their world, Flax would have already offered himself, to follow him, to serve him...to spread for him and let him fuck him senseless.

Flax's lips twitched in a distracted smile as a little fantasy of that played out in his head. Damn. Now he was horny on top of being humiliated. Of course the kid was the captain's lover, his chosen mate. He'd known in a vague sort of way that the captain had bonded with a human, but he'd expected something

51

different—something more—a human of impressive stature and grace. Flax could have accepted that.

He kicked at a discarded cigarette pack as he walked, head down. A cold, shivery hollow had opened up inside him, a strange, almost nauseating contrast to the heat pooling at his groin. *Bad combination. I need to get laid.* When he looked up, he realized he had wandered past his apartment, down the block where a few run-down human gay clubs dotted the street. Snagging a human interested in elf action was easy and usually the cop thing just seemed to add spice for them.

They often wanted him to stay in uniform. Humans had odd cravings. Not that a bizarre request or two ever threw off his game, and Matt had confided that such things happened to human officers too, but it puzzled him when skin to skin was so much better.

A group of young men gathered in a cluster outside the door of *Boho*, a popular dive bar. It was smaller and quieter than some of the clubs, but always packed. One of the young males laughing with his friends spotted him, made brief eye contact then whispered in his friend's ear. As Flax approached, he smiled and leaned back on the railing behind him, canting his hips forward, and looked him boldly up and down.

"Evenin', Officer."

"Evening, young sir." Flax pulled out his most brilliant smile. The young man was tall enough, dark-haired, with sharp features and high cheekbones. He would do. "Are you behaving yourself tonight?" He swaggered close, tucked his hair behind one pointed ear, and propped a booted foot up on the bottom step up to the club. "Or have you been a very bad boy?"

The slight smile on the boy's face bloomed into something warmer—or at least something more knowing. "Oh, I've been real bad." He grinned, turning to put his hands on the railing. "I think you better frisk me."

Flax laughed and was in the act of reaching for his conquest when a hand fell on his shoulder. With so many people in close proximity, it didn't shock him that someone had touched him, but a sudden hum along the magic currents made him whirl around to face the owner of that beautifully manicured hand.

She hardly had to tilt her head up to meet his eyes. Even without the heels, she would have been tall. Heavy lashes blinked at him over sharp, hazel eyes. The stole around her throat slipped for an instant, revealing a prominent Adam's apple, but Flax was accustomed to such things by now.

"Well, hello there. Aren't you pretty?"

"Yes, I am," she said, no hint of humor in her tone. "I have to tell you. I believe you are in terrible danger."

"Oh, for fuck's sake," one of the other guys, not the one still bent over for Flax, said. "Not this again. Would you get lost? No one wants to hear your bullshit."

She sniffed and looked at the heckler disdainfully. "It isn't bullshit. I always speak the truth."

"Yeah, yeah. Take a hike, sister."

She ignored him and turned her eyes back to Flax. "I'm just trying to warn you. If you stick your dick in that, you're asking for trouble—and a terrible itch, too."

Flax arched a brow at her. "A VD soothsayer? That's a rather specific talent."

"You little bitch, go poach somewhere else!" Flax's current 'bad boy' protested.

"I know more things than who's got the clap," she said to Flax, giving the other boy another contemptuous flick of her eyelashes. "I can tell you who your future lover will be."

"If you would get fucking lost, it would be me," the boy at the railing called over.

Flax ignored the snarling knot of club boys and stroked a gentle knuckle over her cheek. Yes. Power. She didn't draw it down. It danced around her. "Can you? But it seems a little silly. I have a lot of lovers."

She waved a dismissive hand, but she smiled coyly at Flax. "No. You have a lot of people you fuck. I can tell you who your real lover will be. Who you'll fall in love with." She paused, looking into Flax's eyes. "Both of them."

Both? He narrowed his eyes and stepped closer, backing her away from the club a few feet. "What do you know? Or what do you think you know?" he growled. "Tell me."

There was some grumbling going on behind him, but Flax ignored it and so did she. She also didn't seem intimidated in the least by his growling as she patted his arm and smiled at him. "They are together, but you will be asked to stay. One is tall—taller than you—the other less so. One is kind and gentle, the other fierce, and both are brave."

Flax let out a snort. "Uh-huh. That's terribly oh so not specific. The boys are right. This is bullshit."

She let his arm go, a little pout pursing her lips. "I'm not wrong. You think you are doing the hunting, but before long you will be the one hunted."

"That sounds like a threat," he said close to her ear, soft and low. "I don't like threats, pretty soothsayer."

"It is a threat. Love is always a threat to men like you."

"You have something specific you want to say to me, you better fucking say it. Otherwise, you keep your vague, veiled warnings of danger away from me. Hear me?"

She seemed completely unconcerned with his irritation and lifted her hand to his cheek, caressing him. "I can't be more specific, because you wouldn't believe me anyway. You won't even believe yourself, not yet. But you will. Oh, and…" She tipped her head back the way they had come. "He really does have the clap. He doesn't know it yet, but he will." She winked at him, patted his cheek and walked away.

"Oh, for all the goddesses' sakes," Flax grumbled. "Someone save me from freak humans."

Whatever she had wanted to accomplish, she had completely ruined his mood, at least, and sure as hell put him off the club boy at the railing. He shook his head in exasperation as he strode away, back toward his apartment.

"Hey! Where are you going?"

The young man called to him, but Flax kept walking. His sharp ears still picked up their conversation for a moment or two.

"Can you believe that bitch? Scared him off with her bullshit."

"No, man, she's not full of shit. She's the real deal. She told my cousin last week he'd fall in love with a doctor and when he went to the clinic, the doc asked him out. Now he's like his sugar daddy."

There were snorts and laughter, then Flax was too far away to hear them anymore.

An early night with some porn. That was the ticket.

He reached up and touched his cheek where her hand had lain and shivered. *Not freaked out. I am not freaked out.*

By the time he made it home, his brain spinning around all the things she had said, he was well and truly freaked out.

Chapter Four

Quinn had never been particularly fastidious about hygiene. He took a shower when he needed to but didn't really luxuriate in the experience or spend too much time scrubbing up. He wasn't particularly unhygienic either, but when he'd been living on his own he had just used regular unscented bar soap and the cheapest shampoo he could find and didn't worry about how he might smell to anyone else, figuring that as long as he didn't smell like BO, he was fine.

Ever since learning that every elf and most crossovers could pretty much tell immediately if he'd had sex in the last twenty-four hours and could smell Val's pheromones all over him, he'd been more conscientious about body scrubs and herbal-scented shampoos.

When he asked Val what he smelled like, he invariably told him he smelled delicious and not to worry about it. Quinn didn't, usually. It wasn't that he was ashamed of anything, but he was a private kind of person. It made him feel awkward that half the people he worked with would know his business as soon as he walked into a room. He just hoped that the shower gel and shampoo were enough of a clue that he didn't want to broadcast his sex life to anyone that they would keep any knowing looks or comments to themselves.

Val also assured him that elves had a different view on these things, which only made sense when you couldn't really hide what you'd been up to. Still, Quinn took a few extra minutes in the shower to lather, rinse and repeat to make sure he smelled appropriately clean and herb scented.

Usually Val was up and gone long before he rolled out of bed, but with Momma Cats dead and everyone still in the dark about how it happened, he figured he had better be up early and get a ride in with Val to take another look at her body, er, statue.

In the kitchen, the coffeepot was finishing its cycle, orange juice sat on the table, and Val was at the stove. He turned with a bright smile. "Pancakes?"

Quinn returned his smile and brushed a kiss across his lips. "Do we have time?"

"We have enough. And I'm the Captain. No one can berate me if I'm a minute or two late." He actually winked at Quinn as he put a plate stacked high with pancakes in front of him. Someone was feeling better that morning. "You need to set up a time with your new teacher."

Quinn had just dropped into his chair and he grimaced. "Shit...I forgot to call him last night. You think I should call him now or wait until we get to headquarters?"

"Now might be best. That way everyone can plan the day. I do have staffing to consider, you know, so if any of my officers have meetings, it's good to know before roll call."

Quinn couldn't argue with that, although if it were up to him he would have procrastinated as long as possible. His jacket was still on the back of the chair in the living room and he got up to retrieve the cell phone from its pocket, hoping that it wouldn't be dead after he'd forgotten to plug the damn thing in as well last night.

It wasn't dead. When he pressed the little button on the side to wake it up, he had a text message.

You were supposed to call last night. Meet me at headquarters at 8:30. Don't be late.

Quinn looked at the time. If he left right this minute, he'd probably make it with time to spare. Val might get on him for not eating again though. Eat first then. He could still make it and maybe be only a few minutes late.

He sat back down and dug in and when Val looked at him questioningly, he explained, "He sent me a text. He wants to meet right before roll call, probably just so he can set up a later time in case you got something for him to do this morning."

"Good. Hopefully he'll suggest early. I need him out on patrol this afternoon."

Quinn did not exactly linger over breakfast but he didn't wolf his food down as fast as he could either. Val was in a relaxed mood and it was nice just to spend some time with him. He wasn't eager to rush into work. Eventually they got there, and not too terribly late. Things were already buzzing and humming along and Val barely got in the door before an officer waylaid him with questions regarding some sort of housing issue for the newly arrived. Quinn didn't see how that should really be Val's problem but he left him to it and wandered off in search of Flax Wolfheart.

He didn't have to go far, of course, since Flax had a desk in the squad room. He was just returning to his spot, maybe to get some paper work done, when he spotted Quinn.

"Not a good start. I'd rather not teach someone who isn't reliable."

Quinn stomped down on the urge to smirk. He had never dealt well with any kind of authority and even less so with nagging and scolding, but Wolfheart didn't know that. Besides, Quinn's issues were not Flax's problem so he tried to cut him some slack.

He glanced up at the clock over the door at the far end of the squad room. "It's eight-forty-five. I don't think fifteen minutes is that big a deal."

"No. Especially not if you arrive on the arm of the captain." Flax's smile was one of those chilly ones, all teeth, no friendliness implied. "But you were supposed to call last night."

Quinn bristled at the implication of special treatment, but it was not altogether unexpected. Flax was simply the first to point it out so blatantly. If it was just his reputation called into question he couldn't have cared less, but he didn't want one of Val's officers to make an accusation like that in front of anyone who would take it seriously.

He was about to snap that he'd been busy last night, but he cut that off too. "I forgot. Sorry, it was my fault." Quinn sighed. "Listen, can we just... I'm not usually 'unreliable'."

Flax's golden eyebrows crept up, and his chilly smile slipped a little. Maybe it was Quinn's refusal to fight that stole his aggressive needling. "Good. Fine. Ten o'clock. Empty holding room up in Research."

"Cool, that works. Val said he'd need you out on patrol this afternoon," Quinn said offhandedly, then wondered why the other man stiffened like his chain had been pulled. He frowned slightly. "See you then."

He turned and headed toward the stairs. He might as well go up and check in with Kai. They had undoubtedly brought in the statue of Momma Cats as well by now and he wanted to take another look at her.

* * * *

Flax seethed all through roll call and the morning briefing. Yes, he absorbed the fact that there had been some human-on-goblin violence around Central Park West. Yes, he got that someone needed to get to Athens later in the day and retrieve a frightened unicorn. But most of his brain ran in circles around what that damn kid had said to him.

Fucking nerve of the brat, giving him orders, as if living with the captain gave him the right. Or maybe the captain had purposefully relayed the order through him. Both of those possibilities sliced into him and made him angry, but the second one was more directly humiliating. The captain had been warming up to him the day before, he thought. So it couldn't have been that, could it?

Tesined Valerian... *Captain* Valerian. How could he settle for a single scrawny human male when he should have had a full *senrist* of warriors at his back? This world was full of supremely stupid shit, as the locals would say, but that? He couldn't get his head around it.

He finished his reports early—no one was going to find fault with his work today—and headed up to

Research fifteen minutes early. He'd teach the kid. He'd do the best he could with it and no one would be able to fault him for that either. The kid would run right to Valerian and bad-mouth him if he did anything overtly nasty, which really wasn't fair. If this human was incompetent or slow, he should have his hands smacked.

Why does everything have to be so complicated here?

On the way to the holding room he'd reserved, he turned a corner too fast and nearly slammed into a white-haired figure in black glowering at something on a tablet. Elvish and drow reflexes saved them from actual collision, but of course it was the head of Research himself.

"Watch yourself, Wolfheart," Hiltas snapped at him.

From him, those simple words could have had several meanings. Flax stepped aside with a courteous bow to let him go on his muttering, glowering way. The drow gave him the shivers, for more reasons than he could tell anyone right now. When he reached the holding room, he left the door open halfway and tried to collect himself. Being angry wouldn't help. Neither would being jumpy. He drew his knives with a sigh and set them spinning in the air, juggling two, three then four. As relaxation techniques went, not something you could really do in the squad room.

* * * *

An hour wasn't a long time to spend looking for any clues as to how a living person was turned into stone, but even so, Quinn had thought he'd maybe get something. Some vibe, some little hint. Kai at least had spared him any belittling comments when he'd come up empty. Or maybe he was just glad Quinn hadn't been the one to find the Cracker Jack prize when everyone else had missed it.

No. As much as he would have liked to believe that was the reason, he doubted it. Kai might have been many things, but a total egotist he was not. He would have been relieved if Quinn found something.

Frustrated was not the way he wanted to be when he met up with Flax Wolfheart again but he hadn't given himself any time for a distraction before he had to head to the holding room. This time he was determined not to be late. The 'not reliable' comment had gotten under his skin more than he cared to admit. Lazy. Impulsive. Undisciplined. All of those he might admit to, but unreliable grated on his nerves.

The door was open and he pulled the cell phone out of his pocket to check the time. Five minutes early. He couldn't complain about that. Nudging the door a little wider, he stopped in his tracks. Flax stood with his back to Quinn, throwing knives around. Not exactly the best time to startle someone.

"I hear you breathing, kid. Come in and shut the door." This was said without Flax turning around or missing a beat with his knives.

Quinn slid through the crack, shut the door behind him, and tried not to envision Flax suddenly turning and flinging the knives at him like some kind of circus act, a test to see if he would flinch. He would definitely fail that one.

Luckily, Flax caught the knives deftly, two in each hand, and shoved them in their holsters, one on each hip, one strapped to each thigh. Like Val, he didn't seem to carry a gun. Most elves didn't take to them, but at least Val's sword was magic. Quinn didn't feel any magic coming from those wicked, curved knives.

"Great." Flax clapped his hands together as he turned, his serious expression giving nothing away, the pissed-off smile from that morning banished. "So let's see what you can do. We'll start with something simple. Go ahead and cast a fireball."

Quinn thought he was joking for a second but his expression didn't change and he didn't suddenly break into a friendlier smile and say 'just messin' with ya'. *Damn it.*

"Uh, I didn't bring a staff or wand or anything," he hedged.

Flax shrugged. "You don't need one, do you?"

Quinn's eyes narrowed. He couldn't be that ignorant. "I'm human, remember? Yeah, I do. If I don't want magic burn, I need something to use as a channel."

The rapid blinks he got in response couldn't have been anything other than genuine surprise. "Well, that's a problem right there. We'll have to work on your inborn magical deficiencies."

Before Quinn could decide whether that was a direct insult or just an elf thing, the damn hunter elf handed him one of his knives. "Here. Silver. Try that."

Quinn suppressed a sigh. He didn't know why he'd even tried the delay tactic. It wasn't like he could go home, practice and show up tomorrow somehow able to throw around gouts of flame. Should he just admit defeat now? He wasn't sure which would be more pathetic, not trying at all or letting Flax see just how little he could actually do.

Gritting his teeth, he turned the handle of the blade around in his hand a few times. Maybe he could manage a little flame this time. He never had before, but he'd never tried to use metal as a channel before either.

With little hope of anything happening, Quinn opened up to the energy inside, letting the flow come, letting it build longer than was strictly necessary for him. Maybe that was the key? Maybe all the times he'd tried before he'd pushed it too hard and fast, hadn't let it grow? He tried to think fiery thoughts. He could feel the amount of power he was coalescing flow down his arm. Candle flame. Campfire. Stove burner. Come on….

The blade started to glow, a faint bluish color that got brighter and whiter, but threw off not even a little heat and no flame at all. He let the energy slide away and scowled. He thought he'd almost had something there for a second, but it was like trying to figure out how to grab an eel. It just went right through his fingers.

"Um. Hmm." Flax stood there with his arms crossed and one eyebrow raised high. "That was surprisingly bad. Really. Shockingly bad. You're channeling enough power to take out an army of trolls and…nothing?"

Quinn forced himself to stop trying to crack his molars. "I can't do fire, okay? It just doesn't come out right." Now he did sigh. "I can work with air or water easier."

"I don't understand why humans don't teach their young from birth. It's like you want to have your children grow up crippled. Fire is the first element you should learn. It's the closest to a direct expression of energy. The simplest." Flax shook his head and scrubbed both hands over his absurdly handsome face. "Fine. I want to see what you *can* do, not what you can't today."

He stalked to the end of the room and set up a folding table. Then he took items out of a bag—an empty soda can, a stapler and a bowling ball. Where the hell he'd found a bowling ball inside AURA headquarters was anyone's guess, but Quinn couldn't worry about that now.

"Wind then. With or without the channel, I don't care. Knock what you can off the table."

"Uh..." Quinn started to say that he should probably stand out of the way, but Flax gave him a quelling look.

"Don't tell me. You can't work with wind unless you're outside? Or is it some other human frailty keeping you from actually producing a result?"

All right, Quinn was just about tired of this shit. He turned his attention to the table and the items on it. Power surged up into him and he wrestled with it as hard as he'd struggled to contain all the frustrated anger he'd penned up since walking into AURA that morning. He tried to force it to do his bidding as he let it go.

A gust rushed past him, ruffling his hair and gaining speed by the millimeter. The soda can flew one way, the stapler another and the bowling ball launched like it had secretly wanted to be a cannon ball it's entire life and embedded itself into the drywall a good six feet off the ground. The table flipped over and slammed into the wall on top of it for good measure.

"That's...great," Flax said dryly from where he'd had to duck the flying stapler. "Not a speck of control. Wonderful."

The table clattered back to the floor and Flax squeezed his eyes shut as if he needed a moment to gather his patience. With exaggerated deliberation, he set the table back up and pulled out a stack of pencils that he let fall on the table like pickup sticks.

He sauntered back to Quinn and held up a finger. "Watch. Not only what happens, but how I do it. Watch the flows. Watch how they move with me instead of me forcing them like an elephant with a magic jackhammer."

Currents of green magic rippled down his outflung arm and as he flicked his fingers, he shoved the pencils one by one off the table, never disturbing more than the one he aimed for.

He turned to Quinn, his expression somewhere between exasperation and amusement. "Like that."

Quinn just barely kept from mimicking his 'like that' while he went and picked up the pencils and dropped them back on the table. This was not going to end well. He already knew it. At least they weren't sharpened.

He tried to focus. He was able to see the traces of magical energy when other people used it, but he had trouble seeing his own. It was more feeling than visual with him. He used the knife as a channel this time, and as an aid to direct the energy. If he took his time and wasn't pissed off or scared out of his mind, he generally managed a little more finesse. He tried to send just a breeze, knowing already that he wasn't capable of the control Flax had, but figuring he might be able to knock one at a time off if he was gentle enough.

The power built and he sent it out, and every pencil was blasted off the table and clattered against the wall, one embedding itself like a spear, sharpened or not.

Flax looked at him contemptuously and Quinn shrugged. "At least the table didn't move."

"Small favors. I can see why they'd want someone to teach you. You're a disaster waiting to happen." Flax cleared his throat, apparently thinking hard. His head jerked up, gaze fastening on the clock above the door. "That's it for today. Out of time."

He retrieved his knife gingerly from Quinn as if he was afraid humans couldn't really handle knives either. "Practice. A lot. Think small. When it doesn't work, think smaller. Thursday. Same time. We'll try again."

* * * *

Quinn had not been the most self-assured person in the world when he'd met Val—not by a long shot— but he hadn't been totally without pride either. Most of the things he was proud of in himself had to do with his magical abilities. Meager as they were by some standards, they had always got him by and allowed him to be self-sufficient. He had also worn the fact that he'd taught himself almost everything he knew like a badge of honor.

Since meeting Valerian and all that had happened to defeat the lich queen, his confidence in other areas had been slowly mending and growing. After one hour with Flax Wolfheart, that newly formed confidence was badly shaken.

It wasn't just that Flax made him feel like an idiot either. If it were just that, Quinn could have chalked it up to the other guy being an asshole. However, he'd pretty much shown him, in exacting detail, how woefully inadequate he was in the whole magic department. He also could not stop thinking that maybe Flax was right. Maybe the reason Kai and Val wanted him under a trainer so badly was that he was a disaster waiting to happen.

Practicing at home was out of the question. There was too much that could get broken. He didn't really want to hang around at AURA headquarters all day either, so he took his handful of pencils and headed to the park.

Several hours later, it was starting to get dark. He had a small pile of splintered wood and graphite that used to be pencils, and he'd forgotten all about lunch — or dinner, for that matter. There were leftovers at least.

Val was home already when he got there, showered and changed into nothing but a pair of sweats, rummaging through the fridge. "There's my Quinn. Everything all right?"

Quinn wanted to grumble and complain about Flax, his attitude and his lack of teaching ability, but he figured he'd sound like he couldn't handle things on his own if he did that. "Yeah, I was just at the park. Sorry. I kinda forgot about making dinner."

"We have plenty to eat." Val pulled him into a distracted, one-armed hug and kissed the top of his head. "I won't tell you I was worried, since I'm not supposed to smother you. But I was a bit... No, that's not the right thing either. You're home. That's all that matters."

He pulled containers out of the fridge, some with a bit of a dubious sniff. "How did it go with Flax?"

Quinn could feel a muscle along his jaw twitch and his head was starting a slow throb to let him know he'd been pushing too much magic today without using a proper channel. Stupid, but he'd thought maybe if he could do it the way the elves did he could get a better grasp on not blowing the pencils to smithereens.

"It went fine," Quinn said. It hadn't been a total disaster anyway, so it wasn't a lie, just a tiny fib. He didn't like it, but he didn't want Val to worry about it either. He had enough on his plate. "Has Kai found out anything useful about Momma Cats yet?"

Val frowned at him, obviously not quite buying the fib or the change in subject, but he was kind enough to let it go. "No. He's terribly frustrated. Keeps running back and forth between the murder scene and the holding room where her statue is. I haven't seen him this confounded in…perhaps never."

"Well that sucks," Quinn said, leaning one hip against the counter. He crossed his arms and frowned thoughtfully. He hadn't really known Momma Cats well, but he did know her enough for it to feel somewhat personal. He wanted to know what had happened to her at least.

"Quinn…"

"Hmm?"

"What's that in your hand?" Val asked.

Quinn had to look before he remembered he was still clutching the remnants of the pencils. He opened the cupboard door under the sink and threw the shards of wood and graphite away. "They were pencils. I was, uh…practicing. I guess my control's not so good." He tried to sound joking rather than frustrated or bitter, but it fell flat.

"Ah. Since I don't think you were practicing murdering pencils, I think I see." Val took him by the shoulders. "Quinn, look at me. You were never formally trained. You shouldn't be able to do any of the things you do. But your abilities are so far beyond normal that some talents manifested almost on their own. Oh, I know you think someone taught you, but that was merely someone showing you that you *had* power. Your control is astounding for certain things. Very specific things. But Kai thinks you can achieve actual control over your abilities. He believes in you. I do too."

Quinn looked up at him and hoped his expression didn't look as cynical as he felt. He knew Val was only trying to be supportive. "Can we not talk about this right now? It's fine Val, really. I'll work it out." He slipped his arms up around Val's neck and gave him a soft kiss to let him know he wasn't mad, not with him anyway.

* * * *

Flax tossed back the wormwood, shuddering at the bitter taste before he could chase it with one of the better beers at Outland. The place was a dive, but a lot of magical folk came here — exiles, outcasts. He'd been in the captain's office again that afternoon, briefly, with other officers, and had been in a position to see the photo on his desk. Valerian, with his arms around that runt human of his, both of them looking sickeningly happy.

"He deserves better," Flax muttered to his beer. His second...third? Strange. No one cared if he used *alcohol* as an intoxicant. Oh, no. But his other issue? That was treated like a crime. Someone slid onto the barstool next to his. He didn't look because he really didn't care right now.

"Hey." The voice was familiar. The intruder dared to elbow him. "Wolfheart. Hey."

Annoyed, he rolled his head to the right. "Oh. Matt. Hi."

"You all right? Drinking alone when you're in a slump is a bad idea."

"Yeah, yeah." He waved an unsteady hand in Matt's direction. "Why'd they have to pick me?"

"Why'd they have to pick you for what?" Matt put a gentle hand on his arm. "Look at me. You drink the rest of that, you're gonna end up on the floor."

"Don't care. Nobody cares." Flax did try to focus on his fellow officer though, just to be polite. "They're makin' me teach that snotty kid. Quib. Quim..."

"Quinn?"

"Yeah. That. How is he a hero, anyway? No control. Can't even direct magic without a fuck...without a fucking wand. Don't think he can *with* one."

"Okay, you're not making a hell of a lot of sense, but I think I'm getting some of it." Matt disengaged Flax's fingers from the beer mug and set it on the bar. "Look, maybe you won't remember this in the morning, but humans are different from elves."

"No fucking kidding. Really?"

"Don't be a smartass. I mean dealing with magic. We're different conduits, if you want."

"I don't. Stupid kid. Saw them kissing in the lobby."

"What?" Matt shook his head. "Never mind. But we don't have the magical insulation you guys are born with. It's really rare for a human magic user to pull down magic wandless and not be in a world of hurt after. It hurts us physically. The wand channels the energy—provides the buffer, the transformer in the system, that we don't have."

"Oh." Flax tried to take his beer back, but it had vanished. "So it's not just him?"

"No, kid. It's just about every human, except the really old, really powerful ones. You build up resistance over time, but Quinn's young. He hasn't had time."

Some part of him, the sober part at the back of his brain, felt terribly foolish. He could've hurt the captain's lover. As much as he felt the human didn't deserve someone so wonderful, harming him would only cast doubt on Flax. Doubt. Suspicion. Possibly would make Valerian hate him. He couldn't have that.

He might never have anything except the few minutes a day in the squad room, but he'd rather that than no Valerian at all.

Chapter Five

It had been a good haul tonight. People were always more generous this time of year, when it was getting cold at night and closer to the holidays, but not so close everyone was broke.

JD had actual dollar bills in his case tonight, along with the change people had thrown in. Enough to score a six-pack and a pack of smokes and probably enough left over for some Mickey D's. Sweet. He whistled brightly as he climbed the steps from the subway and headed toward the nearest liquor store. The tune was one of his originals. Not that he'd ever actually play it while he was busking. New Yorkers were too fickle for that. Play something original and he might sit there all night without two pennies thrown his way. Play old favorites everyone knew and he was at least likely to make enough for a beer. Tonight he'd have more than just a few. He deserved it after flogging his backside all day, singing songs and playing his fingers raw.

Yep, a six-pack would do him fine right now. He turned down a side street that was a shortcut to where he wanted to be and some guy behind him called out, "Hey."

It was probably safer to just ignore it and keep going, but he didn't want to get a shank in the back either so he turned, "What?"

"I heard you playing. Heard what you were saying, man. Not cool."

JD squinted at the guy. "Hey, man, if you don't like the music, just move along. It's still a free country, you know." And who the fuck ran him down just because they didn't like his singing? That was weird, and so was the guy he was looking at. Stupid white boy probably only wanted to listen to that country bullshit anyway.

"I can't let you just go saying those things about me. Can't let you put the word out, you know. Sorry about that."

JD was about to tell the little fucker to go fuck himself, he was seriously starting to get creeped out, but a hand landed on his shoulder. He tried to jerk away but the hand was like a vise and pain started to spread down his arm.

"What the fu..." The pain shot up his neck and the side of his face. Maybe he was having some kind of stroke. He was about to scream when it reached his heart and his brain at the same time, ending any thoughts he had.

* * * *

Kai shifted the bouquet of narcissus to the crook of his left arm, trying to gather himself for the fight he knew was coming before he opened the door to his apartment. At least it was before ten this time. That might work in his favor.

Not a single lamp shone. The ghostly blue display on the microwave was the only light to witness the gut-wrenching silence. Kai's night-adapted eyes still picked out the large white-furred figure on the living room couch, a bottle glinting on the end table to his left.

"Tenzi?"

A soft sigh reached him before Tenzin shifted. Kai wondered if he'd fallen asleep. "Kai, you need to give me some honest answers. Now, without hedging. Or I will be leaving."

The flowers nearly dropped from Kai's numb fingers. "I don't...understand. I haven't been anything but honest with you, dearest—since the lich incident. Tenzi, what's happened?"

A strange laugh, bitter and hollow, reached him. "You're suddenly working late every night. Supposedly working, anyway. I was willing to believe you. I know you work hard. It didn't make me happy, but like the trusting fool I am, I believed you."

"I have been working." Kai closed the door behind him, venturing a few careful steps closer. "The statue murder—"

"Oh, yes. That." Tenzin cut him off, something he never did. "Perfect excuse, wasn't it? But then, your lies were always well constructed. Flax Wolfheart called and left a drunken message about secrets and exposing them. He wasn't terribly coherent, but the gist of it was plain enough. I need some truth, Kai. The next thing out of your mouth needs to be the truth."

Wolfheart? That idiot. How dare he call here and upset Tenzin. Kai's voice was colder than he'd intended as he said, "I have nothing to hide. I've done nothing wrong."

Tenzin heaved himself up from the couch, weaving before he steadied. "Wrong answer, Kai. Oh, not that I didn't expect it. But wrong, nevertheless."

To Kai's horror, Tenzin bent down and picked up a suitcase, the largest one he owned. "Tenzi? You can't... Please don't do this. I'm here now. We can listen to the message together. Sort this out."

Even in the dark, Kai could see his yeti frown, hesitation in the way he held himself. The phone in Kai's coat pocket rang and he risked a peek at the screen. *No, goddesses no, not now!* "I have to take this." He held up a finger for Tenzin to give him a moment as he turned away. "Hiltas."

"Mr. Hiltas, this is Officer Watkins, NYPD. We have instructions to call you if we found another statue victim." The officer gave an address as Kai squeezed his eyes shut, every syllable another heavy, iron nail in the coffin of his relationship.

He thanked the officer and hung up, turning back to Tenzin with a feeling of sinking deep into frozen mud. "Tenzi, I have to go. There's been another death. They need me on scene right now."

"Of course they do." Tenzin shook his head, adjusting his grip on his suitcase as he strode for the door. "That's fine. I won't be here when you get back—or most likely ever. Even if you're not having the affair I suspect you are, I'll never come first with you."

Desperate, Kai clutched his chest where he felt he'd been stabbed and fell to his knees in front of Tenzin. "Please don't go, Tenzi. Please! Give me a chance to make this right. I've been horribly neglectful. I've been under so much stress. Just please don't do this. Don't leave me. I can't manage without you."

"And that's just it, isn't it? You do as you please, to the detriment of your health and our home, and faithful, patient Tenzin will always be there to pick up the pieces. I can't, Kai. No more. I can't watch you destroying yourself while you ignore me and any advice or requests on my part. Goodbye, Kai. Maybe your new lover will pick up after you now."

Kai grabbed his arm in a last, pitiful bid to get him to stay. "There isn't anyone else! There hasn't been since I met you! Tenzi, I love you and only you, with all of my heart. No one else."

The look Tenzin gave him wasn't angry any longer. It was infinitely sad, and Kai's heart shattered.

"Except your work, Kai. You'll always love that more."

Tenzin wrenched his arm free with little effort and left Kai on the floor. The door closing behind him sounded so final, so horribly final.

"Tenzi..." Kai whispered, wiping the tears from his face. He couldn't wallow in self-pity now. He had to get to a murder scene. But oh, it hurt, more than anything else had in this world. He got to his feet, shaking, turned around and left home again to go back out into the night. It was where he belonged, after all, in the dark, where things like love could quietly die.

* * * *

Valerian was talking with some of the NYC cops, but Quinn tuned them out. To him it all just sounded like *blahblahblah* anyway. Thankfully he didn't know this guy. That would have felt too weird. He could have known him though. Easily. He could have been any one of the buskers he knew that hung around the park. At least, he didn't think he knew him. Being that he was a statue and all, it was hard to tell, without color or sound... But no, he didn't look familiar and the statue was so exacting in detail it couldn't possibly be an artist's rendering.

He hadn't touched it yet. He hadn't wanted to. But he didn't think it would make any difference if he did. He could sense nothing—not a hint, not a trace of magic on him.

Another familiar figure arrived, no mistaking him in his long black leather duster and his white braid. Made sense to call Kai to the scene, of course, but something seemed wrong with him. He moved as if his bones hurt.

Kai spoke briefly to the officers and to Val, though he never quite made eye contact with any of them, then turned his attention to the area surrounding the statue, waving everyone back as he started to pace circles around it.

Quinn stayed where he was, propping up the wall opposite the newest victim. He did not greet Kai, figuring it was better just to stay out of his way for the moment. He watched him though, trying to see if Kai did anything special, some trick that might pick up where Quinn had not been able to see anything.

Kai did not acknowledge him either. He kept his head down, eyes scanning the ground, not the victim. Quinn figured that made sense to look around him too, but he had just figured the regular cops had already done that and so he'd focused on the statue itself.

On Kai's third time past him, Quinn finally broke the silence, "Can I help you with anything?" He suddenly felt like he was some kind of store clerk asking such a question. *Do you need help finding anything? Sack of sugar? Olives? Murder weapon?*

"I need you to stay still and quiet, child," Kai snapped without taking his eyes from the ground. The oddest tremor ran through his voice. "Hush."

With a twitch of his shoulders and a sniff, Kai bent lower near the statue's right foot. He picked up a bit of paper, soggy from some unidentifiable spill on the concrete. Eyes closed, he held it between his gloved thumb and forefinger. Then he shuddered and finally turned to Quinn.

"It's faint. The barest trace. But someone who uses magic had this in his possession. Her possession. I can't tell. Do you feel anything?"

Quinn tried to unfocus his vision, see if he could see the same trace Kai did, but he got nothing. Now, if Kai had known he needed to find this little piece of paper an hour ago and told Quinn what he needed him to find, he could have pinpointed it in this alley before any of them had left home. He felt kind of useless though when he didn't know what they were looking for. He shrugged.

"No. I don't—" He stopped and squinted at the piece of paper Kai held by one corner. He changed his mind. "Maybe. Kinda weird though, like…" He shook his head, not knowing how to describe the energy clinging faintly to the paper. He had been looking for a color. Magical energy usually looked like a glow of light to him, and the glows had different colors. This wasn't light or color though, it was more like… "Static."

"Yes." Kai lowered his arm, his voice soft and hollow now. "It's something I haven't felt in a long time. Whether this magic user knows it or not, they are masking. Covering magical tracks. There is power here. Perhaps not well-controlled power. This is very dangerous."

Quinn narrowed his eyes, wondering if that was some kind of crack toward him. He didn't ask though. Instead, he asked, "You think whoever turned them to stone did it by accident?"

"We can't discount it." Kai's gaze wandered. He clearly wasn't entirely present in the moment. "Nor can we discount malicious intent. Either is possible. That I feel this same 'static' around the statue, very faintly, does lead me to believe this is our perpetrator? Culprit? I don't know what to call it."

"Kai." Quinn waited until Kai looked at him and still the drow's eyes shifted away almost at once. "Are you okay?"

For a moment, Kai's gaze snapped to his, anger flaring, and Quinn was certain he was about to be verbally flayed. Then those strange white eyes wandered away again and Kai's shoulders slumped. "No. And I most likely never will be again. Tenzin left me this evening."

Quinn's jaw literally fell open. That was not at all what he'd been expecting. "What? But—" He stopped himself before he asked why. This was obviously not the time or place to ask Kai why he'd been dumped. "Kai, that's... Shit, man, I'm sorry." He might think Kai was a jerk sometimes, but he'd gotten to know him better while working with him, and he'd gotten used to his quirks and his sometimes-bitchy attitude. He wasn't a bad guy really, and he and Tenzin had seemed so tight, so right for each other, and obviously in love. What the fuck could possibly have happened?

Kai ran a hand over his eyes and nodded. He swallowed hard, obviously fighting for control. "You would have heard soon enough, I suppose. AURA gossip is vicious. I don't... It's so hard to think right now."

Uncomfortable with overly emotional displays he might be, but Quinn wasn't heartless. If Val had just left him, he sure as hell wouldn't be at a murder scene right then. He put a gentle hand on Kai's shoulder and squeezed lightly, not knowing what to say. He should probably tell him he should go home, but if Kai wanted to be home, he would be. "If you, uh... If you need anything, you know..." He didn't know how to finish that thought either. It seemed cruel to say, 'Val and me will be there'.' The last thing a person going through a breakup wanted to hear was about another couple.

Kai made it easy for him, though, as he shook his head. "No. What could anyone do? I'll go with the statue to AURA. You and Val..."

He trailed off, maybe coming to the same conclusion Quinn just had. Luckily, Val managed to break away from the police confab at that moment. His jaw tightened the moment he spotted Kai, his long legs bringing him over in three strides.

He shot Quinn a quizzical look before taking Kai's face between his hands. "What is it? Hiltas? What's happened?"

Amazingly, Kai allowed the manhandling without a single snarky remark. He leaned forward so his forehead rested on Val's chest, whispering to him. After a moment, Val closed his arms around the drow, wrapping him up tight as if he could keep him together that way. "Kai... Oh, goddesses, Kai. We'll find a way to fix this. Just hold on."

Both hands clutched in the front of Val's coat, face still buried against his broad chest, Kai nodded and whispered some more.

"I know," Val murmured. "You're too stubborn and mean to do that. So I won't worry too much. Are you going home?"

Kai lifted his head, wiping impatiently at his eyes. "No. I can't. My office is smaller. It will seem less barren. Less empty."

Quinn couldn't even imagine the effort of will involved, but Kai pulled himself together to direct the police and AURA staff in loading the statue into the waiting van.

"Bad business all around, love." Val shook his head. "Kai won't admit it, but he's going to need you on this. He won't be at his best, concentration-wise. It's one thing to have a lover walk away from you. Bad enough. It's far worse to have a bond mate leave you."

Quinn knew that. He knew also that he hadn't liked the way Kai clung to Val, or the way Val had put his arms around him and soothed him. He knew further that he was stupid for thinking that way, but he couldn't quite pretend that the little spurt of possessive jealousy hadn't been there—not that he was a big enough jerk to say anything about it when Kai was so down. He wondered if he should call Tenzin and ask him what the hell had happened, but he figured that was sticking his nose a little deeper than he should into their business.

"I'll keep Kai company at the office anyway," Quinn said. "Who knows, maybe we'll figure out what's doing this."

"Good thought. Thank you, love." Val tipped his chin up for a quick kiss. Too much in the PDA department in front of the cops was never a great idea.

* * * *

Quinn leaned against the wall of the holding room, waiting, as Kai crouched beside the second statue, his eyes squeezed shut. Kai looked awful, his dark complexion a mottled gray, his hands twitching in little spurts and starts, but Quinn didn't want to derail his train of thought if he still had one running.

"Two victims, Quinn. One more and we have a serial killer." Kai's voice was soft and even. "What do our victims have in common, do you think?"

"Other than being homeless you mean?"

Kai looked at him. "How do you know he's homeless?"

Quinn shrugged. "I don't for sure, but not a lot of people that have jobs and can afford an apartment spend their spare time hustling for change."

"Point taken." Kai scrubbed both hands over his face. "Quinn, I appreciate the fact that you came with me, but until the police identify this gentleman, we have nothing else to work with. Perhaps you should go home."

Quinn couldn't argue that there wasn't a lot for him to do here, but he hesitated. It wasn't that he thought Kai was going to do anything really stupid... Well, yeah, it was.

"Kai, what the hell happened?"

With a soft grunt, Kai sat on the institutional tiles of the holding room. "I've been asking myself that all evening, believe me. There was a message on the machine at home. Tenzi got there first...but, no. If this was a simple misunderstanding, he would still be home. I had the most wonderful person in any universe who loved me. I didn't see...until it's too late. Sometimes you don't see."

"All right, all right, forget all that bullshit for a minute. He didn't just walk out without a word, did he? What did he *say*? Did you have a fight about something?"

"Yes. A fight." Kai shook his head, obviously fighting a hundred kinds of exhaustion. "We've argued off and on these past few weeks about my work. My working too much. Tenzin began to suspect that it wasn't all work. That I had been unfaithful." A choked, mirthless laugh escaped him. "Me. As if I had time for an affair."

Quinn looked at him shrewdly for a moment but he didn't think he was dissembling. Also, he knew how much time Kai spent at headquarters. If Kai was getting some on the side it would have to be with one of his co-workers. Not impossible but...maybe he just didn't want to believe Kai would hurt Tenzin like that. Obviously, Tenzin believed he would though.

"Okay, I was all ready to support you and all but...fuck it. Kai, Tenzin is right. You *are* here too much." He held up a hand at the scathing look that got him. "I know there's tons and tons of shit to be done here and no one else to do it. Well, who the fuck is gonna do it all when you start to fade from the loneliness? You can't do it all, Kai. Let some of your staff do the work. They should be here working on this right now, not you. Why don't you go find him and see if you can start making it up to him?"

Kai had crumpled during this speech, knees drawn up to his chest, head buried against them. The small, lost voice that answered sounded like anyone but the arrogant, high-handed head of Research. "I don't know where he is. He doesn't want to see me. I did call. But messages don't help make things better — ones he won't listen to. He said he would always be second with me. I didn't want... I didn't mean..."

He was going to cry. Quinn could feel it coming. His dark face didn't get all blotchy or anything, but Quinn could hear it in his voice. What he wanted to do was slap him one and tell him to go looking and not come back to work until he'd sorted things out with Tenzin, but not only did he not have the authority to do that, he also didn't think Kai would listen to him. What he did instead was ease down next to him, put his arm around him and his chin on top of Kai's bowed head, and ignored the way the drow stiffened at his touch.

"Oh stop it. No one else is here. Just let it go already. I'm not going to leave you here to cry on your own."

It wasn't an ugly cry. Like everything else Kai did, it was soft, oddly elegant and restrained, but it was just as heartbreaking—maybe more—since he didn't make such a big fuss about it. When he finally calmed to a few faint hiccups, he said wearily, "You can't find a yeti who doesn't want to be found. First rule of dating a yeti. But he will have to come to work eventually, even if he calls out tomorrow. I'm just afraid it's too late."

There was nothing for Quinn to say to that. No hope or advice he could offer. He should probably have urged Kai to go home and get some rest but he doubted he'd do that. Instead Quinn ended up just holding him for a while. It wasn't much, but it was something at least, and Kai didn't seem to mind. Quinn expected it to get awkward after a while, but it was oddly comfortable, like it was perfectly natural for him to take care of his kinda-sorta boss and his boyfriend's ex lover. Oh well, there were stranger things out there.

* * * *

Val was looking forward to getting home for the second time that day when his phone rang. *Sweet Mother, what now?* He considered ignoring whoever it was, but he knew that number. If Matt was calling this late, something was wrong.

"Hey, big guy! Where are you?"

"I'm perhaps three blocks from home. Are you all right?"

"I'm fine, Val. One of your officers, not so much. Flax is down here at Outland, wasted on wormwood and beer. Really not a good thing for him to be doing."

"Causing a scene?"

"Not bad enough to call the cops. And Dee will kill me if I bring home another drunk stray."

Val had to chuckle at that, despite the absence of humor in the situation. "I'm on my way. Keep things contained if you can."

When he reached Outland, he found that Matt had at least herded Flax to one of the back booths, away from the bar and most other patrons. At least he wasn't in uniform, though Val knew the hunter would have a knife or three on him, not quite legally. Facedown on the table, Flax appeared to have passed out.

"Not good. Why do they serve wormwood still?" Val asked in exasperation.

"Mostly for the goblins and the trolls," Matt said as he helped Val heave his intoxicated officer upright. "Doesn't affect them the same way."

As soon as Val had an arm around him, Flax's eyes snapped open. "Cap'n. You're here. Oh, you're here—" He turned his face to nuzzle at Val's throat, licking at his pulse line.

Val cleared his throat and put a little distance between them. "You've had far too much, pup. Is there someone we can call to take you home?"

"He lives alone." Matt shook his head. "I can't find anyone to claim him."

"Well, he can't be alone like this. Elves die from wormwood overuse." Val sighed and slung an arm around his shoulders, heaving Flax out of the booth. "I'll put him on my couch tonight. At least we'll be there if he needs someone. If he's mortified about it in the morning, at least that means he's alive."

Matt chuckled and laughed harder when Flax started snuggling closer, even though his feet tangled. "Poor kid. He's gonna have one hell of a hangover."

* * * *

Quinn finally left Kai sleeping in his office, or at least lying down on the couch in his office with his eyes closed and a blanket thrown over his shoulders. He felt bad leaving him there, but he couldn't convince him to go home and he let it go. If Kai didn't want to face his empty apartment yet, who was he to make him?

It was late and he felt grainy-eyed and somewhat down. Another person had died, Kai and Tenzin were falling apart and he had no answers for either of those things. All he wanted was to go home and crawl into bed for a few hours with Val before he had to go to work.

He thought maybe he was hearing things when he got to their door. Voices came from inside, one of them Val's. Who the hell was here at this time of night? Irritated, Quinn opened the door and stopped, his brain unable to process what was in front of him.

Val leaned over a prone figure on the couch, a male figure with an obvious boner behind the zipper of his jeans. This male, no, Quinn caught a glimpse of pointed ear, this *elf* had his arms around Val's neck and looked like he was trying to hook a leg over Val's back.

Quinn hadn't had exactly the most normal life where he'd had adolescent romances or many romantic relationships. Hell, he hadn't had anything he would have called a 'relationship' before Val. He'd never even been in love before Val. Maybe if he had, he would have been more prepared for the surge of blinding rage that boiled up inside him. Then again, maybe not. It was probably a good thing that he was not adept at throwing around fire because he would not have hesitated to fry the guy who was all over his man.

Along with the burning jealousy came another sort of rush. Magical energy coursed through him like a floodgate had been opened, filling him up until he felt he would burst if he didn't do something with it.

"What the *fuck*?" he demanded, and the living room chair went flying across the room and hit the wall as if he'd grabbed it and thrown it. He hadn't meant to do it and it scared him—or it would have scared him more if he wasn't so pissed off.

Val startled, one of his big hands thrown up defensively out of reflex. "Oh, Quinn. Good. Could you help me with this drunken idiot? I swear to all the gods of earth and water, the next one of my officers I catch drinking wormwood is going to be put on duty cleaning out wyvern sand toilets."

Quinn didn't relax. He didn't budge. "What is going on here, Val?" he snapped. He didn't know which of them he wanted to kill—maybe both of them.

"Matt called me to Outland." Val's blue eyebrows crept up his forehead as he met Quinn's glare. "This pup drank enough wormwood to kill a water dragon. I couldn't simply send him home in a cab, love. It's like abandoning someone who's close to alcohol poisoning."

Quinn's jaw was still tight with tension but Val wasn't reacting like someone who had been caught cheating. He looked more confused than anything, which did bring Quinn down a couple of notches below supernova. Of course, Flax chose that moment to caress Val's arm and that was enough.

"Get your hand off of him. Now," he barked.

Which worked for a drunken elf about as well as it would work for a deaf leech. Val seemed to grasp the situation finally and disentangled himself from his flailing, too-many-limbed charge on the sofa. Flax reached for him as Val backed off and ended up falling half off the sofa on his face.

"Goddess, give me strength," Val muttered, running a hand over the side of his face. He turned to Quinn, a slightly belligerent set to his own jaw. "I just want to get his boots off and get him covered. I most certainly don't want someone in that condition pawing at me, if that's what that look implies. What a dishonorable thought, to take advantage of..." He waved a weary hand at Flax, who hadn't moved from his half-header into the carpet. "That."

"I didn't think you were the one taking advantage here," Quinn said, hands on his hips as he regarded Val just as belligerently. Was he still pissed at Val? Maybe not so much. He sure as hell wasn't in a laugh-it-off mood, and the bastard on his couch... He finally looked down and realized he knew the bastard. His head whipped back up to pin Val again. He couldn't be that naïve, could he?

Val didn't look like he was trying to twist things around though, and he couldn't believe Val capable of such games anyway. Quinn shook his head. "He's not your problem." He stomped past Val before he could respond. He slammed the bedroom door for good measure.

Muffled Elvish cursing came from the living room and not thirty seconds later, Val stomped right after him and slammed the bedroom door open since Quinn hadn't had a chance to lock it. Fire blazed in his green eyes—intense anger Quinn had never seen before.

"He is my officer, so he is *my problem*," Val snarled. "I am the commander and the behavior of my men reflects on me. If one of them needs to be rescued from himself, I damn well better do my best to *do* it!"

Quinn lifted his chin and tried not to show any intimidation in the face of that blazing anger. "Right. And how many of them know that? How many know if they do something stupid enough to require a stomach pump that you'll be there to scrape them off the pavement? I bet all of them." He stabbed a finger toward the living room. "I bet that one knew damn well what would happen if he got wasted in a bar where half the squad hangs out and that someone was bound to call you. If he puts another fucking finger on you, I'm gonna break it for him."

Val scraped both hands back through his hair and Quinn saw the dark circles under his eyes in stark relief. "You would be within your rights. I don't suppose I would stop you if you limited yourself to a single finger. Yes, they know I'm there for them. But they also know that such behavior can only be tolerated for so long. If he can't behave like an officer of the law should, he can find another job."

No longer stomping, Val reached into the closet and pulled an extra blanket from the top shelf. "I'm not blind, Quinn. Yes, I know what hero worship looks like. He needs to work through it or he will be dismissed, which would be a shame. He's one of the best we've had come out of the academy in some time."

Quinn knew that. He knew that Val needed all the good officers he could get, too. He didn't buy that this was just hero worship though. But what was he going to do? Insist that he throw Wolfheart out? Val wouldn't do that. Then what? If Quinn backed him into a corner, either they were going to continue to fight or he would have to leave. He didn't want to do either of those things.

When he said nothing, Val finally turned and went back out to the living room. Quinn sat down on the edge of the bed and stewed. His stomach felt like it was full of acid. So. This was what jealousy felt like. He couldn't say he was learning anything good from the experience.

It didn't take Val long to come back with a pair of size thirteen boots in hand. He closed the door more gently this time, put the boots by the closet and came to sit next to Quinn on the bed.

"I'm very sorry," he said, his usual control replaced by simple exhaustion, it seemed. "I shouldn't have gotten angry with you. I won't make a habit of wrestling other males in the living room. I promise. And I will do my best to address this little situation. But not now. He's too drunk to remember anything and I'm too blasted tired."

Quinn ordinarily would have put his arms around Val at such a statement but he couldn't get his arms to unfold from around his middle. The white-hot anger had mostly drained away, seeing as how he couldn't hold onto it knowing that Val hadn't been doing anything wrong. The feeling left in its wake was not a pleasant one.

"I have never felt like this before," he said softly.

Val reached across the space between them and hooked a hand through Quinn's elbow. He didn't pull or move closer, just offered that warm hand. "It's not a happy one. I know. But I'm yours, love. Entirely. Without reservations. No matter who wants to throw himself at my feet, it won't make any difference and for you, I'll happily break hearts. All right, not happily. I'm not cruel."

Quinn rolled his eyes but just that one touch was enough to melt his reserve and he slid closer, putting his head on Val's shoulder. "I'm sorry I blew up. I just... I just saw him touching you like that and saw red."

"Hmm, well, I can't claim I wouldn't have a similar reaction if our positions had been reversed. Better the chair being thrown than a person, too. You probably did better in that regard than I would have."

Quinn half turned and slid his hands up Val's chest, nuzzling the side of his throat. "Really? I thought elves were more, um, relaxed about that stuff."

Val pleased hum rumbled against his ear. "Not with someone's bond mate. Things can get a bit messy in that regard. Oh, we do have arrangements where there are several bond mates, but everyone in those situations has agreed and the bonding is mutual."

Quinn frowned slightly. Given that he was still shaky with the aftereffects of adrenaline and magic from a jealous rage, he was not ready to think about something like that. Instead, he tipped his head back and found Val's lips, kissing him softly but insistently. "I love you, Val. I trust you, too. I hope I didn't screw that up."

"No, love. We've had a long day and had too many strange, upsetting things happen." Val tugged Quinn's shirt off over his head and yanked his own off without undoing the buttons. "In a way, I'm pleased to have elicited such a forceful response. I certainly don't love you less for it."

Val stood, but only to undress the rest of the way before he slid under the covers with a groan. "Climb in, please. I need you in my arms."

Quinn wasn't sure how they could go from screaming at each other to snuggling but he was more than happy to slide in next to Val's solid frame. There had been some misunderstanding and uncertainty when they had met, but this was the first real fight they had had since he'd admitted he loved Val and moved in with him. As he put his head on Val's shoulder and wrapped one arm around his chest, it was not lost on him who the cause of their first fight had been.

* * * *

Pitching on a turbulent sea of wormwood, Flax swam through dreams alternating between erotic and surreal. There were Val's hands caressing him, Val's arms around him. That had been real, though, hadn't it? The memory of his captain's arms around him was far too solid.

Sometimes he would be aware that he dreamt. His hunter's instincts processed sounds and scents as he slept, often warning him of approaching danger. This was different, though. He knew he dreamt in a more conscious way, wandering from one scene to another as a puzzled, disconnected observer.

"He had a senrist before, you know," Quinn was saying to him while he built a tower out of small, lavender eggs.

"I know. I —"

But Quinn had vanished along with the room in which he had stood. Green surrounded Flax. He stood in the depths of an ancient forest so like home his chest tightened with longing. Every leaf vein, every grass blade, every rough line of bark on ancient oaks stood out in such sharp definition that his eyes ached. This didn't strike him as a normal dream. It was too complete, too detailed. Was this a vision instead? A glimpse of another plane? Was this home? He was so distracted by the hyper-reality that he missed the approaching sounds until they were almost on top of him.

An arrow whizzed by his head, then another, narrowly missing him. He flinched, heart pounding as he looked for cover. Then he stopped and smiled. This was a dream or a vision. He couldn't be harmed. Another arrow came through the trees and passed right through his shoulder harmlessly. Flax reached up with one hand and touched the spot. No pain, no blood. He felt its passing through, like an echo far in the distance. His smile faded as figures crashed through the underbrush, a squad of elvish cavalry with a pack of drow right on their heels.

Hooves churned the ground, thundering around him, the sounds of their labored breathing and occasional shouts of warning, or pain, or anguish spilling in the air all around him. Metal rang against metal somewhere in the distance. He pressed himself to one of the ancient oaks as more horses and elves streamed around him in hasty retreat as the woods filled with more and more black steeds carrying drow riders, two, three times the elvish force's numbers. Flax was hard-pressed to remember this was a dream. He could hear the battle, smell the fear and the blood in the air, see every vivid detail of straining horse flesh and panicked elves.

Flax cried out when one of the elvish steeds reared as an arrow sliced through its beautiful throat. The rider was thrown to the fern-strewn forest floor and the horse staggered and fell almost at Flax's feet. Damn drow. Shooting the horses. *Old anger long buried came to the surface in a visceral rush as the drow circled like a pack of wolves closing in.*

The elf commander waved two of the elves on, perhaps to summon reinforcements, but he went back to stand guard over his fallen warrior and the rest of his company followed suit.

One of them dismounted, kneeling beside the fallen elf, pressing a hand to his head and chest, his lips already moving in a chant. The others formed a circle around them, bows at the ready or swords drawn. A brave and shining circle of light in the gathering gloom while the drow drew nearer on their dark steeds.

A black, shafted arrow came from the direction of the drow and one of the warriors flung himself from his horse to intercept it, his quick sword knocking it from the air in a blur of grace and speed. Flax's vision blurred as well, the details starting to waver around him, taking the once hyper-clear and crisp edges from the world as he tried to focus. He couldn't make out their faces though he tried to, squinting as they struggled to lift their fallen brother and escape before the drow could slaughter them. Flax moved, wanting to help, wanting to drag them to safety before it was too late, but the forest vanished before he could reach them.

Flax cried out, his arms still outstretched, reaching for them. No! What happened to them? I need to know what happened!

But the brief glimpse of battle had been replaced by a small room where night had fallen and Flax lay naked on something soft. He blinked, trying to see through the blur as gentle hands caressed him, soothing and yet driven by an obvious hunger. It felt like many hands touched him but after a moment or two they resolved into just two sets, a pair gliding up his chest, another smoothing down his back. He reclined between two deliciously warm bodies, the one pressed to his front taller than his own.

He moaned into a passionate kiss, the unmistakable scent of aroused elf swirling into his confused senses. The bodies pressing him felt so solid, so real. He wanted to touch them, kiss them, move and breathe and love with them. It felt heartbreakingly real. He reached a hand out to stroke the smooth, warm chest in front and everything shifted again, the realness sliding away in favor of something more dream-like.

Their hands still caressed him but felt different now, the smells of lusty elf replaced by the scents of wormwood and a soft blanket. The chest still pressed to his own was broader, and he could only think of one person his drunken lust-addled mind might conjure to touch him like this.

Val? Captain, is that you?

A hand found his cock, fingers closing around him in a firm, sensual stroke that made Flax moan again. He rolled his hips, pushing his aching member into the circle of his fingers. His whole body quivered at the simple touch. Another hand slid between his ass cheeks as he kissed his dream lover fiercely, sliding up and down in gentle, inquiring strokes. Oh, goddess yes, he wanted this. He needed this. Anyway they wanted him he was ready, so hard, so needy, he was going to burst. He bucked faster into the hand wrapped around his cock and he felt soft kisses placed across his shoulder, the fingers teasing between his cheeks growing bolder, pressing into him. He moved frantically, kissing the lips pressed to his own as if this might be the last kiss he could ever have, as if he knew if he stopped for even a moment they would be gone. Val would be gone, and if Val was the one that kissed him, the other body could only be —

Suddenly he was falling, falling forever as if dropped from a great height.

His eyes snapped open as he hit the ground, a gasp pulling him half upright in his dizzy, wormwood-muddled state. Dreams. Just dreams.

His body ached and with more than just the effects of the wormwood. He slid a hand down to his hard cock, needing the relief, but before he could do more than pass a hand over his crotch, the wormwood pulled at his consciousness and dragged him back down. He rolled over and passed out again, the dreams fading into bits and snatches of fog and mist.

Flax woke later to two separate sets of rhythmic thudding, horribly out of synch. It took several minutes of squinting at what he thought was probably daylight and not an interrogation lamp to parse out that one series of thuds was the pounding in his own brain. The other set—

This wasn't his bed. This wasn't his room. Where in all unholy thunder was he? Someone's couch. Not Matt's. He'd been to Matt's house and the living room walls were blue.

Sweet Mother, how did I get here? What did I do?

The thumping from down the hall got faster. He identified it just as he picked up on the escalating moans and grunts. *Oh, crap.*

"Val! Oh, fuck...yeah! Right there!"

A rumbling growl, followed by, "Quinn, love, come for me. Now!"

No. Oh, no no no no! The sexy moans became a gasp and a soft cry of pleasure. Flax's face heated and his stomach rolled. This was some sort of sadistic nightmare. He couldn't be listening in on his handsome captain nailing his human lover. He tried to sit up in a frantic search for his boots. The rolling became a wave of swamp-green nausea and he rushed down the hall, barely making it to the bowl of the toilet before he heaved up what had to be several months' worth of stomach contents.

* * * *

Val sighed into Quinn's shoulder, his softening cock still buried inside. "I think our houseguest is up."

Quinn's eyes were closed, his legs still loosely twined around Val's and his arms flung out to the sides as if he were drifting on a cloud of bliss. The sticky wetness of Quinn's spend was still warm between their bodies and he looked in no way inclined to move.

Val had been the first to open his eyes that morning, and the soft kisses he'd brushed along the back of Quinn's neck he had only intended to be sweetly reassuring, a reminder that their quarrel had not escalated to more than a few harshly shouted words and it was over. However, Quinn's sleepy responses had roused them both and it had been too many days since they had started the morning off so pleasantly.

Quinn rubbed a hand over his face and finally pried his eyes open. "Sounds like it," he agreed as they both heard another round of miserable retching from the hall bathroom.

"At least we know he lived through the night." Val kissed him gently and gave him a wry smile before disentangling himself with a groan. "Why don't you take the shower first and I'll go see if we need to call for medical intervention?"

Quinn gave him a look that clearly said he would rather Val join him in the shower, but he nodded and sighed as he rolled up to a sitting position. Yawning and stretching, he got up and there was definitely a little extra saunter in his step as he made his way toward the en suite bathroom. "Yeah, guess we don't want him keeling over," he said, less than charitably.

"Would be a bit of a scandal," Val said dryly, more than happy to delay and watch Quinn's lovely ass sway on his way to the shower. "AURA officer dies in captain's apartment. Not a good headline."

He got the chuckle he wanted from Quinn and threw on track pants and a T-shirt, not at all concerned that he smelled like fresh sex. If it made Flax uncomfortable, it was the pup's own fault.

The retching had stopped, so he knocked on the door before he eased it open. "Are you among the living?"

Sprawled out on the floor next to the toilet, this was perhaps not the most dignified moment of Flax's life. His eyes were open and seemed to be tracking, though his complexion was an unhealthy gray. "Captain?"

"Yes. I'll save you the questions. You're in my apartment. For whatever ill-advised reason, you drank far too much wormwood last evening and Matt called me, concerned. I brought you here and you seemed to believe I was alternately a popsicle or a stuffed bear. Get yourself up and moving and come into the kitchen."

"I can't—"

"You can. You will. Five minutes."

While he wished he could be compassionate and caring, Val knew caring for Flax with his own hands was a terrible idea on far too many levels. Stern and detached was better and more appropriate to the incident. He shook his head as he started coffee, put bagels in the toaster for Quinn and himself and put the teakettle on. By the time Flax dragged his rather sorry hide to the kitchen and collapsed at the table, Val had a mug of tea ready for him.

"Green tea. Good for you at this point. Would you care to offer explanations?"

Flax stared into his tea, red spots high on his cheeks. "No, sir. I was... It wasn't the best week. I was stupid."

"Indeed you were, pup." The shower turned off but Val couldn't care less if Quinn heard them. "You could have died. I need to have a word with the bartenders at Outland since they should never have kept on serving you. However, the fault lies squarely on your shoulders. Your behavior was disgraceful."

Flax had hunched farther over his tea with every sentence. His voice was a spare, mortified whisper when he choked out, "Yes, sir."

"Now, I'm going to give you cab fare home. I'll excuse you from roll call, since you can't physically get home and back to the squad room on time at this point without teleporting. But you will report for duty today, as soon as the laws of physics allow. If you're miserable, it's your own doing. If I *ever* catch you throwing back wormwood again, I will start proceedings to have you dismissed. Is that clear?"

"Yes, sir."

"Damn it, Flax, you're a good officer. Don't throw your career away before you've even started." Val waited until he received a miserable nod. "Any questions?"

"Do you have my boots, Captain?"

"Yes." Val had to hide a smile as Quinn emerged from the bedroom, fully dressed and carrying the boots as if they were poisonous snakes. "Thank you, love." He took the boots and turned a less tender expression on Flax. "I took them to be sure you wouldn't stumble out of here still drunk."

He handed them over, kept watch while Flax, with his eyes never leaving the ground, shoved his feet in and levered himself slowly up from the table. "Thank you, sir — for watching out for me."

"Don't let it happen again. Are we clear?"

Flax nodded, tight-jawed, and accepted the cab fare Val offered before dragging himself out of the apartment.

"Hmm." Val shook his head as he sipped his coffee. "I hope that wasn't too harsh. Resentment, I don't need."

Quinn poured coffee into a mug and took a careful sip. "He's still got his job. You didn't suspend him or anything. He should be more thankful than resentful."

That was typical of Quinn's practical nature but even so, Val noticed he was perhaps a shade more callous than he might have otherwise been. At least he was trying to be civil this morning. Val had been worried that Quinn might feel the need to tell Wolfheart off, then there would have been no salvaging the situation.

Whatever else they might have discussed was cut short by Val's cell phone ringing.

"Captain Hartgrove," Val answered. A friend would have called their landline. Only AURA used his work phone.

Nestor, the centaur, serving as first-shift sergeant, sounded a bit breathless. "Event sign, Captain. We're pinpointing now, but it looks Pacific."

"Thank you. I'll be there as soon as possible. Do we have a feel for it?" Val tucked the phone between ear and shoulder as he strode back to the bedroom to yank clothes out.

"Not a huge one, Lisa says."

"Good. Send Matt and Aello through for first assessment and possible containment. Keep me updated."

A quick sluicing off at the sink and a brush through his hair were all he took time for. He hurried back out, still buttoning his shirt, and gave Quinn a quick kiss. "You want to ride in with me?"

"Yeah, I need to check back with Kai anyway. See if he's got anything off the paper he found last night," Quinn said.

It seemed such a simple statement, but it made Val's heart swell with pride. A few months ago, Quinn would never have voluntarily taken such initiative and he certainly wouldn't have wanted to help Kai, whom he had seen as a snotty prick.

He made certain Quinn took his bagel along then had no more time for niceties. An Event could be anything—there simply was no way to predict. It could be a creature as small as a water lily sprite or as large as a mountain dragon. As they pulled into the garage, his phone buzzed again with a call from the squad room.

"What do we have, Ness?"

"Pair of elves, Captain. Warriors, Matt thinks. Armed to the teeth and kinda freaked out."

"Where are they?"

Ness cleared his throat, a little whinny escaping with his nervousness. "Tokyo, sir. Shibuya Crossing."

"Lovely. I'm on my way up."

Chapter Six

Quinn refrained from telling Kai he looked like shit, although he did. He had his team of researchers gathered in the room where both Momma Cats and the still-unknown busker were. Every last one of them looked uptight and like they were walking on eggshells. Quinn hung back while theories were posed and shot down, some more than once.

They were getting nowhere standing around examining the statues over and over. After about a half hour of listening to them going around in circles, Quinn said as much.

"This is pointless. There are only so many creatures that turn living flesh into stone and you guys have already been over why it was none of them a dozen times." Okay, so that wasn't the most positive thing he could have said, but he was going to lose it if he had to listen to Jordie kissing Kai's ass and shooting condescending looks at Vicki every time she opened her mouth for even one more minute.

"Yes." Kai rubbed his fingers over an obviously aching forehead. "And if I could move this pack of ninnies in any other direction, I would have." He waved a hand toward Quinn. "Mr. Riley at least thinks. Please take notes."

Quinn was pretty sure that was a jab at him somehow but all of the research assistants turned to look at him as if he were going to suddenly pull a rabbit out of a hat. He almost told them to fuck off, but bit his tongue.

Several seconds ticked by with the assistants staring at him and Quinn staring at the statues and Kai rubbing his temples. At least they had all shut up. He didn't know how any of them could think while talking all the time.

The seconds started to stretch and feet started to shuffle. He counted down in his head.

"Maybe it was an immature basilisk," Jordie said when he'd reached seven.

Quinn sighed. Kai made a sound like a small, suffering animal.

"Okay, look. I'm not a magical creatures' expert and Kai isn't supposed to rip your head off for thinking out loud, but I swear if you say the word 'basilisk' one more time, I'm going to hex you so hard your grandchildren will feel it. It wasn't a fucking basilisk."

"Quinn—" Kai started to say but Quinn cut him off by sliding off the desk he'd been sitting on and stalking over to the statue of Momma Cats.

"Somebody had to see what happened," he muttered, looking into the gray stone of her eyes.

Kai was chewing his lip, obviously processing, but it was Vicki who spoke up next in a tiny voice. "She fed cats."

"She did, Victoria. That she did," Kai murmured. "Perhaps we should talk to some cats."

Quinn whirled around so fast that everyone but Kai took a step back. He was grinning though. He pointed a finger at Vicki, "This one is a keeper, Kai. I can find a cat, if you can find someone who can actually talk to one or read its little mind."

Kai raised a white eyebrow. "My dear Quinn. I'm a drow. Of course I speak cat."

Quinn blinked at him. "Really? Well...cool. Let's get started then."

"Should I reserve one of the ritual rooms? Do you need a pendulum, or did you bring your own?" Jordie asked.

He said it pleasantly enough, but Quinn heard the slightest note of condescension in his voice. "Nah, I don't need any of that stuff." He had practiced a lot with the scrying ability since it had been so useful in finding the lich queen's phylactery and he'd found he didn't need to cast a full circle or chant or do much of anything except sit quietly and concentrate.

However, there was one catch. Cats moved. Unless he caught it sleeping, it might not be where he had seen it when they got there.

"Everyone out," Kai said softly, his tone steadier than it had been all morning. The assistants started for the door, but Kai snapped his fingers. "Except Vicki. I want you to watch and learn how to stabilize someone who's scrying. Quinn, if you can find a location, I'll help you track it. Cats have territories. They don't often stray from them."

"Right. Okay. Just...gimme a few minutes here," Quinn said. Now that he'd waved off any of the props and assistance, he was hoping he'd actually be able to get deep enough in his head to get out of it. That sounded weird, but it was the way it worked.

This was going to be tricky. It wasn't like it was a totally unique and unimaginably evil object he was looking for. If he told his psyche he wanted to find a cat, it was likely to show him a random leopard at the zoo, or maybe it would light up a few hundred thousand strays. That would be helpful. Not. It had to be the cat that saw what happened to Momma Cats, if there even was one. They were guessing. Still, it was a good guess.

Quinn looked at the statue that had been Momma Cats and figured that was the closest he was going to get to some sort of marker to narrow it down. He settled down at her feet, leaned back against her legs and tried not to think morbid thoughts like if she was stone all the way through or if there were still some blood and guts inside. He shuddered. Okay, enough of that.

He closed his eyes and started to breathe in a conscious way, pulling the air deep and letting it out slowly as he tried to tune out the murmured instruction that Kai was giving to Vicki about energy support and anchors and other such shit.

He started to sink. He didn't really, but that's what the sensation felt like at first, like diving deep, then getting lighter and lighter. He opened his eyes and he was looking down at the room. Vicki and Kai were still standing with their heads together. Vicki's eyes looked wide, nervous. He had faith in her, though. She was sharper than those other nitwits anyway. Time to find a kitty cat.

He pushed up and effortlessly he was through the ceiling and above the building. He liked that part. It wasn't like flying in his physical body, where he was scared shitless and could hardly bear to look around. This way he was fearless, and for some reason far more confident than when he was muddling around in the flesh. He did a slow turn, floating, looking over the rooftops of the shorter buildings around AURA headquarters.

The taller buildings blocked his vision, but only because he couldn't yet get his head around how they weren't really there at all when he was like this. In theory, he should be able to see right through them, but so far he hadn't managed that. He looked toward the park, and beyond, toward where he knew Momma Cats had been found and in a blink, he went from floating above AURA headquarters to standing at the mouth of an alley.

Quinn hummed softly to himself. He never did that except when he was wandering around without his body and didn't know why he did it then, but somehow it felt right. "Kitty kitty... C'mon... Where are...you?" He saw a scruffy cat that looked like it had seen its share of fighting. "There you are." Quinn smiled. "Okay, buddy, stay. Don't look at me like that. Just stay there."

He had no doubt that he had zero influence where the cat was concerned and more than likely it couldn't see or hear him anyway, although it did seem to be focused rather intently where he stood. Then he was falling through the pavement and his arms jerked as he landed back in his body.

"Aw jeez..." Quinn said, blinking and rubbing one eye with his knuckle. "It's across the river — Hundred-Forty-Fourth Street."

Vicki nodded, wide eyed, her phone already up to her ear. "One-hundred-and-forty-forth, Mr. Hiltas. Yes. Where they found the body, I think." She covered the mouthpiece with one hand and whispered, "Are you okay?" Then she was listening again. "Yes, sir."

Her hands shook as she looked at Quinn again, not quite directly. "He wants us to stay online."

Quinn nodded, expecting that. The cat was at 144th Street now, but by the time Kai got there, who knew if it would still be there. Even so, it wasn't likely to travel far. Now that he'd seen it once, it should be easier to find him again, tweak Kai's direction if it moved.

He relaxed, settled in and got ready to scry again. This could take a while.

"He's asking what the cat looked like," Vicki whispered.

"Fluffy," Quinn answered, and when she relayed his response precisely he grinned.

"He says more detail would be helpful."

She was totally deadpan and Quinn wondered if she really had no sense of humor or if she was just scared.

"Orange-ish…stripes I think. Got a big chunk out of his ear. Looks beat to shit."

"Um…he said it's an orange-striped tabby with a notched ear and scars," Vicki said into the phone.

Quinn grinned again. He liked Vicki. "Tell him to let me know when he's a couple blocks from the target. I'll check and see if it's still sitting there."

Vicki did the covering the mouthpiece thing again. "He's cursing at the cabbies." For just a second he thought he caught a ghost of a smile. "Some of them are going to be itchy in uncomfortable places."

They waited a few minutes as Kai got across town. Quinn had seen him drive and swore he cheated, using magic to change lights and clear paths.

"He's parking. About a block and a half away."

"Okay…here we go. I'll try and stay with the cat and relay the position at the same time. Don't get freaked out. I sound a little weird when I'm not really here." It was also hard for him to make his mouth talk here while he was technically somewhere else.

Quinn slipped into the relaxed state again, and soared upward. He would never get tired of that feeling. This time he didn't even get the sensation of moving from place to place. In a blink, he was just suddenly on the street.

"He's moved," he told Vicki. "Tell him to go right, toward Riverbank Park."

"Sir," he heard her say from what seemed so far away. "Go right. Riverbank. Yes, sir, I'll tell him." She seemed to be closer when she said, "He'll start calling the cat if you tell him he's close."

"He's not close. Cat has been on the move since I first saw him. Keep going." Quinn's voice was soft, almost singsong. He saw the cat and followed it into the park. "Keep going," he said again. He didn't hear Vicki relay that message and knew he needed to be more specific but once he was actually in the park, he wasn't sure how to tell Kai how to find him. What he needed to do was to find Kai and lead him but... He was suddenly standing next to Kai and completely disoriented.

"Go left," he said after a moment. Kai didn't answer him but he heard his words echoed far away and Kai turned left. Okay, now he needed to find the cat again. Right there, not far. Back to Kai. "Follow the path you're on. It's going to curve to the right but keep going straight when it turns, through the bushes."

Again, the echo of his words and Kai kept walking. He hesitated where the path curved to the right.

"Keep going. Into the trees."

Kai moved again. Quinn checked on the cat's position. He went back to Kai. Things were starting to look funny, blurry and melted. He was confused. Kai

110

stopped and looked up, Quinn looked up too, and there was the cat in the tree.

"That's the one," Quinn said.

"That's the one," Vicki echoed.

Quinn slammed back into his body, no falling sensation, no warning. His head jerked and he cracked the back against Momma Cats' knee. He opened his eyes but his vision was still blurry and everything was tipping sideways.

"Quinn? I mean, Mr. Riley? Are you okay?" Vicki asked him.

"I'm okay," Quinn gasped, then slid sideways and passed out.

"Is he all right?" Kai snapped at the phone. He'd felt Quinn beside him, then he was ripped away, far too fast. *Damn the boy. This is why I want him trained.*

"He's... He seems okay, sir. Breathing all right." Vicki's voice trembled.

"Stay with him. Get a jacket or a blanket if you can." He pulled in a slow breath. "Vicki. You're doing well. Don't fall apart now."

Wonderful. His research team had potential, but one was an arrogant snot from a magically gifted family, one was a brute who approached everything with too much force, one was apparently educated by rote and unable to think. Then there was Vicki. Bright, powerful, insightful Vicki, who had the confidence of an undersized field mouse.

Cat. The cat was staring at him, tail twitching.

"Well, come down here, please. I'd like to talk like civilized people."

The cat stretched and let out a yowling meow.

"No, I don't have any tuna with me. I can procure some for you, but I don't carry it in my pockets."

With little grumbling sounds, the tom descended and sat in front of Kai with his tail curled around his front feet. He was a handsome feline, a champagne tabby with fur that suggested some long-haired breed in his mutt ancestry. The scars simply gave him character and perhaps a bit of swagger since he was a youngster.

"There was an old woman who fed you. She did bring tuna — and other things, I'm sure. But something terrible happened to her."

The cat growled low in his throat, a sound as much anger as it was fear.

"You needn't be afraid. Whatever did it doesn't seem interested in cats."

More growls and some plaintive mews later, Kai stiffened. "That can't be what you saw."

Green feline eyes regarded him with disdain and the cat sneezed in offense.

"But...that can't be. It... You're certain?" Kai shivered as the cold wind picked up. "I don't even know what to do with this. I... Have you seen it again?"

Now the cat got up and rubbed at his leg with little chirrups.

"I suppose it's good that you haven't. For you, not for the investigation." He considered the tom a moment longer before bending down and holding out his arms. "Perhaps you should come with me, after all. Tuna. Yes. I'll find tuna for you."

Kai turned with the cat in his arms, a terrible pit of dread in his stomach compounding his other miseries as he made his way back to his car. *How could this be?*

* * * *

Quinn blinked his eyes open. He did not know where he was but he was warm and comfortable so he wasn't panicked. As he came more awake, he looked into green, almond-shaped eyes, open just a slit, as if it were too much effort to keep his full attention. A gentle rumble vibrated his chest where the cat sat contentedly. He was in Kai's office, on his couch.

"Kai?" Quinn meant to call out his name but his voice rasped and he had to clear his throat and try again. "Kai?"

"I'm here," Kai's voice came from a few feet away, a note of uncertainty coloring his words. Quinn turned to find him at his desk, his usually impeccable braid a snarled mess. "You need to work on your returns."

Quinn snorted softly and lifted his head, dislodging the cat as he sat up. It resettled in his lap. Well, at least someone was friendly.

"I'm not usually trying to be more than two places at once. Did you talk to the cat yet? Find anything out?"

"I did." Kai turned his gaze out the window and Quinn thought he shivered. "It saw something it describes as stone."

"Of course the cat did," Quinn said impatiently. "He saw Momma Cats turned to stone."

"No." Kai shook his head, obviously disturbed. "I mean, yes, he did. But the thing that turned her to stone was...stone."

"Made out of stone, like how? Like someone touched her with a stone or...or a stone was just walking around? How is that possible?"

"The cat was frightened by this thing, whatever it was. Terribly frightened. Images from him are jagged and strange. But it was a hulking thing. Large...and stone."

Quinn sat silently, absently stroking his hand along the cat's back. "Well what large hulking thing made out of stone walks around turning people into stone? Some sort of statue?" He frowned, trying to picture it.

"I don't know." Kai stabbed both hands back through his hair, yanking more white strands from his braid. "Quinn, I don't *know*. And it frightens me as much as it does the cat. One thing I do know. Whatever it was would not have had a receipt for fast food. It would have caused a panic. Someone...either controls it or is in league with it. Someone flesh and blood."

"Right. Hey, Kai, you're a pretty good detective, you know that?" He leaned back into the couch and rolled his neck. The cat purred and he petted it. Kai was silent, like he was waiting for the punch line, but there wasn't one. Quinn meant it.

"So, we've got a troll-sized hunk of stone walking around and someone using magic to possibly control it and cover their tracks. You think that someone is human? You know of any elvish spells that can make living stone?"

Kai shook his head. "I don't. That doesn't mean they don't exist. The magic user could be human. Could be elf or drow. Could be goblin, for all I know."

Quinn tapped his fingers on the arm of the sofa for a few moments but nothing came to him. "All right, well it's more that we had this morning." He stood up and stretched. "Any word from him yet?" Quinn didn't think he had to tell Kai which 'him' he was referring to.

"No," Kai said shortly.

Quinn paused, then put his hand on the back of Kai's neck and rubbed there reassuringly, he hoped. "He'll show up, Kai. Tenzin is too honorable to just walk out on AURA without a word. You'll get another chance to talk to him."

The soft laugh that Kai spat out was stripped of humor. "Yes. I should go down and check with medical. See if he's called in. I'm simply afraid they'll want to keep me there. I don't have time for that."

Quinn sighed. "Kai, how can you be so smart and so stupid? What else are you going to do? Sit up here and stare at the statues some more? At least take Mr. Cat down. He probably needs a checking over to be sure he doesn't have PTSD or something. If Tenzin is there, I bet there are a whole bunch of reasons you have to be down there all day."

"I suppose I could have the interviews for the afternoon rescheduled," Kai said softly and made a moue of distaste. "The cat most likely at least has fleas."

"Yeah and… Wait, what? And you let him sleep on me? Thanks a lot. Go get the goddamn fleas taken care of, and give him a name while you're at it so we don't have to keep calling him 'the cat'," Quinn grouched, already heading for the door himself. His head was starting to itch. Surely that was his imagination.

Chapter Seven

Stupid hands. Stupid socks. Flax stopped for a deep breath, trying for the third time to pull on socks with hands that shook worse than January leaves. He had to hurry. After disgracing himself so badly, he had to work ten times harder to get back in the captain's good graces.

How bad had it been? Had he said stupid things? He thought he recalled licking the captain, but the wormwood haze was too thick to remember clearly. *Sweet Mother, I hope I didn't.*

The pounding in his head was getting worse — the hangover, the stress, trying to rush. He wasn't going to make it like this. Just this once. Yes, he'd promised the counselors that he was clean. But one wouldn't hurt. He needed something to get through this horrible day. Then he'd dump the rest of the bottle.

Acetaminophen. Such a harmless thing for humans, to pop a Tylenol if they had headaches. For elves? An addictive narcotic, on par with meth for humans. The clinic had sealed the records. Because he'd been through rehab, the academy had given him the waiver to apply. No one in the department knew. *No* one. But somehow Hiltas—that sneaky little drow—had ferreted out the records and used them as leverage. For now, it was just to twist his arm into teaching the human kid. He hoped it wouldn't escalate to other things later.

The white bottle mocked him from inside the medicine cabinet. *One. Just one. Maybe two.*

He ended up taking three because the pain was so bad and he had to get to work right fucking now. It only took a few moments for the poison to hit his bloodstream and the wonderful wave of euphoria to wash away all the agony.

Flax smiled as he jogged to the subway. It might not be such a bad day after all.

When he reached the squad room, the place was in a state of organized chaos. Event. He knew the pattern, the rhythm of these things by now. Sergeant Nestor, the centaur, stood near the Event map table, phone to his ear, coordinating the effort, wherever it was.

"Flax!" Captain Hartgrove bellowed from across the room. "I need you briefed and porting five minutes ago!"

"Yes, Captain!" Flax shouted back above the noise and hurried to the table where the twins waited, holding the doorway open. "Sergeant? What's happening?"

Ness stomped a back hoof and tucked the phone between his ear and shoulder as he pointed. "Pair of elvish warriors. Tokyo. Shibuya Crossing. It's one of the busiest intersections in any human city. Matt and Aello are there, but the transitional language thing is an issue. Our crossovers are only speaking Elvish, and we need someone fluent."

"Of course, Sergeant." Flax's heart sank a few inches when he realized the captain had only needed him as a translator.

Ness gave him a sharp look. "If anyone can defuse this without bloodshed, it's you. Careful going through. There's a bow involved and who knows what else."

Ego away, Flax told himself. *Do your job*. Luckily, the acetaminophen took the raw edges off everything, so the hurt he should have felt was distant and unimportant. He nodded to the twins and braced his feet as they cycled the portal. The screams and running feet reached him before he stepped fully through.

He held still as he stepped onto pavement, needing a moment to orient himself in the neon and LED madness of the Tokyo night. It was nearly midnight, so the Event could have been worse. At least it hadn't happened during business hours. He blinked, following the fleeing crowd back with his eyes, across the broad white stripes of pedestrian crossings, to where two figures stood back-to-back in the center of the city square. Matt and Aello had taken up positions on either side, holding a circle closed around the obviously terrified and belligerent elves.

"Matt!" Flax called out as he jogged toward them. He took the time to size up their crossovers on the way. Both were fully armored, the shining plates blood-spattered as if they had been in the thick of battle when the hole in reality had opened under them. They watched him approach, though the one kept his bow trained on Aello and the other faced Matt with his longsword clutched in both hands. The taller one, the one with the wicked recurved bow, was willowy, with a silver braid trailing out from under his helm. The shorter one was broader shouldered, his stance more aggressive, wild evergreen hair hanging over one eye.

"Hey, kid." Matt nodded as he came up. "See if you can talk sense into these boys. They're scared to death. Can't blame them."

Flax held both hands palm out toward the elves as he murmured to Matt, "Hold the circle until I get closer. We're gonna have to give them a show of trust here."

He paced around the outer edge of the containment circle, its magic crackling and spitting as the elves fought to break through. It tugged at his heart to see them, so confused and frightened. It hadn't been so long ago that he didn't remember how awful those first hours had been.

"Sons of Earth!" he called out in Elvish, hoping they didn't come from some strange plane where the language was different. "You have fallen out of your world, out of the battle in which you valiantly engaged! The terrible truth you must hear is there is no way back!"

"Are you of Hellebore's?" the taller one snarled, his voice smooth and melodious still. "One of her illusions?"

"All you know is gone," Flax said soothingly, pacing around to face him. "Whatever enemy you fought, whatever horrors you were facing—they are gone."

"We're dead then?" the one with the sword spat out. "Ash, I think this may be some level of hell."

"You live. I promise. And I am living flesh as well." Flax moved closer to the edge of the circle, hands held out. "My name is Flax Wolfheart. I served a queen named Hemlock, but she… I can't return either."

The tall one, Ash, frowned. "There is no queen by that name."

"Perhaps not in your world. There was in mine. We were torn from our worlds — me some years ago and you now — by a magical storm, one that strikes where it will. This world, this one where you are now, there are no elvish courts, no queens, no grand battles with the drow or rival queens. You must lay down your weapons or you will come to harm."

The bow had begun to droop, now Ash raised it again, taut and nearly vibrating with aggression. "You take us for fools!"

That was the moment the circle failed. Either Aello miscalculated when to drop it or the captive elves broke through. It fell with a strange echoing snap and Ash shifted his aim just over Flax's left shoulder.

Aello.

Without time to think, Flax hurled himself left as the arrow flew. It hit his shoulder with the force of a mailed fist, spinning him halfway around where he stood staring down at the shaft protruding from his shirt. For a moment, it didn't hurt, and he laughed, feeling unbalanced and disconnected. Maybe it was shock or the drugs. Hard to say.

"You shot me."

When the pain did hit, hard and fast, he crumpled to his knees, pleased that the look on Ash's face was horrified rather than triumphant.

"Don't move," Matt said. He wasn't talking to Flax, he was pointing a gun at the newcomers. AURA's regulations stated that all living creatures pulled through an Event portal were to be contained and accommodated as peacefully as reasonably possible. However, force, up to and including deadly force, was sanctioned when lives were at risk.

Matt wouldn't care anymore how scared these elves were. They had just shot a fellow officer.

The one with the green hair spoke a harsh word. He was ignoring Matt. He took a step forward and Flax saw Matt move as well, his arm raised and gun pointed.

"Don't shoot them, Matt," Flax said in Elvish, then swore and said it again in English. He could hear Aello speaking frantically into her phone.

"Please..." Flax sat back on his heels, ignoring the fact that his sight was wavering in and out. "Please put down your weapons. We want to help you, but we can't have you harming innocents. The weapon the human has will kill you. Pierce your armor and *kill* you. Place your weapons down. Come here by me. We don't mean you any harm if you'll just demonstrate your honorable, peaceful intentions. Your enemies are not here."

It was a tense stand off. The two elves had both lowered their weapons slightly, not actively threatening, but Flax knew all too well that they could bring them to the ready again in about the same time it would take Matt to shoot one of them. He opened his mouth to say something more, something to bring the situation back under control, as if it had ever really been that much in control, when Aello spoke, "Backup is coming."

"Brothers, please," Flax said quickly, because whomever they were sending was not likely to be patient and try to coax them into behaving when there was an officer with an arrow sticking out of him bleeding all over the ground. "We didn't bring you here. It isn't something we control. Have we offered any harm? No." Flax answered his own question quickly so neither of them thought to bring up being trapped by magic. "We only want to take you somewhere quieter, to explain and to help you."

The one named Ash moved first. Perhaps Matt saw something in his face, or more likely the fact that he let his bow hang at his side when he could have just as easily have nocked another arrow, but Matt didn't shoot him. He crouched and put his hand on Flax's back, supporting him.

"It is you in need of help, brother," he said, softly spoken. He pulled the arrow from Flax's shoulder before anyone could as much as blink, and pressed his hand over the wound. Flax thought he heard the first murmured word of a healing chant but that was all he got before his vision went black.

* * * *

"Move!" Val bellowed, as he gathered the troops and prepared to storm Tokyo himself. Aello's frantic *officer down* call had the entire department's adrenaline racing. This was one of *his* officers. Val wasn't about to lose a man this early in his command.

His magical sword, Anvar, in hand, a harpy, two humans and a centaur at his back, he strode through the portal the twins held open.

The scene wasn't as bad as he'd feared. Flax leaned against the chest of a tall, silver-haired elf, Matt crouching beside them, weapon holstered. Blood pooled on the ground, but not enough to indicate a fatal wound.

Val's fury had to go somewhere, though. He pointed with Anvar at the green-haired warrior and bellowed in Elvish, "You! Sword on the ground! On your knees! Now!"

It was a voice that had commanded armies, had sent divisions of elves into dire and bloody battles. The young warrior dropped his sword with a clatter and fell to his knees, eyes as big as saucers.

"Sir!" the green-haired one sputtered. "It was an accident! Ash aimed for the winged demon!"

"She's not a demon. She is one of my warriors." There simply wasn't a word for police officer in Elvish. "I am Tesined Valerian Hartgrove. They use the word *captain* here. I expect a name in return, pup."

"Sage Blackdrake, Tesined. First guard in her majesty Queen Hellebore's ground troops. This is my *kalesi*, Ash Bloodroot," the elf said.

There's hope here. Oh, youngsters, you don't know how lucky you are. Val sheathed his sword since no further violence seemed in the air. "Are you both unharmed? The crossing is often difficult and dangerous."

Sage blinked at him from behind a fall of hair so dark a shade of green it was nearly black, and shook his head. He hadn't bothered to rise, and his weapon was still on the ground, but he had a wary look to him that spoke volumes about his state of mind. How did you know who to trust or who to fight when you found yourself in a nightmare?

"What is this place, Tesined? The hunter said we were in a place of no hope—that we needed to surrender. The way he spoke, he did not seem...real."

"You live, Sage. Your beloved is with you." Val came forward a few steps, bent to check on Flax and returned his attention to the kneeling warrior. "Therefore there is hope. What my hunter may have said is there is no hope for return. This much is true. You are in this world now, for all time. I feel for you— the anguish and the confusion that is in your heart. When I crossed over, my battle steed died beneath me.

I was alone and broken. No one cared to tell me what manner of place I had fallen into until much later."

He closed the distance and crouched in front of Sage. "This is a human world—one not normally reached from your own. A magical...accident has caused tears between the worlds. Sometimes beings fall through. They cannot return. We make the best life we can here. The most honorable life we can. To say it is easy would be a lie. But we will help you. We do not abandon one of our own."

"Tesined Valerian." The silver-haired one, Ash, looked up at him. His voice was soft, and had a musical quality that was soothing despite the noise of traffic and people and city around them. "The hunter is poisoned." He met Valerian's eyes. "Not by my doing."

"Poisoned? You are a healer then?"

Ash nodded.

"Enough to cause his death?"

Ash tilted his head to one side ever so slightly, "I am no drow, Tesined. If I had wanted him dead, I would have killed him cleanly."

Val raised an eyebrow at the young elf. "You may need to leave those old hatreds behind. There are drow whom we consider honorable here. I'm asking about my hunter, pup. Is he dying?"

A stony look was returned, but Ash dropped his gaze first, looking down at Flax once more. "I don't think so, Tesined. His heart beats strongly. The wound will heal cleanly. I do not know the poison in his veins. I only sense its presence."

"I thank you for informing me." Val sighed. Poison. It could be the leftover wormwood, but he had to wonder. All AURA officers underwent random screenings for substances that had proved addictive and harmful to non-humans, though perhaps Flax only used whatever it was under stress.

"What am I to do with you, pup?" Val murmured as he slid his arms under Flax and lifted him with a soft grunt. He fixed first Ash then Sage with a stern look, "Come with us. If you stay here, the local guards will *not* be as patient with you. Please help me prevent your deaths."

* * * *

Kai hesitated in the elevator lobby outside medical. Giant spiders? He could face those. Lich queen's undead minions? Without hesitation. His beloved who didn't want to see him any longer? Not so easy.

The cat purred in his arms and he rubbed his cheek against the soft fur for comfort, fleas or no fleas. "Breon. Can I call you Breon?"

A head butt let him know that was acceptable. Breon obviously didn't care since names weren't a cat thing, but he liked the purring sound of it. Kai took a deep breath, squared his shoulders and walked through the doors to medical reception. His heart stuttered at the sight of his yeti manning the desk as he so often did in the afternoons.

Tenzin chewed on his bottom lip but didn't otherwise react. He didn't run away, at least.

"Are you in need of medical assistance?" Tenzin's voice was professional and kind. He was always kind, but so impersonal.

"It's…" Kai swallowed hard, willing the tears back. He had to take two deep breaths before he could spit out. "Cat! I have this cat."

"Yes. You do."

"Breon. The cat." Kai heaved a breath and tried again. "He's helping with an investigation. I need... If someone could check him over for me? Fleas? Worms? Cat diseases? His ear is torn..."

"Of course, Mr. Hiltas." Tenzin pushed a clipboard across the desk. "I'll need you to fill out the intake. Just the basics so we can start a file. Are you certain you don't need a healer yourself?"

Kai ducked his head, shaking it no. This was ridiculous. He filled out the forms dutifully, handed them back then handed over the cat to the healer who came out for Breon. When she had passed back through the inner doors to the clinic, Kai couldn't keep himself together any longer.

"Tenzi, please," he whispered, wringing his now empty hands.

A long silence followed in which Tenzin just stared at him. Kai thought he was going to shatter in a hundred million drow pieces all over the floor.

"It's a lovely cat, Kai. I'm glad you have someone to keep you company."

"I don't want a cat, Tenzi! I want you! Please...please come home. I'll do better. I swear I will."

Tenzin sighed. "Look at you. You're a mess. You're still wearing the same clothes from yesterday, so I know you slept in your office. This isn't showing me you can change. You haven't changed one tiny thing, except picking up a cat. I can't come home, Kai, if you refuse to change. I can't watch you killing yourself anymore."

"But I can't... I can't do this... I can't pretend not to know you. Not talk to you."

"I'm here, Kai. All day, usually. You can talk to me if you need to, just like anyone else who needs an ear. Of course I know you. We can be polite. Professional. I am here to help if you're willing to admit to an issue—which I know you won't. You collapse instead of admitting your body is failing you. You'd rather work than live."

Kai shoved the hair back from his face and tried to stand straighter. It was absurdly difficult, as if his spine were compressing. He wanted to say terrible things, childish things, like Tenzin wanted to watch him die. It would be a lie, though. He knew that. But somehow he had to fix this—

The phone rang. Tenzin held up a finger for patience and answered it. "Medical. Yes, Captain. Nature of the emergency? Oh, dear. Yes."

Tenzin hung up as he sprang from his chair and dashed back into the clinic. "Medical emergency! Code eight!"

Eight... That was an officer shot. Kai stepped back and sank into one of the chairs by the wall out of the way. He had to fix this somehow...

* * * *

Quinn had spent some time in the lesson room blowing pencils around and trying to figure out how Flax so easily flicked one from the pile without moving the rest and was mostly unsuccessful. At least he hadn't pulverized any of them. He really wished he could saunter in tomorrow morning and line them all up just as pretty as you please and impress the hell out of Flax with how much he'd improved, but he seriously doubted he was going to be able to do anything impressive at all.

When he was thoroughly frustrated, he gave it up and went downstairs, intending to see if the Event from earlier was now under wraps and maybe Val could take a break for lunch.

He knew as soon as the elevator doors opened on the squad room floor that was not going to happen. It was more chaos than usual. People were rushing around, phones were being yelled at, and Val was nowhere in sight.

"Ness, what's going on?"

"Minor disaster. Captain has it under control. Two freaked-out elves. Sounds like they were pulled right from the battlefield. We sent Flax in to negotiate in Elvish. One of the crossovers shot him." Ness wound the story out in short, staccato phrases, half his attention on the phone plastered to his ear. "On their way back."

"Shot him? How the hell did that happen? Did he get one of the officer's guns? How did he even know what it was? Is Flax all right?"

Ness spared him a startled glance. "What? Oh, no. Arrow. Shoulder wound. Flax stepped in front of it when the elf tried to shoot Aello. Thought she was a demon, Matt says."

"Oh," Quinn said.

If the squad room was chaos before, Quinn didn't know what to call it when Val stepped back through the portal—or porthole, as Quinn always secretly thought of it—carrying Flax. Matt, Aello and two fully armored and armed elves stepped through right behind him. Whatever the state of the room now, it was worse than chaos. Two medtechs immediately ran up to see to Flax's injuries. Quinn tried to stay out of the way as half the squad room swarmed forward.

He had to tell himself firmly that Flax had been shot with an arrow and obviously had passed out and who else was going to carry his lanky ass back if not Val? It was the stupidest thing in the world to be jealous over that, and if it had been anyone else, he wouldn't have even thought twice about it, other than to think how knee-meltingly sexy Val looked when he was being all heroic. No, he was more in control of his emotions than that. He wouldn't give in to the green-eyed monster. Yeah. If only he could convince the acid in his stomach that twisted his gut that he was not at all jealous.

The medtechs had a stretcher and Val put his armload down on that. He ordered the portal closed, got everyone moving back to work and told Ness, who had a basic command of Elvish, to see the two crossovers made it down to Assimilation. Val in command mode—so hot. Quinn could watch him boss people around all day.

Finally, Val wove his way over to Quinn. "That was messier than it should have been. Maybe I should look into Kevlar for our field teams after all." He gave Quinn a wry smile. "I need to head down to medical with the stretcher."

"Okay." Quinn tried to squash his libido as he had his jealousy and was just about as successful, which was not at all. He wanted to grab Val, pull him into his office and close the door...but duty called.

He watched Val take two steps before he stopped and came back, gripped his chin and tilted his face up for a hard kiss that was absurdly inappropriate in the squad room but Quinn didn't care even a little bit. Without a word, Val turned back around and strode out, his long legs carrying him quickly. Quinn glanced around but almost everyone was pretending they hadn't seen the kiss, everyone except Ness, who gave him a wink. Quinn grinned at him, feeling all sappy with the butterflies fluttering around in his belly.

The two elves standing next to Ness looked at him with expressions that Quinn thought might be surprise or might be hostility. It was hard to tell. The one with the green hair said something to the other in Elvish, too quick for Quinn to catch all of it. Val had been teaching him more words in Elvish but he had to go slow and pronounce carefully. He heard enough to know it wasn't complimentary though, and as green-hair hadn't taken his eyes off Quinn, he figured it was directed his way.

"Welcome," Quinn said the Elvish word and patted himself on the back for getting the inflection right. He pointed a finger in the direction Val had gone, then flipped his hand and pointed at himself. "Tesined Val, he's all mine. Just want to make that clear." It was probably as clear as mud to them since half those words were in English. He might have got the gist of it across though, he hoped. He didn't need any more elves getting grabby with his man. "C'mon, Ness. I'll help you walk these guys downstairs."

Introductions were made on the way. The two crossovers gawked at the building, but that was only to be expected. Quinn had tried to imagine how his world would look to someone who came from a world that hadn't gone through the industrial revolution and he couldn't fathom it. He found it amusing that the elevators were more fascinating than the centaur to them, and he himself garnered more interest than the griffin they passed in the hall. He guessed they knew what a centaur and a griffin were, but elevators and humans were rarer. At least he thought that was why they kept staring at him.

"You are Tesined Valerian's *kalesi*?" Sage asked, perhaps with a hint more disbelief than was strictly polite.

Quinn nodded and tried not to blush. His little possessive display and Val's kiss should have been clue enough, but he couldn't help thinking they probably also smelled the elf pheromones dripping off him that marked him as Val's bond mate.

"Are all of those in Tesined Valerian's *senrist* human?" Sage asked, with less disbelief and more honest curiosity this time, Quinn thought.

"No, just me. Er, I mean there is just me. Just us," Quinn said in his halting Elvish and made a mental note to practice with Val more. It always seemed to take a backseat to other priorities though because elves tended to pick up other languages quickly. Val had told him that it had only taken him about a week to grasp English. Kai had told him much the same. These two had already probably picked up a few of his English words while their heads were still spinning from being yanked into this world.

"He has...just you?" Sage asked slowly, and Quinn thought it was for his benefit rather than any real need for clarification.

Quinn didn't snap at him, reminding himself that culture shock was a bitch sometimes just driving from one state to another, much less one world to another.

"We are both happy with the way things are," Quinn said a little stiffly.

"Forgive my *kalesi*, he meant no insult," Ash said in a soft, melodious voice. It was the first time Quinn had heard him speak. "This is all very strange to us."

Quinn wasn't sure if he meant their surroundings, what had happened to them, his living arrangements or all of the above.

"You'll get used to it," Quinn said. *You'll have to*, he added silently.

"I didn't know a bonding was even possible with a human — or one so young," Sage said, and if that was his way of trying to apologetically explain, it wasn't helping.

Quinn stifled a sigh. It was his height. Five foot ten was not especially short. It was perfectly average for a human male. He had yet to meet an elf under six-two. If he did, he would know they were an adolescent because the newly-crossed elves always thought humans were barely more than children until they got used to being here.

"I'm not that young. I'm full grown, an adult." He struggled to remember the right Elvish words. Elves had more phases in their growth cycle and the concept of 'legal age of consent' was alien to them. Sex and relationships were determined by physical and emotional maturity, not an arbitrary age. He knew to them he looked barely grown enough to have a mate bond with someone, and if they were in their world instead of his, it might be something of a scandal — for more reasons than one. Their lack of reply was telling.

Fortunately, he didn't have to keep up the chitchat. Lysander, the faun, and Aesa, his dryad assistant, met them at the door to the woodland counseling room, which also doubled as the first stop on the way to assimilation. They could get their bearings here, then Lysander would get them into housing and whatever else they would need for the immediate future.

"Quinten, how are you?" Lysander asked with his typical enthusiasm. "And who have you brought to me?"

Before he could answer, Aesa gave him a sweeping bow, which always embarrassed Quinn. "My knight, it is good to see you again," she said in Elvish.

Quinn took her hand, kissed the back, and didn't even feel foolish doing it. Not with Aesa, it was just...appropriate. "I'm well," Quinn answered. "I bought a couple friends for you and Lysander to take care of."

"Ah, I thought I heard the Event alarm." Lysander switched to Elvish and stepped around the counter, his button-down shirt odd without pants, and his little goat tail waving madly behind him. "Welcome, Sons of Earth. We understand how difficult this all is for you, but this is a place of peace, of quiet. Here is where you may ask any questions you need without offense and where your needs will be seen to." He eyed the blood-spattered armor with concern. "Are either of you injured?"

"It is only the blood of the fallen, little brother. Not any of our own," Sage answered.

Quinn thought he detected more than a little condescension in the tone. That was Lysander's to deal with though, and he did a good job at it usually. Personally, if Quinn had to deal with elf arrogance on a regular basis, his eyes would probably roll right out of his head. At least, when it wasn't Val's. Of course, when Val acted all high and mighty, it was usually warranted—and hot.

"Okay, I'm gonna leave you to it," Quinn told Lysander, and tilted his head in a little bow to Aesa, which she returned with a pretty smile.

He wandered off with Ness, Lysander's voice fading in the background as he got names and vital information. Funny how tough it was for elves, sometimes. Well, not really funny, but ironic. Some non-Earth beings, like goblins, didn't have much trouble assimilating. They adjusted, used the skills they had and took the transition in stride. Elves? They were the apex magical predators of their worlds. Finding out that in a human world they were often second-class citizens? Drove some of them off the deep end fast.

At least these guys had each other. They'd probably be okay.

* * * *

Val stopped a tech coming out of Flax's room. "I need a full tox report on him, Kara. Something's off."

"Without consent?"

"Officer of the law. His consent is on file."

"Yes, sir."

The young woman hurried off and Val leaned in the doorway a moment. Oh, to be young and stupid again. Flax could be erratic, moody and borderline racist, but damn it, he was also charming and thorough. Never gave up a chase. Never skipped apprehension procedure. And he was brave with that fierce, blazing courage of the young. His reflexes were fast enough to avoid an arrow. He had stepped in *front* of it rather than out of the way, to save a fellow officer. The boy had issues, but if he could mature a bit... The department couldn't afford to lose him.

Flax tossed his head, teeth gritted on a moan. In two strides, Val was by the bed pulling the visitor's chair up to the side.

"Flax? Back with us?"

"Captain?" Flax tried to sit up and didn't get more than a few inches before he fell back, eyes glazed.

"You lost several flagons of blood, pup. Lie still. That was a courageous thing you did today, though I don't recommend using yourself as a shield too often."

Flax managed a half smile, turning his head and squinting against the light. "Yes, sir."

"I'm somewhat confused, though." Val leaned forward with a hand on the mattress. "You're no novice in battle. Was Ash so swift a shot that you couldn't knock his arrow from the air with a blast of wind? Burn it to cinders before it hit?"

"I guess..." Flax hesitated and pulled his bottom lip between his teeth. "I wasn't at my best this morning, Captain. My apologies."

That had been the most clumsy, pitiful evasion Val had ever witnessed. Probably was better that Flax was a terrible liar. He had no proof yet, so the confrontation would have to wait. "Hmm. I just don't want to have to carry you back again. And I think you scared several years off Aello and Matt collectively."

"You carried me, sir?" The wet sheen in Flax's eyes was trouble. He reached over and stroked Val's arm. "I thought...I dreamt that."

"I do not abandon my warriors," Val answered steadily and held the wandering hand still as he switched to Elvish. No need for random medical staff passing by to hear the conversation. "Flax, I must tell you a thing that I believe might hurt you, but you must hear it. This infatuation is neither appropriate nor will it bring you aught but heartache. I have a bond mate. His name is Quinn. You know this. Also know that I would never entertain the thought of hurting him. Ever. Not for you. Not for all the elves in creation."

Flax swallowed hard and whispered, "But Tesined, you were a prince. *Are* a prince. A single human is hardly your due."

"Once I had a full *senrist*. I loved them with all my heart." Val put Flax's hand on top of the blankets and patted it gently. "The pain of being ripped from them was almost more than I could stand. Quinn has healed my heart—brought me out of the darkness, back from the fading. He is all I need now, in this world. I need you to understand that."

"Yes, Captain," Flax switched back to English as he squeezed his eyes shut.

I've hurt you, pup. I'm sorry. But better now than later. Val rose with a last pat to Flax's shoulder. "Rest, braveheart. I want you back on duty as soon as possible." He hesitated at the door. "Is there anyone we need to call? Someone to send in to help your healing?"

"No, sir." Flax had turned his head away, his words small and choked.

If only he could fix things like this as easily as he solved physical problems. Val shook his head as he made his way back into the corridor and stopped short at the sight of Kai leaning against the wall.

"Valerian, a word."

"You look terrible."

Kai rolled his eyes as he turned to walk beside Val. "So I hear. That one in there. Wolfheart. I, ah, overheard."

"Of course you did," Val said dryly.

"You already suspect and the tox reports might confirm it. He's an aceta head."

Val nodded. It was one of the substances on his list of suspected addictions for Flax. "And how do you know this?"

"Sealed clinic records." Kai cleared his throat. "Sometimes one needs to have things in reserve. Just in case."

"Why tell me now? And when are you going to take a shower?"

Kai sniffed in offense. "I'm taking the afternoon off, I'll have you know. My staff is working on tracking down the restaurant on the receipt in the hopes there might be security camera footage."

"Good. You need rest—and some time to gather yourself back together." Val nudged him with an elbow. "And my other question?"

"Reports of his behavior this morning lead me to believe he's using again. No one bounces back from a wormwood hangover that fast. The hyper-alertness. The lack of judgment. The ability to ignore the pain of being *shot*. These add up to a messy equation. Just…watch him closely. He's been through rehab, but recovering aceta heads are never cured."

"Noted. Why were you down here, anyway? To speak to Tenzin?"

Kai's shoulders sagged. "I tried. It didn't go well, but I had to bring my cat."

"I didn't know you had a cat."

"Apparently, I needed to be adopted." Kai blew a strand of wayward hair out of his eyes. "And besides, what self-respecting drow mage doesn't have a cat? It was high time."

A smiling medtech met them near the front desk to hand Kai a large tabby and a bag. "He's a sweetheart, Mr. Hiltas. No fleas, surprisingly. There are drops for the ear mites in the bag and he could use some feeding up. There's some cat food in the bag, too. But he's healthy and parasite free."

"Thank you, Jennifer." Kai appeared oddly flustered as he juggled feline and bag before turning to Val. "If you'll excuse me, Captain Hartgrove, I'm going home."

Good. Kai was still thinking, still scheming and finally realizing he had to delegate. Val hoped it would be enough to put him back together until he could convince Tenzin to come home.

Chapter Eight

"Albert, what are you doing up there?"

"Nothing, Mom."

"Come down for dinner."

"I'm not hungry."

"You need to eat. Come down."

Albert sighed heavily and put away the magazine he was reading. She was always after him to eat, clean his room or do the dishes. He was only a few months away from turning eighteen and she still treated him like he was eight. She made him so mad — almost mad enough to do something about it. He couldn't do that though. That was his secret and he wasn't about to share it with his family, not even if they were dead after they knew.

He heaved himself out of bed and went downstairs. The sooner he sat at the table and pushed food around his plate, the sooner he could go back upstairs, wait until his parents went to bed and sneak out to go visit his friend.

Not friends. He only had the one. He was his best friend though — the best friend anyone could ever have. He never judged, he never stared or whispered behind his hand. And when they were together, no one dared bother them. If anyone started anything, said anything about him like that old lady had — or that stupid fucker with the guitar — they regretted it. They regretted the whispers and the jeers and telling everyone his secrets.

Mom and Dad sat at the table and Albert sat with them. Mom put food on his plate and gave it to him. He'd tried serving himself a few times, but she told him he didn't take enough vegetables, or he needed to put it on his plate a certain way or that he should have a slice of bread with butter. At least Dad had made her stop cutting up his meat for him a couple of years ago. Now he didn't even bother trying to assert his will over what he would and would not eat. He let her fill his plate and usually half or more went down the garbage disposal.

He wondered what she would do if he stood up and threw the plate, smashed it on the wall, picked up the chair and started hitting her with it. He wouldn't do that but sometimes he heard a whisper that told him he should.

The whispers told him to do lots of things. Mostly things he knew he shouldn't do. But they had also told him how to find his friend.

* * * *

Flax sat with one boot propped against his desk, eyes close to crossing as he tried to clear out his email. Nearly two weeks away from work had played havoc with his obsessive filing system. Physically? He could've been back on duty in two, maybe three, days. Not chase-down-and-tackle bad guys' duty, but enough to clear out his goddess-forsaken email.

But the brass knew. Some test while he'd been flat on his back had come back positive, and his zealously guarded secret was out there. So the captain had set him up with a counselor and two weeks' worth of mandatory sessions with regular follow-ups and daily screenings. And had a stern paternal talk with him about ruining his health and jeopardizing his life and career.

He'd decided to call it the Year of Humiliation. Really, how could it get much worse?

No, stupid. You don't say that. You never say that.

Maybe it was time to think about a career change? But he'd worked so hard to get here. He *liked* his job, blast it all, and he would be abandoning the captain. The thought of leaving the department more shorthanded was unthinkable. The thought of leaving Val and never seeing him again was worse.

Sure, he didn't have a chance right now. He got that. Val was honorable to the core and a good, caring elf who would rather stick a dagger through his eye than hurt his bond mate. Going after him directly as he had previous lovers wasn't going to result in anything but more humiliation and heartache. The real barrier? Quinn. If Flax had been drow, he would have simply killed him off as an inconvenient rival. He shuddered at the thought. It would break Val's heart. He couldn't do that, no matter how bad his own loneliness got.

So, Quinn. He wasn't a bad looking human. Bit on the skinny side, but pretty in a human way. Flax frowned at his screen. There had to be something to the kid for the captain to love him, for his legendary status around AURA. If he could help Quinn solve his control problems, maybe even pique Quinn's interest?

That would be the better route. He'd have an ally. It could be a sweet arrangement, the three of them.

He was distracted by overstimulating thoughts about being the center of a human-elf sandwich and missed the approach of footsteps.

"Hello."

Flax startled and whipped around to find Ash and Sage beside his desk. Since Ash had started in English, more or less, he figured he'd better continue that way. "Oh, um, hi. Good to see you boys getting around. How's everything?"

Sage shrugged while Ash smiled and said, "We came to ask you the same question. Also so I could apologize. I would tell you that I didn't mean it, but..." Now it was Ash's turn to shrug, though his was more elegant and expressive than his beloved's. "The wound has healed well, I hope?"

"Oh, yeah." Flax rotated his arm to demonstrate. "Never better. Hey, it's okay. You thought you were fighting for your life and Sage's out there. It was a damn good shot."

Ash arched one slim eyebrow. "Perhaps, if it had hit the intended target. Although now I am glad that it did not. I have you to thank for that as well."

Sage moved closer while Ash spoke and he rested a hip against the side of the desk, looking down curiously at the papers and items scattered there.

"What is it that you and everyone else in this benighted land find so interesting on these boxes?" he asked, indicating Flax's laptop.

Flax chuckled. "I asked that same question when I came across, almost exactly the same way. I'm surprised Lysander hasn't shown you Internet stuff yet."

"Lysander has offered to show him, but he did not want to take instruction from the faun," Ash said, the slight amusement in his tone coming through.

Sage lifted his chin a fraction and pretended Ash hadn't spoken.

Flax continued his explanation after a moment, "It's like a vast library and communications ring. You can speak to anyone on this planet, by writing to them or even actually speaking to them. You can find answers to almost any question you have about this world if you know how to look. And for us, in this department, it's also how we keep records." He scrunched his nose in distaste. "Not my favorite part, but has to get done. Laws are complicated here."

"Everything is complicated here," Sage said bitterly. "The humans seem to go out of their way to muddle things and make everything far more difficult than it need be."

"Sometimes, yeah. But the stuff they make is incredible. The things they can do. Machines that can fly a hundred people from one place to another instead of having to rely on a winged horse that can only carry one. Food you've never dreamed of. Okay, some of it's vile but a lot of it's wonderful. Ways to live with so many people in one place, relatively peacefully." Flax couldn't help a grin. Defending humans. Who would've thought the day would come? "But this is where we live now. Grousing about how weird humans are won't help much."

"I hate this world and everything about it," Sage said coolly.

Ash sighed. "*Kalesi*, you promised."

Sage switched to Elvish, "They spew poison fumes everywhere. Everywhere you look, there is more filth, and the humans all look the same, like children playing at being grown-up, and we are supposed to bow to their wishes and laws and customs?"

Ash put a hand on his arm and Sage calmed at once, looking away from both of them and cutting off his angry words.

Ash met Flax's eyes but he did not apologize for his mate. "We would both be honored if you would join us for an evening meal, Officer Wolfheart."

That caught Flax off guard. Not what he'd expected as the next sentence in the conversation. "Oh. That's kind of you. I'd..." He'd what? Tell them he wasn't feeling social these days? That would be rude and it would be nice to be just an elf among elves for a bit. "I'd like that. Thank you."

Sage sat rigid with arms crossed while Ash borrowed pen and paper and wrote the address down for Flax. He twirled the pen in his fingers contemplatively, then handed it back. "Useful, and far less cumbersome than quill and ink."

Sage snorted and shoved himself off the desk where he'd been slouching. As he turned, he nearly mowed someone down. He caught him by the shoulders and looked about to snarl something, but he recognized him at the same time everyone else did.

"My apologies," Sage told Quinn, making sure he was steady before he released him.

"No problem," Quinn said.

Sage nodded respectfully and strode off. Ash also gave a little bow of his head before following his *kalesi*.

Quinn watched them go for a moment then turned his attention to Flax. "I heard you were back to work. Are you ready to pick up where we left off?"

"Back to work to four hundred and fifty-seven emails." Flax shot him a rueful grin. "How does that even happen? But I'm plowing through. Should have this under control by, say, ten?"

Quinn nodded, a small line appearing between his eyebrows that Flax interpreted as wariness or confusion. "Okay. See you then," he said in a careful way that matched his expression.

Right. You were an asshole to him. Flax propped his boots up on the desk and offered a smile, not the big, bright one, but one that was just a little embarrassed. "Look, this whole thing started for the wrong reasons. It pissed me off. Sorry about that first time. But I'm intrigued and hope I can help. So, you think we can start over?"

Quinn stared at him for a long moment. A long, hard look that reminded Flax that he was indeed older than he appeared. He nodded slowly and said, "Sure." But Flax could tell he wasn't so easily won over and was perhaps reserving judgment.

"Wonderful. Maybe, ah, bring a wand if you need it. And we'll do something different this time." Flax fought back a sigh when the wary light in Quinn's eyes didn't fade even a hair. A challenge. He had to think of it that way and stop looking at Quinn as if he were a recalcitrant child.

"Okay," was Quinn's only reply and he left Flax to deal with his four hundred and fifty-seven emails, which had gone up by two in the time they had been talking.

* * * *

"Mrrrah."

Kai glanced over the side of his chair where Breon stared at him in a pointed way. "In a moment, my dear. We have a guest."

"Mao-rah!"

"He's a gorgeous cat, Mr. Hiltas." Sterling, the interviewee, had an open, genuine smile. "Can you really understand him?"

"I can and he's being rather rude at the moment. He believes his lunch is hours late when it's an entire three minutes past his usual time."

Sterling laughed. It was a deep, friendly laugh, not the nervous laugh one often got during an interview. He liked this one—his openness, his confidence. "I don't mind, sir, if you wanted to feed him. I have three at home and they definitely rule the house."

"Thank you, but I do think we're finished here." Kai closed the file and stood, offering his hand. "It's been a pleasure. Your work is impressive. I'll have Mindy email the offer and you can let us know if you're still interested. Did you have questions for me?"

Sterling shook his hand, his expression serious again. "I'd only want to know when I can start. AURA's been my goal for years, sir. If you're offering, I'm accepting."

Yesterday. You can start yesterday. "As soon as possible. If you have to give notice, do so. If not, tomorrow would be soon enough."

"I'll be here tomorrow morning, Mr. Hiltas." That infectious grin was back. "Without fail."

Kai waited until his office door had closed before he collapsed back in his chair with a whoosh of breath. *Mother of Night, thank you.* A skilled and experienced computer mage, finally, *finally* he would have one on staff. A more mature individual who could be given projects and not prodded and guided every step of the way.

Someone to replace me, to do what I used to do.

Kai frowned. No one could ever replace him. The world had no computer mage alive that was his peer. They had all been slaughtered by the lich queen. Sterling would be a help, though, could chip away at the pile of work on Kai's desk.

"Mrrrra-ah!"

"Yes, my apologies, oh, emperor of the office." Kai reached into his credenza for a can. He probably didn't need to buy the fancy kind for Breon, but he couldn't bear the smell of the cheap food. Revolting. With his demanding companion chomping away, Kai retreated to his private bathroom to wash his hands and check his hair. Still respectable. No need to re-braid it. No stains on his shirt or ink on his fingers. Good.

His suit jacket hung over his chair, charcoal gray with a bloodred handkerchief square in the pocket. He straightened his vest, pulled on the jacket and gathered the tatters of his courage. What was the worst that could happen? The answer would be no. It wasn't the end of the world, though it might feel as if it were in that moment.

"Mindy, I'll be downstairs in medical for a few minutes," he told his admin as he closed his office door. "I shouldn't be long."

"You're going to do it, sir?"

"I'm going to make a valiant attempt. Should I fail and perhaps suffer an aneurysm on the spot, I'll have someone call you."

"Good luck, Mr. H. You're looking fine. It'll be okay."

Kai gave her a stern look and a sniff of disapproval, which she didn't take seriously. Cheeky girl. Though her support didn't really annoy him. He needed all the borrowed confidence he could find. Straightening his shoulders, he marched to the elevator, trying not to fidget on the way down. Could he do this if people were listening? Could he manage not to make a scene if it didn't go well?

Wrack and storm, I shouldn't have to go through this at my age.

His legs felt numb as he made his way through the double doors into the clinic where Tenzin sat at reception. Tenzin, huge, beautiful Tenzin, whose fur was so thick and soft, who knew just how to pin Kai down...

"Good afternoon, Healer Tenzin." Kai gave him a polite nod, wishing Tenzi would stop frowning at him like that. "I'd like a word with you, if I may?"

"Of course, Mr. Hiltas, how can we help you?" Tenzin's gaze traveled up and down Kai's impeccably clad body. That could only be good.

"Not the medical staff. You, on a personal matter."

"Oh, I see." Tenzin sighed. "Kai, I've already—"

Kai held up a hand. "Please. Please let me finish." He waited until Tenzin sat back again. "I've admired you for some time, Healer Tenzin. Your patience, your kindness, your beauty, your intellect. If you don't find it too forward, I would like to invite you out for dinner and an evening at the theater."

Tenzin hesitated, fiddling with a letter opener shaped like a flamingo. "That might be the stiffest, coldest invitation for a date I've ever received."

"Have you had many recently?" Kai's heart sped in panic until he thought it might leap out of his chest. "No, I didn't mean... I have tickets to the Philharmonic on Friday. It's a lovely program. You can pick anywhere you like for dinner." He took a step forward, spots dancing in his vision. "I'll throw myself to my knees and beg if you like. But it's just a date, Tenzi. Please."

Tenzin straightened the files on his desk, not quite looking at Kai as he said, "I'll meet you downstairs here in the main lobby at six. And if you cancel for anything less than being hospitalized, you can consider this your last chance."

"Thank you." Kai gripped the front of the desk with both hands, pulling in slow, deep breaths.

When Tenzin spoke again, his voice was closer and concerned. "Maybe you should sit down for a minute or two."

"No, I—" *Don't faint. Don't.* The black spots faded and Kai felt he could breathe again. "I'm fine. Thank you. I'll see you on Friday, then."

"Yes." Tenzin still watched him carefully. "And Kai?"

"Hmm?"

"You look stunning today."

A smile blossomed unbidden. The expression felt strange since Kai hadn't tried it in over two weeks. "Thank you, Healer Tenzin. I'll let you get back to work."

It wasn't what he needed yet, not even close, but as Kai strode back to the elevators, the iron bands constricting his lungs loosened a few notches. It was good to draw a full breath again.

* * * *

Quinn squinted at the message on his phone. He'd almost missed it because he still wasn't used to carrying it around. Somehow, he'd managed to turn off the noise it made when he had a text and he didn't know how to turn it back on. He didn't really want to know. He could ask Kai to show him but he cringed at the thought of the look he was sure to receive. Kai had told him more than once that his tech-phobia, as he called it, was rare and strange in a human his age. Quinn barely managed not to tell him to fuck off.

The message was from Flax and it said there was a change of plan, to meet him in the park at ten. In the park, that's all it said. He started to text back to ask if he could be more specific but before he could figure out how to make the keyboard appear on the screen, he realized that Flax might have been purposefully vague.

So he wanted to test him. Quinn was okay with that, especially since it was an easy test. He knew who he was looking for and even his general location. Piece of cake.

Quinn put on his coat, took the elevator down to the main lobby and walked toward Central Park. Talking from his physical body while his mind was wandering around the city looking for the cat that Kai had adopted was the first time he'd tried that trick and he was somewhat surprised it had worked. He didn't know if he could send his mind out hunting and make his body follow, but it stood to reason that it was a possibility. It kind of gave him the heebie-jeebies though, to think about controlling his body from the outside, like he was piloting a remote control car. He might try it at some point, but his plan for now was to find a quiet spot to sit, find Flax and hope he stayed put while Quinn made his way over to him.

By the time he settled under a big maple and got comfortable enough to cast his mind out, he was starting to think this test might even be fun. The hunter being hunted.

Within only a minute or two, Quinn found him. He saw his energy like a beacon, bright among the other people strolling, jogging, or just ambling through. He was near the sheep meadow, nearly the same spot the conspirators had met all those months ago to figure out how they were going to kill a lich queen. He wondered if it was coincidence or if he'd picked it on purpose, maybe thinking he had to make it easy. Quinn dropped back into his body and started walking.

Flax was sitting on an exposed root of a big ol' tree, leaning back against the trunk, looking like he was ready to take a nap. It was still about five to ten. It hadn't even slowed Quinn down to have to find him first.

"Well look at you." Flax's golden eyebrows were almost buried in his hairline. "You probably don't need a circle or a scrying stone or any of that crap, do you?"

"I used to," Quinn admitted. "The tools helped, at first. Now I just have to sit and think for a little while and...I find what I'm looking for."

Flax leaped to his feet and gestured back toward AURA. "And that was what I was trying to say to you in our first lesson. Though I sucked at getting the point across. You shine with power, Quinn. You shouldn't need crutches or cheats like other humans. Like Kai's pack of...um, less competent novices."

Quinn tipped his head to one side as he regarded Flax. It was like he was talking to someone else, someone totally unlike the cocky jerk who acted like he was assigned babysitting duty and couldn't think of anything he wanted to do less.

"Magic burn is real, Flax. I can do certain things without using a staff or wand, but... Well, I don't know why I can scry or hold a circle without using any kind of buffer, but trust me, doing other stuff without one hurts—a lot."

"Right." Flax snapped his fingers, index finger pointing toward the clouds. "Why. That's it exactly. We need to figure out why. I've seen human mages after magic burn. It doesn't look like fun. I get that. But I think it happens to other magic users because they're trying to channel too much. The vessel's too small to contain the fire. I think with you, it might be different."

He smiled at Quinn, a grin that was suddenly real and open and tinged with mischief as he pulled a piece of paper from his back pocket. "Wanna play a game?"

Quinn folded his arms, feet shoulder width apart, squarely planted. The posture wasn't particularly inviting but he said, "What kind of game?"

"Scavenger hunt." Flax settled back into the tree roots and smoothed the paper on his knee. "I've hidden a list of things around the park. Things I've borrowed from people you know, so you have energy signatures to look for. Not a long list. But I'd like to watch you work, watch how your energy shifts and flows as you find them."

"If you borrowed stuff from people I know and you're going to tell me what to look for, this is going to be too easy," Quinn told him.

"I wasn't trying to make it hard," Flax said. "It isn't a test, Quinn. I already know you can do this. I only want to see you do it so that I can learn how you tick. Then maybe I can figure out how to teach you."

"Oh." Quinn still didn't quite believe Flax wasn't testing him, but he eased down next to him, sitting on the grass and leaning back on a spare part of tree trunk. "What do you want me to find first?"

"I borrowed a pen from Matt," Flax said.

Quinn closed his eyes. *Pen. Matt.* He zoomed up. The park lay before him, still the same park he knew but it looked like it was overlaid with shades of gray when he saw it this way, and the pen hidden under a rock nearby twinkled like the sun caught in a chip of mirror.

"It's under a rock by the foot path," Quinn said. "Do you want me to get it, or just tell you where everything is?"

"Just tell me for now." Flax's voice became uncertain. "Unless you can get it without getting up?"

"No, I can't. I'm not telekinetic, as far as I know. What's next?"

"A stapler that belongs to Nestor."

"By a tree that has bushes around it...over there." Quinn pointed, even though his physical body didn't move.

"A paper clip from Aello..."

"In an oak tree, tied to it with a rubber band on a branch," Quinn answered almost before Flax stopped speaking.

"Ooookay. Two more things and I'm not telling you what or who from." Flax laughed helplessly. "You gotta give me a chance to watch what happens, Flash."

"I... I don't know if I can, if I don't know what I'm looking for," Quinn said. "Tell me the next one, and I'll go slow...I'll describe what I see." He hoped Flax didn't want to argue about it because his concentration was already wavering from trying to talk while he was outside his body. The park had gone dim around the edges and he felt heavier.

"All right, I hid one of my blades."

Quinn almost blurted out where it was but stopped himself. "As soon as you tell me what to see...I get a picture of it in my head...then it lights up...like a pin of light on a map."

"A map in your head?" Flax asked.

"No. Like...laid out in front of me. I don't know how to explain." As soon as he said it, as soon as he felt the frustration, he felt a drop in the pit of his stomach, like he was falling. He opened his eyes and looked at Flax. "Sorry...that probably wasn't very helpful."

"More than you realize. You okay? Your color's a little off."

"Yeah, I'm okay." This time it was true. At least he didn't think he was in danger of passing out.

"There's one more thing to find. Feel up to it?"

"Yeah, I can do it," Quinn said.

"Okay, this time I'm not going to tell you. Just try."

Quinn looked at him dubiously but he gave it a shot. He closed his eyes again. It was a little harder to fly up, but he managed and turned in a slow circle. How could he find something if he didn't know what it was? He had to have at least a clue to go by. Nothing leaped out at him as important, no little twinkles of light trying to get his attention. He turned slowly again, searching, feeling his way. Matt. Aello. Nestor. Flax. Of course, Flax would get something from Val.

As soon as he thought it, he had it.

"Val's mug is on the bench by the pond."

"Excellent! Come on back and we'll go retrieve stuff while we talk. I asked the boggle in the pond to watch Val's mug for me, but I really want to return it in the condition I borrowed it."

"Groof wouldn't do anything to Val's mug, 'cept maybe get it slimy. I should get him a couple dogs anyway."

Flax gave him a hand up and clasped his hands behind his back as they strolled. He left the path to pull his blade from the stump where he'd left it, and only started talking again when they started down the path. "What you do is unusual, for any race, but we see it sometimes. You scry in worldview instead of simply in a tight focus for something specific. The world spread out below you. Do you feel like you're flying?"

"Mm-hm," Quinn said. Actually, he still felt a little floaty. Sometimes that feeling stuck around if he was looking too long, of if he shifted in and out several times in a row. "I don't just feel like it though. I do fly. Well, part of me does. I can look down and see myself."

Flax stopped short and stared at him. "Spirit dislocation. That's really...dangerous." He shook his head as if he had to get something out of it. "Wait. But...you were talking to me. That's. Holy fuck."

If Quinn weren't so floaty, he might have thought more of that reaction but as it was, he just figured Flax thought he was stupid, again. "It's hard to talk while I'm looking. I never tried it before until a couple weeks ago when we were looking for Momma Cats' stray." He looked at Flax. "Kai didn't seem to think it was a big deal."

"Damn drow. Of course not. All esoteric magic and sneaky shit. But it's not usual. It is a big deal." Flax continued walking, though his steps were slower. "Though he knows you better. He's seen you work. Maybe it just doesn't seem a big deal 'cause of what he's seen you do."

Quinn shrugged. "Who knows? It's not like Kai would really worry too much as long as I can do what he wants. Why is it a big deal? It doesn't feel dangerous. It's not even that hard."

"Yeah. Long as he gets what he wants. That's his whole MO." Flax snorted and shook his head. "It's a big deal because most magic users can't do it. I sure as hell can't. Bet money that the drow can't. I've only run across one other person who could, and that was in my old life. And she was really old and powerful. There's two dangers, though. One is that if you don't have someone with you—someone who can protect you—an enemy can get to your body while you're outside it. Not good. The other danger is that you could—if something bad happens—get lost and not find your way back."

"I always know where I am though. Even if I'm gone a long time and get too tired to actually go back, I just…I dunno, stop trying to hold myself up and I fall back into myself." He tapered off toward the end because Flax was looking at him with an absolutely horrified expression.

"Um. Yeah… We're gonna have to talk about that. If you've gone that far that you have to fall to come back… Yeah. Try not to do that. I don't know what it's like here, either, since that's not something I do here. But back home? There were…things on the spirit plane. Things that could hurt you. Maybe you don't have them here. I don't know." He cleared his throat, obviously trying to regroup.

At a particular rock, he bent, turned it over and retrieved a pen. "Back to the point of all this. I did get to watch. When you're scrying, you're swimming. You let the magical currents flow through you and sweep you up. You're riding the current. But when you were trying to conjure a fireball or control wind, you were fighting it. Hard. Like it stole something from you.

What we need to concentrate on is getting you to feel the same thing, the same way, when you do any magic, not just the couple of things you do better than probably any other human."

Quinn wasn't sure if that was supposed to be a compliment, a criticism or both. "I'm not trying to fight. It's just when I feel the magic come up, it's like a flood hitting me. If I don't try and control it then... Well, you saw what happened with the bowling ball, and that was trying to hold back. If I just let it go, I don't know what would happen."

"I know you don't feel like you are." Flax ran both hands back through his ridiculously perfect golden hair. "But you are. Hmm. I need to think about this. Is it something in how you learned? Did someone...I don't know, frighten you when they taught you?"

Every muscle in Quinn's back suddenly tightened up but he kept a straight face. "No." He answered too quickly and too curtly.

"All right. We're not friends. I get it." Flax pulled the stapler out of the bushes. "I'm not trying to pry. Just thinking out loud."

Quinn walked away from him. The paper clip was not far and he unwound the rubber band from the branch and put them both in his pocket. He was not about to get into what he had learned under Donovan's tutelage.

They continued in silence until they reached the pond. Flax scooped Val's mug off the bench and sat down with a heavy exhale. "I know you think I'm a jackass. It was a bad start. But it was for me, too."

Quinn rolled his eyes, certain another 'human' dig was coming.

"You know Kai asked me to teach you?"

"Yeah." Quinn didn't sit, eyeing Flax warily again.

"Well, yeah, he didn't *ask* me, ask me. He fucking blackmailed me."

Quinn rolled that around in his head for a second or two. Well, that explained some of the initial hostility. How Kai hadn't known that putting a reluctant teacher with an equally reluctant student wouldn't turn out badly, he had no idea.

"And you're telling me this now, why?" Quinn asked.

"Because he can't anymore. Blackmail me." Flax put the mug down and rubbed at his forearms fretfully. "I'm an addict. Tylenol. The records were sealed because I went to rehab. That...drow dug them up. Threatened to make the records known to the department. Well, more fool him. I fell off the fucking wagon and now everyone knows." Flax shook his head again. It was like his brain wasn't settled in there right or something. "I just wanted you to know it wasn't you. That I was mad as hell. Scared I'd lose my job. And I...yeah, acted like a jackass. So it's kind of a long-ass apology."

Quinn stood with his hands on his hips and debated for a long moment. Finally, he took a deep breath and sighed. "Not everyone knows. Just a couple people. They all think you needed time off due to stress. I know because, well, Val had to tell me why my brand-spankin'-new teacher was outta service for a while and he can't really lie to me. As far as I know, only me, Val and the lab tech that did your blood work know. And one stupid drow."

A crooked smile twisted Flax's lips, though he was still staring at this boots. "Yeah. All right, not everyone. But it's in department records now, so no leverage there. But you were interesting. Your magic. What I'd heard and what I'd seen? Two different people. I knew something wasn't right. It *was* blackmail. Now I'd like to help. If you let me."

"Wait a second, what do you mean 'what I'd heard'? What did you hear? From who?" Quinn demanded.

"Quinn." Flax raised his head, a flush rising up his neck. "You're a hero."

"I am not," Quinn said at once.

"Everyone in the department talks about you. How you saved the city."

"That's ridiculous. There were a lot of people that fought to save the city."

"How you held the lich queen."

"No big deal. Val is the one that destroyed her. He's the hero."

"Oh, I won't argue that. He is. But you are, too. He couldn't have if you hadn't been able to hold that circle. Sometimes they say you did a dozen other impossible things. But, it's hard not to hear about that stuff."

Quinn sighed and rubbed a hand over his eyes. He knew what Flax was saying was true, although he tried hard to ignore the fact that people talked about him. It made him extremely uncomfortable. He always figured the same people who gossiped about how instrumental he was in stopping the lich were probably the same people who whispered behind his back about how he got away with doing whatever he wanted at AURA because he was fucking the captain. That he just happened to be in the right place at the right time to wedge his way in when the sticks were down.

He plopped onto the bench next to Flax like it was too much effort to stay standing and slouched down.

"People will say anything. It doesn't matter." Quinn wondered if he was trying to convince Flax or himself.

"Anyway, I won't hold your being a prick against you."

"Thanks." Flax chuckled, and maybe it was a little bitter but he didn't sound so desperately miserable anymore. He nudged his shoulder against Quinn's. "Whatever people say, you held a lich queen. Not even a stupid drow could've done that."

A little half grin curled the corner of Quinn's mouth. "Not even a stupid drow could break my circle, but I bet no one's told you that little story."

"No, you're kidding?" Flax got up from the bench, a wicked grin lighting up his handsome face. "I'll walk you back, cause this, you gotta tell me."

Chapter Nine

The block of apartments AURA used for temporary housing was just a few streets over from headquarters. Flax went up to the tenth floor, tucked his green button-down into his jeans a little better and knocked on the apartment number Ash had given him. He had a bunch of mixed greens tucked under one arm—fennel, kale, arugula—since he wasn't sure if either of them drank and you just didn't come to dinner empty-handed.

Sage answered the door and invited him inside with a sweeping gesture of his arm. He seemed more relaxed this evening than he had when they had found him to offer the invitation. Perhaps it was just that Sage was in his own space now, or maybe he was starting to accept the situation. Or...maybe it was the wormwood Flax scented.

"Come in. Be welcome," Sage said. He was not slurring his words at all, and his eyes were bright but not glassy, so he must have indulged in only a drink or two.

Ash swept out of the kitchen to greet him as well and didn't they make a handsome pair? Sage, all dark and protective, Ash tall and lovely, his silver hair unbound and falling to the top curve of his ass.

"Hey, you two. Thanks for inviting me. Looks like you're settling in nicely." Sure the place was a little spartan, but it was temporary, after all.

"We are making the best of it." Ash accepted the package of greens that Flax held out. "Thank you, this was very thoughtful."

"Would you like a drink?" Sage asked him.

Flax cleared his throat, trying to tamp down on temptation and embarrassment all at once. *How awkward.* "Um, do you have any beer? Though water's fine."

Sage disappeared into the kitchen and returned a moment later with a bottle of beer for Flax and a tumbler with ice and an inch of milky greenish liquid. Ash gestured toward the living room. "Come and sit, dinner will be ready in a little while, but we can talk first."

Beer in hand, Flax sauntered over and took the single chair so they could sit together on the sofa. "Have you two been together long?"

Oh, yeah, great. Sound like the bitter single elf right off the bat, why don't you?

"Almost two years," Ash answered, seemingly unruffled by the question.

"We had just found a *senrist* that we both thought would make a good match for us when we were pulled into this world," Sage added.

"Oh, crud. I'm sorry." Flax took a pull on his beer. Smuttynose. Not bad. "That had to suck. I wasn't attached or promised or really looking when I crossed."

"How long ago was that?" Sage asked.

Flax tapped a finger on the beer bottle. He had to think about it. "It's been…four years now?"

Sage gaped at him and even Ash looked startled.

"Four years in this place with no bond mates?" Sage looked aghast.

"Sage." Ash gave him a disapproving look.

"I'm sorry," Sage said, and he honestly did look apologetic. "It's just when I think about how it could have happened, if only one of us had been pulled across…" He stopped and the ice in his glass clinked as he shuddered.

Flax nodded. "To lose your *kalesi* that way—I know some elves don't survive it. Val, the captain, lost his entire *senrist*. Even he admits he wasn't sane for some time."

"Do you think that's why he— Ow!" Sage cut off whatever he'd been about to say as Ash stomped on his foot.

It was tough to figure out whether to address that slip or ignore it. *Goddess, I'm out of practice socializing with anyone but cops.* He decided to deflect. "But you're right. It would've been harder for me if I'd lost someone. It wasn't easy being alone here at the start, but at least half my heart hadn't been ripped away."

"Perhaps when you are ready to look you will find the right person, even here," Ash said.

Flax managed a grin. "Yeah, that's the hope."

"Although I've heard that the elvish population is scarce here, that most of the crossovers move out of the city, eventually," Sage said. "Unless you would consider a human mate."

"There aren't many, true. But if you find the right one, it doesn't matter how many, right?" Flax shrugged, fighting the tremor that was doing its best to creep into his words. "Humans aren't so bad—the good ones. Any port in a storm, as they say here."

He kept the smile plastered on and gave Ash a wink. No way he'd show them how thinking too much about mates—and the right mate—would show how flayed and tattered his heart was by now. When he'd first crossed over? Sure. Sex with anything other than his own kind was abhorrent. Now? He'd be a hypocrite to say it when he'd had one-night stands with half the fucking city, species be damned. Time to change the subject before he completely embarrassed himself and fell apart in front of his hosts.

"So, tell me stories of your daring lives and I'll tell you mine," he managed with more cheer as he raised his bottle in salute.

For the next hour or so, they traded war stories and compared notes to see if they could fit together the world they came from and the world Flax came from because it seemed unlikely that they were different. By the time dinner was ready, they still hadn't determined for certain. It could have been that Flax had come from a separate world than their own, or it could have been the same only he had lived on a distant continent and they had different names for the peoples and places in between. The things and places they described were similar enough for the latter to be just as plausible as the former.

He did manage to trot out the story about hunting the Black Beast of Dunlas and even got a laugh from Sage when he told them how the beast had been blinded in the sunlight and had mistaken a stone pillar for him. Poor beast had broken off all his teeth.

When the food was placed on the table and they were all eating, the topic shifted to the world in which they now found themselves. Sage had stopped drinking the wormwood and while he was still under the influence, he was not drunk. Even so, he didn't turn as dismissive and hostile as he had previously, although he was quieter, listening.

They both looked vaguely uncomfortable while Flax tried explaining the finer details of the varying governmental systems—how they traditionally saw each other and dealt with one another. Elvish society was entirely feudal, as far as any of them knew.

Flax cleared his throat, casting around desperately for another shift in topic. "The stew is delicious. Truly one of the best things I've had in months."

Not flattery, it was true. The vegetable stew was thick and savory and someone had discovered hummus as well, which sat on the table nearest Sage. He seemed to have a weakness for it.

"Thank you. I'm glad you're enjoying it. I did most of the cooking for our troop when we were afield," Ash said. "Of course, we are better provisioned here in the quantity of foodstuffs."

Sage shot him a dark look but did not comment.

Ash stirred a spoon around his bowl and waited until Flax had time to eat a few more mouthfuls before he said, "We were discussing the possibility of relocating to one of the elvish communities in the north. Have you visited them?"

"I...ah, used to live in one." Where he'd found too many different sorts of elves and drow all packed in one place. Where he'd started using. "You can certainly visit, but I don't recommend them. It's not like home. Too contentious."

He fixed Ash with a puzzled frown as an odd turn of phrase caught up to him. The *quantity* of foodstuffs, he had said. "Are you having trouble finding good quality food? I mean, I'm happy to take you to the better places for the stuff we need."

Sage made a small noise that might have been dismissive but sounded more wounded. He put his elbows on the table and his head in his hands. "The hunter doesn't hunt but rather goes to the market. This place makes no sense."

Ash looked at him and Flax saw the aching concern and worry on his face in that brief moment when Sage wasn't looking directly at him, there and gone again as if swept away by a stray wind. He reached over and put his hand on Sage's shoulder, then pulled him closer, tucking Sage's head under his chin when the other elf folded against his chest. "Be at ease, *kalesi*," he murmured in Elvish just above his ear.

Damn it, I'm fucking this all up. "I hunt still." He wanted to sound fierce and maybe a little offended, though he wasn't sure how successful that was. "My forest has trees of concrete and glass. My prey are lawbreakers and the evil that tries to hide in the shadows. Oh, I hunt, brothers. And it is a joyful, ferocious thing to save innocents and to serve an elvish prince."

Sage pulled himself together enough to lift his head, and when he looked at Flax, all traces of fierce warrior were washed away. Flax reevaluated his original estimate of his age. Ash was older, probably matching his own years, but if he had to guess now, he would say that Sage had only reached his maturity perhaps a handful of years ago. Clear green eyes several shades lighter than his green-black hair regarded him contritely.

"I'm sorry, hunter. I meant no offense. Please forgive me. I am trying to be more understanding of this world because Ash says I must, but everything seems so alien here."

Flax surged up and strode around the table, his heart breaking for this young elf. He dropped to one knee and took Sage's face between his hands. "I shouldn't take offense. I'm sorry. I'm so sorry. This is so hard, and I'm acting as if it's nothing. You just arrived. You haven't had time and it's so, so hard for us." He felt the tears prickling at the corners of his eyes, but he forged on. "Elves don't do well the first year or so. Some die, simply because they can't bear it. Some take their own lives. Some turn to poisons."

Ash's frown said he knew this. He was fighting for composure as well.

"The wormwood." Flax moved the glass away from Sage and returned both hands to frame that earnest, anguished face. "And others. You feel better in the moment, but you will slowly die if you turn to those. Don't. Fight the despair with every beat of your valiant heart. Learn, adapt, adjust. It will come slowly, but it will be less and less strange and horrible. Don't die." A tear slipped out despite his battle to hold them back. To watch yet another elf wither in this world? He couldn't. Not again. "Please. Don't die."

Sage brought his hand up and long fingers cupped the side of Flax's cheek. His thumb brushed there, catching the tear and whisking it away. He tipped his head down and touched Flax's lips with his own, a softly tender kiss that was more question and comfort than passion.

Oh, yeah, this'll be a pity fuck for them if I go any farther. Poor, lonely hunter. He was lonely, though, and he hadn't had anyone touch him so gently in far too long. Who cared why? Flax glanced up at Ash and didn't find any censure or coldness there, so he tilted his head up and reached for Sage's lips again, so soft and warm, even if they still tasted of wormwood.

The hand cupping Flax's cheek slid back into his hair, long fingers splaying out along his scalp. Sage's lips moved gently along his own and the tip of his tongue teased along the crease, not a hesitant flicker but a sensual stroke, coaxing entry.

Flax took the invitation and surged up on his knees, both hands tangling in the thick hemlock green of Sage's hair, his tongue plunging within as he took control of the kiss.

For all Sage's surly aggression, he did not resist, drawing Flax closer with his hands and opening his lips to his questing tongue. The soft purr of pleasure in his throat invited more of the same and the hand that wasn't tangled in Flax's hair stroked down his chest and tugged his shirt from where it was tucked into his pants so he could get underneath to his skin.

Hands on his naked back sent a shiver down his arms. It felt so good, Flax nearly melted in a puddle at Sage's feet. He pulled back from the kiss and pressed his lips to Sage's forehead before raising his head to catch Ash's eye again. Those pool-blue eyes had heated watching them. Yep, this was something they all needed.

"Bed?" Flax suggested.

Ash smiled and rose gracefully, pausing to place a kiss on the top of Sage's head. It put him closer to Flax and he leaned in to brush a soft kiss along his lips as well. "This way," he said, the warm musical quality of his voice lending itself well to a lower, huskier range.

Both Sage and Flax rose, almost as one, and Sage took one of Flax's hands, leading him as they both followed Ash from the small dining area toward the back of the apartment where there was a bedroom.

The double bed wasn't much, but it got them away from the dishes and the breakables. Flax kept hold of Sage's hand as he tipped his head up to kiss Ash, his flavor clean and sweet, like mountain water. He found himself between them suddenly, with Ash pressed up against his front, his calm demeanor giving way to something more primal as he answered Flax's kiss, teeth nibbling at Flax's lips. Sage's hands circled around from the back to undo Flax's shirt buttons and he realized there was a conspiracy to get him naked as Ash's hands went to his belt.

They were certainly efficient in accomplishing their goal. Sage peeled his shirt down his arms at the same time Ash got the button and zipper of his pants undone. Sage placed a line of kisses from the center of his shoulder blades up his spine all the way to his nape and Ash folded to his knees, dragging Flax's pants down with him. The shirt still dangled from his wrists and his pants were now around his ankles, leaving him hobbled.

Not something he was accustomed to in the bedroom, but, goddesses, it felt wonderful, to be surrounded and attended to this way. His cock, half hard already, filled when Ash breathed over it, so fast that Flax moaned and leaned back into Sage's strong, circling arms. Oh, yeah. He wasn't going to complain.

Sage nuzzled into Flax's hair, kissing the tender skin just behind his ear, but not touching there yet. He got Flax's hands free of the shirt and slid both hands around him, stroking up his chest as he pressed into him from behind. His thumbs brushed lightly over Flax's nipples, as gently as he had wiped the tear from the corner of his eye.

"Your skin is like moonbeams, so very beautiful," Sage murmured into Flax's hair.

Ash was running his strong hands up and down Flax's thighs and he caressed over his hips then dipped his head so that he could lick a wet line up the underside of Flax's rising shaft.

"Sweet Mother, yes." Flax hissed, arching his back to thrust his hips forward, his cock a demand and a plea as it pointed straight at Ash. He stabbed one hand into Ash's hair, afraid if he didn't have a point on which to steady himself, he would collapse. With far more flexibility than any human had, he reached his other hand back over Sage's shoulder, scrabbled up a handful of shirt and tugged it up Sage's broad back.

He wanted everything, now, five minutes ago, but he wanted the slow torture of gentle hands and skin on skin more. "You're both so beautiful. I want to kiss every inch of your skin."

With the little bit of concentration he had left, he focused on Ash and slowly began undoing his shirt buttons without touching them.

That earned him a soft chuckle from Ash, which vibrated where his lips touched just under the head of his cock. When he moaned again, Ash took him into his mouth, enveloping him in wet heat, digging his strong fingers into his thighs. He felt Sage move his hips back, but it was only to release his own trousers and he was back, pressing nakedness to nakedness. The thick feel of his shaft pressing into the valley of his cheeks and rubbing there proved he was every bit as turned on.

Flax leaned his head back on Sage's shoulder, even as his mind coaxed the shirt from Ash's body and, oh, that glorious fall of silver hair fanned out over bare skin nearly was the end of him. "I want you to take me," he whispered close to Sage's ear. "Hard as you please."

Those words must have held more magic than what Flax was weaving around Ash to divest him of his clothes because a soft growl escaped Sage. He nipped where he had been kissing and tonguing and moved his mouth to the lobe of Flax's ear, sucking the nub of flesh between his lips as surely as Ash sucked his cock deeper into his mouth.

The gentle brush of Sage's thumbs was replaced with the pads of his fingertips, pinching and tugging more roughly. "Here, or on the bed?" Sage breathed over his ear.

"Beside the bed," Flax grinned wickedly, despite how hard he panted. "Ash can lie on his back on the mattress with his head by my thighs and I'll lean over him." He stroked Ash's hair with reverent fingers. "To give you a way in and so I can taste him."

Ash seemed on board with that idea and he lifted his head, slowly drawing lips and tongue along Flax's throbbing cock before releasing him. He stood and merely had to step out of the clothes Flax had unfastened, and kissed Flax, equally slow and deep before he went to the other side of the bed and lay across. His long body meant his legs were draped over one side when he lay crossways, and his hair spilled over the other side in a silvery curtain.

Sage hummed a passionate moan behind Flax's ear as they both watched his lover, the way he placed himself so gracefully, the way his hands glided up and down his own chest to toy with a nipple, the way his cock lay thick and straight on his belly.

"He's glorious, isn't he?" Flax whispered to Sage, just to hear that growling moan again. He held back the chuckle that wanted out and disentangled himself gently so he could get out of his boots and jeans. His patience was running a little on the thin side with such an incredible buffet laid out for him.

When he knelt on the bed, knees either side of Ash's head, Ash reached up around him, long arms snaking around his waist then his thighs, hands caressing and pulling him. That hot wet mouth was immediately back on him, opening and drawing him in, tongue swirling around the crown of his cock in a way that made him shiver.

Another pair of hands moved down Flax's back, kneading his muscles, digging thumbs in almost painfully as they dragged down either side of his spine. When his hands reached his ass, Sage massaged there as well, fingers parting the globes, then he knelt behind him and Flax had his equally hot wet mouth tonguing his rim, circling and fluttering then pressing inside.

For a brief, whiteout moment, Flax wondered if his head could truly explode from pleasure. An embarrassing sound escaped him, more whine than groan as he tried to push back against the invading tongue and down into Ash's hot mouth at the same time. He spread his knees farther and leaned down on his elbows so he could reach Ash's beautiful erection.

He licked the top, catching the pearl drop there. "So sweet, so lovely," he moaned as he closed his lips around the head.

The muscles of Ash's thighs flexed and so did his hips, pressing up to meet his mouth. The answering moan he gave reverberated up Flax's shaft and Ash arched his neck, pushing his mouth up onto Flax's cock until his nose nudged his balls. Sage's wriggling wet tongue was there one moment and replaced the next by the much thicker, heavier dome of his cock head, pressing firmly to his opening.

Flax pushed back in invitation. It had been a long time since he'd let someone fuck him, but he wanted this so badly he thought his skin might catch fire. A whimper caught in his throat as Sage pushed steadily forward. His cock was thick...broad like the rest of him, but Ash laving at his cock distracted him and a heavily suctioned pull took enough of his attention that he didn't care if he was being split in two.

He swallowed Ash's cock down, taking the head into his throat to catch the heavy groan as he was impaled.

Sage was relentless but slow. He didn't just ram it home. He did make Flax feel every inch of him sinking deeper until the tops of Sage's thighs touched the backs of his own and his sharp, winged hipbones ground into Flax's ass. He held there for a moment, then started to move, short thrusts that were quick and satisfying without causing too much friction. He had definitely done this many times before. It wasn't like the convenient silicone lubricates you could get at any drugstore were readily available where they were from.

Sage gripped his hips, fingers digging in hard and Flax could feel the strength in his body, the way he held himself taut, keeping everything firmly under control. He was holding back, Flax could tell, but he was still enjoying himself if the ultra hard shaft piercing him and the heated groans coming from him were any indication.

Fuck control. Flax wanted him to lose it, to give him the ferocity he had seen in Tokyo. He rocked his hips back and took Ash in hand to free his mouth for an instant. "Faster, Sage. Let me feel the storm within you. Obliterate me with it."

There was a moment's hesitation then Flax felt wetness around his ring where Sage must have drooled a line of spit to ease the way. The first few strokes after that were longer, but still slow, letting the natural lube do its work before he began to pick up the pace. Sage's hands slipped up Flax's sides, over his heaving ribcage and he leaned into him, arching over him, pressing him down even lower over Ash. They moved together like that for several sensual minutes before Sage shifted, and Ash followed the movement almost as if they communicated telepathically, turning Flax onto his side.

The maneuver was so smooth Sage was spooned up behind him and back inside almost before Flax registered the absence. Ash too turned to his side, still facing Flax nose to tail. Sage pushed a hand between Flax's thighs from behind, lifting his top leg so that he bent his knee. He nuzzled back into Flax's hair as he found his rhythm again, sliding more easily in and out. Their bodies made little slapping sounds now, punctuated by the soft growls and groans Sage made. Sage turned his head, rubbing his jaw and the side of his cheek, then his ear along the side of Flax's.

The position gave Flax less leverage, but the haze of pleasure overrode any need he had for control. He returned to Ash's cock with a vengeance, scraping his teeth along the sides, alternately licking and taking him deep into the tight confines of his throat. Ash's desperate moan around his erection thrilled him and nearly sent him over with the vibrations.

Sage gasped raggedly and rubbed the side of his head along Flax's again, the scent of elf pheromones rising and mixing with the scents of musk and sex. The arm Sage had around him tightened hard and his hips drove his cock into Flax harder and faster. A spill of Elvish words, little endearments and encouragements fell from Sage's lips into Flax's ear. The body pounding against Flax was no longer taut and controlled. His breathing was ragged and his fingers dug into him, clawing at him almost hard enough to break skin and the cock impaling him was leaking copiously enough that no other lube was necessary now.

That's it...Sweet Mother, yes. Flax pulled hard at Ash's cock and got a strangled, muffled scream. That long, beautiful body arched and bucked as Ash came, so suddenly, so violently, he almost knocked Flax off.

He waited until the bucking slowed before pulling off, stroking Ash's belly and whispering to Sage, "Let go, let the gates open. I'm right behind you."

Sage sank his teeth into him, at the last moment diverting his mouth to the muscle of his shoulder rather than his ear, which would have caused far more complications than any of them needed. His breath hitched in his throat and he drove deep, holding there as the intense spasms gripped him, then groaning and shuddering, thrusting again in long, smooth strokes.

Ash chose that moment to refocus and sucked hard on Flax's cock, while pressing two fingers against his perineum. That was the last drop that sank him. With pressure on his gland inside and out and that incredible mouth sucking him, he howled as his balls pulled up tight, heavy pulses shooting from him as he came. He bucked between them, begging, pleading, spouting nonsense, until he finally settled, gasping, laughing.

"Oh, that was...yeah. There isn't a word for what that was."

Sage was still rocking gently behind him, not ready to pull out of the warm snug channel making him tingle all over just yet. Ash reeled around so that he could kiss Flax and snug up to his front.

"Stay here with us, tonight?" Sage murmured along Flax's nape, stroking him up and down his side with one hand.

I should say no. There are a hundred and seven reasons I should say no. The memory of Sage's anguish was too fresh, the knowledge that the young warrior was happy for a moment all too present.

Flax turned his head to kiss Sage softly, then turned back to kiss Ash as well. "All right. I'm too comfortable to get dressed anyway. But I have to get up super early and if you're both sleeping, I am sneaking out. No way that I can show up to work in jeans."

Sage licked along the smattering of tooth marks he had left in Flax's flesh and Flax could feel the smile on his lips as he kissed there.

"Who said anything about sleeping?" He purred in Flax's ear, rubbing his lower half more suggestively along Flax's backside, his still half-hard cock slipping back and forth.

With a laugh, Flax flipped onto his back so he could speak to both of them. "Someone has a bit of stamina, I see. But if we're starting up again..." He reached over and stroked Ash's jaw. "We're switching."

Chapter Ten

"Repent ye Sinners and listen to the Law of Our Lord and Savior!"

Albert's stomach churned, his dinner sitting ill in his belly. The shrill voice of the man yelling at passersby hurt his ears.

"Trust in the Lord Jesus Christ!"

No. There was no trust. He couldn't trust in anyone because they all wanted to hurt him. He could tell by the way they looked quickly then looked away, so he couldn't see the blackness of their hearts shining in their eyes. They would kill him given half a chance. Lock him away and torture him first.

"Reject the demons contaminating our world. Cast them out into the barren lands!"

Albert started to hyperventilate. They wanted to kill him and his friend as well. Hurt him...or worse, take him away. Albert would not let that happen. This one had to die. He was ready to die anyway. He could see the blackness in him, eating him from the inside out. Spewing that poison in the form of words. Borrowed time. That's what he was doing. Spreading the poison enough so it wouldn't take him down. Filling the ears of others to do his evil.

"Turn to the Lord Jesus for the answer. He will tell you it is unnatural for a man to lie with non-human devils!"

Albert covered his ears. All the people walking past were ignoring the preacher, giving him looks of disgust or outright hostility, but Albert could tell. He could tell it was all an act. They were taking on the poison. Taking it and they would spread it like disease and they would know, they would know what he did, what he hid, and they would come after him and his friend.

"Understand that He is all powerful! He will do what He wants regardless of whether you believe in Him or not! He will strike those down who befriend His enemies, those not of this world."

Albert moaned softly where he stood in the darkness of the alley, his hands clamped over his ears but still able to hear no matter how much he tried to shut it out. He had to stop him, stop him from saying more, telling more of his secrets. But people would see. They would see and they would catch him and hurt him and his friend. Too risky. He couldn't stand it though. Had to shut him up.

"Go," he whispered. "Go. Stop him."

His friend stepped out from the alley, towering and lumbering, his footfalls slow and crunching on the sidewalk. Albert watched from the shadows as his friend touched the preacher and his words choked off. The people looked relieved at first, then scared, then they started to run and scream. He called his friend back to him and they ran too—ran away, where they would be safe.

* * * *

"Is this all right?" Kai asked as he opened the cab door for Tenzin. He'd dressed in his best black Armani for their date, shoes spit-shine polished. *Please let this be all right.* "I should have asked. I'm sorry. But I'd hoped you would say and then you didn't call—"

"It's fine." Tenzin waited on the sidewalk while Kai paid the cab fare. "It's always good here."

Junoon had been one of their special occasion restaurants, a place to go to celebrate things like anniversaries and surviving lich queen attacks. That had been his one fear, that Tenzin would see the choice as manipulative, but he couldn't think of anything better that he knew Tenzin would like.

At least Tenzin took his offered arm as they went inside to speak to the hostess. Yes, he had a reservation and he discreetly gave her incentive in the form of cash to find them one of the more private tables, with the high back wall. Tenzin was quiet, letting Kai order the vegetarian tasting menu for both of them. Seven courses, *prix fixe*, expensive, but well worth it. By the second course, the rainbow chard paneer, Kai had begun to despair that his beloved would remain silent the entire evening. Finally, Tenzin spoke.

"Are you going to tell me?"

Kai's heart hammered in his throat. One misstep now and all was lost. "Tell you what, Tenzi?"

"What Flax was talking about when he called the other night?"

"Oh. That." Kai swallowed hard. "You will most likely be angry with me."

"No more angry than I have been the past weeks, I'm sure."

"I suppose that's fair." Kai put his fork down. "I, ah, resorted to extortion. That's why he called drunk and angry."

"I see." Tenzin took a bite of paneer, chewing thoughtfully. "And why would you blackmail an officer of the law?"

"Ah. Well...I needed an appropriate teacher for Quinn. Someone who would be able to see his way through the boy's issues."

Now Tenzin looked at him, perhaps for the first time that evening. "You couldn't simply ask him?"

"Flax is...young. He would be able to connect better with Quinn. But he's a bit of a bigot. I knew he would say no. So I threatened to expose his drug addiction."

Tenzin shook his head. "There is so much wrong with that series of sentences, I don't even know where to begin. Can you really, honestly, accuse someone else of bigotry?"

A strangled sound caught in Kai's throat. He had to take a long drink of water before he could speak. "I'll have you know, I'm a recovering bigot, thank you very much."

There was a long, terrible silence. Then something wonderful happened, something miraculous and astounding. Tenzin began to laugh. He rolled in his chair, he laughed so hard, finally dabbing his eyes on his napkin and covering Kai's hand with his huge, furry one.

"Oh, my love. What am I to do with you?" Tenzin waved a hand helplessly, trying to recover his power of speech. "Here I am thinking you were having affairs at the office, and you were merely engaging in illegal activity."

"Well, if you want to be technical." Kai sniffed, though he felt he had won through some terrible barrier. "But it's not as if I asked for money. It was to help Quinn."

"I know...oh, I know." Tenzin reached across the table and stroked his hair. "You are incorrigible, Kai Hiltas. The world must bend to your rules."

Kai managed a ghost of a smile. Having Tenzin touching him made him dizzy with joy. "Everyone except you, Tenzi. You are my anchor. My beacon. The only one who can tell me no."

"I wish it was the case," Tenzin said sadly, returning to his food. "Maybe I've had some influence, but you don't really listen to me either."

"Tenzi?"

"Yes?"

"I'm sorry. I'm terribly, horribly sorry for being such a terrible mate."

"I know, dear. Eat your dinner."

They did, and conversation became more constant, though still a bit stilted. Kai told him all that was happening in his department — the new hires, the help he now had, the way he was practicing how to delegate. See? He listened. He talked about Breon and about Victoria, how he was worried she would never blossom, and about the murders. Tenzin, as he so often did, mostly listened, though he did at least divulge that he was staying with friends.

The dinner was wonderful. The concert was lovely and Tenzin allowed Kai to lean against him when the lights went down. Though his fingers itched to do so, Kai never once reached for his phone. Not once, until they were getting back in a cab to take Tenzin to the AURA building, since he still refused to let Kai know where he was staying.

Still humming a tune from the concert, Kai pulled out the phone and froze. "Tenzi..."

"Let me guess. Work?"

"There's been another murder. There are eyewitnesses reporting a monster turned a street preacher to stone."

Tenzin nodded and leaned down to kiss him. "And you're going to send one of your people to the scene?"

"I... Tenzin...this is one of those times..." He couldn't finish the sentence. Tenzin had already pulled away.

"All right. I suppose I can't expect a full recovery overnight. Go, Kai. Because only you are competent enough, only you are skilled enough to do this."

"People are dying. I can't simply not be there."

The deep voice was gentler when Tenzin spoke again. "I know. This time, I think you're actually right. It doesn't make me resent the world less for taking you from me again."

Tenzin closed the cab door and the car drove off, weaving into the busy 24th Street traffic. Almost. He'd almost been there, almost managed a reconciliation.

He supposed that couldn't happen overnight either.

* * * *

"Captain." Cypria, their one griffin officer glided down to meet them as Quinn and Val exited his car. "We've isolated several of the less hysterical witnesses."

"Good. Same pattern as before?" Val strode toward the newest statue, a street preacher caught in mid-sermon, his hand still raised, pointing at the sky, his face contorted with rage.

"Not quite, sir." Cypria paced beside him. Unlike some of the larger male griffins, she was more compact, her head at eye level when she walked. Val's eye level, at least. "Murder by stone, yes. But this happened right in the open, on a crowded street."

"Who do we have questioning witnesses?"

"Mr. Hiltas insisted. He's over there." Cypria pointed with a wing and Quinn winced.

Kai was in one of his fancy suits, great for a wedding or some hoity-toity restaurant, but not for police work. *Came right from his date with Tenzin. Damn it.*

Val lengthened his stride to bring him to Kai, but the drow turned away from the witness in obvious frustration and came to them.

"At least they agree that it was large," he spat out in disgust.

"Do we have anything useful?" Val peered over at the witness, a middle-aged man in a trench coat, pale and visibly trembling.

"Precious little. Something large came out of that alley." Kai pointed to the dark passage between buildings. "It moved in a clumsy way, but somehow wasn't slow. It touched the preacher. The man turned to stone. But as for descriptions? I'm getting everything from a giant stone bull to a dragon to the devil himself."

"Do we have someone tracking?"

"I sent Wolfheart after it."

"Best choice. Alone?"

"He's on open channel. We can reach him quickly if he runs into trouble."

Val let out a slow breath. "Check with me first, will you, before you start giving orders?"

"Sorry. I'm sorry." Kai scrubbed both hands over his face. "If only I could've arrived here sooner."

"I only just got here myself. Stop that."

"I can try and find it. Now that we've got some idea what 'it' is," Quinn said. "Just let me talk to one of the witnesses for a minute."

Val nodded. "Which one is the least traumatized, Kai? The one who may actually recall something other than a panicked hallucination?"

"That one." Kai pointed to an older woman with a messenger bag slung over her shoulder and a fedora pulled tight on her head.

Quinn nodded and walked over to her.

"Hi, um, I hear you saw what happened?" he asked.

"I saw," the woman responded. "I already told them what I saw. Don't know if they believe me though."

"Can you tell me what you saw?" Quinn asked.

She narrowed her eyes at him. "What difference does it make, just look at all them notes the other one took."

"Well, I kinda wanted to hear it from the source," he said carefully. "I need to hear it from someone that actually saw. It'll help me track it." This was mostly true. He could still try just from Kai's notes, but unless the thing was giving off a truly evil vibe, he wasn't likely to find it, seeing as how he'd already tried.

The woman sighed. "It was big. About seven or eight foot. And about yay wide..." She held her arms out as wide as they would go. "Heavy. Gray. Looked like a statue come to life—an ugly statue. Like they have on churches and buildings, the old ones."

Quinn frowned at her. "You mean like a gargoyle?"

"Yes. That's exactly what I mean." She nodded once, decisively.

"All right. Anything else you can remember about it?"

"Yes. It didn't move like a normal...being. Like a living being would. Its joints were in the right place but it didn't bend them."

Quinn tried to picture that. It was an awfully specific description, so he tended to think it was accurate.

"Okay, thanks."

She waved him off as he turned around and headed back to Valerian and Kai.

"Did you hear all that?"

Of course they had. Elvish ears. Val nodded, "Yes, but I don't follow how that could be true. We certainly haven't had any living gargoyles come through any Events."

Kai stared at the woman, then fixed Quinn with a wide-eyed, anxious look. "No. We haven't. Quinn...from what we know, what does this say to you?"

Quinn shrugged. "I dunno. I mean...I'd guess maybe someone had...animated a gargoyle?" He stopped short of saying someone had brought one to life, because that just was too crazy. You couldn't bring stone to life. No one could.

"I've walked the crime scene, Quinn." Kai's voice was hushed and trembling. "The magical...signature we had from the receipt? It's nowhere near the victim. Would you like to know where it's lingering? In the mouth of that alley. We have someone of such enormous power that they can, as you say, animate stone and then direct it from the shadows and this mage does...this? Killing random victims without purpose?"

Quinn looked at the latest victim, taking in the long coat that looked ratty even in stone, and the bushy beard and wide crazy looking eyes. Had someone said he was a street preacher? Quinn could believe it. "Maybe. Maybe not. Maybe the victims aren't so random, or without purpose. Whoever it is seems to have some kind of problem with street people. That's pretty obvious. And not the quiet ones that just sit around and try to be invisible. Momma Cats was well known because she was always walking around talking to everyone about her cats. The guy with the guitar? I bet he wasn't just quietly singing to himself. And this dude, I mean you can't get much louder than these assholes. Right? So..."

That's where his train of thought apparently derailed because all of those things were true but he still didn't know how they were supposed to fit together or why anyone would kill them.

"Dangerous to draw lines where there may be none," Kai murmured. "But even if we make the assumption that we understand who the victims will be, how does this help us find them? Can you find them, Quinn? This gargoyle and his...creator? Controller?"

"I guess we'll find out," Quinn said.

Kai suggested Quinn go home, or to AURA headquarters to scry for the killers, but Quinn was feeling confident and he borrowed the backseat of a cruiser. He relaxed and closed his eyes and Kai opened the door.

"Quinn?"

"I can't do this if you keep talking to me, you know?" Quinn said.

"Perhaps you should have a circle for this," Kai suggested.

"Why? I didn't need one to find your cat. I just need to focus and—" He snapped his fingers. "Off I go."

"Yes, well. Be careful."

Quinn looked at him. "Why have you never told me to be careful before? Has Flax said something to you?"

Kai made an exasperated sound. "You're not tracking a cat! You're tracking a mage, one perhaps more powerful than anyone we have on staff. If he or she detects you, sees you as you scry, you could be in terrible danger."

Quinn snorted. "I doubt I'll be seen. No one's ever seen me before. Besides, even if they did see me or sense me, it's not like they can hurt me when my physical body is back here."

"And Tenzin says I never listen to anyone. Just watch yourself. Come back if there's any sign you've been seen. Quickly. No, most mages could *not* harm you on the spirit plane. But this mage...*this* mage brings stone to life. No one should be able to do that either."

"All right, all right. Just relax. I don't even know if I'll be able to find them anyway."

He ignored the huffy way Kai sighed and though he didn't slam the door, he did close it harder than was strictly necessary.

Quinn took a deep breath and let it out, then closed his eyes and tried to relax himself, now that Kai had got him all off his game with his 'be careful' talk. Damn it.

It took Quinn longer than it had been taking him lately to feel the sensation of floating free of his body, rising up high into the air. When he was finally looking down over the city spreading below, he had to take a few moments to focus. Gargoyle. He fixed the description the woman had given him firmly in his mind.

At first, he thought it wasn't enough, that it wasn't going to work. Maybe the mage was casting some kind of concealing magic. There was no telltale twinkle at the corner of his eye begging for attention. He turned slowly, started off in one direction, then another.

Gargoyle...a big stone gargoyle...walking around. How hard could it be to find?

He thought he saw a shimmer. It wasn't like the normal wink of light he got when he was looking for something, but it was something. He blinked and he went from one place to the other.

Total blackness engulfed him. He was conscious, he thought he was, but he couldn't see his hand in front of his face. He was totally blind. His chest hitched and he started to panic. He twisted his head, looking left, right, up, down. Nothing. He couldn't see. He reached out with his hands, hands that weren't even physical but the motion was instinctual, groping around in the dark. His heart hammered in his chest. Okay. He couldn't find them. Not like this. Fuck it, he was scared. He was going back.

Only, when he thought it, nothing happened. Now he was really freaked out. *Okay, okay, calm down...* Before he could even try to calm himself, try to reorient himself, something slammed into him from behind, like he'd taken a baseball bat to the back of the head. Stars exploded in his vision and he screamed, then he was falling, bile rising in his throat at the pain and the sickening drop. His body jerked as if he'd been hit with an electrical shock and he screamed when he was back in his body and he still couldn't see.

He heard the door beside him open and Val was there. He could smell Val before he started bellowing. "Quinn! Quinn, are you all right? Damn it, Kai! Do something!"

There was a crackling of magic, a sudden powerful surge and Kai's voice spoke through the static snapping. "I've thrown a circle round the car! You should be safe inside!"

Val's hands were on Quinn's face. "Quinn? Talk to me."

Quinn panted liked he'd just sprinted the quarter mile. He blinked, trying to get his eyes to work again. Val's hands burned on his cheeks. He gulped more air. "I'm gonna be sick..." He didn't know how he managed to spit the words out but Val turned him, opening the other door and Quinn hung his head out. The acid burned the back of his throat and his eyes watered but nothing came up. When he blinked his eyes open again, his vision was blurry with tears but he could see the asphalt and the side of the car.

"Okay, okay... I think I'm okay," Quinn whispered. He was shaking all over but he no longer felt like he might vomit.

Val threw a blanket over him and wrapped him up tight in his arms, rocking him for a moment. A strangled sound caught in Val's throat and he turned his head to bellow out the car door. "I want medical here, now! Hiltas! What's out there?"

A police radio crackled somewhere, an officer radioing back to headquarters. Kai called out from nearby, "Ether is clear, Captain. No imminent threats."

"Drop the circle, Kai. Let medical through when they land."

Quinn clung to Val, pushing his face into his chest and clutching at him. He needed him. Needed to feel him. He didn't think he'd ever been more afraid in his life, not even facing the lich queen. He felt wetness on his lips and wiped at it with the back of one hand, thinking it was just mucus but a bright red smear was on the back of his hand when he took it away.

"Uhh...shit. I couldn't see. I couldn't see anything, Val." He had meant to just describe what happened but his voice sounded strange to his own ears—too breathy, too fast.

"Easy, love. Your nose is bleeding." Val pinched his nose to try and stop the blood flow and stroked his hair, apparently not caring one bit that there was blood on his shirt. "You can see now, though?"

Quinn nodded against his shoulder.

Then Val was bellowing again. "I want a report from Wolfheart! More than immediately! And I want him back here! Where the hell is medical?"

Wings beat the air overhead, several sets, and suddenly Sinistrus stuck his head in the back of the cruiser. "Hey, kiddo! How are we doing here? Cap, can we maybe get him out of the car so I can see him better?"

Quinn heard him, looked right at the incubus paramedic and understood every word, but when he told his limbs to unbend and get out, he couldn't do it. His fingers tightened on the material of Val's shirt and he cringed. "C-can't." His teeth were chattering now. "I couldn't see anything."

"S'Okay hon." Sin put his medical satchel down and got out a penlight. "Cap, maybe put him on your lap and turn this way? There we go."

Sin actually winked at him, though his smile was gentle as he tucked his huge black wings in tight to his back and crouched beside them. He shone the light briefly in Quinn's eyes, making him flinch. Then he put his forehead against Quinn's, which, yeah, not normal for human medics, but most of Sin's magic came through touch.

"All right, you're a little on the shocky side. Think I can convince you to come back to Medical with me? Free griffin ride and everything. Or our handsome Captain can drive you. I mean, I understand if you don't wanna leave him. He's still got a stick up his butt, but he's hot as hell."

"No, it's okay," Quinn said softly. "He has stuff he has to do. I can go with you." He said the words reasonably, but then he just sat there on Val's lap, not moving.

"Okay, we'll get you a ride then," Sin said. "C'mon out, hon."

Quinn tried to. He actually scooted a half inch in that direction, and he started to shake all over again. His hand was wrapped around Val's arm and he couldn't make himself let go. "I-I can't. No." He backpedaled, turning his torso so he could wrap his arms around Val's neck and cling to him again.

"Got it. More than a little shocky," Sin said quietly. "Cap, maybe hang onto him and bring him in soon as you can."

"I think that's best," Val murmured, though he did manage to turn Quinn far enough so Sin could help with the nosebleed.

"Captain!" Cypria winged down to them. Damn street was full of wings. "Wolfheart is on his way back. He reports hitting a 'blank spot' during tracking. A place where he suddenly couldn't think straight and couldn't move forward. He's coming in now."

Across the street, Flax staggered out of the alley, and medical pounced on him as well, though he didn't look as bad off as Quinn felt. Maybe he hadn't been outside his body, at least.

"Something hit me, when I couldn't see," Quinn said, remembering. He was struggling not to fall apart but he felt pummeled from all directions, physically and emotionally. When he started to shake again and felt panic rising, he turned his face into the crook of Val's neck and breathed deep. That helped. That helped a lot. He took several deep breaths and felt the panic ebb. As long as Val had him, he would be okay.

"I'm sorry I couldn't find them."

"Hush, none of that," Val murmured against his hair. "I'm just grateful you're here. Never mind the rest right now. I don't understand how something could hit you without a body, though."

"I don't know either. But I think that's what knocked me back into my body. I tried to get back to myself, a- and I couldn't." That terror was fresh enough to make his throat tighten and his teeth clench.

"Captain, I think he should be sedated," Sin suggested quietly.

"Quinn?" Val questioned gently.

Quinn thought he should say no. Everything was chaos right now and he might be needed. That thought was absurd. He didn't think he could help sharpen a pencil right now. He couldn't even make himself let go of Val, who actually was needed and if he couldn't have Val, he didn't want to be able to think about it. He'd rather just be knocked out.

He nodded slowly, not lifting his head from Val's shoulder.

"Gonna hurt you more than it does me," Sin warned as he wiped down a bit of Quinn's arm with alcohol and stuck the needle in. "Just a nice warm blanket to help you sleep, okay?"

Quinn nodded again as warm fuzzies overran his body. Val was talking. Someone was lifting him, and that was it.

* * * *

For a brief moment, Val wanted nothing more than to forget his responsibilities and simply hold Quinn. Something terrifying had happened out there, and he had no way to protect Quinn from it. His sword was no use against things in the spirit realm. Reluctantly, he handed Quinn's limp frame off to Sin.

"Make sure he's not alone." Val hadn't meant the tone to be so abrupt, but he was still reeling from Quinn's scream.

"Not for a second." Sin got a better grip on Quinn and hurried back to his team where the aerial stretcher waited. Some distant part of Val's mind registered how serious and professional Sin was when he needed to be—not something he ever would have expected from an ex-con and ex-promiscuous troublemaker.

He shook his head and strode over to where several officers surrounded Flax, who sat on the curb with his head on his knees and his right arm tucked close. All of his people were jumpy, edgy, scanning the shadows, and Val couldn't blame them one bit.

"Are you hurt?" Val crouched down in front of Flax with a hand on his shoulder.

"No, sir." Flax shook his head without raising it. "Yes. Sort of. Don't feel so good. Arm's numb."

"He ran across some sort of barrier field, sir," Cypria filled in the blanks. "Tried to reach past it. He's shaken pretty bad. Said he felt like his brain was melting."

The medevac team lead, a huge, golden griffin, shouldered his way through. "Captain, I think he needs to come with us, as well."

Flax finally raised his head. Even with glazed eyes and a face pale as milk, he protested, "I'm fine, Captain. Please. I don't need—"

"Go with Hal. No arguments. You've done what you could here." Val took his arm and helped him up onto Hal's back. "And don't fall off on the way."

In a flurry of wings, the medevac crew took off again, leaving Val to deal with the NYPD and the rest of the mess on the ground. He advised, as strongly as possible, that all precincts put out a 'do not approach' order. If anyone spotted the gargoyle, following at a safe distance might be helpful, but no one was to attempt to make contact or to detain.

The whole evening disturbed Val profoundly. None of it made sense — not the deaths themselves, not the agent of the murders and certainly not the nature of the mage in question, who might or might not be the powerful entity in the mix.

Once again, Kai was supervising the loading of a formerly human statue into one of the AURA vans. While he didn't have the lost, drowning look he'd had the night they'd found the busker, he still seemed...reduced, less than he should be.

"Are we clearing the scene, Captain?" Kai asked as Val came to stand beside him.

"We are. Go home, Kai. You know you won't get anything useful from the statue."

Kai nodded, chewing on his lower lip as he did when he was distressed.

"Did you ruin your date with Tenzin?"

"Not entirely." Kai shot him a guarded look, then pulled in a sharp breath. "It was, actually, a lovely evening. We had left the concert hall before I saw the call. But he was still annoyed at me for rushing off."

"I'm sorry. Though this time, I was glad you were here."

Kai sniffed in offense. "You should always be glad I'm here to offer my expertise."

"Of course. How could I misspeak so dreadfully?" Val smiled and bumped his shoulder against Kai's. "Go home. I mean it. You're just starting to look healthy again."

A bare few months ago, Kai would have responded with real offense, brittle and nasty. Now he simply nodded and patted Val's arm. He turned to go but then turned back.

"Don't let Quinn go looking for our suspects, Valerian. When he wakes up, he'll want to try again. Forbid it if you have to," Kai told him.

"I'll... I'm not sure I can prevent it, but I'll do my best."

There wasn't much more Val could accomplish, either, but he certainly wasn't going home. He got back behind the wheel and drove to AURA, desperate to get to Quinn.

* * * *

Sulking probably wouldn't help. Worrying wasn't much better. Flax sat in the bed in the emergency section of Medical and tried to piece together what had happened. The trail of almost magical scent, that puzzling, barely there trail and the stranger trail of moving granite. He'd managed to follow them for several blocks. Somewhere in there, he'd gotten too close, maybe, or the weird field might have been a protection this person, mage, monster — whatever — always had up.

Dr. Nagi, one of the few goblin doctors in the city, tapped her tablet screen. "I want to keep you for observation, Officer. The numbness concerns me — and the dizziness. We may be looking at neural damage."

"Great, doc, thanks? But can't I just rest at home?"

"You have no one there to watch over you. The only emergency contact you have in your files is the department dispatch number."

"Oh."

"Is there someone we should call for you?"

Who the hell would care? Goddesses, I hate this world sometimes and how often you get to be reminded you're alone. Then he had a thought, one born of his leftover panic. "I...I have a number. Could someone call Ash Bloodroot for me? Um, see if he's willing to, you know, collect me?"

"Write it down. We'll call. If he doesn't come, you're stuck with us for the night." Dr. Nagi waited until he'd scribbled the number on the paper she offered. "In the meantime, you can be useful and keep someone else company who shouldn't be alone."

That statement puzzled Flax until they wheeled him into a clinic room where Quinn lay on the other bed, out cold. *Ah. Got it. Well, at least if the kid wakes up, we can compare notes.*

Flax watched him sleeping, his skin pale against the sheet. He had known what Quinn was doing was dangerous. Maybe now he would take more caution. What was that drow thinking, letting him go after a mage that powerful with no protection? Did he want to get rid of him? But that made no sense, seeing the trouble he'd gone through to find someone to teach him, to keep him safe. He supposed he was as much to blame as Kai for Quinn lying in a drugged sleep now. He had warned him, but he should have been firmer about it. If he had died, Valerian would have been crushed.

Even as he thought it, Flax felt guilty. He shouldn't only think in terms of how his death would have affected Valerian. He might not be close to Quinn, but he was trying to change that.

Not too much later, a soft tap on the jamb of the open door interrupted his musings. Ash stood there, tall and willowy, his hair braided neatly down his back. A step or two behind him was Sage.

A rush of warmth suffused him to see them, gratitude and mortification all in one combo package. "Oh, hey. Thanks for coming." His throat tightened and he felt like a child suddenly, close to tears for no good reason. Instead, he forced a smile. "I'm sorry to drag you out here, but the doc said I had to give her someone's name."

Ash moved into the room with a smooth grace that was uncanny, even for an elf. He went right to Flax, pulling his head to his chest and bending to kiss the top of his hair. "What have you been doing, my hunter? Your color looks faded."

That *my hunter* sounded kind of nice, and wasn't that the stupidest thing he'd ever thought? What was wrong with him that he only reacted to males who belonged to someone else? Flax pulled in a slow breath and let it out again before he trusted himself to speak. "Hunting monsters. It did something I've never seen before, and got away from me while I was..." While he was what? Panicking? Disabled? Completely disoriented? "Um, distracted."

"Mm. You should stay away from this monster." Ash advised in such a way that said without saying that he didn't expect to be listened to in the least. He started to hum softly, almost under his breath, while his fingers gently glided along Flax's hair. Warmth started to trickle through Flax, making him realize he had been awfully cold.

"What's wrong with the boy?" Sage asked as he moved up closer.

"Same monster." Flax shivered and Ash's arms closed tighter around him. *Goddess, it feels wonderful to be held.* Not that he would admit to feeling steadier and safer in Ash's embrace. "I was chasing it in the physical realm. Quinn was chasing it on the spirit plane. His encounter was obviously worse than mine."

"He's a spirit walker?" Sage asked, not a trace of his usual disdain in his tone. He hadn't taken his eyes off Quinn and looked like he was studying him carefully.

"He got closer to your quarry," Ash said, not making it a question. "How powerful is the medicine they gave to make him sleep? Sleep is good for the initial healing, but he needs to have his spirit grounded — and soon."

Flax glanced from one to the other, trying to keep up with the conversation. "He is. He did. I don't know."

A violent shiver started at his numb shoulder and raced through him. Ash pulled him in tighter, running a hand down the numb and aching arm. How those two things could happen at once, he didn't know, but yeah, arm non-responsive plus bone-deep ache. At Ash's touch, the pain subsided.

"Oh, that feels so good. You don't even know." Flax tried to relax. He did. It just wasn't happening yet. "Quinn came back blinded and panicked. Something awful happened out there. They had to sedate him to get him out of the car. I really don't know how long he'll be out. I guess we could ask one of the med folks when they come in."

"No, it won't matter. He will wake when he wakes." Ash still caressed Flax gently. "I take it the healers you have don't do spirit healing?" He didn't wait for Flax to answer, probably because if they did, he wouldn't have to ask. "I can help him while he is still asleep. You as well, if you will lie beside him."

"Would you? That would be... Thank you. You're amazing." Flax really didn't want to leave Ash's arms, but he forced himself to sit up. "We do have one spirit healer on staff, but Tenzin's not here right now."

Carefully, with Sage rushing forward to wrap strong arms around him, Flax made his way to the other bed and stretched out with Quinn. "Like this?"

"Closer is better," Ash said.

Sage helpfully lifted Quinn's head and shoulders until Flax scooted closer and laid him back so his head was on Flax's good shoulder.

"Good. Now just close your eyes and relax. I will sing to your spirits, and they will settle more peacefully," Ash said.

Sage must have assisted him before because he moved without being asked to the opposite side of the bed and planted his feet as if on guard. When Ash started to sing softly, Sage joined him, his deeper voice making a lovely harmony.

It was like melting into a river of warmth. Flax felt muscles relax that he'd forgotten he had. The sharp, sick feeling of panic faded, flowing down that warm river of rainbow-colored light. Maybe it should've felt weird to hold Quinn in his arms, but it didn't. Comfort, shared heat, shared pain, these were what he received from the contact.

The sedative was probably too powerful for Quinn to fight free of it already, but he must have been aware on some level because he snuggled into Flax's side like a puppy seeking warmth. Flax could feel his body relaxing as well, although it wasn't really a physical thing he could measure.

The ache and numbness in his arm started to ease and Flax's eyes drooped drowsily. Ash and Sage both moved. Still singing, they touched gently along their bodies, Sage stroking his fingers lightly along Flax's arm and Ash brushing his feather soft over Quinn's hair.

"Thank you," Flax whispered as he let his head sink back against the pillow.

He was just drifting off when a sharp voice came from the doorway. "What's this, then?"

Oh, shit. Val's here. Even with that thought zinging through his brain, he couldn't quite wake up enough to move away.

Sage tensed, ready to protect, but the reaction seemed automatic rather than him detecting any real threat in Valerian.

Ash removed his hand from Quinn's brow but looked completely unruffled. "A healing, Tesined Valerian," he answered, as if it should be obvious.

The sound from the doorway put Flax in mind of a bull about to charge. When Val spoke again, his voice was soft but tense. "While I thank you for your efforts, I would very much appreciate being *asked* before anyone lays hand or anything else on my Quinn."

"Sir, I didn't—" Flax started to protest.

"Shh." Val waved a hand to cut him off. "You're hardly in any shape to think sensibly right now, pup. Lie there a moment and get your bearings."

At least he would be keeping all his limbs and his head. That was a good thing. Slowly, Flax disentangled himself. "It wasn't anything more, Captain."

There was a charge in the air, a tension that wasn't there a minute before as the four elves stood and faced one another. Flax fought returning shivers, while Sage looked uncertain and Valerian was scowling. Only Ash still looked calm. At last Valerian broke the bubble of tension by sighing.

"I know there was nothing more, or you wouldn't be standing there with your arms still attached to your body."

Ash grinned at this, completely unabashed, before he sobered again. "I could see that your *kalesi* was in distress, Tesined. Whatever manner of creature he came across in the spirit realm left him...ajar—like his spirit was not at ease within him. He should be fine now."

Flax's knees chose that moment to buckle and three sets of hands shot out to catch him, though he ended up supported against Val's side. The captain shook his head in an exasperated way, put him back in his own bed and turned back to Ash with a calmer expression. "I thank you. Truly. He was so frightened he forgot how to command his own body when he returned. I have no shame in telling you I was frightened as well."

Ash tilted his head in a little bow of acknowledgment. "The spirit realm is a dangerous place, frightening even for those who know it well. You should rest with him, Tesined. There is no better healing for him now than the comfort of his *kalesi*. Sage and I will take Flax home and tend to him there."

A twinge caught in Flax's chest as Val bent over Quinn and kissed him, oh, so tenderly. "Best advice of the whole damn day," Val said with a weary chuckle.

He threw his coat over a chair and kicked off his shoes, while Sage and Ash flanked Flax on either side and got him moving. Maybe he shouldn't have looked back. He really shouldn't have. The sight of Val curled protectively around Quinn, the contented smile on the human's face, nearly took him out again. A little bit of jealousy, he understood. He'd had a desperate thing for Val since the first time he'd seen him. But this terrible gray pall sending out roots deep inside him? *It's happening. I didn't think it ever would to me. The fading's started.*

He shivered, leaning against Ash. It would take time. He had time before it reached a level of despair so great his heart would stop. Years, probably. He'd just never thought he really needed anyone.

* * * *

Despite the fact that Flax had been living in his current apartment for a little over two years and Ash and Sage had only just been assigned their temporary housing, they still had managed to make the place feel more lived in, more like a home, than Flax's apartment. Since the last time he had seen them, they had been busy. Plants of all sorts in pots of all sizes occupied windowsills and the end tables, crouched in corners and even hung from the ceiling.

The furniture in the living room had been rearranged so that one corner was empty except for a bamboo mat and a knot of wood in the process of being shaped into something.

Flax took these changes in at a glance as he cradled his arm and Ash ushered him inside.

"I really appreciate you coming for me." Flax propped himself up against the wall beside the kitchen. He'd managed the short taxi ride without much more than a headache and had stood on his own two feet on the elevator, but now the damn floor decided to play games, bucking and twisting.

"I didn't know…" Flax's voice trembled and he let the thought trail off. *I didn't have anyone else to call* sounded too damn pitiful.

"We take care of our own," Sage said, putting a hand on Flax's uninjured shoulder.

"Of course we would come for you," Ash added.

Flax dredged up a smile. He thought he found one, anyway, before the room decided to tip on its ear. One moment he stood, the next he stared up at Ash, a strange humming in his ears. Oh, there was concern in those beautiful eyes, and something that approached pain. Had he done something? Said something? But the momentary worry vanished and Flax told himself he'd imagined it.

"What happened?"

"You seemed to be having trouble staying on your feet, so Sage carried you in here," Ash told him. "How do you feel? Still light-headed?"

The whole time he spoke, Ash stroked gentle fingers up and down Flax's arm, barely touching him, but still Flax could feel the tingle reaching from Ash's fingertips into his aching muscles.

Before he could answer, Sage appeared in the door, carrying a mug that had an absolutely delicious herbal aroma.

"Since I don't seem to be on speaking terms with the floor yet, I guess the answer's yes." Flax scooted toward the head of the bed and tried sitting up, with Ash helping and fussing to stuff pillows behind him. Damn, he'd never felt so spoiled.

Sage sat down on the edge of the bed and handed him the steaming mug. "This should help," he said.

A smile of thanks and a sip were all Flax could manage since his throat had closed up. *Stupid, getting so emotional about someone simply being kind.* He supposed it was the leftover shock, residual effects of whatever evil magic he'd smacked into that evening. Ginger, peppermint, chamomile...maybe a hint of mistletoe, and where Ash had found that in the middle of New York, he had no idea. But he sipped and snuggled back and felt...better.

"I'm keeping you from things." He patted Ash's hand. "I'll be all right here."

Ash hesitated, then stood. "Just call if you need anything," he said, and kissed Sage, brushing his fingers through his hair on his way out. Sage didn't follow him.

"It would make him feel better if you stayed tonight," Sage said. "He's worried about you."

"Well, we can't have that." Flax shot him a grin, hoping it didn't look too ghastly. "Don't think I'm going anywhere right now, don't worry."

"Are you in a lot of pain? Is there anything we can do for you?" Sage asked.

"It's bearable now. I feel ridiculous, having to be coddled like this." *But it's really nice. And I shouldn't be enjoying it this much.* "You busy? Want to climb in here with me for a bit?"

Sage smiled and took the cup from him to set within easy reach on the night table, then slid down beside him. "What else do I have to do? I'm sorry you were injured but it's nice to have someone to 'coddle'. It makes me feel useful."

"Glad to be of service, citizen," Flax said in a too-serious voice, then ruined it by laughing. He slid his uninjured arm under Sage's shoulders and pulled him close, nuzzling at his throat. "Mmm, you're so warm."

Sage tangled his legs with Flax's and put his arms around him, snuggling back. After a few moments, he turned his head to kiss Flax, nothing demanding or even overtly sexual, just a soft kiss, like you would give to your lover before bed or upon waking, comfort and pleasure and unity all conveyed in the simple touch of lips to lips.

Flax closed his eyes as he burrowed closer, his head resting in the crook of Sage's throat. Odd whispers of guilt nagged at him, that he should be up and doing something, that he shouldn't be taking up so much of his friends' time, but his exhausted body took the whispers by the elbow, shoved them out of the door and told them not to call. Warm and secure in Sage's arms, damn it, he needed this. He wasn't moving until he felt like he could face the world again.

Chapter Eleven

Quinn woke slowly, his head groggy, and that was the only reason he didn't jump when he didn't immediately recognize where he was. That, and the heavy, familiar weight of Val's arm wrapped around him, the warmth pressed to his back and his breath stirring his hair. If Val was sleeping beside him, he was safe. Funny how he'd never known how unsafe he'd always felt until Val showed him what it was not to have to be constantly on guard.

He still didn't know where he was, but he was warm and comfortable and still sleepy and so he closed his eyes again and just drifted.

"Quinn?" Val whispered sleepily. "Are you awake?"

"Mm? Sort of," Quinn murmured back. His arm was on top of Val's and he moved his hand to cover Val's hand where it was resting on his ribs just over his heart.

Val nestled closer and nuzzled at Quinn's hair. "You scared several decades off my life last night, love."

"Believe me. I scared myself just as much," Quinn said, then after a moment added, "I'm sorry I scared you."

"My heart, my own." Val sighed and stretched. "You need to tell me exactly what happened. And then you need to listen to all the elves who tell me what you're doing is horribly dangerous."

Quinn really didn't want to relive all the details, but he knew the longer he waited, the more likely it would be that he would forget something, and who knew what might be important or not? What might point them in the right direction?

He pushed his fingers in between Val's and curled them around his palm, holding his hand and pressing his arm in place around him.

"I kept the description of the creature the woman described in my head, and I went looking. Everything was normal at first. I rose up above the city and cast around. I didn't see any lights, no twinkles to tell me where it was, but I saw something blurry, out of place, so I told my conscious self to go there and…I moved and everything went black. No light. No sound except my own breath. I think I was cold, but I started to panic so fast that it's hard to tell. I didn't know which way was up or down and I tried to abandon ship, so to speak, and go back to myself, but I couldn't. I was just stuck there, blind…so I started to feel my way, and then something hit the back of my head so hard I saw stars, and I was back in my body."

He could feel Val tense behind him. "How could something hit your head when it wasn't a physical head?" Warrior, good with wind and fire, Val had never left his body in his life. Quinn understood why he sounded so out of his element.

"I don't know. I felt it, though." That was all the explanation Quinn could give. He had no idea how to interact with the world when he wasn't in his body. He could look but he couldn't touch things or move them, so how could he know how someone else had done it? Maybe they hadn't. "Maybe it was some kind of spell, and that's just how it manifested."

"Perhaps." Val hugged him tight. "I hear the shift changing. I should probably get up and try to get presentable for the squad room. If the doctors say it's all right, you should think about talking to Kai. And…ah, continuing your lessons."

Quinn dropped his shoulder and wriggled around so he was facing Val. "Don't go yet." He kissed Val's lips softly.

"Quinn…" But Val cupped his face and returned the kiss with a hint of heat. "Five more minutes."

Quinn didn't waste time arguing for more time, he was pretty sure he could convince Val to stay longer without any words at all. Then again, they might not need more than five minutes.

He pressed his lips back to Val's and trailed his hand down his chest. He hadn't stripped completely before getting into bed but a flick-flick of his fingers and he had Val's fly undone and he slid his hand inside.

"You're trying to get me thrown out of the clinic," Val whispered against Quinn's shoulder, a grunt obviously standing in for a stifled moan. Despite his protests, he pulled the blanket up around them and shoved the scrubs someone had put Quinn in down to the bottom curve of his ass.

Quinn kissed along his jaw and the tender skin below his chin, nipping with his lips covering his teeth when he reached just above his Adam's apple. He pushed his fingers deeper, then skated along Val's thickening shaft and pulled him free of his trousers.

"If we're quiet, no one will know," Quinn whispered over his collarbone.

Val chuckled, the deep sound more of a turn on than any dirty talking. "I'll do my best." His long fingers closed around Quinn's cock, thumb stroking gently along the underside.

Quinn shivered, even though he was toasty warm. The pleasure that trickled down into his groin felt almost ticklish. He brought his mouth back to Val's lips, kissing him deeply this time, his tongue pressing between Val's lips while his hand stroked him. He flexed his hips, pushing his stiffening cock into the curl of Val's fingers and rocking back and forth.

Normally, Val talked during sex. A lot. This time, he buried his face against Quinn's neck, breathing hard through what sounded like clenched teeth as Quinn tightened his grip. Val threw a leg over Quinn's hip, giving him better access to whatever he wanted.

It probably would have been smarter to stop and have Val take his pants off so they didn't leave any incriminating evidence on them if he was going right to work, but stopping what they were doing for any reason was the farthest thing from Quinn's mind. This wasn't going to take long anyway. It never did first thing in the morning when they were still relaxed and sleepy, not the first time around anyway.

Quinn stroked his hand up and down Val's thick shaft, his thumb swiping over the crown with each up stroke and squeezing tighter on each down stroke. He pulled his cock away from his body slightly so he could press the head to his own throbbing erection, mingling the slickness of their pre-cum. He was breathing as hard as Val was now, panting as he kissed his cheek and toward his ear.

A soft growl vibrated the bed and Val wrapped his larger hand around both cocks, speeding the strokes, growling incessantly as Quinn started to lick at his ear.

Quinn brought his now-free hand up to Val's chest, flicking his thumb rapidly back and forth over his nipple. He could feel his balls starting to tighten and draw up already. It just felt so amazing to rub the underside of his shaft against Val's while he jerked them off.

"Uuh...oohh..." He kept the little sounds that escaped him a bare whisper and they sounded almost fragile. He kissed the delicate, sensitive ridge of Val's ear, sighing over the dips and curves. "Ohh, Val, I'm so close..." He hardly breathed the words.

Still Val shushed him, tenderly, as if the act of asking for quiet was sensuous on its own. He closed his lips over Quinn's, panting through his nose against Quinn's skin as he speared his tongue into Quinn's mouth, his movements demanding, possessive. Val's hips jerked erratically, his moans barely muffled in their passionate kiss.

With the hand half-trapped beneath them, Val twitched the sheet up over their twinned cocks, shuddering against Quinn as he came. The hot, wet splash that hit his skin was more than enough to tip Quinn. He sucked at Val's tongue and lips, squeezing his eyes shut and the groan of pleasure he would have normally released came out only a soft gasp into Val's mouth. He could feel his own heart beating in his throat, strong, steady and fast, then Val's joining his, washing the rest of the world away.

Val released his lips, nuzzling under Quinn's jaw. "I needed that so very badly."

"Mmm...yeah." Quinn purred. He opened his eyes and tipped his head forward until their foreheads touched. "I love you."

Val's breath hitched. "I love you, too. Please be safe today."

Quinn kissed the bridge of his nose and his lips and his chin, then pulled back enough to look at him. "What do you mean?"

"I mean don't do anything that's going to stop my heart today."

Quinn gave him a crooked grin. "You're afraid to tell me you don't want me to go looking again, aren't you?" He said it with absolutely no accusation in his voice. "Don't worry, Val. I may not be the brightest bulb in the box, but that scared the shit out of me more than I even know how to describe. I'm not going looking for that thing again anytime soon, I promise you."

"Good." Val searched his face and finally gave him a soft kiss. "Good. I'd better at least pull a comb through my hair before I go down. There won't be any hiding what we've been up to from certain people, but I don't think I care."

Quinn's grin widened and turned mischievous. He might feel weird about people knowing his business just by getting a whiff of him, but if he didn't have to look them in the eye himself, he didn't mind so much. In fact, Val smelling like sex to half the squad room was kinda hot. Okay, he had better stop those thoughts or Val was never going to get to work.

With a little grunt, Val heaved himself up, checked to make certain his uniform pants had escaped any stains and gave Quinn a last kiss before he swaggered off. Oh, yeah. He swaggered. A wolf whistle sounded out in the hall and Quinn had to snicker when he heard Sin call out, "Way to make the best use of the patient rooms, Captain!"

* * * *

The research team sat wide-eyed at their desks that morning. Kai knew this wasn't the normal order of things—or hadn't been—but he wasn't going to apologize for sweeping in on them like a storm first thing in the morning. If they didn't come prepared to work, they didn't need to be here.

"Jordie, I want a spell developed to enhance that security footage from the fast food place." He rapped Jordie's desk as he strode past.

"But, sir—"

"No excuses. Rudy can help you." Kai paced farther into the room to the next terrified employee. "Terrence, you're on the street. Keep your ears open, mind listening. If you hear any whiff of anything off, even if it's a blank spot in the ether where none should be, you call in."

The big lug nodded, tight-jawed but with a gleam of determination in his eyes.

"Victoria!" Kai called out as he strode to her desk in the corner. "You're working with Sterling today. Magical sweep of city Internet addresses."

She actually gave him a shy smile. "What are we looking for, sir?"

"Evil, my dear. We are looking for evil. If you build your programs correctly, you'll know it when you see it."

Sterling gave him a salute, then his fingers were already flying over the keys as Vicki rolled her chair over to join him. Kai gave him a nod. He had no need to worry about that one. When he made his way to his office, Mindy was grinning at him.

"What? Are you one of those Cheshire cats now?" Kai scowled at her.

"I like the new you, boss."

"Oh?"

"Look at 'em in there." Mindy nodded at the flurry of activity in the main Research room. "You provided them with purpose, Mr. H."

That gave him pause. Is that what he'd been doing all this time? Robbing his employees of purpose? Making them feel not at all valued? He gave Mindy the usual sniff but shook his head at himself as he went to his desk. He was a fool. How could he have lived so long and still be such a fool?

Kai sat down at his laptop and for the next hour focused on the work that needed doing outside of the tasks he'd already assigned, and found that it went remarkably smoothly when he wasn't trying to do ten things at once. He was nearly ready to start on the architectural grid he was planning to map when Mindy buzzed his phone.

"Quinn is here to see you, Mr. H."

"Please send him in." He probably should leave standing orders to let Quinn in whenever he came up. Next time he went out there...

Quinn opened the door and Kai looked up, noting that he still looked rather pale but otherwise okay. He certainly smelled recovered.

"Hey...I've got an idea," Quinn said.

It was tempting to say something about Val's scent, but Kai managed to force it back. "Tell me. Any idea at the moment, I'll entertain, no matter how improbable."

"Thanks for the vote of confidence." Quinn rolled his eyes.

"I didn't mean that." Kai ran a hand back over his braid. "Truly improbable ideas are often the most ingenious."

Quinn's eyes were positively in danger of rolling out of his head if he kept doing that.

"Okay, so, you got that little scrap of paper that had the trace of magic on it, or I should say, the trace of non-magic on it. I figure if the guy is paranoid enough to cast a Romulan cloaking shield on a piece of paper, it's likely that he'd try and erase any traces of his magic from me after I came into contact with it. Only he'd have to use a lot bigger dose on me, so maybe you can crack it and get inside the fucker's head."

Kai knew his mouth was hanging open. Carefully, he closed it and was horrified that the first thing that leaped out was, "You watch *Star Trek*?"

Breon chose that moment to meow at him, allowing him to regain a grain of sanity. "Perhaps I can trace it at that. Oh, this should be interesting."

"There's just one thing though." Quinn said. "Val says I can't do anything today that will give him a heart attack, so if it's going to be dangerous, we should wait until tomorrow."

"I will endeavor not to give the captain a coronary," Kai said dryly. "No, we'll concentrate on the traces left on you and I'll go looking. Discreetly. Carefully."

He rose and held out his arms to Breon, who leaped into them. "We'll go to one of the holding rooms. Unlike some young, wild mages, I need a circle—and my laptop."

Quinn looked at him hard for a moment, but if he sensed any sort of rebuke about using a circle, he kept his mouth shut. Would wonders never cease?

"Let's go," was all Quinn said.

Kai closed his laptop, let Breon climb onto his shoulders and tucked the machine under his arm as he strode out. Poor office wasn't getting much use today. "Mindy, we'll be in holding room five. Standard protocol. Have someone check in an hour." He was about to stalk past when he stopped and backed up. "Oh, yes. And whenever Quinn comes looking for me, let him come right in. Unless I'm in the middle of an employee, ah, evaluation." He stopped again. "Or with Tenzin."

"On my discretion, Mr. H. Got it." The girl had the audacity to wink at Quinn. If she hadn't been the best admin in the known universe, she would have been fired a hundred times daily.

Quinn wiggled his eyebrows at her when he thought he couldn't see him, and Kai barely kept from telling them both to stop acting like children—as if it would do any good. At least Quinn kept up when he stalked off again.

"Something bothering you?" Quinn asked, as Kai reached the door.

Kai lifted an eyebrow. "Why do you ask?"

"'Cause you seem huffier than usual."

"I have no idea what you mean." Kai stiffened his spine, eyes forward. "Though some people might find it unprofessional to come to work reeking of elf captain."

"I didn't have time to run home and take a shower," Quinn said defensively. "And I didn't know if showering would, you know, wash off any of the magic hiding stuff."

Kai opened the door and stepped in and Quinn followed him. He didn't look exactly shamefaced but

Kai could see the extra color on his neck and around his ears.

"Is it really that bad?" Quinn asked.

Humans and their deficient sense of smell. "It's noticeable to any elf you might pass at perhaps twenty yards. And to me. And probably most non-human species." Kai couldn't help a tiny grain of satisfaction at discomfiting Quinn just a bit. Petty revenge, yes, but parading his successful, sex-filled relationship in front of those who were forcibly celibate? Kai couldn't feel too badly.

"All right, all right, I get it. I stink. I'll go home as soon as we're done here," Quinn said, and Kai noted the red color had crept up to his cheeks.

Kai cleared his throat softly. "Quinn…it's not *stink*. It's a heady scent. Some might see it as, ah…" He struggled for a human equivalent. They didn't openly issue sexual challenge. "A bit in your face?"

Quinn just looked at him blankly.

It was hard not to smack his face with his palm. Kai stopped, back against the open door and fixed Quinn with a hard stare. "Sex. Val. Lots of it. Often. And it's obviously enjoyable, the scent says. Screams. And some of us are living alone. Do you really need to ask why I'm a bit, as you say, huffy?"

Quinn dropped his gaze and now his face was positively scarlet. "Oh, um… I didn't… I mean, I'm not trying to flaunt it or anything. Geez."

The snort was automatic, but Kai shook his head and continued into the room. "Just something to be aware of. Moving on." He indicated a stool in the center of the room. "If you could sit there, I'm going to cast us a circle. Mostly a precaution, but it helps me as well."

Quinn sat on the padded bar stool and mercifully let the subject of what he smelled like go.

"I could cast the circle if you want, so you can just focus on looking for trace," Quinn said.

"Thank you, but the circle is, shall we say, part of my process. Not everyone can walk out of their bodies as you do. Every mage with a finding talent operates in his or her own way. I need a circle, with my energy in it, and I need a program. The code helps me...focus."

"How did you do it before you had a computer?" Quinn asked.

The question engendered a wave of anger and sorrow, but it was old. Distant. Maybe at one point, he would never have considered answering, but Quinn needed to understand that magic took many different shapes. "I... Before I came here, I had a bond mate. The love of my life. Since childhood. Terik was brash and bold. Never hesitated to say what he thought, never..."

He had to stop and close his eyes. Perhaps the pain wasn't as distant as he'd thought. "He was the matrix I used for certain spells. His blood, his life, the rhythms of it, the mathematical beauty of it... He was a vessel for my work and the strength that kept me safe. Not so different from a well constructed program, in some ways."

"I'm sorry," Quinn said simply, but Kai could tell it was sincere. It was not his fault of course, but Kai understood humans used this particular phrase of apology also as a way to express empathy.

He waved a hand. "It was a long time ago now—a different lifetime. I only tell you so you understand that I do not simply sit down and fly out of my body as you do or picture the world as a forest to hunt through as Flax does. Or even spirit walk through meditation as Tenzin does. We all come to it in our own way."

"Right," Quinn said, apparently eager to steer the conversation on to more immediate topics. "So, do you want me to do anything? Or just sit here?"

"Just sit there and be your charming self," Kai said in his driest voice.

Quinn shot him another of those looks of his, the one that said he was trying hard not to release several choice profanities. Good. That was better than the sympathetic looks.

"Breon, please go in the circle with Quinn." Kai was about to settle with his laptop when a flurry of wings stirred the air overhead. The traitorous pack of flower fairies twittered invective at Kai before they dropped a packet on his head and winked out again.

"Ow. How many times must I apologize?" The packet was from Tenzin, though, and contained an invitation, more of a demand that Kai join him in the third floor atrium for lunch. Despite his flower fairy-induced irritation, Kai's heart thudded and skittered on the realization that Tenzin was willing to make the next move.

"I thought they liked you," Quinn muttered.

"They left with Tenzin, saying I had made him cry. Which might be so, but they had no right to take sides."

"Guess Brianna figured she did." Damn the boy, mimicking Kai's dry delivery.

Kai ignored him and settled in, casting his circle around cat and human. Breon wouldn't help with the spell, but he would act as a barometer for dark intentions. Relaxed cat equaled safe Quinn.

The spell matrix booted up and Kai sank into the coding, the perfect beauty of the logical system surrounding him and clearing his mind. Quinn shone as a shining nexus at the center of the matrix, a mass of bright, ever-shifting code. Mostly bright. Amorphous, dark anomalies blighted the otherwise vibrant hues. Some of these were part of Quinn, integral to the coding. Others…odd bits of out of place, dangling code did not belong. Kai concentrated on those.

He sank further into the spell matrix, chasing these strange bits out, following the trail toward the source. A hot trail, still connected to the source would have been dangerous, but this trail had cooled. He followed the dark strands, the whispering, hissing threads. Even at this distance, they frightened him, the malignant, angry feel of them.

Closer to the source, he knew he was ferreting too close when the darkness became oppressive. He stopped, hovering in the ether, retreating far enough to observe without his soul being overwhelmed by panic. As it was, it was a close thing. The strands whispered terrible things about a world full of hate and danger, a world where everyone was the enemy. Conspiracy, dark terror, black rage… The strands whispered all these things.

He whimpered, even without a voice. The only place he had encountered such self-perpetuating, encompassing rage before had been in the drow courts where politics were often deadly and smiles often hid scathing hate. Movement caught his attention. Blackness marshaling on the edge of awareness. Too frightened to think clearly, Kai fled, shifting code behind him as he raced away, hiding his trail as best he could.

The holding room was suddenly in his vision and he hugged his arms around his chest, gasping, bent over his knees, unable to think past the single-minded primal need. Escape. He had gotten away.

Breon jumped into his lap and looked at him intently.

"Kai? What's up? Did you find anything?" Quinn asked him.

For a moment, Kai couldn't make sense of the words. He realized he had dropped the circle in his panic. Quinn stared at him as if he expected something. What did the boy know? What did he suspect? Would he have to be rid of him?

Kai gasped as if his head were breaking frigid water. "Goddess have mercy on us all." The strange too-vibrant colors of the room faded and he realized he had been seeing through the killer's eyes.

"I don't know...who." He shook his head hard. Quinn wasn't the enemy. Quinn was a friend. More or less. A colleague. *He* was not the darkness. He was Kai Hiltas. "But I know what."

Quinn joined him on the floor, his expression concerned, but Kai held up a hand.

"I'm well enough. It was not a good experience but I'm whole. Our killer is young, frightened of the world, certain he is persecuted. Powerful, yes, but untrained. Raw power driven by his terror. He is not well. His thoughts diseased. Schizophrenic, I believe your doctors name this."

"The guy's a nutjob?" Quinn summed up.

"Always so eloquent." Kai did a good impression of Quinn's eye roll, he believed. "He is not sane. But simple insanity would not produce this. Our mage is frighteningly intelligent. Resourceful. Cunning. He is mad, but his madness is calculating and has purpose."

"Great," Quinn said, making the word sound exactly the opposite. "It does help though. I got the impression that he was male, for no real reason I could put my finger on, but you seem to have gotten the same thing.

And, if he's 'mentally ill' he might be diagnosed. It could help narrow the search. You gonna tell Val?"

"Yes. I'll call him with the details and keep my people searching. And then I have a lunch date." *A real, goddess be praised, I-will-not-be-interrupted-even-if-the-heavens-fall lunch date. Sweet Mother, so help me, I will not be.*

* * * *

Quinn left Kai to inform and organize, and headed downstairs with the intention of going home and taking a shower. He wanted to stop in and tell Val but after his chat with Kai, there was no way he was going through the squad room.

The elevator dinged on the first floor lobby and the doors slid open. He was just starting to believe he'd make it out of the building without running into anyone who might find his current perfume of horn-dog elf offensive when he just about plowed into Flax.

Flax wasn't looking at all himself, pale and frowning, clutching his right arm to his chest. But he quirked an eyebrow at Quinn. "Best kind of healing."

Quinn grimaced and tried to force himself not to blush. "I was just heading home. What's wrong with your arm?"

"I touched that... Whatever it was last night. The thing you ran into, except in physical form. Still doesn't feel so great."

"Oh." He was trying to remember if he'd even seen Flax last night after his little run in, but it was all a blur. He felt bad now that he hadn't thought to ask if everyone was okay. He hesitated, then said, "I guess you were right about what I was doing being dangerous."

"Damn straight I was." Flax managed a crooked grin and a wink. "You gotta listen to your elders."

"Right. 'Cause you're such an old man. How old are you anyway?"

"Oh, about seventy or so. Who keeps count?"

"Uh-huh. You're like the same age as me in elf years," Quinn said.

Flax laughed. "Yeah, just about."

"If Val doesn't send you out today, did you want to meet up later?"

"I'm on desk duty," Flax told him with a disgusted snort. "Like I need both arms to do my job. So, yeah. I'm available."

"Doesn't desk duty mean you need to stay at your desk?" Quinn asked, only half teasing. It wasn't like there was much Flax could do sitting on his ass all day.

Flax pulled his cell phone out of his pocket and held it up. "This is pretty much my desk. It goes where I go."

Quinn chuckled. "All right. I'll go home and get a shower so you don't have to keep holding your breath around me. Be back in about an hour."

"I don't mind the scent," Flax called after him, "even if it makes me a little nuts."

Quinn stopped and gave him a puzzled look. He understood why Kai had practically told him off for rubbing his nose in it. After all, he and Val had once upon a time been lovers and he was going through a rough patch with his current lover. Flax, though, acted like he didn't want him to run off so fast. He was going to ask him why, but what came out was, "What do I smell like? I mean, I *know* what I smell like, but you guys get so weird about it."

"Oh, you just don't know the deliciousness of Eau de Happy Elf. It's um...rich. Intense. Like really good Indian food and your favorite pastry all rolled into one. It sets off a lot of automatic reactions—very primal reactions."

Quinn crossed his arms and thought it was more than a little strange to be having this conversation in the middle of the lobby, but it was fairly empty right now and he didn't know if he'd get the opportunity or the courage to ask again. Of course, he could just ask Val but...he just wanted to know.

"I don't get horny from smelling Indian food. There's got to be more to it than that."

"It's like trying to describe blue to someone who can't see color," Flax said with a crooked grin. "It's really hard to get the sensation across. And it's not so much horny as it is a...longing? Walk down a hall full of elves smelling like Val's pheromones and every head will turn. We can't help it. Val is...kind of the pinnacle of elf? His scent alone makes us want to drop to our knees and declare allegiance." Flax's frown of concentration flipped up into a wicked grin. "Wait. Wait. You're asking cause Hiltas flipped, aren't you?"

"Sort of," Quinn said. "He acted like I was rude or something."

Flax nearly collapsed laughing, leaning on the wall to hold himself up. "Oh....oh goddess. He is such a prude. Oh...sorry. He'd probably chew you out for holding hands."

"He's not that bad," Quinn said, trying not to grin, but even he knew there wasn't much conviction behind the words. "So, it's not all elves that get that kind of reaction? Just Val? Or, like, alpha dog elves?"

"Yeah. You hit it on the head there. Alpha dog elves."

Quinn hadn't known that. He knew it was an elf thing, but not a specifically Val thing. "Huh...well, that's interesting. And it's not all just about sex." He was more or less just thinking aloud. "Coulda fooled me." He shook his head.

"To be fair, okay, I don't like the drow much. It's personal. But he probably reacts the way he does cause he's sort of a drow alpha dog — which is a weird animal and I can't believe I just said that."

Quinn lifted his eyebrows. Well, this might not have been what Kai had planned, but he was certainly getting an education. Again, he could have just asked Val, but they didn't talk much about elvish stuff. Val got melancholy talking about the world and the life he had been ripped away from, and he had been so focused for so long on learning everything human and trying to fit in that Quinn hadn't wanted to bring it up. Flax didn't seem to have any problem letting him know.

"So, you want me to go take a shower first, or are you okay to just get on with it?" Only after it was out of his mouth did Quinn realize how that sounded.

Flax choked on a laugh, handsome face turning scarlet. "Look, I'm fine with it. But you probably feel grungy. I can wait." He snickered again.

Goddamn blushes. Quinn hoped his cheeks weren't red again. This was getting ridiculous. "Okay. Where do you want me to meet you?"

"Let's do the park. I'm happier outside anyway."

Quinn had a lot of occupy his thoughts on the way home and while he got cleaned up. By the time he was getting dressed in fresh clothes, he was thinking that maybe when Val wasn't elbows deep in trying to find a killer that he'd figure out a way to ask him some more about how elves ticked.

Considering the night he'd had and all that was on his mind, he would have thought another 'lesson' and probable failure would not be high on his list of things he wanted to do, but he found instead that he was actually looking forward to it. Now that Flax wasn't being such a jerk, he had a lot of interesting theories. Maybe he would even find something useful to help him get better control over his magic, and if Flax could teach him how to throw a fireball, that would be badass.

He was in a pretty good mood by the time he found Flax in the park.

"Okay. I had a thought," Flax said when Quinn sat beside him under the same tree from before. "And you might think it's kinda weird."

"What else is new?" Quinn said. "Shoot. What's your idea?"

"I think I can, uh, shadow you? When you try to control your magic? Sort of like a double control yoke in a training plane, right? If I'm in close contact with you, I can maybe guide you? Help you see how it's supposed to feel. Damn it. There was no way to say that not suggestively."

Quinn quirked an eyebrow. Maybe there was and maybe there wasn't. He wasn't going to put any stock in it though. He knew Flax had a thing for Val, but he had backed off after Val set him straight. He wasn't in the least worried that Flax had any interest in him, so he figured it was safe enough to experiment.

"What do you want me to do?" Quinn asked.

Flax cleared his throat, obviously uncomfortable, and said, "I think if you kinda scoot here between my legs and put your arms on top of mine...that way I can follow the same flows you're pulling down."

Quinn looked at him dubiously. If it were just about anyone else he'd swear it was some kind of come on, but he was pretty sure the discomfort he saw on Flax's face was real and probably because he didn't find him in any way attractive. Okay. This was just work — or training. Or whatever you wanted to call it. They were both adults and there was nothing sexual about this, Quinn admonished himself. He scooted over and parked himself between Flax's knees and Flax slid his arms under his.

"Ow, ow, fuck fuckity fuckington," Flax muttered, but he seemed to settle once he had both arms straightened. "Stupid arm. Start with something that comes easy to you. Start with wind. Just try for a gust to pick up those leaves on the ground."

Quinn took a breath and wondered if he was adult enough to do this after all. When Flax spoke, he was just above his ear and it felt more intimate than it should. He pushed the thought roughly aside and focused on what he'd said rather than the tingle that crept down his spine. He put his hands on top of Flax's hands and let the power flow into him, rushing up from below and surging through him.

"Okay, we're not trying to take down trees," Flax murmured. "You're fighting it so hard. Little sips. Relax. Feel what I feel."

The rush of power reduced to a trickle as Flax gently eased into control. Quinn was sure that tiny bit wouldn't do a damn thing. He struggled for more, but Flax had a tight rein on the flow.

"I've got you, Quinn. Everything's okay. Easy. Easy."

The trickle of magic whispered out across the grass, soft, almost tentative, and the leaves stirred, then rose in a column, dancing to the tune their magic played. It was strange, almost sensual, and felt more like play than serious magic.

"Okay, now you take the reins," Flax said.

As soon as Quinn felt Flax start to pull back control, the flow of magic amped up. He tried to get a grip on it, keep the little trickle of power flowing without letting it blast across and obliterate something.

"Breathe, Quinn," Flax murmured.

He was trying to, but he was afraid to twitch so much as a muscle. The wind picked up, getting stronger, rushing down the thread of power that was more like a rope now. The small playful whorl of leaves was turning faster and getting ominously larger, more like a small tornado.

"You're trying too hard. Relax," Flax told him.

Relax...just relax, Quinn. Close your eyes and this won't even hurt.

Power roared through him, blowing every leaf, twig and even a few stones across the empty space in front of them and pelting the trees fifty feet away with debris. Quinn shut down quickly, his shoulders slumping.

"Okay... It's okay," Flax murmured, no censure, no taunting in his tone. "We're stirring up something in there you've been fighting a while, I think. It's all right."

But Flax wasn't going to let him get away with quitting either, apparently. "Let's try again. I'll start. You ride my wave until you feel like you can do it. I'm right here. It's gonna be okay."

They tried again, and again, and again, but every time Quinn took control, he quickly lost it. By the end of several hours, Quinn was thoroughly discouraged that he could not manage this simple task. Flax on the other hand seemed more optimistic than he had been to start.

"Don't be so hard on yourself. You couldn't maintain control for a handful of seconds when we first started. Now you can go almost a minute."

"Oh, whoop-de-doo. A whole minute."

Flax sighed. "Look, with as much power as you channel, I'm not surprised that you expect everything you try to happen instantly, but that's not how it usually works. It takes time and practice."

"I guess so," Quinn grumbled, but even he could see the wisdom there.

"Elf kids don't learn overnight, either." Flax hissed and pulled his arm back into his chest. "But I have to stop today. I know I'm supposed to be all badass and shit, but it hurts."

"It's okay," Quinn said, getting up and stretching. All the muscles in his back felt stiff and sore from sitting so long and focusing so hard. "I need to get home and figure out dinner anyway." He hoped that didn't make him sound like he was Suzy Homemaker.

The smile Flax gave him was...what? Wistful? Was that the word? "You did good today. It'll get better. Promise."

Chapter Twelve

Cold glass and steel. Once, the building had been a source of terrible sorrow for Val. Coming home every night to a place he was supposed to call home, an empty, gray, lonely place had been his greatest despair. Now? This was truly home, where he came home every night to someone who loved him more than any other.

Quinn had left a message that he was at the park, so this afternoon, Val had the rare privilege of arriving home first. He hummed as he unlocked the door and wandered to the kitchen to put groceries away. Little cues that he no longer lived alone—the cereal Quinn liked, the Zachary Quinto coffee mug, the note scribbled about being out of eggs—warmed Val's heart.

A few minutes later, he was out of his work clothes, changed into track pants and a Mekons T-shirt, and still humming as he started a vegetable stew for dinner.

He heard the telltale sound of keys scrabbling against the door before being slotted and turned. A moment later, he heard Quinn step into the entry, then pause.

"Val?" Quinn poked his head into the kitchen. "Hey! I didn't think you'd be home before me." He came smiling into the room and put his arms around Val. "Smells good."

"Ness had things under control and I'm tired of spinning my wheels, so to speak, on this stone murder issue. I left a few minutes early. How was your day?"

Quinn considered the question rather than simply answering, which told Val all he needed to know, even if the little line that appeared between his eyebrows hadn't.

"It was mostly frustrating, but kind of interesting too. Flax thinks he's figured out a way to teach me how not to be such a menace to the neighborhood."

"Oh, yes?" *Clever pup. Of course he did.* Val kissed Quinn's nose. "What would that be?"

"Well, just telling me what to do wasn't getting anywhere, so he took control of the energy I was building, so I could feel what it felt like when he was directing it." Quinn's face said he wasn't sure if he was explaining the process correctly.

An odd twinge made Val's heart stutter. "How did he manage that?" He was certain of the answer since Flax's scent clung to Quinn, certain he didn't like it and annoyed with himself for the feeling.

"I don't know exactly," Quinn said. "He sat behind me and told me to try and bring up a wind to move some leaves and when I did, he put his hands under mine and just sort of...took over."

"Ah." Val hugged Quinn close to hide his expression. If his lover had been an elf, said elf would have smelled the jealous possessiveness rolling off him. With his voice carefully controlled, Val managed to ask, "Was it successful?"

Quinn snorted and buried his face into Val's shoulder. "A little, I guess. Every time I would try to hold onto it, just keep it gentle, it would get away from me. After a few hours of trying, I could keep it together a little longer than when we started, but not by much."

"A beginning, love. More than you had before." The growl crept into Val's voice. He couldn't hold it back any longer.

Quinn might not have been able to smell the shift in chemistry that would have told any elf nearby that Val was a hair away from putting the smack down on someone, but he wasn't blind, or stupid. He lifted his head and leaned back, looking at Val curiously.

"What? What's wrong?"

Val squeezed his eyes shut and breathed deeply of Quinn's scent but it was laced with Flax's, so it didn't help. "He was touching you. I know it was innocent. He was helping you. But he was touching you and I can smell it. I'm so sorry. It's not something I can help."

Quinn didn't say anything but he didn't pull away either. Val could feel Quinn's hands on his chest, just resting there, but even that felt like a barrier, like he was holding him away. He should open his eyes and see what expression Quinn wore but he was afraid he'd see anger or defensiveness, when all he wanted to do was rip his lover's clothes off and claim what was his.

After a moment or two, Quinn tapped his fingers on Val's chest and leaned up to kiss him.

"I'm going to take a shower—another shower. You elves are getting ridiculous. I've never been so clean in my life. I love you, babe. Nothing happened."

Val opened his eyes and gave him a sheepish smile. "I know. And I assure you, I feel quite ridiculous as well."

Despite feeling ridiculous, Val didn't tell Quinn to forget about the shower. He finished dinner preparation while Quinn disappeared into the bathroom. He was not a slave to hormonal urges, but he knew he wasn't going to be able to relax until Quinn smelled like Quinn, and not Quinn plus another male.

Quinn emerged ten minutes later, his hair wet and wearing different jeans.

"Flax said that the scent thing was like, something to do with alpha dogs and it was more or less that you just happened to be top dog around. So was that not right?" Quinn asked, it having obviously been on his mind.

Val processed quickly. Quinn had said 'another shower'. Not a singular shower. Flax must have reacted to the scent of morning sex. "It is correct, but there's more to it. My scent on you is a claiming and a proclamation, I'm afraid. Marking territory, which then becomes anywhere the scent is. Before elves were civilized, we were essentially herd animals. Groups of females living together with one clear leader. Any male who wanted that herd for his had to fight for it— other males and the females as well. So the scent of a successful powerful male had two purposes—to warn off rivals and to allow weaker males to find protection if they were willing to, ah, roll over and show their bellies, as it were."

Quinn grinned and shook his head. "That's really not so different from humans, you know. Except I suppose with us it's more posturing and words. It must be easier to just tell everything you need to know from a smell."

"It is an exceptional social shortcut. Though this is also where the need for the *senrist* arises—males who enter the sphere of a more powerful male and happen to prefer their own gender. It becomes a group attachment, a group bonding, almost like the old female herds, in a way."

Quinn's thumbs were hooked into the belt loops of his jeans and his fingers flexed a couple of times. He rocked forward slightly, onto the balls of his feet and back down in a way that Val had come to associate with Quinn thinking heavy thoughts.

"It's more than just for protection or sex though, isn't it?" Quinn asked, obviously picking his words carefully. "You all get more powerful from each other too, when you're bonded like that."

Val nodded, fighting to stay in the present. "True. It's something like a feedback loop of power. And it is more than simply sex. Truly polyamorous."

He watched the way Quinn chewed on his bottom lip and could almost see the wheels spinning in his head. Val braced himself.

"Do you want that again, Val?"

"I have what I want." Val leaned back against the counter, speaking carefully. "If you loved someone in addition and I did as well, that would be the only way it would ever happen again."

Quinn's eyebrows drew together, a look of consternation on his face, but also determination.

"Yeah, but how would that ever happen if you didn't look? I just… I don't want to think I'm holding you back from anything."

"I don't feel that way, not in the least. But if you came to me someday and said you had an interest in someone for us, we would make the decision together."

Quinn leaned back on the counter opposite from Val and crossed his arms over his chest. He was looking down at the floor so hard Val wondered if he was about to make a confession.

"I don't like that you're leaving it all up to me. Why would I be the one to find someone I was interested in? I doubt that would ever happen. You though... You've got people chasing after you all the time. You might find someone you were interested in." He finally looked up at Val and there was fear and worry in Quinn's eyes but also something else. Something that said he'd do anything to make Val happy.

That looked pierced through Val's heart. He managed a spare whisper through a swiftly closing throat. "You're what made me whole again. You and you alone. How could I look for anything else when I have a whole heart with you?"

"I know... I know you love me," Quinn whispered back. "But you can't, you know, fight biology."

Val crossed the room to hug Quinn tight. "I promise. You will be the first to know if I have the need to rebuild a *senrist*. But understand, it only happens if all parties wish it. You would need to want this person in our lives as well. A *senrist* is a mutual bonding. If we took a third, the bond would flow through all three of us."

Quinn pressed close to him and slid his hand up Val's chest, his neck, and into his hair, holding there and looking into Val's eyes. "Okay. It's all—you know—theoretical. I just wanted to make sure we talked, about things. And now I'd really like a kiss."

Val's knees nearly gave out in relief. "You needn't even ask." He tipped Quinn's face up and seized his lips in a kiss full of hunger and fire. It was a close thing. He almost did rip Quinn's clothes off there in the kitchen. "Mmm, love, I need to finish dinner."

Quinn pushed a knee between Val's thighs and pressed closer yet, riding up on his thigh and bucking slowly against Val's hip.

"Turn the stove off," he murmured in Val's ear, pulling the lobe into his mouth and pinching it between his teeth. "It'll keep. Take me to bed, now."

Val chuckled as he turned to shut off the stove. He swept Quinn into his arms and carried him to the bedroom.

* * * *

It had been an interesting day. Flax stopped at a corner to check his messages. Bit of a pain with the sharp ache running from shoulder to fingertips still. Fine. He was supposed to be resting it and he hadn't. Oh, well. He'd enjoyed the day's lesson, though, really enjoyed it. Strange how nice Quinn had felt in his arms.

He should have been on his way home. He really should. But the warm, fuzzy feeling? He didn't want to lose it. Instead, he turned left instead of right and headed for Ash and Sage's apartment. Good chance they were home and he had promised to take Ash shopping. Yep. Shopping. That's all he was after.

Keep telling yourself that.

His heart shouldn't have been hammering so hard, but it was as he knocked on the door.

Ash answered the door this time. His hair was braided neatly and he looked as serene as always, but there was a strain around his eyes that hadn't been there the last time Flax had seen him, and the smile on his face was faint.

"Flax, hello. What brings you here this evening?" Ash asked.

"Well, I thought I'd stop by on my way home and see if I could take you shopping. Did I come at a bad time?"

Ash hesitated, the faint smile flickering. "No, no, you didn't. I would love to go out with you. Let me get my coat," he said, pointedly not inviting Flax inside.

Oh, crap. Have I done something? Not done something? Flax stepped back and didn't intrude. When Ash reappeared and shut the door behind him, he fell into step beside Flax without a word.

It was only about half a block before Flax couldn't stand it anymore. "Ash? Is everything all right?"

Ash turned his weary smile on him once more, then looked away again. "No. Nothing is right, at the moment. For all that we can't return to our own world, this one still offers many escapes. Sage made himself sick with wormwood the last two nights, and so today he tried the capsules that Lysander warned against."

"Aw, fuck. Fuck. Fuck. Fuck." Flax reached out and took Ash's hand as they walked. "I tried to warn him, but it's a tough road. I'm still struggling with it too some days. But I've been alone. If I'd had you..." He stopped, feeling himself flush. "I can help. He needs to face it head on, and not discount the faun's advice just cause he's a faun. But it's not easy—never that."

"Sage did not ignore Lysander's advice because he is a faun. He ignored him because he knew you had taken this poison and lived. He wasn't afraid to try it.

He's young, and he's always been fearless. There is no battle for him to fight here, so he's created his own."

"Damn it, I'm so sorry. He just… It nearly killed me. And it's nearly ruined my life several times now. I'm not proud of being an addict. I'm not happy about it. I'm mortally ashamed that I could be so weak." He peered into Ash's face. "You want me to talk to him?"

Ash laughed softly, although it was anything but amusement Flax heard in the sound. He shook his head but said, "You can try, if you want. I doubt he will listen. I doubt he even thinks he's doing anything dangerous or wrong. He's only fifty-some summers old. Did you know? I resisted creating the mate bond with him. I told him he was too young and should wait a few more years, but he was so insistent." He squeezed Flax's hand. "He acts very brash, very aggressive, but he isn't a leader, Flax. He isn't even a hunter. He's a soldier and there is no one to give him any orders."

Flax got that. A lot of young warriors were lost without a strong commander. "I wonder if he should think about the academy. I mean, working for Captain Hartgrove. You couldn't ask for a better commander."

Ash chuckled again, and this time there was a slight bit of humor behind it. "Sage has trained his whole life to be a warrior. I don't know if his pride will stand being told he must now learn from those he sees as little more than children. Even so, he might be tempted. But that will take time. Of course, if Tesined Valerian told him to drop to his knees and suck his cock that would be a much swifter remedy."

"Would be for me, too," Flax muttered. *Oh crap. I said that aloud.* "Though I guess it's kinda obvious."

"Perhaps we should ask him then," Ash suggested.

Flax gaped at him, a strangled sound escaping. "Um…" Just ask him? But then… "Maybe…maybe we should."

Some undefined tension went out of Ash and he seemed more like himself when he looked at Flax. "How about if we invite him to dinner? That seems to work well." He flashed a teasing smile. "Him and his *kalesi*, of course."

Flax shot him a grin. "Works for some of us. But then, you're so freaking gorgeous. Hard to resist." Could it really be that easy? Though now that he and Quinn were on more friendly terms… "We will then. Why not? Val deserves a full *senrist* more than any elf I've ever met. Could handle one better, too." He leaned in to plant a quick kiss on Ash's cheek. "Quinn's an amazing human. You'll like him, since you're pretty amazing, too."

Ash put his arm around Flax and returned the kiss with a brush of his lips on his temple. "Shall we see how everyone gets along in bed first before we discuss forming a *senrist*?" he teased. "Speaking of which, are there any precautions to take? Humans seem so fragile. I wouldn't want Quinn to be injured."

"I think the key is to make sure you take your cues from him. He's smaller, so one would need to be a bit more gentle. But he's certainly not fragile." Flax still felt that astounding influx of power, so wild and tempestuous raging along his nerves.

They walked for a few moments in silence before Ash said, "So you've already thought about how to seduce him then?" That was definitely a teasing glimmer in his eyes now.

"I've been working on being friends first. But…it doesn't seem that far to go." *Not since I've held him in my arms.*

"Have you had human lovers?" Ash asked curiously.

"Oh, yeah. Dozens. They come in all sizes and flavors. The basics are the same. The ears aren't as sensitive, but the palms are incredibly erotic."

"The palms? Really." Ash made a face as if he might be storing that information for future use.

"Yeah." Flax waggled his eyebrows. "Lick a human's palm and they nearly melt at your feet. Not just any random human on the street, of course, but one you have in the bedroom."

"Hmm, I will keep that in mind," Ash said.

Their conversation continued, although in a slightly less candid way when they reached the Asian market. Flax could tell it was a welcome break for Ash, which made him feel both worried for Sage and a less defined sort of anger that he didn't know how to express without being hypocritical.

They returned to the apartment laden with bags, mostly containing fresh produce and various herbs and spices. Ash had cooed over the variety and preservation methods of the spices and herbs, many of which he planned to make into various healing preparations as well as use for cooking.

Ash invited Flax in this time and they put the groceries away together. There was no sign of Sage but Ash did not seem concerned.

"He's in the bedroom, if you still wanted to talk to him."

Flax gave Ash's shoulder a squeeze and he marched back to the bedroom where Sage was sprawled on the covers.

"Get up," Flax snarled. "Get up and face me like a grown warrior. You should be ashamed."

Sage rolled over onto his back, a familiar glazed look to his pretty green eyes. "And here I thought you would be happy I finally found something I like about this world," he drawled.

Flax pounced, seizing Sage's shirtfront in his fists and hauling him up. He slammed Sage against the wall. "I said up! And I expect you to listen! This will kill you. Not today, not tomorrow, but slowly, after stealing your dignity, your pride, your strength and your health! Meanwhile, your love watches you in anguish as you wither to nothing. Is this how you show your love? To make this hell for him?"

Sage grabbed at Flax. Snarling, he twisted and reversed their position, driving Flax back to the opposite wall. "You dare judge! What have you done? What have you said to him?" He shook Flax, his strength still remarkable, despite the drug coursing through him.

Flax was older, cannier and sneakier. He feinted left and swept Sage's feet out from under him, taking him to the floor and pinning him on his face with his right arm twisted behind his back.

"I judge because I know. I judge because I've lived the hell and nearly died from it. So you listen and listen well, you beautiful, headstrong pup. I was alone, in terrible pain, and slowly dying from lack of purpose. You...you have someone who loves you deeply, so deeply your actions cut him to the bone. Think, Sage! Think what happens when you die or have to be taken from him because you live only for the pills!"

Sage struggled against him but only briefly before he gave up, going limp as Flax railed at him. He bent his free arm up and put his face into the crook of his elbow. Flax thought he was ignoring him, tuning him out like a child tunes out a parent he doesn't want to hear. Then he felt the shudder run through the body beneath and heard the small catch of a sob.

He relented, turning Sage and pulling him into his arms to hold him tight as he wept. "Don't go down this dark road. There's only shame and loneliness down there. I can help you. Ash can help you. Let us. Don't shove us away. Don't break his heart like this."

Sage said nothing, but he clung to Flax, snuggled into his arms and accepted the comfort there. If he was not ready for promises and reassurances, perhaps that was for the best. It would be better he said them when he was sober anyway.

Ash appeared quietly beside them and he helped Flax to stand and place Sage back on the bed. "Stay with us," Ash whispered, kissing the back of Flax's ear. "Stay, help me with him. Let us heal each other, Flax."

His arm was throbbing now that the adrenaline was wearing off. Part of him, the angry part, wanted to tell them to fuck off so he could go home and be miserable in peace. The angry part was quieter than it used to be. "I'm staying. I am. Can't leave you to deal with this alone."

Ash kissed the shell of his ear, rubbing his cheek there lightly, and his hand reached around to loosen the buttons of his shirt. It was not an entirely sexual thing though. There was intimacy, friendship, caring certainly.

When they were down to their underclothes Ash lay down on one side of Sage and Flax on the other and Ash gently ran his hands over them both, singing softly, warmth and healing energy drawing up into all three of them.

Flax pulled Sage close, letting him curl around him like a vine. *I'm going to stop this from happening. I'm not letting this beautiful young elf die – neither one of them.*

The fierce strength of that promise to himself shocked him, even frightened him a bit, but there it was. He would fight for them, and that had to mean something.

Chapter Thirteen

"Albert, honey, are you still feeling ill?"

"Leave me alone."

"All right, but if you're not up for school tomorrow, I'm taking you to the doctor. You hear? Albert?"

He didn't answer her and after a few moments, he heard her walk away. He couldn't go to school. No way. His mom and dad were stupid but there were people at school that were smart. Mr. Cantorie, Mrs. Argustine. They would know. They had evil in them and they could feel what was inside Albert. If he went to school, they would get him.

Maybe that was the plan. Maybe Mom and Dad were only playing dumb. Maybe they were in on it. Maybe they were working with the police right now — the ones that had almost caught him the other night.

Albert's stomach clenched, his throat tightened and he had to fight down the urge to run to the bathroom and be sick again. They had come after him, hunted him. Invisible, but there, he could tell. He'd felt the presence chasing him until he'd been backed into a corner and had had no choice but to fight back.

He had fought the idiots at school the same way for so long he couldn't remember when he'd started. Closed his eyes and imagined the abyss around him, and he was calm and hidden at the black heart. Of course, those asshole bullies had no magic so they only avoided him, like they couldn't see him—walked around him untouched. But the one who had come after him the other night, the one who was with the police, he had walked right into his world as if it were nothing.

Albert had panicked. He had felt the net dropping over him, dragging him down. They would do such horrible things to him. He knew they would. The whispers never stopped now, always telling him what would happen when they caught him. He had no choice but to strike out. Just as he'd slammed a wall of darkness into the one chasing him, another had reached for him. He and his friend had barely gotten away and Albert had not left his room since.

The headache that had seared his mind as he'd run from them had been like nothing he'd ever felt before. He was so sick he had thrown up in an alley behind his house before he could stumble inside. They had done it to him somehow. Made him sick. Punished him for being stronger than they were. He was so sure they would find him when he was weakened, but they didn't come again, and the more time that passed, the more he was certain he'd lost them.

Maybe not forever though. Maybe they were looking for him even now. He had to get out. Keep moving. He would buy a bus ticket and leave, but he didn't know how he would get his friend on the bus, and he would never leave him behind. If he couldn't leave, then he would have to fight. He would get up and pretend to go to school. He would go to his after-school job washing dishes and get his pay. Then he would find a place to hide—a better place than here. Somewhere he could be with his friend all the time. Then they would hunt the cops that were looking for them and he wouldn't have to worry about them finding him.

* * * *

Kai stared out of his office window on the top floor of the AURA building. The original founders of AURA had placed Research on the top floor, not because it was the most important, but because it was the department most likely to have magical disasters occur. It was isolated in its top floor aerie, alone in its hazardous miasma of experiment and schemes.

The stone mage still eluded them. He had a general location—as in which borough—and a general profile, but their inquiries into schizophrenia patients who might fit said profile were going nowhere. Frustrating.

Still, he made certain every member of the department had something important to work on, something to challenge them, help them learn. He made certain he ate more than vending machine snacks, and that Breon had everything he needed. He made certain he went home on time and went to bed at a decent hour.

He sent presents. He called regularly. Courted with little notes and invitations, and here he was, doing everything right and still at such a loss in every aspect of his life. Lost. Without Tenzin, he would be forever lost.

There were voices outside his office. He didn't feel he could muster the strength for one more crisis today. Not right then. His phone rang.

"Hiltas."

"Mr. H.?" Mindy's voice was oddly hesitant. "You have a visitor."

"No games, child. I don't have the energy."

"You should probably come out here, sir."

With a sigh, Kai lifted Breon from his lap and let the tom ride on his shoulders. He smoothed a hand over his hair, straightened his tie and drew a deep breath. All right, most likely some government official. He could handle this. Cool. Professional.

When he opened his office door, no one stood at the high semicircular counter around Mindy's desk. He quirked an eyebrow at her and she nodded toward the floor in front of her desk. Puzzled, Kai stalked around the desk and his heart decided it was a butterfly instead of a cardiac muscle.

Tenzin was on one knee, and though that barely put him below Kai's eye level, it was unexpected, to say the least.

"Tenzi? What's this?"

"I've decided there's only one way to fix this," Tenzin held up a black velvet box and took Kai's hand. "I know you're mine, in every way important to a drow. But in this world, there's a piece we're missing. I would like you to be mine in the eyes of society here—in the eyes of the law. What is mine is yours and not even the government can separate us."

"I don't..." Kai shook his head, still unable to draw a full breath.

"He's asking you to marry him, Mr. H. Say something smart, damn it!" Mindy squealed. "Say yes!"

Tenzin smiled up at him, opening the box to reveal a lovely onyx and diamond ring. "Listen to your admin, Kai. She's very astute."

Kai could only gape for several seconds. When he said yes, it was in such a spare, choked whisper, he wasn't certain he'd said it out loud, but Tenzin heard. He swept Kai up in his big furry arms and crushed him close, whispering soft endearments.

"Tenzi? Does this mean you're coming home?"

"Yes, my angel. I'll be coming home. And I expect you home as well, please."

Kai wiped at his eyes, feeling foolish that his staff had seen everything, but not able to drum up any real irritation. "Get back to work, everyone. Haven't you ever seen a yeti propose before?"

There were some giggles, but Kai ignored them as Tenzin carried him into the office and shut the door.

* * * *

Flax glared at the contents of his medicine cabinet. If he was serious about staying clean, why did he keep the stuff around? How could he keep Sage from sliding down the same path like this with his security blanket still right in reach, waiting to reach out and softly strangle him at the next weak moment?

"No, damn it. If I'm telling him one thing and doing another, I'm worse than useless to him."

But it was more than that. He had to show Sage, show him he was serious and that he wouldn't be alone if he ended up having to fight it. He swept the bottles into a paper sack and ferreted out all the sample packs and small stashes he had in bureau drawers and under kitchen utensils. Every last damn one was coming with him.

He stomped into his boots, grabbed his jacket and swept out the door with his bag of whispering little demons under his arm. They murmured to him the whole way there, but he refused to listen. Sage was more important.

At Ash and Sage's place, he ran a hand back through his hair, pulled in a deep breath and knocked.

Ash answered, and he looked as serene as always, if a little sad, although he smiled at Flax. "Well, this is a pleasant surprise. Come in."

"Hey, gorgeous." Flax leaned in to plant a kiss on Ash's cheek but his nervous energy propelled him inside. "I need to talk to Sage. I need... I need him to do something with me."

That flash of sadness and pain flickered in Ash's eyes again before he turned his head to shut the door. "I don't know if this is a good time, Flax," he said softly. When Flax's eyes widened, Ash hastily added, "No, he hasn't taken any more of the drugs since you came the other day. But he tells me he wants to."

Flax nodded. "All right. Good. I mean, not that he wants to, but this is the perfect time for me to be here, then."

He strode down the hall to the bedroom where Sage sat hunched on the end of the bed, a dark frown on his handsome face.

"Hey. You and me. We need to talk. Now." Flax dropped to his knees so he could see Sage's eyes and placed his bag on the carpet beside him.

"About what?" Sage asked.

Flax snorted as he took both of Sage's hands. Good, strong hands, powerful and still so gentle. "About what, he says. About your wanting to take what you think is the easy way out. Sage, my dear Sage, the pills, the wormwood... They're evil. They tell you it's easy. They whisper to you and tell you they'll take the pain, make everything better. They lie. Oh, they lie."

Sage sighed. "You and Ash are both overreacting. I took them the one time." He shrugged.

"He says you want them again." Flax lifted one of Sage's hands to kiss his fingers. "And you still have them here, don't you? Letting them sit in the cabinet and sing to you."

When he shifted, the bag beside him crinkled. "I brought mine—all of them. You and me, we're getting rid of the demons. Tonight. Right now. Sure, you could get more. But it makes it harder, that one step harder, if they're not right under your nose."

Sage finally lifted his eyes to look at him. "Why? Why are you doing this? Why do you care?"

"Because I can't watch you make the same mistakes I did without trying to help." Flax swallowed hard. The intensity of those green eyes nearly made him choke on his words. "Because you've both been so good to me. Looked out for me. Because you're my dear friend, and I can't stand to see you do this to yourself. Because Ash needs you and this is causing him so much pain."

Only that last part seemed to touch Sage, making him drop his gaze again and look away, the shame all too apparent in his expression. He wiped a weary hand over his eyes. "Do you know how many would have bonded with him if he'd chosen them?" he asked so softly it was almost a whisper. "He had his pick. There wasn't anyone who didn't want him, at least in their bed. Not just because he is beautiful. I have never known anyone as kind, or brave. I chased him long and hard, persistent as any hunter." His lips twisted into a wry grin. "He probably should have chosen someone else, someone stronger."

"I should slap you. Or put you over my knee and spank you." Flax shook his head in exasperation. "He chose you because he loves you, because you're the one who completes his heart—not one of the others. You are an elf, right? You do know how this works?"

Now there was a flash of anger in those green eyes as Sage glared at him. "I'm not a child."

Flax patted the air with both hands. "I know, oh, dear goddesses, I know. I was teasing—sort of. The point is, Ash did choose you and he loves you so much his heart is cracking. He tries so hard to hide it, but he can't. Not all the way. But it's all right. You don't have to break his heart. Come help me banish the demons. We'll do it together. So much better than trying to do it alone."

He stood to give Sage some space. "Gather it all up. Whatever poison you have in the apartment. Do this with me now or break his heart. It's your choice."

During the long moment of silence, Flax thought it was not going to work—that this would be harder, take longer, be more of a fight. Then Sage stood and he opened the top dresser drawer, pulling out a familiar white and red bottle. He rolled it in his hand for a second, looking down at it, and Flax could tell by the rattling of the pills in the plastic bottle that it was mostly full. That at least was a good sign. If Sage hadn't lied—and Flax didn't think he had—then maybe the stuff hadn't gotten its hooks into him so deeply yet. Maybe he could flush it away and never look back.

Together they went into the bathroom and emptied the contents of Sage's bottle, then all of Flax's stash as well, into the toilet. Sage pushed the lever to flush them.

"The wormwood, too, sweets. Bring it here."

A slow blink was the only response Flax got before Sage walked out. He held his breath, hoping that he hadn't pushed too far and he wanted to faint in relief when Sage's soft tread returned. He held up the bottle for Flax to see, almost a salute, before he dumped the wormwood as well.

Flax took him by the shoulders and kissed him softly. "Well done. Now." He took Sage by the hand and brought him back into the bedroom. "Get your sword."

Sage looked at him curiously but he didn't question, merely got the sheathed blade from its place under the bed.

Flax hauled him into the kitchen where Ash fussed with some concoction on the stove. "Now for the other part of this. You need to take oath, on your sword, your honor, on all you hold sacred, that you will never seek your own ruin this way again." He turned Sage toward Ash when the young elf opened his mouth. "Not to me. To him. To Ash, who loves you more than life."

Sage gripped his sword and looked at Ash, who looked back at him with such tenderness and understanding. Sage cleared his throat then he turned slightly and took Flax by the arm, moving him gently to stand beside Ash.

"I swear to you both. I won't take the poison anymore." His voice was rough with emotion, but clear and there wasn't any hedging or hesitation. "My word of honor."

Flax flung his arms around Sage and pulled him into a rough embrace. "And I give you my word that I will do everything in my power not to turn to it again, too. If I start to weaken, I'll come here, and I will be there to strengthen your resolve if you do."

Ash wrapped his arms around them, and Flax and Sage both snaked an arm out to bring him into the fold. "I am proud of you both." He lifted a hand to Sage's cheek and kissed him. "I did not choose unwisely, *kalesi*," he said, proving that it was a little too difficult to have an entirely private conversation in such close quarters. "Flax is right. I chose you for my mate because I love you." He turned his face to kiss Flax as well. "And you, my hunter, thank you." He whispered into his ear, kissing there softly. "Thank you."

* * * *

Flax was still on desk duty and no real progress had been made in finding the ones responsible for the three deaths that they knew of, so it was an opportune time for him and Quinn to work on Quinn's lessons. They upped their schedule to daily meet ups in the park and usually got so engrossed they spent the better part of each day there.

Quinn did make it a point to head home before dark so that he could get dinner on and shower before Val got home. It felt a little weird, almost like he should feel guilty washing the smell of another elf off him, even though any touching they did stayed strictly platonic. Even so, Val had been more protective than ever since his run in with a killer in the spirit plane, and if smelling clean and only like himself made him feel better, Quinn wasn't going to complain about so much showering.

"Easy, easy... Quinn, you've got this. You've felt how it's done a hundred times. Stop struggling," Flax encouraged him.

Quinn tried. He was focusing so hard he could feel a bead of sweat on the back of his neck roll down his spine, and still he felt the control slipping through his grasp, gaining momentum until the wind rushed around them, flicking leaves, dirt and small stones into the air.

"Damn it," Quinn cursed in frustration. All week they had been working on this exercise and Quinn had not made much progress beyond what he had the first day. A minute was about the longest he could hold it together before the power rushed into him, his adrenaline spiked and he was shoving all that power out like a man frantically bailing a sinking rowboat.

"I can't do it, Flax. I don't know if I'll ever be able to do it."

Flax hitched a breath, a thing Quinn realized he did when he was trying not to sigh. "You can. You really can. But there's something in your way."

"Yes," a deep voice said behind them. "I believe there is."

"Captain!" Flax practically dumped Quinn on the ground as he scrambled up.

Quinn rolled his eyes. "Don't act like we were doing something fun."

"Perhaps it wasn't fun," Val growled. "But it certainly was a little too close for my tastes."

Quinn stood and brushed away the little bits of grass and leaves that had caught in his hair from his latest try at making a tiny whirlwind. He could feel Val's tension, even from where he stood, but avoided looking at him until he was sure he wasn't going to snap something defensive. Finally, he lifted his eyes to see if Val was as pissed off as that little growl had suggested. Only he wasn't looking at Quinn, he was pinning Flax with those piercing green eyes. Uh-oh.

Quinn cleared his throat. "Am I late? I didn't think it was past five yet," he said, trying to distract him.

"What?" Val growled, still glaring at Flax, whose complexion was edging toward green.

Right. Roll over and so on.

"The time, Val? Is it after five?"

Val's head whipped around, the glare subsiding as he fixed on Quinn. "No, love. No... I wanted to check on your lessons, since I know you're struggling."

Quinn heaved a sigh and felt his shoulders slump. "I might as well go now anyway. I haven't been able to do any better."

"I'm sorry, sir," Flax murmured to his boots. "Quinn's trying so hard. We just can't get past whatever's...um, stopping him."

"Hmm." Val folded his legs, settling on the dry grass. "Sit, pup. I'm not going to rip your head off just this moment." He gestured to Quinn to join them. "My love, my heart, do you *know* what's standing in your way?"

The way Val said it implied that they both knew. He was really asking if Quinn was going to admit it.

Quinn clenched his jaw stubbornly. Ever since he'd told Val that Flax thought his problem with control had something to do with the way he had first been taught to use magic, Val had latched on to the idea as probably true, but Quinn wasn't convinced. He didn't want to believe that Donovan had affected him so much and for so long, and was still messing with his head.

He sat down next to Val and picked at the grass. "No," he forced out at last.

From the corner of his eye, he saw Val and Flax look at each other, just a glance but it was enough to prick his temper. "Stop that. Don't look at each other like you know better than I do when I'm sitting right here."

Val raised his eyebrows. "My apologies. But I know the thing you won't say in front of Flax. I know how deep those scars run. And I know how you prefer to turn away from them rather than remember."

Quinn pushed his fingers into the dry grass, pressing his palm down, digging his fingertips into the dirt. He refused to look up at either of them. Not remembering was a skill he had cultivated to perfection. Cracking open his memory and taking a look inside gave him the same cold, clammy fear as opening a creaky old door into a dark basement full of whispers and slithery sounds. He swallowed hard and dug his fingers deeper into the soil.

Would spilling his guts actually help at all? He didn't see how it would. It wasn't like it would change anything. It wasn't like talking about it would go back and erase any of it. The question then was if he wasn't willing to go down this road, how long before Flax gave up on him as unteachable? Even if telling them how he had been taught did nothing, at least he was showing he was dedicated enough to give their idea a try.

The ground under his fingers was as dry as the grass and hard packed, but when Quinn flexed his fingers he could feel little grooves forming, letting him dig in, hold on. He took a deep breath and let it out.

"When I was first figuring out that I could do things—that I could feel magical energy, and was trying to figure out how to use it—I met a man who told me he could show me how. Only, he wanted me to do things that I didn't know if I wanted to do. He kept nagging at me and pushing and calling me a coward until I agreed just to get him off my case.

"He had a gang of kids that did petty stuff, picking pockets, shoplifting…stuff like that. So he got us all together and had this plan and it all hinged on me being able to send a big gust of wind down a street and knock some people around, make them drop things, create confusion. I stood at the mouth of this alley and he was telling me to focus and how I had better not screw up and if I couldn't earn my keep he was gonna throw me out. I was all jacked up, totally high on adrenaline. Scared I couldn't do it, scared I could. Then he gave the signal and I just blasted a gust of wind as hard as I could and people tripped and coats went flying and purses dropped and half a dozen kids ran out and snatched stuff up and ran away before my knees even started knocking over what I'd done.

"He fucking went ape shit. He thought it was the greatest. I was his star." Quinn shook his head. "I was so starved for the tiniest bit of attention. I lapped it up.

"After that success, Donovan wanted to see what else he could get me to do. I remember one time we were doing the wind trick and some cops were right around the corner and spotted us. We ran and they chased us and Don was yelling at me to do something. My heart was about pounding out of my chest and I didn't have any time to think. I was just going on sheer terror and so I pushed as much energy as I could until every dumpster and trash can in the alley went smashing behind us and into those cops, and we just kept running.

"One time we were up on a rooftop, scoping out potential areas we could set up a good wind tunnel, and he claps me on the back as says he figures I'm so good at this wind thing I should be able to fly. Before I knew it, he's got me hanging off the edge and telling me just to raise the wind under me or he's gonna drop me and..." Quinn took a shaky breath.

"Let's just say I didn't learn to fly. I managed to break my fall but it took everything I had and I still landed flat on my back. I didn't know then if I was more scared of failing, or what he would do to me if I didn't do what he wanted. I don't even know how many more 'lessons' like that happened. I just remember I was in a constant state of fear. My heart would pound and I'd get sweaty, and whatever he told me to do, I threw everything I had at it. He about drowned me in the bathtub when he started trying to figure out how to get me to use water."

Quinn finally shut his mouth. All that buried shit. Actually only a little bit of it, but he had to stop because he didn't want to look into that cellar anymore.

Val reached over and placed a hand on his knee — not crowding, not demanding. "That man should have had his balls cut off and fed to him. There can be no doubt there. Keeping him in the dark places of your memory gives him power, though. Power he does not deserve. Power you give to him. Forcing him to stand under the sun... This is how you reclaim what is yours. I love you. I believe in you. But I would never love you less simply because you cannot speak to the wind in anything close to a whisper."

Quinn smiled at him, though it felt harder than it usually did, and he put his hand over Val's and gave it a squeeze.

Flax cleared his throat softly. "I think I have another idea."

Quinn chuckled at the hesitant tone, so unlike Flax. He waited and Flax held up a dry twig.

"I've been asking you to use wind because it's what you know best, but now... Well, maybe we should try something else that the bastard that abused you didn't terrify you with."

Quinn gave him a narrow look but just waited.

"I want you to focus on the end of this twig. You've been feeling all week how to push only a little bit of power. This time I want you to tell that power to be heat, to be fire, instead of air."

"Flax, take a look around us. It looks like a blast zone. I'm surprise you even found that twig. Do you really want to hold onto it while I take aim and hope I don't accidentally set your hair on fire? Not that it's likely to happen, but still."

"You can do this. I know you can," Flax said, his confidence returning. "You trusted me enough to show your fear, and I trust you enough to control it. Besides, my hair would grow back."

Quinn sighed. "You're crazy. You know that? Crazy damn elf." He sat up straighter though and figured there was no harm in trying, since he'd yet to be able to produce even the smallest flame. Still holding onto Val's hand, he concentrated. Felt the power start to rise. He focused on that power, tried to remember exactly how it felt when Flax guided the most delicate trickle from his fingertips, and he narrowed his vision down to just the tip of the twig Flax held up. Just a tiny bit of heat…that was all he wanted.

A small curl of smoke lifted from the end of the twig and Quinn gasped, his jaw hanging open. It burst into flame like the head of a match and he quickly cut off the flow of energy, just as smooth and easy as you please. He was so stunned that he was speechless.

"Look at you," Flax said softly with his normal grin. "Didn't even singe my handsome eyebrows." He waggled the eyebrows in question and beside Quinn, Val let out an explosive laugh.

Quinn grinned too and when Val stopped laughing, he leaned in and kissed him and Quinn slid his arms around his neck. He thought it was just a brief celebratory kiss but Val wrapped his arms around him, hauled him into his lap, and kissed him so thoroughly Quinn forgot they had an audience. He was thinking back to a much more pleasant memory — or dream rather — one where the two of them were in the park naked together. When Val finally let his lips go, he was breathless and he snuggled into Val's chest as Val tilted his head and rubbed his cheek along the top of his head.

It was only then Quinn realized what he was doing and laughed. "Geez, are you going to pee on my leg, too? 'Cause seriously, I will smack you with a newspaper if you try and mark your territory like that."

Flax made a strangled, choked gasp and Quinn realized he was trying not to laugh, trying so hard his face was heart-attack red. Val grumbled something in Elvish that didn't seem to help Flax's fit one bit.

"See, though? You can. Quinn, you did so good," Flax said when he could speak again. He got up, brushing the grass off his uniform pants, still smiling. "I think we should celebrate. Captain, Ash and Sage would like to have you both over for dinner. Would you do us the honor? You and Quinn?"

Quinn realized even though Flax had directed the question at Val that he was waiting for Quinn to answer for them. He didn't see any reason not to accept, other than he and Val didn't really do the whole dinner date thing often — or at all. They both had friends of course, but most of them were co-workers and once the workday was done, they didn't really hang out together. Funny how Quinn had never considered that until Flax's suggestion.

"Sure," Quinn said.

Flax swept him an elaborate bow, his smile bright and devoid of irony. "My thanks, oh mighty Quinn. I'll let Ash know."

* * * *

It was only after they were home, changed and headed back out that Quinn thought about the fact that Flax hadn't exactly invited them spur of the moment, nor had he invited them to his own house or apartment. Wherever he lived, Quinn didn't know. Val assured him this wasn't strange, that Flax had been spending a lot of time with the new crossovers — when he wasn't monopolizing Quinn's time, that was. He said it casually but Quinn still looked at him sideways and wondered just how much all the time he'd been putting in with Flax had been bugging his man.

He didn't want to get into a lengthy discussion about it though when they were headed out for their first social event together. Their first social event, and he would be the only human. Would it be weird? He hoped not. It wasn't only his magic he'd been working on. He'd been working on his Elvish the last few weeks as well. He still had trouble with a lot of words, but he understood it better than he spoke it.

"What should we bring?" Quinn asked, not knowing if elves had particular customs like that.

Val gave him a wry smile. "Bunny food."

Quinn rolled his eyes. Of course. Once they were in the store and Val had chosen several bunches of greens and things, Quinn spotted the bouquets of flowers and pointed them out, "Should we get some of those?"

Val went still and Quinn turned to look at him questioningly. The look on Val's face was so serious and searching, Quinn had to ask, "What?"

Val cleared his throat. "Not unless you are planning on courting one of them."

"Oh...*oh*... Um, okay, the salad stuff is enough," he said quickly.

"Easy to make missteps in any culture." Val kissed the top of his head. "Though I realize I had been solitary so long, before you. It takes effort to think of social niceties."

"Right. Well, we give flowers to our sweethearts too, but it doesn't always mean you *like*, like someone. Sometimes it's just friendly."

"That's one of those things that are a little more stringent for elves. A gift of flowers would only be given to a lover or an intended lover."

They left the store sans flowers and with plenty of bunny food instead.

"Anything else you might want to fill me in on so I don't trip over my own feet when we get there?" Quinn asked.

"I'm unclear whether Flax is simply friends with Ash and Sage, or if it has become something more. I doubt it would create issues either way, but something to be aware of."

Quinn snorted. "I could have told you that he was knocking knees with them."

Val chuckled as he opened the car door for Quinn. "Sex is one thing. Flax is a young elf. He most likely has a variety of sexual partners. But whether he's courting them or not, I don't know."

Quinn got in the car and waited until Val pulled away from the curb before he asked, "Can't you smell it on him?"

"I can scent sex. He has slept with both of them—at once. I would be able to scent the difference if they bonded, which they have not. But I can't smell courting."

"Oh," Quinn said simply, then rolled the idea of Flax courting around in his head for a while. That led to him thinking about him rolling around with Sage and Ash and he had to distract himself by playing with the radio. He wasn't going to walk into their apartment and instantly turn flame red. Not going to happen.

Val found a spot not half a block from the building. It was like some special parking spot radar he had and Quinn wondered if it was a magic thing. They took the stairs to the third floor, and Flax answered when Val knocked, which was kind of weird.

"Hey, Captain, Quinn! Come on in. Ash is in the kitchen. Gods, his cooking is to die for." He waved them in and turned with a frown for Sage. "That better be water, hon."

Sage looked offended in a way that only elves could manage. He didn't answer but moved his fingers so Flax could see that the contents of the glass were clear. Quinn thought for a moment things might get awkward, but Sage smiled a greeting at them and gestured for them to come into the small tidy living room.

"Welcome, Tesined. Welcome, Quinn. Would you care for anything to drink?"

Val greeted Sage with a brief embrace and seemed to take his cue from Flax. "Water is lovely, Sage. Thank you."

Whatever was going on, Flax rewarded Sage with a bright smile and a kiss to his jaw before Sage vanished into the kitchen.

He returned a minute later with two tall tumblers of ice water and handed them to his guests. Quinn took his with a thank you, and made no comment that he hadn't actually said what he wanted, but he would have said water anyway so it was no big deal.

Ash came out of the kitchen a moment later to greet their guests. "Tesined, you look well. Thank you for coming. And you look much improved as well, Quinn. No lasting trouble since you were attacked in the spirit realm, I take it."

"No. I'm fine," Quinn said. "I wasn't really attacked. More like I ran into something."

Ash looked at him as an adult might look at a child who said something precocious and hadn't gotten it quite right. "You might have found yourself in the wrong place at the wrong time, this is true, but make no mistake that what was done to you was a deliberate attack. A little more force, a little more skill, and he could have killed you."

Quinn frowned. "Are you sure about that? I mean, it was scary but it didn't feel particularly malicious."

Now it was Ash's turn to frown. "The blindness might have been simply defensive, but what I felt in you the night Flax called us to the medical ward was a spell that was meant to sever you from your body and destroy your spirit. If you were not as strong as you are… If you had not been able to return to your body when you did, you would have died."

Quinn sipped his water and mulled that over.

A wounded sound came from Val. Quinn turned to see him frost white and swallowing hard.

"I apologize, Tesined." Ash cringed as he said it. "That was insensitive of me. Quinn is well. I made certain that night."

This was news to Quinn but he was more concerned with Val right now. He moved to his side and slipped an arm around him, "Hey, big guy, I'm fine. Right here." He stretched up to brush a soft kiss on his cheek.

"Yes. Yes, of course." Val pulled in a slow breath. "Do you... I think I'll sit down a moment."

Flax was right there. "We'll all sit for a minute. Only civilized, right?"

The living room was small, even smaller than his and Val's. There was a love seat and a chair. Val took the chair and pulled Quinn down into his lap. Quinn sensed he just needed him close and put an arm around him. Ash and Sage took the love seat and Flax settled himself on the floor nearly at Val's feet.

Well, they were off to a great start, Quinn thought.

"So, Ash is looking into city healer certification," Flax said in an obvious Hail Mary bid for a conversation topic.

"They can always use more healers at AURA," Quinn said. Holy shit. He'd just advocated for AURA.

"Very true. Our medical department has several different sorts of healers, but no elvish healer yet." Val gave him an encouraging nod. "Would have been more than helpful during the lich disaster."

"Flax has told us that story," Ash said.

"Although it was second hand," Flax said.

"Did you actually entrap a lich queen by yourself?" Sage asked, looking at Quinn.

"Well, sort of," Quinn said. "I held the circle, but there were a lot of people that worked to get me set in place to do so."

"Ah, so you were the focus. Now it makes sense." Sage smiled.

"No one used him that way," Val said.

Quinn looked at him, then looked at Sage and back. Had he missed something? Sage looked contrite. Val looked vaguely hostile. Quinn didn't know what he meant by being a focus, but he figured it was something like letting other people channel magic through him.

"I did have some help from Tenzin. He kept me hidden until I had the circle up. After that it was just a matter of holding it in place until Val found and destroyed the psy-thingy."

Flax waved one hand over the other, drawing attention as he shook his head. "No, Sage, you have to understand. Quinn's one of the most powerful magic conduits I've ever come across. Ever. He can pull down more than three of me. Practice, he needs. Control, he's getting that. But pure, raw power? Yeah. He's got that."

He glanced up at Val, who just nodded, before he went on. "Way I understand it, the battle was a joint effort. Warriors held the lich's undead slaves at bay. Tenzin and the incubus distracted the monster. The drow, ah...Kai, unearthed the phylactery and held the hordes back so Val could destroy the thing. But Quinn, and only Quinn, held that monster in that circle. Alone. Without help he faced that abomination."

"Geez, shut up would you." Quinn chuckled. "You make it sound so..." He shook his head.

Ash laughed. "A modest warrior. This world's wonders never cease."

Sage nudged him in the ribs but Ash looked unrepentant.

"It sounds heroic," Flax said stoutly, "because it was."

Quinn put his head in his hands. "Stop. Please. Really."

Sage reached over and put a gentle hand on Quinn's arm, pulled it down until he had his attention. "Watch," he said, and stood. He crossed his arms and straightened his shoulders, giving his head a small shake that sent his hair cascading down his back. He looked completely composed and slightly bored. "It was only what needed to be done," he said in a somber tone. Then he winked at Quinn. "That is the proper response when we are sitting around the hearth and the warriors are singing each other's praises."

Quinn laughed. These elves were absurd.

"Flax's heart is bruised because he was not at that battle," Ash said gently. "So he, what is the word? Overcompensates?"

Flax snorted. "I don't overcompensate. I've had my share of good hunts."

Quinn was actually starting to enjoy himself, even if Flax had made him a little uncomfortable. It was interesting to see them all interacting like this. In their element, so to speak. He leaned back against Val, relaxing.

"You are very brave," Ash said as he rose. He kissed the top of Flax's head as he passed. "My apologies. I must finish in the kitchen."

Funny how Sage didn't bristle or growl when his bond mate kissed someone else.

They heard the sounds of Ash working in the kitchen then his soft humming floating out from that direction. Sage and Flax both smiled and after a moment Flax picked up the melody with soft hums and trills and even whistles that sounded remarkably like bird song. Sage joined in too, singing words in Elvish, half of which Quinn didn't know but it didn't matter because they wove into the subtle music and Quinn swore he could have closed his eyes and easily pictured they were all in a sun-dappled forest rather than a living room in an apartment building. It was beautiful.

Even Val joined in, humming softly, the deep notes resonating against Quinn's back.

When Ash popped back out of the kitchen with a long flat cutting board stacked with all kinds of edible finger foods, the singing wound to a halt and Quinn felt the urge to applaud. He didn't, because everyone else acted like it was nothing, like they had all just been singing along with a tune on the radio or something.

The atmosphere grew more relaxed as they noshed on bunny food and Flax told outrageous stories, waving a carrot as he gesticulated, vegetables alternately standing in for weapons, opponents and even a giant bird.

Quinn had to admit he was entertaining. When he'd first met Flax, he would never have believed he'd be sitting in his company and enjoying it so much or that Flax could be so charming. Ash and Sage too were gracious hosts, pressing choice tidbits on him and Val both until Quinn wondered if they were planning on getting them so stuffed they couldn't move.

By the time Ash called them to the table, Val was more relaxed than Quinn had ever seen him around other people. Maybe this whole social thing wasn't bad. Dinner was an assortment of sauces and dips with all sorts of vegetables, fruits, breads and cheeses to scoop them, some cold some hot, all delicious. It seemed to Quinn as if Flax, Sage and Ash fed each other as much as themselves, but he only really noticed it the first few times. If he'd had someone describe it to him, he would have pictured it like mushy-gushy stuff or like a dominant feeding a fawning pet. Weird. But it wasn't weird. It seemed natural, somewhat tender, the flow of the conversation not in the least interrupted by the offering or acceptance of little morsels.

Trying not to feel self conscious about it, Quinn selected an olive and lifted it to Val's lips.

Val took the offering without hesitation, as if it were the most natural thing in the world, and he reciprocated with one of the cheeses Quinn had made pleased sounds over.

It was all going so well. Something bizarre just had to happen. When Ash brought out dessert, cue the weird.

Flax cleared his throat and dropped to his knees beside Val's chair.

"Tesined Valerian, we recognize your strength and your valor. We would come to you as a triad, to offer our devotion, our strength, our love. There is no other we admire as we do you. Please, Tesined, we offer our hearts, ourselves."

Quinn felt something cold drop into the pit of his stomach. What the fuck was going on here?

A strained moment of silence stretched almost to breaking. Finally, Val put a hand on Flax's shoulder. "This is rather unexpected. Very sudden. I'm touched. But this is not something I've—we've—had time to consider."

"There is no need to make a decision tonight, Tesined," Ash said in a low, soothing voice that was almost a purr. "There is plenty of time to spend learning each other's ways and desires, and then if everyone is agreeable, perhaps there will be more."

It was Sage, who was sitting on Quinn's other side, who took his hand and lifted it to his lips in an oddly old-fashioned gesture. "And we understand how deeply you feel for your *kalesi*, Tesined. We would cherish him as well, and he would always be your First."

That was somehow significant, Quinn felt, as it started to sink in what was happening here. The words Flax spoke were too formal to be just a simple expression of admiration. They were offering to form a *senrist* with Val. Quinn also realized they had planned this. Flax he could almost have expected it from. He had shown more than once how he felt about Val and suddenly all the time he and Flax had spent together, practically wrapped around one another, and sharing the feel of each other's magic felt a whole lot more intimate. He had been fooling himself that it was all done in total innocence. He could have smacked his forehead. He had been so stupid.

He should probably feel angry at being manipulated, but as he tried to sort out how he felt, he didn't think anger was a big part of it. Worried, yes. Maybe even a little flattered. Was he interested though? He hardly knew Sage and Ash. And, was he seriously sitting there considering this? His heart felt like it was beating too hard and too fast. Shouldn't he stand up and maybe stomp out? At least tell them all to back the fuck off. He didn't though. It felt awkward sure, but it didn't feel threatening. None of it did.

As a matter of fact, Flax's eyes were wet and shining and Quinn felt kind of bad for him. Val hadn't rejected him outright, but he sure as hell hadn't said yes.

"A *senrist* at both your backs," Flax whispered. "Protection. Love. Never having to feel alone."

Ash stood and moved to Flax, stroking a hand through his hair. "He needs time to consider, my hunter, my heart," he said gently.

Quinn felt a little shock run through him at those words. He knew as well as Val did that Flax was sleeping with the two of them but he'd braced for a surge of jealousy from Sage, only there was none. Sage still had his hand and now he leaned closer and murmured in Quinn's ear, "Flax has a very high regard for you as well, and Ash and I both see why. You are lovely and powerful. Won't you grace us with your thoughts?"

"Um..." Quinn said intelligently. He let a breath out he hadn't even known he was holding and it made his middle shake with tiny flutters. "We, uh... We hardly know you," Quinn said. There. That was something that made sense.

"Which is why we will court you and Tesined Valerian, if you will allow it," Sage said. "Show you both all the pleasures we have to offer." He rubbed his cheek lightly on the back of Quinn's hand, almost pressing his ear there, but not being quite that bold.

Quinn chuckled and again it sounded shaky. "That's, um... I dunno." He looked to Val helplessly.

Val came to his rescue. "The offer is generous, and we are both overwhelmed. I think it best if we retire for the night, Quinn and I. We will discuss your offer."

Flax stood as Val did. "Captain? I hope..."

"It was a bold move, pup." Val actually reached over and ruffled his hair. "Perhaps a bit of subterfuge on your part, but only a small piece. This will not, no matter the decision, affect your position in the department or our working relationship. I won't allow it. Hear me?"

He got a snuffle and a nod in answer, and Val held out his hand to Quinn. "Come, love. Best we get home."

Sage rose with Quinn and said, "Must you leave, Tesined? We knew you would need time to decide but had hoped you'd stay with us tonight. You are both welcome."

Quinn bit his lips to keep from chuckling. He'd all but came out and said, *let's just have some sex, huh? No strings attached.*

"It is not so simple for everyone, Sage." Val spoke gently, but he tucked Quinn under his arm. "While coupling might occur without attachment here, to do so with people one would like to consider friends? It comes with emotional consequences. We will leave you in each other's company, though, so I need not fear we leave anyone alone and grieving."

"Why would we grieve? You have not said no. And how could you possibly resist?" Sage said with a teasing grin and a sexy pose.

Quinn laughed. He couldn't help it. The man was outrageous.

Even Flax managed a watery smile. "Thank you for hearing us. Thank you for considering. It's all we can ask."

Again, Ash was there, hand on Flax's back and Sage finally got the memo, too, moving around the table with a concerned frown so he could take Flax's hand.

"Goodnight, my dears," Val murmured. "I will speak with you soon."

Quinn was silent all the way down to the street and back to the car. He wasn't angry or brooding, just thinking. The night had been both interesting and strange, in a lot of ways. He had no idea how to feel about most of it. Even with Flax and Val's explanations about what a *senrist* was and how it all worked, he hadn't expected it to be so blatant—so plainly put out there, like a contract. Sure there had been some wooing going on, even Quinn had realized that after a little while, but it wasn't exactly like humans flirted.

If he looked deep enough, Quinn could admit he had been curious, interested. But outside of the sex there was something else that kind of bothered him. Flax had seemed so desperate. And Sage and Ash while less so, had also obviously been willing to bow down and follow anything Val wished of them. He was so independent. He had a hard time getting his head around that. Of course, there was then the issue of sex. Quinn's libido was just as strong as the any healthy young guy, but it was the intimacy with another person where things got complicated for him.

It had taken quite a lot of fixing for him to feel like he and Val had a normal sexual relationship, and even now there were some things that blindsided him and left him shaken and he and Val would have to slow down and talk before they could continue. That was with Val, whom he loved and trusted with his life. He didn't know if he could let anyone else touch him that way.

Val put his hand on the center armrest, palm up, and Quinn automatically put his own hand into his.

"So," Val began.

"Don't ask me what I'm thinking." Quinn cut him off. "Everything is just rattling around in there and none of it feels screwed down too tight. Tell me what you're thinking first."

"I'm thinking that I have been slammed between the eyes with a war hammer—and wonder how long they have been planning this. And I worry for Flax. Part of him is not well."

Val heaved a long, slow breath, his chest expanding until Quinn could practically hear the ribs creak. "I've explained the fading. Unbonded elves seem to be hit harder with it in this world than our original ones. His has begun. If he remains alone… Well, he's young and strong. He does have time."

"But he's not alone. He has Sage and Ash. They all seemed pretty cozy with one another," Quinn said.

"Sage and Ash are bonded mates, my love. He may be having sex with them, but he is still alone."

"He's practically living there. He didn't act like a guest. He was comfortable. I'd say it's only a matter of time before they are all three bond mates. I mean, why not? Since they're so eager to hook up with you."

"He would bond with them as well as part of a *senrist*, yes. They most likely considered it in the first place, since they seem to be compatible. It is, of course, vital to a *senrist* that all parties trust and love each other. Mine, they were all warriors. My bodyguards. My caretakers. But each other's as well. It was… They quarreled sometimes. But what family doesn't? And that's why a *senrist* has, as you say, an alpha dog and a First."

Quinn's fingers tightened on Val's, knowing how hard it was for him to talk about those he had lost. Val never made him feel like he was only a replacement, but Quinn didn't think Val would ever fully recover from the grief of losing them. If it were any other day, this would be the point where Quinn would distract him, change the subject and soothe the hurt from his eyes. But Val was speaking calmly, not getting lost or agonizing over memories, and so long as it wasn't hurting him, Quinn wanted to slake his curiosity as much as possible.

"What does that mean? First? Like a rank or something?"

"It is like a rank or something, and is exactly as it sounds. The First is the first love of a Tesined. As such, he has precedence, is regarded as head of household in many ways."

The most obvious question to ask next would be who had been Val's First before, but Quinn could feel the way Val's fingers had tensed, all the way up his arm. He was not willing to push him on that score, especially not while driving, and he also knew if he did that it would most likely end this discussion.

"Does there always have to be sex involved? With everyone sleeping together?" he asked instead.

Val quirked a Prussian blue eyebrow at him, but if he had some smart remark on the tip of his tongue, he kept it to himself. "No. It's not always part of a normal day. Sleeping? Yes. Elves tend to sleep close. Puppy piles, Matt called it when I tried to describe living arrangements to him. But there do tend to be pairings and triads even within *senrist*s. And if one partner prefers no sexual relations — rare, but it happens — no one is offended."

This was a piece of information Quinn really wished he'd had a long time ago. Suddenly his mind was switching gears from total resistance to actually thinking about how that would all work. Instead of it sounding to his way of thought like they were just offering to put together a convenient orgy group, now it seemed more like what Val had been trying to describe — an extended family. If he took the sex out of the equation, it didn't seem so bad.

He must have been quiet for a long time because Val finally spoke and asked him, "Are you ready to share your thoughts now?"

"Yeah, I think so," Quinn said, picking his words carefully. "I think...maybe you should think about it."

Val shook his head. "*We* will think about it. This must be a joint decision, since you will be First. So. All right. We will consider. But I can't make a decision quickly. This would be an enormous change to our life together. At the moment? I'm too tired to decide anything."

Quinn turned his head and looked at Val thoughtfully. "By thinking about it, I don't mean you should avoid them and go into your shell to literally think, Val," he said knowingly. "This courting thing is like dating, right? It's getting to know one another and seeing where it leads, and if it don't work out then it don't work out. So, maybe we should let them do that."

Val lifted the hand he held and kissed Quinn's knuckles. "This is why I love you so. You keep me from being a snarling old hermit. Thank you for being so sensible."

Quinn laughed and shook his head, then leaned closer and put his head on Val's shoulder. "I'm not sensible — or I don't feel very sensible. I'm just trying to keep up. I used to think I was cynical enough to know what people were up to but I didn't see any of that coming until they were practically on their knees offering to blow you."

Val snorted. "Would have been interesting to let them all try at once."

That put a mental image straight into Quinn's head, one with a lot less clothes and a lot more mouths than had actually been involved. He figured picturing Val naked with a bunch of other men all touching and kissing and sucking on him would have made him sick with jealousy. Instead... Well, interesting wasn't the word he would have chosen. More like hot.

Fortunately they were already pulling into the parking garage. Quinn might even manage to get Val upstairs before ripping his clothes off.

Chapter Fourteen

"Pretty sure the boss man got some last night," Rudy whispered.

"Maybe he'll be less of a bitch." Jordie's lips were pursed in a sour expression.

"The boss is a drow and can hear a flea sneeze at a hundred yards," Kai called over as he swept out of his office. "Please keep that in mind, gentlemen."

Both youngsters paled and flushed by turns, but Kai had no time for their grousing. His mind was clear for the first time in weeks. Amazing what a bit of a hard yeti fuck could do for the brain. *A yeti who loves me, of course. Probably wouldn't be pleasant otherwise.*

"Staff meeting. Soonest possible moment. Conference room. Let's move, please."

It did his dark heart good to hear the scramble behind him. At least one desk chair overturned with a crash as his staff rushed to comply and catch up. *Ah, minions.*

When they had assembled — Terrence rushing in last, out of breath — Kai folded his hands atop the oak conference table. "So. We are no closer than we were before, but we will be. At some point we will be. And when we send staff after this menace, we must be prepared. Something concerns me terribly about any arrest. What might that be?"

The usual suspects stared at him blankly. Vicki raised a hand and Kai managed not to sink his head into his hands.

"Victoria, this is a closed staff meeting, not a school room."

"Sorry, sir." She lowered her hand but her head stayed up, thank the goddess. "The officers. He could kill them. We almost lost two already."

"Precisely so. I would prefer that we limit casualties as much as possible."

"Can we protect them?" Sterling's frown was his thoughtful one. "As a circle? All of us together?"

"What are we gonna do, follow them?" Jordie snorted.

Kai leaned his head against his fist. "'Yes, in a way. I want crystals on every officer and operative who might be involved in an arrest. Crystals keyed to our computer matrix here, where we can monitor and through which we can send spells of protection if necessary. As a circle. Our power combined and enhanced through the program."

"That's a plan I can get behind." Sterling grinned. "Where do you want us?"

It took a bit more explaining and convincing for some of them, but in the end, they all had it and there might have even been some enthusiasm. Good and better.

Even Mindy got involved, getting the right crystals sent up from storage. By one in the afternoon, Kai and his staff invaded the squad room and burst into Val's office.

"Hiltas? Knocking? It's usually done?" Val said at his most ironic.

"No time. Officers. All of them who might be in the field. Call them in. I need them all here—and Quinn. Definitely Quinn. Especially Quinn."

"I'm happy to oblige. But on a bit more information."

Kai pointed to the chest Terrence carried. "We're going to save lives, Captain. Is that enough?"

He parked himself in the center of the squad room with his staff around him like an invading army and waited while the urgent recall went out over dispatch and Val called Quinn.

He waited, ignoring questions as the officers trickled in from patrols. When Quinn appeared, he finally rose from the desktop on which he had perched.

"Quinten. I have a gift for you," he called over the heads of the waiting officers.

"Are you sure you're not actually a drama major? 'Cause, you know, the theatrics are usually excellent when you're around," Quinn said in a mild grumble as he came forward.

"Some things call for a bit of theater," Kai told him softly as he came close. "Your captain won't be at all happy with me in a moment."

He flung open the lid of the chest and retrieved the first blue crystal on a silver chain, which he hung around Cypria's neck. "These crystals are keyed, if you will, to the Research department. If you are involved in arresting or containing the stone mage, call us and we will be with you every step of the way."

He continued around the room as he spoke, placing the crystals on the officers who allowed it and handing them to the ones who didn't. Flax, naturally, didn't let him that close. Kai handed his over with a bow. "Hunter, best to trust me on this one point, even if it's the only thing you ever trust from me."

"Captain?" Flax called over his head. "You authorizing this?"

"Wear the damn thing, Flax. It would most likely be you on that arrest. I'd rather give you any advantage we can."

The damn boy preened—he did—and slipped the chain over his head. Finally, Kai came to Quinn, though Val seized his wrist before he could hand over the last crystal.

"Not Quinn. He's not going after that monster again."

"You don't know that, Val," Kai murmured. "Better if we can help keep him safe."

Quinn stood with his arms crossed and tried to ignore the stabbing feeling that he was pretty sure was his pride taking a hit. He wasn't usually the macho type that had something to prove. He was more in the camp of be smart and live to fight another day—or at least live. Still, it stung to have Val put him on the sidelines in front of what amounted to the entire department.

He heaved a sigh. "Even I know my limits, Kai. I can't avoid or fight something I can't see." There. That wasn't too big of a cop out, was it?

"This."

Kai held up the crystal and now Quinn could see his was different. His was a deep blood red. It sang as Kai let it swing through the air and he realized it wasn't an audible hum. It was power, like Val's sword sometimes sang. "This will pierce the dark as well as let us protect you."

"You will *not* send Quinn." Val loomed over Kai. "I forbid it."

Kai turned to Val, head up, eyes blazing. "You know Quinn's the best chance we have of catching him. Are you willing to cripple us all because of your overprotective nonsense?"

"Hey!" Quinn snapped. "Don't try that bullshit, Hiltas. You don't try and guilt him into doing what you want or I'll take that pretty gift and flush it."

"It's not guilt. It's proper use of resources. If you are the best man for a job, he has no business standing in your way," Kai snarled, though the snarl was directed at Val. "You start checking your personal feelings at the door, Tesined, or you may as well resign."

Val took half a step closer so he stood toe to toe with Kai, taking full advantage of the height difference. "You forget yourself, Hiltas. You invade my department and make demands. You insult me and hurl veiled threats. I suggest you amend your tone and your tactics."

Kai backed up a step, clearly taken off guard, then another until he smacked into a desk.

Val didn't pursue, though storms still brewed in his eyes. "Nevertheless, Quinn's a grown man and not even part of my command structure. He makes his own decisions on this."

"Yeah, well, I'll tell you right now I'm not too keen on being your guinea pig, Hiltas," Quinn said, still pissed off about how manipulative Kai could be. He did take the necklace though, and almost threw it back at him when he saw the triumphant gleam in the drow's eyes.

"Quinn," Val murmured close to his ear. "He only means to keep you safe. I don't approve of you in danger. I don't approve of his approach, but at least this gives you an edge. And if he's feeling a bit ornery? Is that the word? Look at his hand."

It took Quinn a second to process this apparent non-sequitur before he frowned and looked down at Kai's hand. There was a ring on the second to last finger of his left hand. Quinn's eyebrows lifted slowly. "I don't see why that would make you bitchy."

"I'm certainly not bitchy," Kai said, though his eyes had softened as he gazed at the ring. "Assertive is not the same as bitchy. Today, I suddenly feel as if I can face monsters again."

"You have a strange way of celebrating getting a ring put on your finger," Quinn said, then more cautiously, "Tenzin did give it to you, right?"

"He did." Kai's smile was oddly shy. "On furry bended knee."

Quinn blinked. He hadn't been sure if the ring was just a ring or if it was something more and hadn't wanted to ask, so he was glad now he hadn't blundered. He looked down at the ring again and nodded. "It suits you, but Tenzin is smart like that. Congratulations, Kai."

"Thank you." Kai heaved a little sigh, obviously thinking of other, more pleasant things and Quinn was about to rag on him when Ness called from across the squad room.

"Captain! We have another one!"

"Location, Sergeant?" Val strode across to where Ness consulted with dispatch. After a flurry of quiet exchanges, Val turned back to his officers. "Ladies and gentlemen, we have another stone murder on East fifty-eighth. Owner of a small diner there. The Sergeant has the address and a witness. Flax, I want you with Matt, Aello and Cypria. Let's see if we can't get an ID on our murderer. He may or may not be on scene still. Do not approach or pursue without my approval. I want those crystals on until further notice. Kai, are your folks ready to monitor?"

"We'll head up now, Captain. We'll be with them every step."

* * * *

Matt and Aello took one car and Flax and Cypria took the squad's van to investigate their latest crime scene. NYPD was already there securing the area and awaiting them. Before they cleared the parking garage, Flax's phone rang. He looked at the caller ID, expecting the captain or dispatch with further instructions but it was from a landline—Ash or Sage. Technically he shouldn't answer while he was investigating, but he knew there would be no time later, and since they weren't actually at the murder scene yet, he picked up. It was Ash.

"I will say the communication systems here are one of my favorite wonders this world has to offer," Ash said. "Will you be here for dinner this evening, my hunter?"

"I'm kinda doubting it right now, hon. I'm on a call that might take a bit. Hard to say. I don't want to make promises I can't keep."

"The same case?"

"You know I can't tell you that."

"I see." Ash paused. "Please be careful, my dear."

"Anything for you, beautiful. I'll be by as soon as I can. I'll call you if it looks like we're going past midnight."

"All right. Be safe, *kalesi*." Then he was gone.

Flax gaped at the phone. Luckily he was at a stoplight. *Kalesi*? Ash must have misspoken. He wasn't... Or was Ash saying...? No. That was ridiculous.

"Wolfheart. The light's green," Cypria said from the back.

"Sorry. Sorry." *Mind on the job, stupid. Mind on the job.*

He drove.

When they arrived at 58th Street, he parked, got out and opened the back door for Cypria. *Must be sucky not to have opposable thumbs.* They joined Matt and Aello with the police detective and several milling uniforms who were keeping news crews and the curious away from the alley.

"What's it look like?" Flax asked Matt.

"The same as the others," Matt said. "Solid stone. Look of pain and terror on his face. He must have stepped out from the kitchen to throw out the trash and our perp got him. First non-street person. That might be significant."

"Timeline?"

"The kids who found him are afternoon shift. They saw Mr. Rizzo alive and fine when they left work last night. He's apparently always last out."

Flax considered this, though when he looked at the list NYPD provided, the 'kids' were all waitstaff. "So who's with him after the front of the house leaves?"

"Sounds like it's just one kid, dishwasher. Name is..." Matt consulted his notes. "Albert Warren."

"Have we found him yet?"

"No. Mom is frantic. He's not home and according to his school, he didn't show up there either."

"Damn." Flax chewed on his top lip. "Good chance he's one of two things."

"Yes." Aello nodded. "He is either stone as well or he is..."

"Don't even say it yet. We just need to talk to the kid." Flax checked the address for Albert's house. "Cypria, can I bum a ride?"

"Gonna see if you have a trail?"

"I'll start here, but there might be *more* of him at home."

"You want me to call it in to the Cap?" Matt asked, as Flax was the officer assigned to the case and responsible for making the decision in the field. What Matt was really asking of course was should he tell Val they might have a hot trail here and to put Quinn on it as well.

Flax nodded. "Do it. If this pans out, I don't want to be out there alone again."

Matt ambled away, already pulling his phone from his pocket. Flax watched him for a moment and told himself not to worry. Quinn was far better protected within the walls of AURA headquarters surrounded by other mages that would hold a circle for him while he went wandering in the spirit world.

He spent a few minutes trying to pick up Albert in the diner and the alley behind it, but he didn't have a good starting point, something that was only Albert. Too many other scents, both physical and psychic, too many people trampling over each other's trails all day long. Cypria took him up, her strong wings able to bear him easily. One of these days, he would have to ask her for a ride just for fun. Flying was so freaking cool. He slid off her back while she was still landing and sent her back toward Matt. Any hunting he did from here would have to be on foot.

Albert's house was a little semi-detached in Queens—nothing special. Just another relatively well-kept middle-class house in a sea of others. But as soon as Flax walked up the steps and touched the front door, his knees nearly gave way. The heavy, oppressive darkness eeled around the doorway, oil slick pervasive and thick. Instead of knocking right away, he pulled out his phone first.

"Hiltas, you have me? I think I'm at the mage's house. Not a hundred percent on the identity yet." He couldn't make assumptions. Their culprit might be the father or a brother.

"We have you, Wolfheart," the drow came back, his voice clipped and harried. "Whatever else you do out there, don't lose that blasted crystal."

"Aww, he cares," Flax drawled. "I got it. Tell Quinn to be extra fucking careful."

Hiltas wasn't paying attention to him, though. The drow was barking out orders as he hung up. Great. Let the bossy little bastard rule his kingdom, so long as Flax was nice and far away from it. Flax knocked on the door and a harried looking woman answered. The overwhelming darkness wasn't coming from her, though.

"Mrs. Warren? Flax Wolfheart, AURA enforcement. I'm here about Albert's disappearance."

"You're one of those elves," Mrs. Warren said with a gasp. Flax wondered if she'd forgotten to put on her clutching pearls that day. "I can't imagine what my Albert would have to do with any of you."

"Ma'am, there was magic disturbance where Albert works. We're just trying to make sure he's okay. Could I see his room?"

"I… I suppose that would be all right, though Albert doesn't like anyone touching his things."

He followed her up the stairs and as soon as she opened the door, Flax knew. This was the lair of their stone mage. The darkness was so heavy here he wondered how Albert's mother could see anything. But she just stood there, headblind and stupid, while Flax had to fight rising nausea.

"Thank you, ma'am. That's all I need."

He raced downstairs, Mrs. Warren calling after him, "But you didn't even go in!"

Out on the street, Flax closed his eyes and opened his senses. The trail was faint, but he had a direction. The magical signature would grow stronger as he went.

A trilling sound like a bird whistle got his attention and he looked around.

"Ash was worried about you, so he did some scrying to find you," Sage said. "I told him I would keep you safe while you hunted your prey."

"Damn it, Sage, you can't be here. This is police business. Go home. Please."

Sage crossed his arms. "I won't interfere with your police business, but you need someone to keep you from sticking your arm where it doesn't belong," he said pointedly. "I promised Ash I wouldn't let you get hurt, Flax. We have already given our pledge to Tesined Valerian, all of us. How could I let our *kalesi* go into battle alone?"

"I don't have time for this," Flax muttered. There it was again. Now Sage was talking like they were already bonded. "I can't stop you from running with me, but I move fast. No complaints."

Sage nodded, his jaw set, and Flax took off down the street, heading toward the faint trace of his quarry. Part of him was absurdly pleased that Sage kept up so well.

When he stopped at a corner to reorient, he asked softly, "So it was Ash who was worried about me, is that it?"

Sage did not deign to answer but Flax saw the smile he was trying to hide when he simply nodded.

"I see. Well, as long as you don't really care. We have to have someone with professional detachment."

They started to run again and Flax almost missed the words Sage whispered under his breath.

"I care."

* * * *

"I still don't get why you need to do this through the computers," Quinn said.

"It allows us to broadcast much farther than we could without them," Vicki told him.

"Uh-huh," Quinn said, unconvinced.

"Look here." She pointed to the little dots on the computer screen that were traveling along a map. "That's Flax over here and Cypria up there. All we have to do is push the signal out to the crystal Mr. Hiltas attuned to them and the circle will expand to encompass them. A mobile circle! Isn't that exciting?"

It was certainly the most excited Quinn had seen Vicki about anything. He'd say that.

"The computer matrix also allows us to track multiple targets, something we couldn't do in a normal circle," Sterling said with a smile for Vicki. "The computer languages go well with certain types of magic. They mesh perfectly and give us the ability to do more at once than we would with our brains alone."

"Uh-huh," Quinn said again. Whatever they said. But then, he didn't even like having the damn cell phone Kai insisted he carry, so what did he know about what they could do with computers?

"The circles seem to be suffering some structural integrity when people move though," Terrance said. "It's like it's sucking more energy to keep up."

"Uh-huh." Quinn was starting to think he should have gone with Flax. He was used to working alone. Being cooped up in here while everyone else seemed to know what they were doing was making him feel like a major fifth wheel.

"We just need to adjust faster, maybe write code to adjust for the flux when someone moves. That should take care of the fluctuations in power."

"We need more power, Captain!" Quinn said in a horrible Scottish accent. They all looked at him like he'd grown another head. "Oh come on. You're all huge computer nerds and you've never heard of *Star Trek*?"

They all turned back to what they were doing. After a moment Vicki said, "I liked the new movies."

Quinn sighed. "If you're having trouble with keeping the juice up, I could help you with that. What do I got to do, just push it into one of the computers?"

"Don't you dare!" Kai said. "You'll blow the motherboard out, at the very least. We do *not* need a system collapse right now."

Quinn sighed again, feeling less than useless now.

"He could push the energy through one of us," Vicki said. "As a buffer."

"Yes." Kai sounded testy, but Quinn peered over at him and realized the drow was feverishly tapping away at his keyboard while keeping up with the conversation. "Quinn, with me. Vicki, there's your bit of code. Add it in. Flax is moving at warp speed. We must keep up. Quinn, I need you ready to support him on the ethereal side of things." While Quinn settled, Kai murmured, in a better Scottish accent, "And you canna change the laws of physics, Captain." In his non-Scotty voice, he added, "Even though the show regularly did. Not that I mind."

Quinn fiddled with the crystal attached to the chain around his neck. It wasn't that he didn't trust Kai, but Kai had not been in that absolute blackness. He hadn't felt the creeping terror being lost there had caused. Quinn wanted to help, but the truth was he was scared. He had not so much as attempted to scry since that night.

Just as Quinn was working up the courage to close his eyes and let his spirit slide free of his body, there was a soft tap on the door and it opened without waiting for any sort of answer from within. Val came into the room and behind him the tall, lean silver-haired Ash. Kai whirled around, a snarl on his lips, but Val held up a staying hand.

"Ash has offered his assistance. He will go with Quinn into the spirit realm as a guardian." The tone Val used was the one he used when giving orders, the one that said no argument would be tolerated. His expression softened though when he looked at Quinn, "If that's all right with you, Quinn."

Quinn thought about it for a second. He didn't even know if it could be done, but he didn't really see any harm. The worst that could happen was Ash wouldn't be able to follow him. He shrugged. "I don't see why not."

Some of the tension in Val's shoulders eased, and he gave Quinn a reassuring smile before he looked at Ash. "You ready to go hunting?"

Ash gave Quinn a shallow bow. "Ready when you are, *Milani*."

"Valerian." Kai arched an eyebrow at Val, finally allowing his focus to shift from the screen. "Is this wise? Newly crossed and all?"

"We've spoken." Val patted Kai's shoulder. "He promises not to shoot you."

"Oh, that's *very* comforting. Thank you so *very* much," Kai grumbled, but he turned back to his screen. "Sit with Quinn, Bloodroot. Don't touch the screens, the keys or any of the computer mages, if you please."

Ash moved toward Quinn but otherwise gave no other acknowledgment that Kai had spoken. He was about to settle next to him when he noticed the pendant around Quinn's neck.

"That is unnecessary." His tone was bland but there was something about it that caught Quinn's ear, something like Ash had just smelled something unpleasant or seen something rude.

"Quinn, the elf obviously doesn't consider me a person, so I won't even try to explain to him." Kai's gaze was glued to the screen again, but his voice shook. Anger, probably, but there might have been some hurt there, too. "I'd rather you have all the protection we can give you. His. Ours. But it's up to you. I can't force you to wear it, of course."

Quinn sighed. "It's fine. Ash, sit down. Kai wouldn't give me anything that was going to hurt me. He might be bossy, but he's one of the good guys. Let's get this show on the road, huh? We're wasting time." Which was funny for him to be the one nudging things along now, since he'd been dragging his feet since they'd come up here.

Ash sat next to him and said no more about the pendant. Val took a chair at the side of the room, out of the way of the computer mages, but where he could see Kai's screen.

Quinn drew another breath, let it out, and looked over to Val with what he hoped was a reassuring smile—then he closed his eyes. He opened them again when he felt Ash place his hand on his thigh. Ash removed his hand at once when Quinn looked down at it.

"Touch will help me to follow you," Ash said simply.

Quinn suppressed the urge to sigh yet again. "Fine."

Ash settled his hand again, a little lower this time, which was better. Quinn closed his eyes, took a breath and he was above the building looking out across the city. The gray on gray tones he always saw were less washed out for some reason, hints of color popping from the plants and trees.

"This is how you see the world?" Ash's soft melodious voice filled his ears. He had never had that happen either. Usually voices sounded far away and tinny, echoes coming down a tunnel. Ash sounded like he was standing right beside him. Then Quinn saw that he *was* standing right beside him. He didn't look like the Ash he knew was sitting next to his physical body. He was dressed head to toe in elvish armor, silver and gold and polished leather. A bow almost as long as he was tall was slung on his back, along with a quiver of red fletched arrows. His long silvery hair was plaited on either side of his head and pulled back from his handsome face. Quinn took a moment to pick his jaw up off the ground.

"Yeah, this is how it looks to me when I'm not in my skin anyway," Quinn answered.

Ash didn't seem to have any further comment on that. "I don't think I've ever entered the spirit realm so quickly," he said, sounding bemused. "Shall we go searching now, little hunter?"

Quinn gave him a hard look. "Not sure I like being called that."

Ash bowed low. "My apologies, *Milani*. I meant no disrespect."

"What does that word mean?" Quinn asked.

"It would most closely translate to Tesined's First. It's an endearment."

"Oh." Quinn looked out over the city, feeling suddenly flustered. "We need to get going." He reached out and took Ash's hand, the one on this side of the spirit veil. He thought of the inky darkness—the magic he had touched so briefly before—and he let his vision unfocus and expand, looking for the telltale trace.

"Remarkable," Ash whispered.

Quinn saw it. The smudge that was not a twinkle of light calling to him, but whose absence was just as much of a beacon. He was trying to hide, but not enough to fool Quinn. "Hold on." It was all the warning he gave before he focused on the thought that would move him from one place to the other.

In the distance, he could still hear the activity in the Research department. Kai's sharp voice called out, "He's tracking! Stay with him!"

"But Officer Wolfheart?" a younger voice, he thought it was Rudy, called back.

"Stay with both—never mind. I've got Quinn. Stay with Wolfheart. Concentrate on keeping him safe."

Strange how he heard them so clearly, but they seemed a thousand miles distant.

* * * *

"That bastard Rizzo! This is all his fault!" Albert wailed.

His friend did not respond, of course. It was still daylight and he slept during the day. Albert had tried to get him to move when the sun was up and no matter how much energy he put in, it was no use. He stayed solid stone. Once the sun went down though, that was a different story.

Like last night. He had been finishing up the last of the dishes and washing down the sinks in the kitchen when Rizzo had come through and said something weird. He'd told Albert that he was doing a good job, he could always depend on him. Steady as a rock.

Albert had felt his heart lurch in his chest and his throat tighten in fear. Why would he say that? What did he know? Had he seen his friend waiting for him in the alley? He must have. That was the only explanation for that sly comment. He had seen. He knew.

Albert had no choice. When Rizzo had dragged the bags of wet garbage into the alley to throw in the dumpster, Albert had followed him, and all it had taken was a nod and his friend took care of Rizzo.

Albert had gone back into the restaurant, thrown up in the toilet, washed his face and went back out into the alley.

He could hear a clock ticking, one of those big old-fashioned clocks, tick tick tick… His time was running short. This wasn't like any of the other ones. Rizzo knew him—knew where he lived—and other people knew that Rizzo knew him. His secrets were leaking out around the edges and the tightness in his throat started to strangle him. Choke collar. They were hunting him like a dog.

In a daze he took his friend to a hiding spot, then went home, went through the motions. He needed as much of a head start as he could get and he had lain in a cold panic the whole night. But if he had left right then, left as soon as Rizzo was taken care of, then his parents would have given him up to the police instantly. Let them think he was in school all day. As soon as the sun was down, he would take off with his friend.

He paced and paced and murmured reassurances to his friend and when the tick tick ticking got too much in his head, he slapped his ears and tore at his hair until it stopped. Taking huge gulps of air, Albert tried to calm himself. It wouldn't be long now. The sun was already starting to sink. They would be safe—very soon. They had slipped the net. He was sure of it.

Then he felt it. The tug that wasn't real. The prickle along his skin like ants. They knew where he was. They were coming.

Albert moaned. "No...no, no, not yet!" He put his arms over his head and flung out a wall of darkness. *Drown them. Smother them. Don't let them see!* He pushed it as viciously as he could.

* * * *

It was so sharp and sudden, Flax had no warning. Not like that first night where he knew he was approaching something dark and dangerous. This time the black wall hit him so hard, he couldn't breathe.

He stumbled and crashed to his knees on the pavement, clawing at his throat. Sage, who had been several steps behind, was there immediately, throwing up a wall of air and wrapping his arms around Flax.

The crystal nestled against his heart began to hum, warmth washing through the terrifying chill of the blackness. He drew a breath and another, his sight clearing, Sage's worried questions finally understandable again.

"Flax! Flax! Please, please say something!"

"'M okay, hon. I'm…yeah. I'm okay." He fought his way back to his feet with Sage's help, pulling in huge gulps of air. The crystal kept humming, so whatever spell the stone mage had hit him with was still out there. He sent a silent thank you to a sneaky drow and the Research kids, then he spat out a curse.

"What is it, *kalesi*?" Sage cried out. "Are you wounded after all?"

"No. Worse. I've lost the damn trail."

Frustrated, he cast out into the ether, but his own frustration and shock stood in the way. He couldn't focus well enough, his insides still shaking from the attack of black fear.

Just as he thought he was going to have to give up or go back and try to pick up the trail again, his phone vibrated in his pocket. He pulled it out, looked at the caller ID and answered, "Captain?"

"Quinn says you need to go left," Valerian told him. "He says don't trust your eyes. He'll guide you."

Flax sucked in another slow breath, trying desperately for calm. "You up in the…where they have the circle, Captain?"

"I am."

"They know I was attacked?"

After a moment's hesitation, Val's voice was soft and concerned, "They know. They tell me you're all right. Are you? Can you go on?"

"Shaken, Captain." Funny how Val's voice alone gave him extra courage. No. Not funny. It's how he was hardwired and he knew it. "But not broken. I'm on it. I'm moving."

Chapter Fifteen

It took Quinn a few trips back and forth before he knew where he was in relation to where Flax was. Street signs were useless in the spirit world. They didn't make any sense. If he traveled to a place he already knew, it was easy enough to tell someone where he was, but if he'd never been there before, he had to keep jumping back and forth between a place he knew and the location of what he'd been looking for until it made sense to him.

Ash seemed fascinated by the process and at the same time, he was looking paler and paler. Quinn wasn't sure if that was because he was getting tired or because Ash was. Finally he got Flax close enough to the location where their rogue mage was hiding that Quinn knew where he was.

"Tell Flax it's the church at the end of the street. He can't possibly miss it. He's going to need backup," Quinn said in the airy singsong voice that he used when he was in two places at once.

"Kai, where is he?" he heard Val ask in that command tone he used.

Tapping. More tapping. "Riverside Drive...ah, I see what Quinn means. Riverside Church. No, he really can't miss that one."

"Flax," Val barked into the phone. "Riverside Church. It should be...yes. That one. The one with all the gargoyles. You need to wait for backup. Do not attempt to apprehend. You hear me?"

In his strange, two-place state, Quinn got both sides of the conversation.

"I'll go in as close as I can. But if he spooks, Captain, no guarantees. We have to stop this one."

"Quinn, where are you going?" Ash asked. They could see Flax with Sage on the street, and the church was in sight. They had their prey cornered and there was really nothing left for them to do here, so Quinn was not surprised by the question when he moved toward the huge edifice.

"It will help if they don't have to search the building. We can pinpoint him so when backup arrives, they will know exactly where to go."

Ash considered this for a moment. "He knows we are out here, Quinn. If you enter his lair, he will either fight or flee. Neither is a good choice."

"He won't see us. Kai's charm is keeping him from throwing that wall at us. I can get in and out before he knows we're there."

"This is not wise," Ash said, but he continued to follow Quinn.

"You're not gonna tattle on me?" Quinn said.

"I can't."

"What? Honor won't let you?" Quinn asked.

"No. I can't speak in the physical while I walk in spirit. I would have to leave you to tell Tesined Valerian that you are being foolish."

Quinn grinned and kept going.

The church was huge and covered in stone carvings and sculptures. Quinn couldn't help wondering which of them came to life and wandered around killing people. As soon as he thought it, he was pulled into the building. It was a large room, high up, Quinn could tell that much, but the trip he hadn't even meant to take had disoriented him. Ash gasped softly beside him and looked paler than ever.

Quinn didn't have time to ask if he was all right, though. They weren't alone. A young man paced frantically back and forth on the dusty floorboards, both hands clutching his hair in handfuls that looked painful. He let out a screech and whirled toward them, one hand thrust out. Quinn shoved Ash behind him and felt the pressure hit him, but it was brief, and parted, flowing past and leaving nothing in its wake other than a cold, uneasy feeling. Kai's necklace was awfully spiffy.

Ignoring him, Quinn went to the window and looked out so he could get the location.

"That's enough, Quinn. We must leave. Now," Ash told him, grabbing his shoulder.

"Okay." He thought about going back, braced for the feeling of being dragged down, and it didn't come.

Ash cursed in Elvish. "He's using a different spell. Like a circle. A binding. We're trapped."

The part of him in the physical world still heard the staffers holding the circle and Kai's inventive cursing, followed by Val's bellow.

"What do you mean he *has* them? Hiltas, do something!" Val's voice went on, obviously not to Kai any longer. "Yes. Trapped them, wherever he is in that building. That's what I'm getting out of this fiasco. No…he seems all right so far. Yes. Damn it, Flax! You can't do that! Flax!"

It was a good bet the hothead had hung up on Val. Great. Trapped in some weird spirit world tar pit, with a crazy-ass, valor-obsessed elf charging toward them. This was gonna get fucking interesting.

* * * *

Flax turned off his phone. Backup was on the way. Plenty of it. But he couldn't wait. Quinn and Ash were both trapped up there. Somewhere. He was honorbound to protect the one, and damn it, Quinn was his friend, and he wasn't about to lose the other, the one he loved.

Wait, what? Where in all Hell's pits had *that* come from?

No time. Just no time. He strode up to the front of the church with Sage on his heels and placed both palms flat against the stones.

"What are you—?"

"Help me. Lend me your strength. We have to find them."

Sage blinked at him, since Flax hadn't shared what was happening yet. He really couldn't afford to have Sage freak out right now. But the pup took orders well and placed his hand on Flax's shoulder—all his raw, youthful power pouring into Flax. He flitted mentally through the church, the main floor, then up. It just felt darker there. If Albert had gotten his stone friend here—and it was a damn good bet he had—the gargoyles were up higher. Up toward the top bell tower floors.

There...there...up near the top of the single bell tower. Convenient that there was only one tower. Made it easier. Flax turned and took Sage's face between his hands.

"You can't come with me. Stay here."

Sage's green eyes widened. "I *must* go with you. I promised."

"This is the police business part. I can't involve you."

"Well and fine. Don't involve me. What can you do if I follow you?"

Flax growled. "I can arrest you."

"You have no time." A smile blossomed on Sage's face. "You have no time and only one set of those metal wrist binders. You cannot arrest me."

"I don't want—" Flax stopped himself. No, he didn't want Sage hurt, any more than he wanted Ash trapped by a psychotic killer. But Sage was a warrior and to tell him no to keep him safe would trample on his pride. He wouldn't listen. "Fine. Stay behind me."

"I will guard your back. Gladly."

Flax rolled his eyes and pulled one of his knives as he went in. The church was strangely deserted for this time of day, though maybe the kid's darkness unconsciously drove people away. He made his way through to the elevator, the only way up to the tower, where the sign said the observation platform was closed indefinitely. *Yeah, for anyone else, maybe.*

He put a hand over the call button and summoned the elevator the hard way, by magic. It rumbled down its shaft, taking its sweet time. But once they were inside the car, the floor buttons only went to the twentieth floor. There would be a staircase, since this tower was certainly taller than that.

"Just gets better and better." Flax sent the elevator back up, watching the indicator lights. "I want you at least fifty feet behind. We're gonna come up on a tight passage, I'm thinking. He hits me with something, you need to be far back enough not to have me knock you down the stairs."

"Understood." Sage nodded, his grin gone now. He wasn't armed, since he didn't have a license to carry, but the magical backup would be more important here than blades.

"I know you're there!" A voice echoed from above when Flax was nearing the top of the stairs.

"You can't touch me now, can you? Got you like a little bug." The voice was filled with rage. Flax could hear no answer but the voice went on after a moment. "Got you trapped in there. You can't spy on me now. You were with those cops, weren't you? I felt you that night we took care of the stupid Jesus freak. I thought I got rid of you then but I guess not. I'm gonna take care of you now though—soon as I figure out what you're doing to block me, I'm gonna crush you good."

"Who is the madman talking to?" Sage whispered so softly it barely carried to Flax's ear. He turned and glared at the younger elf in a way that clearly said 'I-thought-I-told-you-to-stay-back'. Flax mouthed, "Quinn."

It wasn't ideal, but at least Albert was distracted. Could only help. Flax started his walk up the stairs on silent feet, quieting his mind and his breathing enough to sneak up on the most sensitive creatures. Even the unicorn he had trapped for Queen Hemlock hadn't seen him coming.

They were almost there. Flax ducked down as the landing to the observation platform came into view. This was one of the few times he wished he had accepted the offer of firearms training, though a mage like this one could turn the weapon against him. Make it explode in his face.

On the last five steps, Sage scraped against the wall. Albert turned, fear and fury in his eyes.

"You! You're that damn cop I couldn't get rid of!"

Construction debris surrounded him. Albert stretched out his hands and a head-sized chunk of stone flew toward Flax. He flung himself off the stairs into the room and rolled to the side, hoping Sage had gotten out of the way.

The stone hit the iron railing of the staircase and bounced down the empty stairs. Sage had leaped as well when Flax dodged and now stood opposite where the staircase led into the room. Flax snapped his wrist, sending his blade spinning toward their target, hoping to disable, but the boy raised a wind and knocked the knife from the air.

The fact that there were two of them had the enraged young mage panicking, turning his head back and forth between them. He lifted his hands and Flax prepared to duck more flung debris but he turned his wrath on Sage this time, sending out a black wall toward the elf, who wasn't wearing one of Kai's protection charms.

Without thinking, Flax launched from his crouch, using his body as a battering ram and net to take Albert down. He couldn't stop the psychic wall though, which slammed into Sage and smashed him hard into the tower stones.

Fury ignited in Flax's veins that anyone would dare harm his Sage. Even enraged, he knew just where to hit an enemy and how hard. Always. He braced his arm against Albert's throat, ignoring the blows being rained on him from hands and feet, and punched the boy behind his right ear, just hard enough to take him out.

Panting, he sat back on his heels, flipped Albert over and cuffed him. More would need to be done, but that would do for now. He hoped Quinn and Ash were safe now. He had no way to tell without calling headquarters, and right now he had more immediate concerns.

Sage had slid down the wall and lay in a heap on the floor, one arm bent at an unnatural angle. Nearly sobbing with relief that Sage still breathed, Flax stroked his hair back from his forehead as he fumbled the phone from his pocket.

"I need medical! Riverside Church, top of the tower, and where the hell is my backup?" he bellowed at dispatch. Not the operator's fault, but he'd had just about enough for one day.

Even as he was yelling into the phone, he could hear sirens on the street.

"They should be arriving now," Nestor told him.

"Sergeant, thank goddess you're there. Medical?"

"On the way. Are you injured?"

"No, it's…someone who was trying to protect me."

"Oh, damn it, Wolfheart. Civilians? This is not good."

"Sorry. I'll explain later." *This is so not my fault!* "I take full responsibility." He bent over Sage and kissed his forehead. "You in there, hon? Help's on the way. You need to be all right, you know. Ash is gonna kill me it you're not. I'm gonna kill me if you're not. Sage?"

Green eyes blinked up at him, a flicker of recognition for a moment, then his face scrunched in pain. Sage gasped and clutched at his arm as he spat out a particularly foul Elvish curse.

"Try to keep still, sweetheart. It's broken," Flax said gently. "I'm sorry. Didn't move quite fast enough."

"Not your fault," Sage said through gritted teeth. "Did you stop him?"

"Yes. Cuffed and out cold. The Miranda rights will have to wait." Flax moved to let Sage's head rest in his lap. "Help's coming. I'm really mad at you, but probably couldn't have done this without you here, so don't do this to me again. I hate feeling all conflicted."

"I'm sorry you're angry, *kalesi*," Sage murmured. "But I would do so again, to protect you...only I didn't do a very good job of that."

"You did. I'm not even bruised. For me, that's a miracle." Flax gave him a soft kiss on the lips. "And when did you and Ash begin calling me beloved? We're not even bonded. It's not exactly kosher."

"I don't know that word. Kosher," Sage said. "Whatever it means, you are still our *kalesi*. Kosher cannot change that."

Flax's stomach did a drop and roll on those words. Really? They loved him? How in all of creation had that happened? He knew they liked him, liked spending time with him and found him acceptable as part of a proposed *senrist*. But more than that? He hadn't...

Though maybe he should have. Maybe he was an incredible fool, though Quinn would have been sure to tell him that, had he asked. The way Sage looked at him when an evening drew to a close and said *stay, please stay*, the way Ash had taken to calling him *my hunter*.

Not something he could sort out right now. The elevator hummed in the shaft and help was on the way up. Anyway, he loved Val. Right?

Just the fact that he had to ask himself made his mind churn in confusion. When had everything gotten so damn hard to figure out?

Sage started to struggle to his feet when they heard the elevator coming and Flax couldn't convince him to lie still and wait. He had to stop himself from rolling his eyes. The suspect was secured and that was help rattling up the elevator shaft, but Sage would not even consider not meeting them on his feet if he was able to stand. He was gray with pain and his face was set in a hard grimace by the time he was up and the elevator doors were opening.

The medtechs swarmed them and more officers poured up the stairwell. They unfolded a stretcher, which Sage refused disdainfully, but at least he conceded that he needed help back down the stairs to the elevator. Their suspect was strapped down to the stretcher instead.

"We'll need more than cuffs for this young one," Aello said. She directed the comment at Matt, obviously seeking his advice—a marked change from when she could hardly speak to him. "I can sing him back to sleep if he wakes in transit, but I can't always stay with him."

"Should be able to get some kind of containment up around him." Matt's eyebrows drew together. "Kai and his folks should be able to come up with something." He glanced over at Flax. "You okay, kid?"

"Fine. No broken bones here."

"You look a little shaky."

"Didn't say I wasn't scared for everyone involved." Flax shot him a grin that didn't feel natural at all. "Quinn and Ash...we have word yet?"

"Not yet. You can call headquarters downstairs," Matt told him.

* * * *

Quinn lay on the floor with a cold cloth pressed over his eyes while everyone else in the room tried to celebrate quietly around him. His head was pounding and he could feel the telltale ache inside that let him know the magic burn was going to sink its teeth into him but good this time. He would be fine, soon. He didn't feel anything broken seriously, but he was too tired to try and talk or explain, so he let Ash do it for him.

"When we saw Flax and Sage come up the stairs, we tried to break the circle," Ash was telling Val. "It was very well constructed, a lot of power sunk into it."

Quinn would have snorted if it wouldn't have hurt so much. That was an understatement. That circle had felt like it was made of stone—as strong as one of Quinn's own.

"I tried to tell Quinn that there was no point in tearing down the circle when there was not much we could do in our spirit forms anyway, to wait, but when the young mage attacked Flax and Sage, there was no stopping him. He tore the circle apart, but by then Flax had incapacitated the mage."

Yes, he had. And there had been nothing left for them to do there but go back to their bodies when they saw both Flax and Sage were not in further danger at that point. Quinn reached up and pulled the wet cloth from his head and squinted against the brightness of the room. Gingerly, he tried to sit up.

"Might want to stay down, love," Val said gently, stroking a soothing hand over his head. "I'm just relieved you're safe. And it's possible that your struggle to break the circle distracted the boy enough to let Flax get close. My only question at this point is where was the gargoyle? Why didn't it come to assist him?"

"Maybe there isn't one," Quinn said, giving voice to something he had been trying to work out in his head since he and Ash had found the mage alone in the tower room. "Maybe he projected it, like a glamour. Or hell, maybe he shifted into it like the Incredible Hulk. Or maybe it just wasn't around and we still have one half of a killing team on the loose. I don't know. I can tell you I didn't feel any other magic drawing me when I was trying to find him."

"Huh." Val's eyebrows drew down. "All possible. We can't let our guard down until we know. We can question the boy when he wakes, but I have my doubts about him giving us anything useful." He walked out into the hall, but he could be heard making a call down to the squad room for extra patrols that evening.

Quinn forced himself up to a sitting position with a groan and Ash put a hand on his back between his shoulders. "You would have been well suited had you been born an elf, Quinten. Our stubbornness is also legendary."

Quinn chuckled softly and winced. "Don't know if that was supposed to be a compliment or an insult."

"Both," Ash said. "You should have listened to me. I was there to protect you, yet you insisted on trying to destroy yourself." He sounded peevish to Quinn's ear, but maybe that was just worry he was hearing.

"I wasn't trying to destroy myself. I knew I could do it if I just put enough 'oomph' into it."

Ash just shook his head.

Kai made a wide berth around Ash to crouch on Quinn's other side. "Risky, but it was well done. The power fluctuations showed a definite weakening on Albert's side at the point where yours was at its strongest. It took both you and Wolfheart to take him down."

"Are they okay? They were both conscious when we came back here, but...?"

Kai edged away from Ash a little farther, so it couldn't be all good news. "Wolfheart's fine. No injuries. The young elf who shouldn't have been there? Managed to get away with just a broken arm. Could have been much worse."

Quinn felt the small hairs on the back of his neck rise and his skin prickled like the barometric pressure just dropped and he realized Ash was gathering power. "Ash, don't."

"Watch your tongue, drow. Do not speak so dismissively of our warriors," Ash said, as coldly as Quinn have ever heard him speak.

"You may as well watch yours," Kai said in that too-soft voice that Quinn knew meant he was well and truly pissed off. "This is not the old world. I am not your enemy. This is my department and my organization. Your boy put himself in the middle of police business, where he did *not* belong. And while I'm certain he's very brave and he thought he was doing the right thing, what he did can be grounds for *arrest* here. Wolfheart's going to be lucky if the board doesn't put him on suspension for letting Sage be there."

Quinn did not have the reflexes to stop him. He barely saw him move. Ash grabbed Kai by the throat and slammed him to the floor so fast it was just a blur. And here he had been thinking Ash, the gentle one, was the pacifist in their group. Fuck. "Ash! Let him go!"

Power of a more dangerous sort was gathering. Kai's sharp teeth were bared in a snarl. Things could have gone so very wrong if Val hadn't stomped back into the room then, having obviously heard Quinn shout.

"Ash!" he bellowed. "Out! Now! You will not manhandle one of our department heads! Out, or I take you out myself!"

Ash swore in Elvish and Quinn happened to know those words—not something said lightly. The translation was something like 'smug drow' but with a racial inference that made it a dire insult. "He threatened Sage and Flax, Tesined," Ash snarled.

Val ran a hand back through his hair in a frustrated gesture. "He did no such thing. I heard. Oh, yes. He was telling you truths about this world. Sage had no business being there. Civilians involved in police business can have consequences here. I'll speak for Flax, though it will be the board's decision. And I won't insist on charges for Sage, but another police department wouldn't look the other way."

He disengaged Ash's hand from around Kai's throat and helped Kai sit up. "As difficult as it will be for you to hear, Kai is my friend. He's prickly and annoying sometimes, but he's saved my life and risked his more than once to keep the world safe. I suggest, strongly, that you begin to think in terms of *this* world."

That saying people use about tension being so thick you could cut it with a knife? Quinn had never figured it was a real feeling until that point. The three of them stayed tensed as if even a twitch might set any of them off. The lights had dimmed, almost as if a dark shroud lay over them, Kai's magic snapping and hissing at his fingertips. Then Val's phone rang.

Ash stood stone-faced and Kai glared while Val answered, spoke a few words and disconnected again. "Flax and Sage have arrived in the infirmary. Perhaps you should go see them," Val said in a way that everyone knew was not a suggestion.

Ash bowed his head to Val. "Yes, Tesined." He turned on his heel and stalked out.

Kai lifted a hand with a snarl, a dark ball of spitting lightning hovering over his palm. The charge in the air thickened until it was hard to breathe, a fretful magic wind tugging strands from Kai's braid and whipping loose papers into whirlwind eddies.

"Stop," Val said softly. "Kai, don't risk everything for this. It's not worth it."

"*Iskental aelfe!*" Kai snapped, which Quinn was almost certain meant *fucking elf*, but with nastier implications. The wind's murmuring rose to a tortured shriek.

Undeterred, Val put a hand on his arm. "Kai, think. Please."

The research staff cowered behind their computers. Rudi had gone so far as to dive under the table. Kai glared at the hand on his arm, then gave a frustrated huff and let his dark magic dissipate.

Quinn let out a shaky breath.

"I don't think he likes me," Kai said in his driest tone, his rage settled into simple bitterness.

Val gave him a quick, one-armed hug. "Are you hurt?"

"Pride, ego, feelings, all wounded and bleeding out on the floor. Physically? No."

"The rest will recover," Val said with a chuckle. "It takes longer than a few weeks to overcome decades of racial tension. Ash doesn't strike me as the most stubborn sort, though. He'll adjust eventually."

"I hope to live that long," Kai muttered, rubbing at his throat. "*He* should hope to live that long."

Quinn had got to his feet and he patted Kai's shoulder. "He didn't mean it, Kai."

"He most certainly *did*." Kai snorted. "Though he's not the first. There were enough nearly deadly fights when Val and I both lived on the elf reservation. So, yes. I have work to do. Ladies and gentlemen, we need to construct an amulet curse to contain our stone mage's magic."

Quinn could have offered to help, but he knew he was pretty much useless in the magic department for a day or two. He consoled himself with the fact that at least it didn't take him weeks to recover like most mages suffering from magic burn. He moved into Val's orbit and gave him a hug. "I think I'll go down and check on them too."

"Thank you." Val kissed the top of his head. "Make sure Flax is really all right. He tends to underreport physical injuries."

Quinn nodded and gave him another squeeze before heading out into the hall. He thought he might catch up to Ash at the elevator but he'd either already caught one or he'd taken the stairs. That was all right. Maybe a few minutes to himself would be enough to cool Ash off. As he waited for the elevator himself, he wondered why he was even worried about it. Kai was right. They had broken the rules. He physically cringed when he thought it. When had he started giving a damn about rules? This... This was what happened when you made a bond mate out of a cop. He sighed. He was going to have to throw out his anarchy badge. It would be too hypocritical now.

He got into the elevator and took it down to the infirmary. He'd known as he'd been saying it that it was absurd to tell Kai that Ash hadn't meant it. Kai was right about that too, Ash had definitely meant it, but he'd felt the need to...to what? Defend Ash? To make it out to be not as bad as it was? Or maybe it was just wishful thinking. Elves. He was up to his eyeballs in them and nothing ever seemed to be straightforward.

Flax was leaning a hip on the intake counter, a hand on Ash's arm, when Quinn entered medical. He looked bone-tired, but he still had a smile for Quinn. "Hey! Good to see you're back in your body. What the hell happened up there? Ash won't say, but, yeah, something happened that wasn't part of the apprehension."

Quinn waved a dismissive hand. "It's not important. We're here, and so are you and Sage. The bad guy is caught—or one of them anyway. Let's just chalk this one up as a success and move on. Are you okay? Don't lie. Val asked me to check, so don't try to play macho."

"Like Ash would let me get away with it." Flax rolled his eyes expressively. Most elves couldn't get that expression down quite right, but he did. "I'm a little banged up. The kid had a mean kick and was wearing heavy boots. But it's just bruises. Promise."

"Uh-huh. Where's Sage?" Quinn asked.

"In X-ray—which Ash doesn't approve of."

Quinn arched an eyebrow and looked from Flax to Ash. "Don't knock modern medicine. It can help a lot of things that even magic can't do on its own."

"He's an elf, Quinn. He will heal a broken bone fairly quickly with rest and my help," Ash said.

"Yep. He will. So there's no need to resist help that can set the bone straight and help him heal even faster. Plus, the pain meds they'll give him will make his suffering a lot less. And don't worry, they know better than to give elves acetaminophen."

Flax turned an interesting shade of scarlet at that and he muttered something to his shoes, but he managed to pull himself together to agree. "Elf or no elf, broken bones are a bitch. If it were me, I'd take all the help I can get. Human medicine, you, me... Whatever works that won't be a problem later."

"C'mon. Let's go storm the castle and keep him company. If Sin's working on him, he's a sucker for letting loved ones stand around and coo, even when he's trying to work."

"Ha, true. Even an incubus has soft spots," Flax said with a grin as he shoved off the counter. "Hope he's forgiven me about the spider silk thing."

Quinn looked at him from the corner of his eye as they started down the hall. "I'm not sure if I want to know what the spider silk thing means."

"Pretty sure you don't. Wasn't my best moment ever."

It was only a casual stroll down the hallway but as they neared the big double doors that led to the diagnostics area, Quinn became aware of how they had automatically fallen into a formation, with Ash and Flax flanking him, letting him take the lead. It was weird. What was weirder was it sort of felt right.

Sin was indeed the tech on duty and was just rolling Sage back from the X-ray room, talking to him in his cheerfully irreverent way. Sage was either on something good, in too much pain or Sin had completely charmed him, since he was allowing himself to be wheeled. There was no way Quinn could see Sage letting his pride bend that far otherwise.

"Oh, and hey, you can't do your own hand jobs for a bit either, so someone's gonna have to help. Bet they'll beg to, since they'll feel all bad for you."

He spotted Quinn and waved as he turned a corner. "Hey, Quinny! We're in six if you're coming to see this handsome hunk of elf. Or you could leave him with me. I won't complain."

Quinn trooped in with his mini-elf squad and damn it, he was getting tired of tense rooms. Sin and Flax stared at each other, hard-eyed, arms crossed over chests, but Flax, thanks the gods, broke first.

He did that thing where he stared at his shoes. "I'm sorry I...tripped you."

Sin cocked his head to one side, his ridiculously handsome face pretty, even when he frowned. "Well, I'm sorry for calling you a goldilocks who couldn't even handle one bear. Sort of."

Flax snorted and threw a mini-whirlwind to muss Sin's hair while Quinn tried hard not to laugh. He failed.

Ash ignored all of them and went to Sage's side to press his hand to his forehead and leaned down to kiss his temple. Sage verified for Quinn that he was doped up to the eyeballs by murmuring a string of sappy, slurred Elvish. He didn't catch all of it but enough to know it was something about how beautiful Ash looked naked and moaning.

Almost instantly, there was a different sort of tension in the room. Sin's eyes had gone glassy and Flax tried to be discreet about adjusting himself.

"Well. Ah, yeah." Sin took a deep breath through his nose with a little smile. "I do love the smell of horny elf in the evening... Anyway, doc says the forearm's broken in two places. She'll be here in a few minutes to set it and then she'll probably cut him loose since he has someone to watch over him."

"Right," Quinn said and looked at Flax. "If you're not injured, you should probably go up and talk to Val, give your report—or whatever you cops need to do. Kai is working on some sort of containment for the dickhead that was trying to kill us. Once that's up, I'm sure Val's gonna wanna question him."

Flax gave him a little salute that was only a tiny bit mocking, though he did stay to give Sage a soft kiss on the lips, which brought about another round of interesting drugged observations from Sage on Flax's bedroom prowess. Flax chuckled and kissed Ash before he went to the door.

"I'll see you both at home," he said, with a suspicious hitch in his words.

When he was gone and Quinn was sure he was out of earshot, he looked at Ash, "You know he's totally twitterpated, right?"

"I don't understand that word," Ash said with a frown.

"It's from a movie that we use to emotionally damage young children. It means he's in love," Quinn said.

Ash gave him an odd look, as if he had more questions about that statement. Instead, he shook his head. "I know the cultural references will take time, and sometimes I think what I hear from humans is humor, but it's difficult. Flax enjoys our company. His heart lies elsewhere."

"C'mon. I thought you guys were the poster children for the polyamory movement. He's got the hots for Val, sure, and that might have a little more to do with how his brain is wired, but once he gets around to admitting it to himself, you're gonna see. He's totally in love with you guys."

Sometime during this conversation, Sin had slipped out of the room. He wasn't always a total jackass. Ash turned away, but not before Quinn saw his eyes fill. "He holds himself back from us. We would accept him as ours, but he seems unable to make that leap, to give us that trust. Perhaps someday…"

Quinn snorted softly. "Perhaps sooner than you think."

* * * *

"Feeling up to accompanying me for the interrogation, pup?" Val asked, half distracted by whatever was on his screen.

Flax sat up a little straighter. He'd expected a chewing out, at least a Very-Stern-Talking-To as only Val could do. "More than up to it, Captain."

"Hmm. Don't be too eager." Val sighed and stood to pull on his suit jacket. As their ranking officer, he was more often in jacket and tie rather than in uniform and, dear gods, talk about suit porn. He'd make any designer want to sign him to model.

"Captain?"

"Kai was present while our suspect was being booked. He is being very uncooperative and hostile. A psychiatrist has been called for an evaluation, but based on Kai's observations and that of a couple veteran officers, they don't believe he is acting. A professional diagnosis will need to be made, of course, but it's fairly safe to say he's suffering from a psychological illness."

"So you don't think we're gonna get much about motive or an accomplice's whereabouts."

"Correct."

They walked down the stairs to holding—the lawbreaker holding on the fourth floor rather than the one in the basement. That one was for crossovers deemed too dangerous to allow loose, like certain dragons and the less sane dire wolves and such.

The front of the cell was barred, cinder block walls on the other three sides. There was a window, high up on the wall and too small to crawl out, but at least light would come in during the day. Val took a chair in the hall facing the cell and Flax took position at his shoulder.

"Albert," Val said gently. "Do you know why you're here?"

The young man in the cell sat with his shoulders hunched sullenly and his lank hair hanging around his face. The temperature was controlled and neither too hot nor too cold for a human being's comfort, but he was sweating bullets. Fear scent rolled off him in noxious waves. "You're all in on it," he said in a harsh whisper.

"Can you tell me what *it* is?"

Flax wouldn't have been able to keep his voice so calm. The boy made his skin crawl and maybe that was unkind since his mind was so obviously unwell, but it was still true.

Albert looked up at them, a sneer on his face, despite the all too obvious fear. "You know. Don't try and trick me. I know you know. All of you. All of you have been after me. You all want to kill me."

"We have no interest in killing you, Albert." Val pulled a photograph of the restaurant owner out of his file. "Do you know this man?"

The sneer grew more disdainful. "Don't play stupid. You know I know him. You know everything. You've been watching. Spying. *On me!*" He suddenly lunged toward them, enraged. He reached through the bars, his fingers forming a claw, as if he were clutching an invisible ball. The same gesture a mage would make to hurl a gathering of power. Flax flinched but nothing happened. No black wall.

"Sorry. I should have warned you," Val murmured. "Kai reworked an amulet to nullify any energy he draws on. It can't be removed."

Albert flung himself back, raking his hands so hard through his hair that he pulled out clumps. He screamed obscenities at them.

"This is going well," Flax murmured.

"I didn't have high hopes that it would." Val stood, pulling himself straight to use the advantage of every inch of his impressive height. The gentle, coaxing tone vanished and Val's voice boomed through the corridor as he asked, "Albert, where is the gargoyle?"

The obscenities cut off like someone had thrown a switch, mid-curse. Albert crouched on the floor, glaring at them balefully. He said nothing, the only sound his harsh panting.

Val gave Flax a nod, giving him permission to try. "We're going to find him, Albert, just like we found you. If you let him run loose out there, without you, there's no telling who he might kill. Maybe you think we're in on some horrible cabal that wants to kill you, but you can't want your gargoyle to just kill random people. Innocent people."

"No one is innocent," Albert said. "They are all filled with hate. They whisper hate all day and all night. They think I don't know, but I know. I hear them. In here." He tapped the side of his head with one shaky finger. "I hear them all the time. Next time you won't be so lucky. Next time I'll get you. Take care of you and the ghosts, too."

Flax was about to ask who the ghosts were, but it came to him. Quinn. Ash. Anyone who had come after him on the spirit plane. "You didn't do such a good job today, did you? Look, Albert, if we wanted to kill you, we would've done it in the bell tower. We don't want to hurt you. We just want to keep you from hurting more people."

"Liar! Liar! You'll pay. You're the one that hurts people. *You're* the bad one." He turned his back on them, hunching down and covering his head with his arms.

Val put a hand on Flax's shoulder. "We can't reason with him. His world doesn't operate under the same rules as ours. I think we're finished here."

The captain looked so tired. Flax wanted to hug him, but that just wasn't done on the job. His brain spun in circles as they walked away. "You think anyone can help him?"

"It's possible. My research tells me there are medicines that might do some good, though it also says that young patients should be seen as soon as possible. I don't know. Perhaps he hid it well and his parents were unaware. Or perhaps they simply didn't see or didn't want to see." Val sighed. "Our focus now needs to be twofold. One, find the gargoyle and two, convince the DA that the magical traces we uncovered are enough to hold him. Otherwise, he goes back to his parents' custody."

"But…we can't do that!"

"We do as we have to, pup. If our evidence collection has been solid enough, we will be able to hold him—at least for the psych evaluation."

Albert heard them talking about him like he was some kind of lab rat as they walked away. He wasn't fooled. They were only pretending to go away. They were still watching. He was in their trap now and there wasn't any way out. It was only a matter of time before they began the experiments. Maybe they had already started. He had been unconscious. They could have done anything to him. Given him injections. Put tracers under his skin. Anything.

It was too late. Even if he managed to escape, it was too late. He was contaminated now. He wrapped his arms around himself and rocked, as he lifted his head to look up at the bar covered window. It was dark outside and had been for nearly half an hour now.

Darkness had always meant freedom. He could surround himself in the darkness and be protected. It was how he had discovered his friend — hiding in the darkness, hiding from all the loud people, the ones who threatened him and told him to do things. He had been ready to give up. He had been ready to jump from the bell tower all those months ago, until his friend told him to stop. That big gravelly voice had cut through all the others and when he turned to find who had spoken, there was his friend, waiting for Albert to release him, waiting for Albert to give the cold stone movement and life. His friend had been born in darkness, created from darkness and only in darkness could the stone hold on to life.

The curse they had placed on him could not stop him from reaching his friend once the sun had gone down. They were linked, mind-to-mind, ever since Albert had first awoken him. He had felt the stretch of stone as his friend shook off the paralysis of daytime and felt him coming. His friend was close now and Albert knew exactly what he needed to do. He would be free soon.

Standing on tiptoes and holding onto the bars, Albert could just see out into the sprawling parking lot below his jail cell. The two elves emerged from the building and he almost decided to attack them. A dark shape, even darker than the twilight sky, moved above them and two heads jerked upwards. He could kill them first, but really that wasn't important now. It was better to be free than to risk a final revenge.

Albert couldn't hear them shouting through the thick glass, but he could see them pointing, before they were blotted out by the massive shape of wings and body, the horrible grimace of his only friend's face that filled his vision. He clutched the cold bars as the gargoyle smashed the thick glass and some of the pieces rained down inside, cutting Albert's arm. He could hear the shouting from outside and somewhere behind him now. His friend reached inside and bent the bars as if they were made of taffy. Albert took his hand.

Thick gray fingers bent around his own, taking his hand gently. The craftsmen who had originally carved him had made him a monster, a fearsome countenance of heavy ridges for brows and lips, a shortened snout for a nose and pointed bat-like teeth and ears. But for Albert, the dark hollows of his fearsome eye sockets held understanding.

"It's okay. It's okay now. Do it," he whispered.

He felt the pain in his hand and clenched his teeth. He had made it. They were too late to stop him. The pain spread up his arm, his shoulder, and Albert threw back his head and started to laugh. He'd fooled them all. The laugh cut off a moment later, nothing left behind but an echo that bounced around the stone walls and died.

Chapter Sixteen

Tenzin was staring at something in the living room and had been for several seconds. Panic tried to claw its way up Kai's throat. Had he moved something? Done something? Not done something? Tenzi was finally home. He couldn't possibly have screwed up already, could he?

"Dearest, what are you looking at?" he finally managed to ask in a cracked voice.

"Hmm?" Tenzin turned and blinked at him. "Whatever's the matter?"

"You were... I didn't... Did I do something wrong?"

Tenzin crossed the floor into the kitchen and took Kai in his arms. "My poor angel, we can't have you walking on eggshells. I was looking at the flower fairies' nest."

"The nest?"

"You didn't throw it out. I was sure once they left, you would throw it out."

Kai sagged against him and buried his face against warm, white fur. "Oh, thank the goddess. That's all. No. I hoped you'd be back someday. And if you were back, they'd come back and Brianna would give me no peace if I threw it out."

"Good thinking. We do want to sleep at night." Tenzin kissed the top of his head. "Are you truly all right, Kai? After everything?"

Everything. Yes. There had been a bit of everything. "I think so. The nightmares should stop now that you're here."

Tenzin pulled him over to the sofa and sat him down, both his hands vanishing in Tenzin's huge ones. "What nightmares?"

"I keep seeing that boy. Albert. The way we found him in his cell. Stone, but still so animated—the look of triumph, of just unholy joy... It was so eerie, Tenzi."

"You've surely seen darker things in your time."

"I suppose I have," Kai murmured. "But this wasn't evil. This was... I just feel as if it didn't have to be this way. His tortured, brilliant mind. How it could have been so different for him."

Tenzin pulled him close again, rocking him. "What happened to the gargoyle?"

"It fell from his window and crashed to the sidewalk. In pieces. Would have flattened Val if Flax hadn't tackled him out of the way. The gargoyle must have turned to stone the moment Albert did, lost its grip on the outside wall. And that too...disturbs me. There was life in that stone. Perhaps it was only life that Albert put there..."

"It's very sad, love. It is. But there was nothing you could have done."

Kai burrowed closer, fighting off a sudden chill. "I hate those words. Oh, more than anything that was ever said."

"I know, my angel. I know. But sometimes even your indomitable will can't bend the world in the right direction."

They were interrupted by the soft *pop-pop-pop* sounds of a troop of flower fairies arriving in their living room. Four of them each clutched a corner of black cloth while Brianna scolded them in sharp chitters to be careful. They lowered their burden to the coffee table and let the cloth fall open. Brianna landed on one edge of the cloth, which was covered in the blossoms of fresh flowers and swept her arm over the pile in an inviting gesture.

"What's this?" Kai asked her.

She made an impatient sound.

"I believe 'this', is their engagement gift," Tenzin said.

"Oh, they are lovely," Kai said amiably.

Brianna preened and stepped back. The other fairies came zooming in over the cloth, their wings a blur, and the flowers lifted in a colorful swirl which settled toward the edges and revealed what lay beneath. A perfect moonstone about the size of a robin's egg gleamed on the dark velvet.

Kai gasped and ran his forefinger reverently over the stone. "It's beautiful. It's perfect. Thank you, Brianna, Timon, Briac, Tara and Artis. This is a handsome gift indeed."

The troop bowed their acceptance of his gratitude as one, then all of them, lifted into the air and made their way over to the nest.

"Good thing I left it there," Kai whispered in Tenzin's ear.

Tenzin laughed against him, all of that huge, furry bulk that, despite all Kai's knowledge and power, was what actually kept him safe, protected him from the ravages of a capricious world. Their home was complete again. The world could do whatever it damn well pleased that night.

* * * *

Sweat dampened Quinn's temples and the nape of his neck and his brow was furrowed in concentration. Five whittled staves were set up with about a foot of space between them. One by one Quinn had magically set the ends alight and Flax had put them out perhaps a dozen times, until now they were charred and about half the size as when they had started.

"Okay, now gently...push the same amount of energy toward the stave, but change it to wind," Flax told him.

So far Quinn hadn't managed to do it. He'd blown them all out, blown them over—created a whirlwind of debris that was on fire, but blowing out just one like a candle on a birthday cake was beyond him. He was determined though. He was not going to let Donovan's poor handling of his training haunt him all his life. He *would* overcome it.

He let go a small amount of magic fire energy, and as he directed it out, he changed its nature. *Wind. Wind. Wind.* He narrowed his focus and a streamer of wind flowed from his hand and the fire crackling at the end of the stave went out. He let the energy go before it could do any damage. He had been so prepared to fail yet again that he didn't even realize he had done it perfectly.

"Yes!" Flax whooped and punched a fist into the air, grabbed Quinn and whirled him around in a mad, joyful circle. "Yes! You fucking did it!"

Quinn's stunned disbelief dissipated like the smoke rising from the end of the stave and suddenly he whooped too. Caught up in the surge of triumph he jumped around, then grabbed Flax in a fierce embrace.

"I am so proud of you," Flax whispered as he hugged Quinn hard. "So damn proud."

In that moment there was nothing more to the embrace than the shared joy of accomplishment. It wasn't until Quinn started to feel his throat getting tight with emotion, something he never let anyone see but Valerian, that he felt a little awkward and gently pulled back, drawing his mantle of cool, calm and collected about him. He grinned at Flax. "I did it. I don't think I ever would have been able to without your help, Flax."

Much more demonstrative in everything he did, Flax didn't seem to have any hesitation about wiping tears away as he laughed. "It's all you, hon. Nobody could get past that but you. Glad to play catalyst."

"I need to call Val," Quinn said, still smiling. "He's gonna flip. He'll be so happy."

Flax waved a hand at him, "Call, goddess, yes. We need to celebrate."

The phone was in Flax's hand almost before he finished speaking and Quinn shook his head with a smile. Of course he called Ash. When was he gonna stop being so dense?

Val was just as ecstatic as Quinn knew he would be. This was a major breakthrough and not just because he was getting a better handle on his abilities. He also agreed with Flax that a celebration was in order.

"Ash says dinner tonight? He'll cook," Flax called over from his own phone call.

Quinn relayed the message, unnecessarily since Val had heard Flax and told Quinn to accept the invitation. When they had both said their goodbyes, they decided that Quinn's success was how they wanted to end the lesson—on a high note.

"I'll see you later." Quinn waved over his shoulder.

"Yes, see you soon," Flax replied and they both headed their separate ways.

* * * *

It was past seven before Val managed to disentangle from work and make his way to Ash and Sage's apartment. He'd sent Quinn over earlier, something he would never have done a few weeks ago, but he and Flax were good friends now, comfortable with each other, and Quinn seemed to relate to Ash and Sage better than he did many humans.

There was laughter coming from within when Val knocked and it warmed his heart to hear. After all the fear and the frustration of recent days, they all needed to laugh. Ash opened the door, greeting him with a kiss to his jaw, gracefully accepting the wine he brought and taking his coat at the same time.

Warmth, companionship—this was a good place to be.

And of course there was Quinn, who nearly knocked him over with the force of his welcome when he came into the living room. Quinn locked his arms around Val's neck and stretched up to kiss him and while that might be how Quinn greeted him at home, it was more demonstrative than usual for him in front of others.

Val fanned a hand out on the small of Quinn's back and answered the kiss with grateful heat. The day's tension melted away as those soft lips pressed and nibbled against his. He chuckled as he finally raised his head to find everyone watching with carefully tamped down smiles.

"Hello, my dears. Congratulations, love, on your wonderful success today." He took Quinn's hand and pulled him toward the room's single chair. "Sage, how are you feeling?"

"Much improved, Tesined. Almost good as new." He smiled. "I've had the best healers attending me after all." His sly smile left no doubt as to what sort of healing he'd enjoyed most.

Flax, once again sitting on the floor, leaned his head against Sage's knee. "Well, it's a hell of a lot more fun kind of healing than that stuff humans call physical therapy. Ugh."

"Poor Flax." Val patted his shoulder as he passed by. "Human nurses aren't permitted to perform fellatio on the patients."

"Only because the hospitals would be overrun with mysterious illnesses and inexplicable injuries if they were." Quinn snickered as Val pulled him down into his lap.

Val chuckled as he accepted the beer Ash offered. A flood of scents soaked the apartment, Ash's wonderful cooking, beer that everyone had at least two bottles head start on, and elf—what Quinn would refer to as horny elf. The pheromones saturated the air, such a strong undercurrent under the other scents, Val was amazed that Quinn couldn't smell them. He was helpless to keep his body from reacting, not that he thought Quinn would mind the erection prodding at his thigh. Not too much.

Quinn slung his arm around Val's shoulders and leaned in to kiss him, just a soft kiss of acknowledgment, and a slight shift of his hips that was a shadow of how he would have rubbed and ground against him if they had been home alone together.

"Quinn, could you...?" Ash stuck his head out of the kitchen, his usual calm marred by a wrinkled brow.

"Yep, be right there." Quinn hopped off Val's lap. "He's making veggie lasagna and some kind of complicated pumpkin-squashy soup thing. But he's never seen a lasagna, so he's kinda struggling with the directions."

"Ah." Val considered offering to help since he'd become rather good at lasagna, but Quinn was already there and the kitchen was the narrow galley sort, not big enough for three people.

"You look suddenly lonely over there, Tesined." Sage patted the empty half of the love seat beside him. "Come sit with us and be warmed. The nights are so terribly cold here."

Val obliged, moving over to the love seat and letting his arm settle along the back. "This time of year, yes. The winters are colder here than what you're most likely used to. The summer nights can be uncomfortably warm, though, so one goes through both extremes."

On the floor between them, Flax leaned back against the love seat, resting his head on Sage's thigh. "Spring is nice. I like spring."

Flax sounded so comfortable and sleepy, Val reached down to ruffle his hair. "Ash will be disappointed if you fall asleep before dinner."

It was meant to be a companionable gesture, though Val should have known better, especially with the pheromone-suffused air. Flax transferred his head from Sage's thigh to Val's, nuzzling at the wool of his dress pants with a soft growl.

"Ah...hmm." Val's brain developed several short circuits as Sage pulled a foot up on the love seat and snuggled into Val's side. *All right. Cuddling. I have no objections to cuddling.*

He closed his eyes and could hear Ash and Quinn in the kitchen together, chuckling over something, the clinks and scrapes and sounds of food being prepared. The comforting sounds and smells and the feel of warm bodies pressed against him invited a flood of memories. He held them at bay though, not wanting to let his emotions carry him away into regrets and loss.

The preparations in the kitchen continued for a few minutes and Val opened his eyes again just as Quinn and Ash returned. His eyes went right to Quinn's face, noting his eyes were wide but not angry. He had stopped moving and Ash put his hand on Quinn's back, not pushing but guiding him to continue to the chair, where he settled and pulled Quinn down into his lap almost exactly as Val had when he had arrived. Quinn didn't jump back up but he didn't look nearly as comfortable as he had sitting on Val's lap.

The last thing he wanted was Quinn becoming edgy. He held out his hand and Quinn crossed over to take it and settle on the arm of the love seat beside Val. Better. Much. Ash didn't appear the least bit offended. He rose and stood behind the love seat, letting his hands fall on Val's shoulders to knead the taut muscles there.

That feels good. So good. Such gentle hands.

There had been tension between them, yes. But Ash had apologized for the near-murder in the Research department. Mind you, he had only apologized for the disturbance. He hadn't said a word about being sorry for trying to kill Kai, and he certainly hadn't apologized to Kai himself, but Val understood. Ash and Sage obviously came from an elvish domain at war with the drow, likely all of Ash's life. He had never asked, but he suspected they had been facing drow forces when the Event had pulled them through. Hard to be raised to see them as the enemy, then suddenly be told the rules no longer applied.

"I leave you alone for a second and come back and you're wearing elf accessories," Quinn teased him, leaning over to kiss the top of Val's head.

"Puppy pile," Val murmured with a little smile.

Quinn looked at him and Val tried to read his expression but there was such a mix of varying emotions flicking across his face from moment to moment that it was hard to tell what he was thinking.

"You look so relaxed. If I didn't know you were on your first beer, I'd say you were on your way to tying one on."

"Hmm." Val's hum was nearly a purr. "Ash's hands. Oh, there…right there." He let his head fall forward as Ash worked on the knot at the base of his neck, vaguely aware that Flax was stroking his thigh in little circles.

Quinn's hip was pressed against Val's shoulder, his fingers threaded with Val's. He was right there with them but Val still felt some distance. He wasn't sure yet if it was reluctance or just uncertainty. The warmth and comfort being generated was almost as Quinn said, intoxicating. It made it harder to think. That was not the only thing harder either. There was a subtle shift in the flow of energy around them. Flax's gently stroking hand moved higher on his thigh, Ash bent and placed a kiss on Val's hair.

Sage reached over and caressed Val's chest and tipped his head up, pressing a kiss to his lips. It could have been overwhelming but it was so skillfully done, as if the three of them were moving in harmony, performing a dance. When Sage lifted his head from the kiss, he was smiling and he reached over Val to Quinn, hooking his hand under his knee and tugging so Quinn slid off the arm of the love seat and into Val's lap.

He still had not made a sound of protest, nor given any indication that he wanted what was happening to stop. When Val moved to kiss him, Quinn kissed him back with heat, lifting his arms around Val's neck. Val circled his own arms around Quinn, pulling him closer and felt the fine tremors under his hands emanating from Quinn's ribs, felt his heart beating hard and fast. Excitement? Or fear?

He lifted his head to look at Quinn again, look into his eyes and make sure. If Quinn was afraid, he was hiding it well, but he still didn't look nearly as comfortable and relaxed as everyone else. His eyes were still wide, but trusting. Oh so trusting. And Val recognized that look, the one that said Quinn would do anything for him.

There, right there, lay the crux of the issue. Flax's hand wandered to Quinn's knee and he stiffened, oh, so slightly. No one else would have noticed, but Val knew his fear-induced reactions all too well.

He stood slowly with Quinn still in his arms, gently, carefully disentangling himself from the pile of beautiful elves. With a shaky sigh, he deposited Quinn in the chair and paced away a few feet. He needed distance. He needed reason to return with so many emotions clamoring for attention in his brain.

Arvad...my lovely Arvad... Quinn isn't him. It's wrong for me to try to make Quinn into him, even in a superficial way.

"My dears," he began softly, every face in the room turned to him, expectant, anxious. "My beautiful, kind friends. I can't—"

Flax pulled his knees up to his chest as if he'd already received a physical blow. But it was better now than if this went further, he had to forge on.

"I can't do this. I simply can't." He spread his hands wide, palm up. "Once I had a *senrist*. They all loved each other dearly. My First was more than merely my chosen to them. He was our rock, our comfort. But I was torn from them and nearly died in my grief."

He stopped again, wishing he could do this without hurting them. It simply wasn't possible. "The comfort you offer, so openly, tempts me. But I cannot start again. My heart was stitched back together bit by bit and given wholly to the one who healed it. My Quinn, my *kalesi*, my own... He might come to love you all. I think he does in his way. But he cannot be the First you need. It's not in his nature, and I cannot ask him to change who he is because he wishes to please me, nor can I be the Tesined you desire. The memories you invoke, it will begin to cause me pain. The complications of intimacy, they will begin to cause Quinn pain, and I can't have that. I won't have that."

Someone let out a shuddering breath. He was afraid to look directly at any of them, afraid to see the hurt. "I'm so sorry, but this can't be."

Ash came over to him first. He took Val's hands in his own and lifted them to his lips. His smile was disappointed but understanding. "Sometimes the best decisions are the ones that hurt the most, Valerian."

Sage joined them, standing at Ash's side. He put a reassuring hand on the small of Ash's back, and the other on Val's shoulder. "Better we all learn now that this cannot be, so that we can remain friends," he said in a gentler tone than Val had ever heard him use.

"Thank you." Val leaned forward and kissed Ash's forehead then Sage's. "I most likely should have come to this conclusion sooner, but it was all too confusing."

Flax had gotten to his feet and he too came forward, although his face was much more drawn and downtrodden, his shoulders slumped in defeat. "I understand, Captain," he said, and the words rang hollow.

"Flax...if we had done this," Val said gently. "I would have needed to ask for your resignation if we bonded."

"Yes, sir. I suppose I didn't think of that," Flax murmured to his feet. "I guess I should still have my letter on your desk in the morning."

"Why would you do that?"

Flax raised his head, his eyes swimming with tears. "How can I see you every day, sir? How am I supposed to do that?"

"Like any other professional." Val patted his shoulder, and it stabbed him more than he thought it would when Flax pulled away. "And the hurt will fade. Your career is too important. You're too good at what you do to throw it away. If you need some extra distance for a bit, I'll give that to you."

The anguish in those beautiful lilac eyes—eyes the color of snow crocuses—stabbed at Val, but there wasn't much he could do. To comfort Flax would simply confuse things. To offer words of reassurance would ring hollow and false. Instead, he stepped back.

"Quinn, I'm sorry. I know this was supposed to be a celebration dinner for you, but I think it's best if we go."

Quinn rose, but he didn't move to Valerian's side. Instead he stepped in front of Flax. They'd had a rocky start, Val knew, but he also knew that a closeness had developed between them over the last several weeks that Quinn shared with few people. His precious mate looked almost as despondent as Flax.

"Are you giving me your resignation as well?" Quinn asked him quietly.

Flax nearly broke on those words, his expression crumpling, but he wiped a hand over his eyes impatiently and yanked Quinn into a hard embrace. "No," he whispered. "I won't."

Quinn wrapped his arms around Flax and squeezed his eyes closed, a rare shimmer of moisture trapped in his lashes. "Why can't you be Tesined, Flax? With Sage and Ash."

"I'm no prince, Quinn. No leader," Flax whispered into his shoulder. "It's not like I've led in battle. I've always been alone."

"Uh-huh," Quinn said, easing back from the fierce embrace so he could look at Flax. "And hunting the stone mage wasn't a battle? Or teaching me, for that matter? I won't pretend half the stuff you guys do isn't way more complicated and confusing than it needs to be, but if a Tesined is supposed to be the alpha dog, you fit the bill. It's something to think about anyway."

"Is that the kind of thing you'd want me to tell you if you couldn't have Val anymore?" Flax asked, though the words were sorrowful rather than bitter. He managed a ghost of a smile. "I'll be okay, Quinn. It's okay."

Quinn pulled away from him and his expression had gone from unhappy to grim as he joined Val.

With a heavy heart, Val gathered up his coat, tucked Quinn under his arm and coaxed him out of the door. There was probably something in all that he could have handled better, but he hadn't the slightest idea what.

"Quinn?" Val cleared his throat as they neared the car. "Are you still speaking to me?"

Quinn reached out and took his hand. "Why wouldn't I be? I'm not mad at you, Val. You didn't do anything wrong."

"But you're still upset."

Quinn sighed. "Yeah, I'm still upset. It's not your fault I'm upset though. You were the one that was smart enough to figure out it wasn't going to work and brave enough to say so. I can't help feeling bad though. You looked really happy for a little while there, and they did too. And I know Flax won't ever say so, but I know somewhere in his head he figures this is more my fault than yours."

"It was a lovely dream. And for a moment, I let myself forget…many things." Val gave Quinn's hand a gentle squeeze. "Flax…I feel terrible for hurting him. He's carried a torch since he first came to the department, I'd guess. But it was an infatuation for someone older and stronger. He needs… Well, I can't tell him what he needs, but I hope he sees he has love right under his handsome nose if he allows it."

"He'll figure it out, hopefully," Quinn said.

When they got into the car, Quinn leaned over the seat and kissed him. "I guess I'm not the elven orgy type."

"I don't think I am either, any longer." Val shook his head. "But it was more than that. Sorry. I know you were trying to lighten things a bit. I just hope… I hope everything will turn round right."

Quinn laced his fingers through Val's and squeezed. "I love you, babe. I know you can't help worrying, so I won't tell you not to. It's part of what makes you Tesined—and my *kalesi*."

"Thank you." Val lifted Quinn's fingers to his lips to kiss each one. "No one has ever understood me better. One of the reasons I love you so."

* * * *

Flax's hands were numb as he gathered his jacket from the closet. He supposed, in a way, he had expected the rejection. Val still saw him as an immature elf, maybe someone to mentor, but not take as a lover, and certainly not as a bond mate.

It shouldn't have been such a shock to his system, but Val's words had hit like multiple lightning strikes and left scorched earth in their wake. Right now, he just wanted to go home and be alone and maybe cry where no one could see his shame—which just proved that Val was right about him. He couldn't even handle this in a mature fashion.

Could he still keep his job and be effective? Sounded like a pipe dream. With Val there as a constant reminder, a constant reopening of the wound, and with the fading taking hold...maybe Elvenhome was the best choice. He could decline on the reservation in peace. No one would give a flying fuck.

"Where are you going?" Ash asked.

"Home," Flax said.

"Why?" Sage asked.

"I...I just need to go home." He couldn't look at either of them. Couldn't do this now. He hurt so much and he didn't want to explain or talk things out or have someone try to make things better. Everything was so raw. "I'm not feeling very well."

"Yes, we know. Which is why you should stay, *kalesi*," Ash said.

Flax leaned his forehead against the door. "Stop. Please, stop. You love each other. You're bonded to each other. *Please* stop calling me that."

"I don't see what loving each other has to do with how we both feel about you, but I will respect your wishes," Ash said, his tone wounded.

"You are not the only one hurting, Flax," Sage said. "We knew if Valerian declined the *senrist* that you would leave us, but…it still hurts to lose you."

"I don't even understand what you're saying anymore." Flax still spoke to the door, trying to convince his hand to turn the knob and leave. But it wouldn't listen. Stupid hand. "You can't love me. It's ridiculous. You haven't known me long enough. I'm an addict—and a troublemaker. And a selfish, arrogant fool."

"You are a recovering addict, and you stop more trouble than you create," Ash said.

"You give more time to your student and your occupation than most would," Sage added.

"Flax, when we decided to ask Valerian to form a *senrist*, we had every intention of following through with our pledge, but these past weeks it hasn't been his touch we have yearned for," Ash told him.

"You made us love you and now you're leaving," Sage said, more resentfully this time.

"Sage, hush," Ash said.

"Well it's true, Ash. He wanted the *senrist* with Valerian. He didn't really want us."

Flax slid down the door. He knees wouldn't hold him anymore. Was that what he had done? Just used them like he had everyone else? He'd used Quinn to try to get to Val. He'd used Ash and Sage to try to make the impossible happen. He'd manipulated. He'd schemed. And this was where he ended up—on the floor, too broken to even leave like he should.

"You're both so good. So honorable and clean," he whispered. "I'm not worth it. I'm just a reject. Always. I wouldn't be any good for you."

They were both so quiet behind him that Flax thought they had finally given up. Now he just needed to muster the strength to stand up and leave.

Hands gripped him from behind and pulled him up—Sage's strong hands, Ash's every bit as strong but somehow also gentle.

"Stop this, Flax. We discussed our feelings for you weeks ago, but have only waited for you to realize your own feelings. This self-pity is beneath you," Ash told him.

Weeks ago? How is that even possible? "I can't do this right now. I can't think straight." He turned, at least he could face them. The looks of accusation, of anger and, yes, compassion in those eyes broke him. Blue and green pools of such fierce emotion…all for him. The first sob escaped before he could stop it, and he had to bury his face in his hands, unable to stop any of the ones that came after.

He didn't remember moving, but he must have because when he finally opened his eyes again, he was on the love seat. They all were, which was quite the tight squeeze. Ash sat to one side, one arm wrapped around his chest, pulling him back up against him, and Sage pressed to his front, his head on Flax's shoulder. They held him tight, Sage murmuring soothing words and Ash humming softly.

Sage lifted his head and while he didn't exactly glare, his gaze was intense. "You are not well. We are not letting you leave here to be on your own."

They were so warm. So wonderfully warm. It would be harder and harder to leave as the minutes ticked by. "I do love you. I love you both," he whispered. "I think I did from the moment I saw you in Tokyo, frightened, disoriented, but standing back-to-back, willing to die for each other. You're so brave and beautiful—and deserve so much better than me."

Sage snorted. "You seem to be under the impression that you know what we want better than we do. I assure you, you are wrong. I could not love you if you weren't a worthy person to love."

"Back home..." Flax began softly. "My old home. I was always alone. I wasn't disciplined enough for the warrior bands. I wasn't powerful enough to train as a healer. So I hunted. Haunting the forests alone, listening, watching, learning stealth. That's who I am. That's the part you've never seen."

He shifted, his hand stroking Sage's still-healing arm. "When I came here, I realized I didn't know what *alone* meant. And in my desolation, I was weak. So weak, and nearly died from my addiction. Even now, sometimes I'm still weak. And do dishonorable things. And remain alone, because this is how it's always been. If I don't have someone stronger to keep me in line, how can I be trusted to be something better? To do what's right? How can I be trusted not to hurt you?"

Ash smoothed the damp hair from his forehead, his voice low and soothing. "You have more strength than many of the battle princes in our old world. You have enough honor to admit when you are wrong. Enough fire to keep living when others have given up and died. Enough courage to fight this addiction that tried to consume you. Enough to take an arrow meant for another. And enough love in your generous, caring heart to pull two lost souls in from the dark and help them see that all was not lost. To teach the bond mate of the one you wished to have for yourself. To accept those that our upbringing, our histories tell us are anathema to us. You *are* what we want, the one we would follow."

"But—"

"You simply have been in too much pain to see."

Flax turned in Ash's arms to see that beautiful smile directed at him. *My hunter,* Ash always said. Mine. Flax tipped his head up to kiss him, a gentle touch of lips just to soothe the hurt he had caused, so much of it.

Ash welcomed him into his arms like he had been lost for days and only now returned. His lips pressed and parted, inviting him to deepen the kiss to something more passionate.

It didn't take much. He knew he was pitiful. But that gentle promise of heat, that little bit of need for him was enough to set a torch to the empty, hollow places inside. Flax seized Ash's head between his hands and plunged in, his tongue demanding and hungry, his lips desperate as he sucked and nipped at Ash's mouth.

Ash clutched at him, his hands gripping at his back as he yielded to Flax's flare of fierce passion and Flax felt that yielding like a spear of lust. He felt Sage's hands on him a moment later, the pads of his fingertips gliding up his back under his shirt then around his ribs and chest. Sage moved his hands down his front, tracing his abs and coming to rest on the button of his jeans. He didn't hesitate to open them.

Almost. He almost told Sage to stop, but the warmth surrounding him eased into the cracks of his brittle nerves. It felt too good and he was too selfish to call a halt. A soft whine escaped him as he tried to tug Ash's sweater off, despite the weight of two full-grown elves in the way. But Ash, graceful, flexible Ash, arched his back and reached around to help, until the black and silver sweater flew halfway across the room.

Flax turned, sitting up in the V of Ash's thighs, to yank Sage's shirt off as well. He wanted skin and more skin, skimming his hands over the shivering muscles of Sage's back as Flax kissed him hard.

He pulled back when Sage didn't take it any further, didn't rip Flax's pants off and maul him like a young buck normally would. There was a plea in those green eyes, but for what? Behind him, Ash stroked his back, equally hesitant to escalate for some reason. Slowly, he undid the buttons of his own shirt, giving himself a moment to think. He turned to find an identical plea in Ash's eyes.

You are what we want, the one we would follow.

Did that mean...? Was Quinn, whose only knowledge of elvish society was through hearsay, was he right? Was that what Flax wanted? Could he handle the kind of responsibility they seemed to want to give him?

"Ash...Sage..." He took the long-fingered, elegant hand on one side and the stronger, blunter fingers on the other. "Am I such a fool that I've misunderstood all along? Everything? Do you truly want me to *claim* you? *Both* of you?"

"You haven't been a fool the whole time, but maybe a little single-minded in your pursuit of one thing, when another was right in front of you," Sage said.

Ash pushed himself up on his arms so he could better reach Flax and kiss him at the corner of his jaw. "We both love you, Flax, and we both want you to be our bond mate."

Trembling started in his belly, working its way up to his hands. "Sage? I need a yes. A real yes. I'm not chomping on your ear without one."

"As if I would let you if it wasn't what I wanted," Sage said with a haughty lift of his chin. "Now you *are* being foolish. Of course I want you, *kalesi*. I have wanted you for a bond mate since the first night I asked you to stay."

Flax kissed his fingers. He couldn't stop shaking. "Not foolish. Not in this. I needed to hear it. From both of you. Consent." He closed his eyes and Ash's arms wrapped around him again. "It's overwhelming. I didn't... Why can't I stop shivering?"

Ash ran his fingers gently through Flax's hair and over his shoulders. "Perhaps this is something you would like more time to think about?" he suggested gently.

"No!" Flax turned again to burrow into Ash's embrace, embarrassed by the vehemence of that single word. And where had that come from? "I... You're both so wonderful. Please don't tell me to stay and then send me away again. I can't do this anymore..."

"Shh," Ash soothed him, caressing his shoulders. "That's not what I meant at all. We aren't sending you away—only giving you room to think so you don't feel so overwhelmed."

It was the hollow place inside. That's what was making him act like a mad, wounded hare. "The fading… I think it's making it hard to *think* sometimes."

"Fading?" Sage's voice had gained a desperate edge. He curled up against Flax's back, holding tight around his ribs. "You're too young. It can't happen yet. Ash, tell him it can't happen yet."

Ash frowned and stroked his fingers through Flax's hair then Sage's, but he didn't offer false words of comfort. "Perhaps it comes sooner in this world." He bent and kissed the top of Flax's head, then disentangled himself enough to stand. "Come help me bring the food to the table, Sage. Don't smother him. He knows how we feel. He has to make his own choice now."

Actual physical pain shot through Flax when first Ash, then Sage let go of him. He managed not to cry out, barely. He watched in a strange haze of confusion and frustration for a moment, trying to restart his brain. The evening had been a celebration. It had seemed it was heading toward what he'd been chasing all along until it all fell apart.

But this…this…

He took the chair he normally had here, the one at the head of the table, he realized. That didn't have much significance for elves, but there was something symbolic in the placement. Ash on his left, Sage on his right, as always, head and heart.

Always? Since when is it an always?

But as Sage brought out bowls of soup, glorious, wonderful soup, and Ash brought the dish of marvelously spiced lasagna, he counted back. He'd been here for dinner almost every night for the past two weeks, barring strange late nights at work and the couple of nights someone was in Medical. He hadn't always stayed the night, but often. There was a toothbrush in the bathroom for him, for all the gods' sakes. In every way that mattered, they were already a household. In every important way, Sage and Ash supported him, encouraged him, nurtured him.

They ate in silence for a few tense minutes that stretched too long. *This is comfortable and warm. They know me better than I know myself. I know their strengths, their faults, those places where they need some extra help. They make me laugh and sometimes tear up. Crud. They even know my favorite flavor of ice cream.*

He looked up from his plate, gazing from silver hair to evergreen, and his heart lurched painfully. There wasn't a strong enough word for idiot, in Elvish or any human language, that would describe him. *I love them. I do. And I would never be able to choose between them. I need them both.*

He dug a bit of yellow squash out of his square of lasagna. Holding it out to Ash with his free hand underneath to catch sauce drips, he cleared his throat and said, "Try one of these. They're really good in this."

Ash glanced down at his own plate. He had his own pieces of squash, of course, and for a moment, Flax was afraid he wouldn't take the bait. Finally with a soft smile, Ash leaned forward and took the offered bit off the fork, licking the sauce from his lips slowly.

Mesmerized by that beautiful tongue, Flax's mouth went dry. Not the time to lose focus, though. He leaned to the left and licked a bit of sauce from beside Sage's lip.

"That would taste good on your ear, I'd say," Flax managed in a husky growl.

Sage didn't respond immediately. He lifted his eyes and looked at Flax with such a smoldering expression it was a wonder they didn't all catch fire. "I'd let you cover me in it, if you lick it off."

"Now wouldn't that just be ridiculously decadent and messy." Flax got up from his chair and realized he'd never re-buttoned his shirt. Maybe his smile was a little shaky, but his cock was screaming at him to get the hell on with it. He took a sip of beer, eyes never leaving Sage and murmured, "Strip for me. All the way down."

Carefully, Sage pushed back in his chair and stood. He looked at Flax searchingly, those spring green eyes locked on his before he lifted both hands to Flax's cheeks and drew him in for a kiss that was every bit as hot as the smoldering look he'd given him moments ago. When their lips parted again, Sage moved back a fraction, enough to pull his shirt off and unfasten his jeans, letting them slide off his hips and down to the floor. He wasn't wearing anything beneath and stood naked after kicking his jeans aside.

"So strong. So lovely," Flax whispered, as he trailed a finger down the center of Sage's smooth chest toward the soft trail of down below his navel. He reached over and hooked the dish of lasagna closer with a forefinger, which landed squarely in the sauce. With a soft smile, he drew a spicy red line along Sage's right collarbone. "Ash, come help me paint."

Ash came around the table but instead of following Flax's lead, he moved behind Flax and removed his opened shirt, draped it over the chair, then unfastened his pants, drawing them down his long legs. When he was all the way down, he paused to place a nip and a kiss on Flax's cheek.

"Bad thing. Not following instructions at all," Flax purred as he shivered and painted a line up Sage's throat. He reached back with his clean hand to stroke

Ash's hair, indicating he wasn't at all serious. If he was going to do this, yes, there needed to be arousal and climax involved, but he wasn't particular about how they got there. Not quite yet, anyway.

He painted a lily on Sage's chest, making certain to paint over each nipple at the apex of the petals. Sage stood still, though he was panting, barely visible tremors running up his legs. Flax wanted to draw sounds from him, though, hopefully louder and louder sounds. He leaned in and licked the sauce from Sage's collarbone with the flat of his tongue.

Sage sighed softly, a little hitch of pleasure at the end. His arms came up around Flax and he yanked him close, melding his lips to Flax's. Still on his knees, Ash chuckled, "Now you see why I wanted to get you naked. Well, one reason."

"Well, yes," Flax murmured against Sage's lips. "Thank you for saving my jeans."

He moved his lips down Sage's jaw to lick the line of sauce from his throat, sucking and nipping at the pulse line. Now Sage moaned softly and pressed his hips forward, rubbing his swiftly hardening cock against Flax's. All very nice, but Flax was so keyed up, he was afraid he might come from the frottage alone.

His hands on Sage's hips, he moved him back far enough to lick the remaining sauce from his chest, working his way down Sage's well-muscled frame until he had sunk to his knees before him where he could kick off his jeans the rest of the way and reach for Ash.

Flax curled his fingers around the back of Ash's neck and pulled him closer. They shared a kiss, passionate but brief, before both turned their heads to lick a wet line up either side of Sage's cock. This time the little sigh Sage released quavered, becoming a soft, welcoming moan. Sage pushed his fingers into their hair, right and left, gripping them both.

"You best get undressed, too," Flax said with a wink at Ash between long licks up Sage's cock.

Ash only needed to flick the button on his pants and unzip to let them fall, although he didn't seem in too much of a rush to unburden himself of clothing. He caught Flax's chin on the edge of one finger and pulled him closer again for a kiss. "Let's go the bedroom, *kalesi*. Tonight I want you to take me," he murmured against Flax's lips.

"Goddess, yes," Flax whispered, spearing his hands through Ash's silver fall of hair to steal another demanding kiss before he rose and faced Sage with a quirked eyebrow. He indicated the random, Jackson Pollock sauce designs on his own chest. "Though I think someone needs to clean this up first."

There were only traces left on Flax's chest but Sage bent his head and industriously applied his tongue, chasing each of the streaks in slow, lazy, thorough licks. Ash joined him, licking his way up from Flax's navel. Their two wet tongues worked in tandem, bathing Flax's chest and nipples even after there was not a speck of sauce to be found. Sage moved to his neck, licking and sucking there while Ash still toyed with his nipple and pushed a hand between his thighs to gently caress his balls.

Flax had no hesitation about letting his head drop back on a hard groan, a hand fisted in each head of hair to keep him steady. "Thank you," he panted out. "I think that about does it. Bedroom. Now."

Several days before, Sage had decided he couldn't deal with the small lumpy mattress and had gotten rid of it. In place of the bed now were several layers of thick carpeting, pillows by the dozen and more layers of blankets, more comfortable than the bed, especially for three. It was more like home, too.

Ash pulled Flax along by the hand and Sage followed them both until they all tumbled naked together into their nest. Flax landed on his back between them and neither wasted any time pressing him back, Ash with a fierce kiss to his lips, and Sage aiming lower, kissing down his belly and licking around his cockhead.

For a few luscious moments, Flax allowed it, letting Sage get his erection all nice and wet and enjoying the hell out of Ash's fire. But he had the urge to have Ash writhing and moaning beneath him. There was nothing more sensual than Ash's moans. He wrapped his arms hard around Ash and rolled them, careful not to kick Sage in the process. Ash's eyes were wide, his pupils nearly swallowing the blue.

Flax settled between his legs, stroking the back of one of Ash's thighs. "Are you ready for me, love?"

Ash settled his hands on Flax's back. "So ready for you, my hunter."

Sage shifted beside them and reached under one of the pillows to bring out a small bottle of sweetly scented lubricant.

"Look at you, all prepared." Flax gave him a soft kiss and held out a hand for Sage to squeeze a bit of lube there. Citrus and spice filled his nostrils, but his head was too full of the heady, erotic scent of aroused elf to parse it further.

With a sweet sigh, Ash pulled his knees up to let Flax reach between his legs and slip a finger into his tight channel. Most of his human lovers had needed careful preparation. Ash, already squirming beneath him, could take him without. A little to ease the way was just more pleasant for everyone involved.

Flax leaned over to stroke Ash's hair, gazing deep into those desire-blown pupils. "You're so beautiful. I love you so." On the last word, he pushed forward, gasping as the head of his cock popped through Ash's tight ring.

Heat gripped and squeezed him and Ash arched under him, his head tipping back and his fingers digging into Flax's back harder. Sage reached between them, sliding his hand around Ash's long, throbbing dick, slicking him with another dollop of lube. He kissed Ash as he stroked down his shaft firmly, swallowing his hiss and moan as Flax sank deeper. After a moment, he lifted his head and turned to kiss Flax, plundering his mouth with a hungry kiss that had nothing to do with the meal they had abandoned.

Fingers tangled in Sage's hair, Flax kept him there while he pushed into Ash and pulled out in little forays that made Ash lift his hips, seeking more. Flax flicked his fingers at the portable stereo in the corner, pleased when his Cocteau Twins CD started to play. *Gotta love how tech responds to magic.* Elizabeth Fraser's ethereal, haunting voice rose and fell through her improbable range, the notes sliding around them like ghostly hands on naked skin.

He wished he had extra hands, wanting to hold Ash, wanting to pull Sage closer, but he needed to have them both right there. This he had to do right. He'd screwed up so much where they were concerned already.

Supporting himself on his left arm, Flax drove in hard, a surge of heat washing through him as Ash cried out, his body arching up to meet him. His right hand, still slick with lube, wrapped around Sage's cock and he gripped tight, not giving any quarter as he jacked him. He had to hang on, at least until they climaxed. *Goddess, I'd give my left thumb for a cock ring right now.*

Neither of them were helping to give him any semblance of control either. Ash bucked under him, whimpering for more while he rode between Flax's cock and Sage's pumping hand. Sage was just as eager, his cock thrusting into the circle Flax's fist made. He felt Ash's hand join his for a moment on Sage's cock, then Ash moved his hand and must have pressed his long digits between Sage's cheeks because the younger elf began kissing Flax hard enough to bruise his lip, panting hard and giving voice to ragged moans.

"So close... Oh we're so close, *kalesi*. Can you feel it?" Ash whispered huskily. "Bite him. Claim him first, my hunter."

Through the haze of lust and need, Flax retained enough sense to know Ash was right. Their heartbeats fought to synch, and Sage's scent had taken on a sharp, desperate edge. He leaned over, dragging his tongue along Sage's jaw. He was so keyed up, the moment Flax licked over Sage's ear, he came, bucking hard against Flax's fist.

"I love you, my brave, stubborn Sage. Thank you for standing by me," Flax whispered into the shell of his ear before biting into the lobe with one sharp canine.

Sage cried out, jerking through his orgasm and stilled against Flax with a long, poignant moan. Their hearts beat in time, their breaths were drawn in tandem, and while he felt the bond, there was no peace for him yet as there was for Sage. He wasn't finished yet and his body told him so.

Fingers trembling, he kept hold of Sage's hand and bent over Ash, his hips pistoning faster. It was agony to hold on, the pleasure nearly melting his brain. The sounds rising from Ash were sensual enough to make a stone come. Sage had collapsed next to Ash, a blissed-out smile on his face, though he went back to stroking Ash's beautiful, pale erection.

"Ash, look at me," Flax whispered. His heart sped at the intensity of Ash's longing, the love shining in his eyes.

"Now, my hunter," Ash's whisper was perilously close to a whimper.

Flax slammed into him as he bent close to lick over the shell of Ash's ear. He shivered as wave upon wave of pleasure rushed through him, and as Ash cried out and clamped around him in climax, the savage need overwhelmed Flax and he bit down hard.

The world vanished in a whirlwind of heat and pleasure-pain so intense, Flax was certain he howled. A distant part of him hoped the neighbors wouldn't call the police. Gradually, the tempest settled, his heart beating in time with his two beloveds', the rhythms of his soul matching theirs. The *kalest*, the heart's peace, settled over him, flooding the terrible empty places deep inside, holding him in its warm, settling embrace. He rested his head on Ash's shoulder and wept in relief.

* * * *

The delicious celebratory dinner that Ash had prepared ended up not going to waste after all. When they had all finally floated down from the physical and emotional high of the shared *kalest* enough to think sensible thoughts, all three were ravenous. A little warming in the oven and they all sat down together to enjoy the meal, not at the dining room table, but sitting on the floor in the living room around the low coffee table where it was easier to reach and touch one another.

There were fewer words spoken during that meal than any of the others they had shared, but the lack of conversation did not matter. A new closeness had replaced the need for immediate conversation.

Once they had their fill, no one wanted to be separated for long. That was an expected part of a new mate bond, but also simple desire. They snuggled back down into the nest of pillows and blankets in the bedroom, a mass of draped limbs over one another.

Sage was curled on his side and Flax spooned behind him, with Ash pressed up to his back, making a deliciously warm cocoon around him.

Ash's lips kissed the nape of his neck and he murmured, "Is it all right if I call you *kalesi* now?"

"You know, I think it is," Flax answered with a sleepy smile. He snuggled back against Ash, kissing the hand that rested on his shoulder. "But you know, this is getting stupid. We can't keep doing this."

Sage surged up and turned to fix him with a gaze filled with such anger and fear, Flax knew he should have started that thought differently. "But we just...you can't...Flax!"

"Sorry...sorry." Flax laughed and took Sage's hand. "I mean the two apartment thing. It's silly. My next day off, we're moving you both to my place. It's bigger. It has a nicer kitchen, and a better TV." He patted the blankets. "This, though... This can come with us. I like this bed."

Ash chuckled and Sage settled against him once more. "I am so glad that you have ended your hunt with us, *kalesi*."

"I don't think I've ever had any other hunt where I went so far after the wrong trail," Flax sighed, letting this new contentment settle in his chest. "Thank you for being such patient prey."

From despair to this feeling of wholeness in one evening… The world never ceased to surprise him. He closed his eyes and let the warmth of new love sing him to sleep.

About the Authors

Angel Martinez

The unlikely black sheep of an ivory tower intellectual family, Angel Martinez has managed to make her way through life reasonably unscathed. Despite a wildly misspent youth, she snagged a degree in English Lit, married once and did it right the first time, (same husband for almost twenty-four years) gave birth to one amazing son, (now in college) and realized at some point that she could get paid for writing.

Published since 2006, Angel's cynical heart cloaks a desperate romantic. You'll find drama and humor given equal weight in her writing and don't expect sad endings. Life is sad enough.

She currently lives in Delaware in a drinking town with a college problem and writes Science Fiction and Fantasy centered around gay heroes.

Bellora Quinn

Originally hailing from Detroit Michigan, Bellora now resides on the sunny Gulf Coast of Florida where a herd of Dachshunds keeps her entertained. She got her start in writing at the dawn of the internet when she discovered PbEMs (Play by email) and found a passion for collaborative writing and steamy hot erotica. Soap Opera like blogs soon followed and eventually full novels.

The majority of her stories are in the M/M genre with urban fantasy or paranormal settings and many with a strong BDSM flavor.

Angel and Bellora love to hear from readers. You can find their contact information, website details and author profile pages at http://www.pride-publishing.com.

PUBLISHING